The Thief of St Martins

Dottie Manderson mysteries book 5

Caron Allan

The Thief of St Martins: Dottie Manderson mysteries book 5

ISBN: 9781713458470

THE THIEF OF
ST MARTINS

DOTTIE MANDERSON
MYSTERIES BOOK 5

.

Chapter One

Sussex, England, Thursday 3rd January 1935.

Dottie sat on the hard bench and made up her mind she would be here a while. She couldn't give way now. To keep her nerves steady and her eyes dry, she fixed her attention on the cell itself.

First, she measured with her eyes the length and breadth. About eight feet by six or seven, she decided. More or less the size of the small staff cloakroom off the scullery passage at home. Then she looked at the way the two benches were attached to the wall—presumably so no one could pick them up and throw them at anyone else, the immense, terrifying female warder for example, or another inmate.

She glanced at, then quickly away from, the other two women in the cell. She wondered vaguely if one could catch fleas from being in prison. She had been so itchy since her arrival. She scraped at a spot just behind her knee. Then, itchy again, she risked a further covert look at them from behind her hand as she scratched her temple.

The woman on the other bench was hunched up against the wall, concealed beneath a huge ragged shawl, apparently asleep. Her shoes—holed and heel-less—lay beneath the bench, one resting on top of the other. One bare grubby foot poked out from under a skirt or some other dark voluminous garment.

On the opposite end of Dottie's bench, the other woman leered at her, open-mouthed and gap-toothed. She was a red-faced greasy-looking creature in what appeared to be just her underclothes—and none too clean either—with a blanket wrapped around her. She was clearly amused at the idea of a well-to-do young lady in jail with a couple of 'women of ill repute'. She looked strong and aggressive. Her bare arms, poking out from under the blanket in spite of the chill, were muscular and solid. Dottie felt a knot of anxiety in the pit of her stomach.

It seemed a lifetime later that the outer door opened, very slightly thinning the darkness with a little grey light from the corridor beyond. Before the warder—a woman of almost six feet in height, and not much less in girth—had even begun to unlock the gate, she was bellowing orders at them. Dottie's two companions took little notice; it was Dottie she'd come for.

'Manley, get up. You've got a gentleman caller.'

The red-faced woman along Dottie's bench laughed.

The 'sleeping' woman called out, 'And not for the first time, neither!' then cackled at her own wit. So not asleep after all. The cackling gave way to a paroxysm of coughing and hacking that made Dottie feel ill.

Dottie approached the bars with caution, then seeing they were all laughing at her timidity, she straightened her back and lifted her chin.

'It's Manderson, thank you very much. Not Manley.'

But they only laughed harder. Dottie bit her lip. She would not cry. She wouldn't give any of them the satisfaction.

The warder pinioned her by the arm and chivvied her out into the draughty corridor, pausing to handcuff her. The corridor was almost as dark as the cell, and Dottie was slow to see where she was to go or understand what the warder wanted her to do. As a result, she got slapped twice by the warder, who clearly believed in the adage that actions spoke louder than words.

A door on the right was thrown open, and Dottie was thrust, blinking, into a room brightly lit by an electric light hanging low over the table. A figure across the room rose, but with the light in her eyes it was half a minute before she found the chair and sat down. Then she looked across the table into the eyes of Inspector Hardy.

It was so unexpected. It broke her composure entirely. The tears ran down her face, and with no handkerchief to check them, the prison uniform rapidly became spotted with damp patches.

Hardy was aware of a rage greater than anything he'd ever felt in his life. He glared at the warder.

'Get those handcuffs off her at once! Then get out. This is a private interview.'

The warder threw the keys onto the table and giving him a filthy look, banged out of the room.

He came around the table to unlock the cuffs. It concerned him to see bruises on Dottie's wrists, and it made him feel ten times worse when she said very quietly, 'Oh no, those aren't from just now, those are from yesterday when they first brought me in.'

He removed the handcuffs and threw them down on the table with a bang. He had to do that, or he would have taken each wrist in his hand, stroked each bruise then kissed it. He forced himself to get his temper and his emotions under control. The loud noise of the handcuffs falling onto the table helped, as did the swift action of it. He took a deep breath, resumed his seat, and, not knowing what else to do, began to shuffle his papers.

When he glanced up, her lovely hazel eyes, with the dark smudges beneath them, were resting on his face. She'd stopped crying but tears streaked her cheeks. He was dismayed by how pale and fragile she looked. He looked down at his papers again, then cleared his throat.

'So, it seems you're being charged with murder.'

'Yes,' said Dottie Manderson. She couldn't think of anything else to add.

Chapter Two

Friday 30th November 1934

Dottie Manderson twirled in front of her dressing mirror, observing with satisfaction the way the long skirt flared and flowed about her legs. It would be perfect! She reached for the matching opera gloves and began to ease them on.

Half an hour later she was feeling less sure. Her mother, encountering her on the stairs, had given her a slight frown and said, 'Dorothy dear, that frock's rather daring, don't you think?'

Dottie had stuck her chin in the air and said, 'Exactly!' and continued into the room where the dancing would take place. It was really both the drawing room and the dining room, thrown together by the opening of the adjoining doors to create a large space, then rolling back the carpets. A little band was tuning up in one corner. Her father always liked to have a modern dance band for special occasions.

She could see Gervase over in the opposite corner, a little gaggle of people around him, hanging on his every word. But before she could reach his side, another man, closer at hand, spoke to her.

'Good Lord, Miss Manderson, are you trying to give every man here a heart attack?'

William Hardy. Police inspector, almost-boyfriend, and now, to Dottie's mind, an odious man she had been taking great pains to avoid. Her family, it seemed, took delight in annoying her by inviting him to this or that event or occasion, and not warning her in advance. He stared at her, his eyes light with amusement—and—with something else she couldn't quite name. She felt irked. She had forbidden him the use of her first name some months ago, and therefore she now had no recourse to his.

'Is it any of your business, inspector?'

She knew she sounded waspish and this was not at all the way one addressed a guest in one's parents' home. A guest presumably invited to the house by those same parents. But...damn the man! Why did he make her feel she had to lash out at him all the time?

He hid his annoyance by taking a sip of his drink. 'I suppose not, though as a police officer I'm very much against vice, and the top of that thing you no doubt call a dress is practically pornographic. I'm fairly sure a bathing dress would cover more.'

She couldn't deny the top of the ruby silk dress was almost non-existent. With no sleeves or bodice in the conventional sense, her shoulders and back were completely bare. At the front, modesty was just barely maintained by two triangles connected to the waistband of the dress with long narrow bands, leaving a tantalising triangle of bare midriff, and that was it. The narrow bands that went up from the triangles formed the straps around her neck that held the thing up. She looked down at it, moved her hips and felt the skirt swooshing around her calves and ankles, then met his eyes with a laughing, joyous look.

'I designed it myself,' she told him with pride. 'It'll be heavenly to dance in.' She gave a quick twirl.

'For you? Or your partner?' He could imagine all too well the feel of her soft warm skin. Surely she had no idea how men would be affected by the almost complete lack of a bodice to the dress, not to mention the little window in the centre to her midriff, and the truly gorgeous satin gloves that reached to the top of her arms, her smooth shoulders so bare and alluring. He was furious at the thought of any other man touching her. Of Gervase Parfitt touching her. He was forced to hide his temper yet again and adopted a polite social smile. 'I hope your dancing partner has warm hands.'

'Can you believe I almost thought of hanging a label on my back saying, 'other shades available, fourteen guineas'.'

'Fourteen guineas! My word!' He grinned at her then, and it was the old William, before all the anger and pain had come between them. She caught herself smiling back, then pulled herself up. She couldn't stand here and let him grin at her. Across the room, Gervase acknowledged her arrival with a smile of his own.

'Excuse me, inspector.'

Then as she began to turn away from him, he said softly, for her ears alone, 'No one else will look half as good as you in that dress.'

That threw her. She couldn't help glancing back at him. He seemed sincere. His eyes, shadowed, almost grey in this light rather than the deep blue she found so appealing, regarded her steadily. Unable to think of anything else to say, she repeated herself. 'Excuse me, inspector.' She walked away. She felt his eyes on the bare skin of her back; she fidgeted with the top of the gloves. She no longer felt quite so happy about the dress. Her mother had been right, it was too much for a little party like this.

William watched her go. He watched as she approached Parfitt. She leaned in against Parfitt's body, her hand going into the crook of the man's arm. Parfitt gave her a quick glance then returned to his anecdote. Dottie smiled as they all did at the culmination of the tale.

With a sigh, Hardy looked down at the wine glass he held. He'd snapped the stem clean through. Arthur Greeley, Dottie's sister's butler, on loan as he often was from the other household for special occasions, came over and relieved him of it, handing him a replacement.

'Don't worry about it, sir, it's not just you. That's the fourth we've had in the last two minutes.' He too turned to look at Dottie across the room. 'Any chap who buys his wife a dress like that will find himself faced with a very heavy glass bill whenever she wears it.'

'Yes,' William said. 'I imagine he will. Not that any other woman will have the same devastating effect as Miss Manderson. If I could afford to buy my wife a frock like that, it would be worth every penny of the fourteen guineas.'

'Very true, sir. Do excuse me.' Greeley moved off to the next gentleman, thinking to himself, I can't wait to get back to the kitchen and tell them they were right about the inspector. He's as smitten as ever, if not more so.

Gervase's eyes told her he approved the dress. She clutched his arm and became part of the chatter that centred around him. Men and women alike took in every line of her dress, though perhaps not for the same reason. Dottie hoped she might receive some orders over the next few days; that would probably be the only good thing to come out of wearing it tonight.

Since Mrs Carmichael's death, the fortunes of the warehouse had gone into a slight decline. Dottie could only hope her plans for the next two seasons would change all that. In bleak moments of doubt, usually in the middle of the night when fear nibbled at her self-belief, she felt afraid the business would fail because of her incompetence. She still had so much to learn.

If only the music would start, and they could dance. She acknowledged a secret treacherous thought that the dress was very decorative—but it was not very warm, and after all, they were almost in December. Even with the fire lit and all these bodies in the room, she was rapidly growing cold. She folded her arms over the non-existent bodice and wished she could put on a coat.

This gave her an idea, and as Gervase's latest anecdote came to an end, and he took a smiling step back from the knot of laughing men and women around him, Dottie's imagination was busily fashioning a dress exactly the same as the one she was wearing but with a matching dainty, miniscule wrap to go about the shoulders, perhaps with spangles of some sort.

'A drink, Dottie dear?'

Thrusting her designs aside, she beamed at him. 'Oh yes please.'

He took his own empty glass and went to get his

refill along with a drink for Dottie. A friend of Dottie's mother, a woman in her late thirties, made a comment to Dottie about the dress, and her mood soaring, Dottie began to tell the woman about the warehouse. It quickly became clear she had a new client. Dottie's 'professional' eye took in the woman's dated and slightly rusty black gown. A glance about the room showed that most older women still favoured black, and the younger women largely wore white evening gowns. One or two wore other colours, but they were of sombre, muted shades. There ought to be more colour, Dottie thought with passion. Women needed some colour in their lives.

Gervase stood waiting for the servant to bring the drinks. Every now and then he sent a glance back towards Dottie, closely observing everyone she spoke to or laughed with. He was pleased to see she was conversing with a slightly dull-looking woman of his own age.

Gervase glanced to his right. He was standing beside a tall, fair, well-built young man, though definitely not well-to-do if the fellow's evening attire was anything to go by. Nevertheless, he was clearly a guest, so Gervase was inclined to be pleasant.

'William Hardy,' said William Hardy, holding out his right hand to Gervase. 'A friend of the Mandersons. Mr Manderson knew my father years ago.'

Gervase shook his hand. 'Ah. Nice to meet you. I'm Gervase Parfitt, the Assistant Chief Constable of Derbyshire. I'm engaged to Mr Manderson's daughter Dorothy.'

Hardy knew that of course. It was the reason he'd come over. It intrigued him that Parfitt felt the need to give his professional rank as he introduced himself. Did he think it made him seem powerful? It was common for men of rank to make sure everyone knew how important they were. It chimed perfectly with the impression he'd already formed of the man.

But Hardy simply smiled and nodded. 'Delighted to meet you.'

'Quite a dress she's wearing this evening, don't you think? My fiancée, I'm talking about, of course,' Gervase said, casting another proprietorial glance in Dottie's direction. His eyes narrowed as a man halted to speak with her. She gave the fellow a smile, the chap nodded then moved on. Gervase relaxed once more.

With some hesitation Hardy agreed it was quite a dress.

'Designed it herself. She dabbles a little in dressmaking. Always looks very decorative. That's important to someone in my position, of course.'

'Yes, indeed. Congratulations, you're a very lucky man. Have you set a date?'

'Not officially. She won't even announce the engagement until she's twenty-one. That's in March, so not long to wait, though I confess I'm rather impatient to be on my honeymoon. I'll probably have the engagement given out in April or May with the wedding to follow as soon as possible after that. Wait until the weather's likely to be half decent, and of course, I'll need to take plenty of time off for the honeymoon, as I'm sure you can imagine.'

'Indeed,' Hardy said again. He already didn't like Gervase. In fact even before he'd met him, he had formed a deep dislike of him. Out of a mixture of curiosity and sheer green-eyed jealousy, Hardy had set out to discover as much about the fellow as he could. What he had found out confirmed his worst doubts, and he could have cheerfully knocked Parfitt down. But he knew that was mostly personal, although some of it was professional pride. The way the man undressed her with his eyes... The self-satisfied smirk on his face... And talking to a complete stranger about his honeymoon... Everything Parfitt said and did added fuel to Hardy's dislike. But he hid all that and said simply, 'And shall you live in London?'

'Good God, no. Can't stand the place. And there's my work, of course.'

'Of course. I suppose Miss Manderson will relocate her fashion warehouse?'

If Hardy sounded too well informed about the lady, the other man luckily failed to notice. Gervase took the drinks from the servant and prepared to return to Dottie's side. He frowned over Hardy's words. 'I hardly think so. My wife will naturally be very taken up with supporting me socially, and of course there'll be the nursery to think of. She'll hardly have time to play about with her dressmaking then. In any case, it would hardly be fitting for the wife of a man in my position to wear some dress she'd made herself, no matter how revealing.'

'Of course. Well, many congratulations. I'm sure you'll both be very happy,' Hardy said, unable to resist adding, with some facetiousness, 'A man could *hardly* wish for a lovelier lady on his arm.'

His sarcasm went unnoticed, however.

'Oh definitely. She's quite the little charmer, and she'll be the perfect little wife for a man in my position. She's young, but teachable, if you catch my drift.'

Anger pushed Hardy to say, 'The lady has considerable charm. I'm certain you're the envy of every man here tonight.'

'Damn well hope so,' Gervase said with a smirk. He

winked at Hardy. 'And between you and I, she's a saucy little minx behind closed doors. As you say, considerable charms. And not too shy about using them.'

Hardy almost choked on his drink. Could Parfitt have said anything less appropriate to a complete stranger? If he had the luxury to follow his own inclination he would have called Parfitt out there and then, like some slighted suitor of the middle ages, he admitted to himself. But once again, he forced down his temper and said simply, with a man-to-man grin, 'As I said, you're the envy of every man here.'

'Thanks,' Gervase said. 'And now I must get back to her. Got to keep the other men away. One needs to give girls plenty of attention in these early stages of courtship. Of course, later on one can ignore them a lot longer.' He guffawed at his own joke.

'Nice to meet you,' Hardy gave him a curt nod and turned away, his blood boiling. He turned back briefly just in time to see Dottie look up and smile as Parfitt reached her side. The way her whole face lit up, the way her lovely smile reached her eyes... Hardy had to turn away. How dared Parfitt talk about her in that disgusting way?

Later, as Herbert Manderson proposed a toast to his lovely wife and publicly thanked her in the warmest terms his daughters had ever witnessed for their twenty-five happy years of marriage, Dottie couldn't help noticing that while William Hardy was focussed wholly on Dottie herself from one side of the room, Gervase Parfitt, official escort and unofficial fiancé, was stifling a yawn and looking everywhere except in her direction, from his position on the other side of the room. It was most aggravating.

She thought back to the beginning of the summer and the first time she had seen Gervase at a hotel in Scarborough where he'd been staying with his newly-widowed sister-in-law. Dottie had glimpsed his fair hair, his tall, lean build, and for a moment had thought he actually was William. She shook her head slightly in exasperation. Inspector Hardy. She must stop calling him William, even in her thoughts. Sooner or later it would slip out in conversation, and she could not let that happen.

Looking at them now, she couldn't think why she had ever thought them alike. Will—Inspector Hardy was an inch or two shorter than Gervase. Gervase was slightly taller, he was thinner, and had a slight stoop to his shoulders, no real surprise for a man who spent the majority of his time working at a desk. And of course Gervase was eight or nine years older than Will—Inspector Hardy. Gervase's fair hair was just touched with grey at the temples—most distinguished. Whereas Inspector Hardy's hair was lighter in colour and both fuller and thicker. What a shame she couldn't have Hardy's hair on Gervase's head! And of course, Inspector Hardy was more athletically built than Gervase, with more solid muscle, broader shoulders, and...

She was distracted from her thoughts by the enthusiastic applause that greeted her father's rather rambling, but beautifully tender speech, and along with everyone else Dottie raised her glass and repeated the toast: 'To dearest Lavinia, the love of my life.'

Her mother, never one to encourage emotional outbursts in public, for once didn't reprove her husband but simply said, 'Oh Herbert, you dear, dear man!' and kissed him on the cheek. The little band in the corner struck up a waltz, Herbert and Lavinia took to the floor, then after a few bars, other couples began to file onto the dancefloor around them. Seeing Gervase go by with a buxom lady of forty-five in his arms, Dottie ended up dancing with an older family friend, Montague Montague, known to herself and her sister as M'dear Monty for his habit of calling all women 'M'dear'.

Later that night, when the guests had gone, the Mandersons were alone in their drawing room with their son-in-law and both their daughters. Even Gervase had left fairly early, pleading the long train journey back to the Midlands in the morning and a full week of work ahead of him. Dottie, now with a negligee over her revealing dress, sat in the opposite corner of the sofa to her sister Flora and huffed a sigh of frustration that sent her hair bouncing into the air and settling again about her temples.

'What's up, poppet?' George her brother-in-law asked.

Mrs Manderson managed to restrain herself from criticising her son-in-law's use of the popular idiom. If one of her daughters had said it, Dottie thought, they would have been scolded. But not George. Since George—once considered by his in-laws as frivolous and lacking in maturity—had proved himself to be a loving and supportive husband to his wife during her first pregnancy, then an equally loving father to his and Flora's first child, and a loving brother to his late sister in committing himself to raising her baby daughter as his own, his mother-in-law's regard for him had gone from strength to strength. Dottie was half-convinced her mother now preferred George to either of her daughters.

But that was not the reason for the huge sigh. Unable to put it out of her mind, she said, 'Why did you insist on inviting Inspector Hardy this evening, Mother? It makes everything so uncomfortable.'

'Nonsense,' her mother said. Dottie could have almost predicted that. Mrs Manderson continued, 'He's a very pleasant young man, and we needed as many young men as we could get, with so many single ladies requiring dance partners. He may not be prosperous, but he is a decent, hard-working young fellow, and very presentable. And he waltzes beautifully.'

'Knew his father,' said Mr Manderson from behind his newspaper, his romantic leanings carefully in check once more.

'Yes, I know, but all the same...' Dottie gave it up. She couldn't win this argument. There was definitely a conspiracy at work here.

'He's certainly better looking than Gervase,' her mother added. 'And has far nicer manners.'

Unable to think of anything to say to this, Dottie glared at her and went up to bed.

She brushed her hair vigorously, enjoying the scraping of the bristles against her scalp, bringing her scalp to life. When she had finished, she pulled the loose hairs from the brush and dropped them into the waste basket beside the dressing table as always. Glancing up slightly as she did so, she surprised herself, catching a glimpse in the mirror seemingly of someone else, someone she knew yet who seemed slightly strange to her, like a friend she hadn't met in a while.

She leaned forward to look at herself. What could she see?

A pale face, grown thinner of late with the anxious times she'd been through. She felt she could see the ghosts of tiny lines about her eyes and mouth—the tiny tell-tale lines of life, that usually kept away until a woman turned thirty at the least—that vast age! But Dottie knew with a little care and rest, her complexion would recover its youth. It was the expression in her eyes that told the story of age and experience. A perfect stranger could look into her eyes, Dottie thought, and immediately see that she had known death and sorrow: too much for a young woman still not quite of full age. Too much death. Too many funerals. Too much sorrow.

She bit her lip. She was turning maudlin, she thought, and it simply wouldn't do.

She patted some cold cream carefully into her skin and caught up the hairbrush once more to try again to coax her curls to be neat and orderly.

Chapter Three

A week later they all met again.

It was the first week of December and usually the weather in Britain could be counted on to remain quite mild until the turn of the year, but Saturday the 8th of December proved to be very cold. A chilling wind snatched at the guests as they hurried, hats clutched on their heads, coats gripped tightly across their chests, into the church for the christening of Flora and George Gascoigne's twins.

Only a handful of people knew that the twins were no such thing. In fact, they were first cousins. The little boy, Freddie, now a little over five months old, was George and Flora's own child, but the little girl Diana, almost four weeks older, was the secret illegitimate daughter of George's sister, Diana, who had died in childbirth. It had been George and Flora's decision to raise the little girl as their own, and to keep her shameful origins hidden from the world. George's and Flora's parents all knew, of course. Gervase knew, because Dottie had told him, and no doubt the servants of both the Gascoigne and the Manderson households knew as well. William Hardy knew, because George's sister had been a witness in a murder case, the victim being her married lover. And obviously Dottie knew, not because she and Flora told each other everything, but because she had been with Diana as she gave birth to her daughter, only to die after placing one gentle kiss on the baby's cheek.

But society at large knew nothing, and so Flora and George stood at the front of the church proudly holding their two babies as the ceremony began.

Dottie had not been looking forward to this event. Ordinarily she loved any celebration or occasion, but once again, *that man* was involved in her family's intimate affairs. She couldn't help wondering if it was to spite her that Flora and George had asked William Hardy to be godfather to Freddie and Diana Gascoigne, and Dottie to be godmother.

She had to admit he looked very nice in his new grey suit. It wasn't an expensive, hand-made suit like Gervase's, and it didn't fit him with Gervase's suit's perfection. It was a good colour for him, though, and he looked—she grudgingly admitted—he looked really rather gorgeous in it.

Gervase was good-looking, there was no denying it. But the colour of his jacket was less flattering. That this particular shade of fawn was fashionable was beyond doubt. However, it wasn't a colour that flattered Gervase at all. Rather he looked fawn all over—his hair, his skin, his clothes, his features had become indistinguishable and uninteresting, a kind of beige mass.

Dottie glanced at Flora, who raised an eyebrow at her, signifying her amusement at Dottie's discomfort.

Yes, Dottie thought, they definitely did this on purpose.

She stepped forward and in her clear contralto, made her promise before God, the vicar and those present as godparent to the fidgeting baby boy and the quiet baby girl who watched everything with such interest. Hardy did the same.

The babies were so good, Diana looking about her, Freddie soon falling fast asleep amongst all the lace and frills thought necessary for the christening gowns of infants. It really was quite difficult to tell them apart, Dottie thought, not for the first time. That gave weight to the success of the 'twins' idea. It helped that although tiny Diana was a crucial twenty-six days older, Freddie was a big fellow, so they looked the same age.

The peace was not to last though. As soon as the vicar took the first baby and bathed its head with the chilly water from the font, the deafening wails of protest told everyone who knew the family that it was Freddie being baptised.

When they left the church, hurrying to their cars, the first few flakes of snow began to fall. It was a relief to reach Flora and George's and be welcomed into the house by roaring fires and a glass of warm punch from Greeley, their butler, back in his own domain once more.

Gervase was being very possessive of Dottie, keeping an arm about her waist or shoulders at almost every moment, and continually dropping hints about having christenings of their own. It was such a relief when they took their seats for lunch and she found herself sandwiched comfortably between Charles and Alistair, George's good friends, with Gervase seated at Flora's right hand further along the same side of the table. But her relief was short-lived when she found herself staring across the table into the eyes of William Hardy who took a seat opposite. Dottie made a mental note to have a serious discussion later with her sister.

Charles and Alistair were something of a double act. They made it their business—having been coached by Flora and George the day before—to keep Dottie occupied, entertained and distracted from Gervase Parfitt for the rest of the afternoon. Her eyes were drawn several times to glance across the table. She wasn't sure why she was so surprised to see Hardy chatting in that relaxed, very animated way with her mother. Surely that didn't bode well? But with Charles and Alistair talking nonstop nonsense, she couldn't hear what was being said on the other side of the table, although she caught the name Eleanor once: that was Wil—Inspector Hardy's sister. If any last doubts lingered, they were now completely banished. There was a conspiracy afoot among her relations to include Hardy in everything they did as a family. Which could only mean one thing: they didn't like Gervase, and wanted Inspector Hardy in their family.

That night, Gervase took Dottie dancing. It should have been the perfect end to an enjoyable, happy day. But Dottie felt irritable and scratchy, whilst Gervase spent too much time criticising her family and their guests. Dottie tried to smile and say the right things, but she was immensely relieved when after a relatively short kiss he said goodnight and returned to his club.

In his room at his club, Gervase was feeling pretty pleased with himself. He felt confident that he had shown Dottie how much happier she would be once they were married and moved into his home in

Nottinghamshire. The sooner she was removed from her sister and parents' controlling grasp the better. Among the guests there had been one young fellow he hadn't taken to, the same one he'd talked to at the anniversary party. Oh, the man had talked about being a friend of the family, but Gervase realised now that it was more than that. He obviously had designs on Dottie. The way the chap looked at her! Gervase tried to remember what he'd said to the fellow at the anniversary party but could only remember the odd look in his eyes when Gervase mentioned Dottie. Clearly the man had an infatuation for her. Not that someone of his class could ever hope to win a girl like Dottie, but all the same, Gervase knew he'd be able to relax once he'd got her away from all these influences. And the sooner the better, he couldn't afford to waste too much more time away from his business interests or his position as the Assistant Chief Constable of Derbyshire.

As Dottie got ready for bed, so grateful to Janet, the Mandersons' maid, for the fire in her room and the hot water bottle in her bed. She was also deep in thought. She felt depressed. Where should she turn? Usually she would talk to her sister. Or *in extremis*, to her mother. But with the current slight reserve between them now, everything was all too difficult.

With the visit to her Aunt Cecilia and Uncle Lewis in Sussex looming as soon as Christmas was out of the way, she had a sense of being overwhelmed by everything that was happening. If she could only go back a year, to when her heart belonged—briefly, before being crushed—to Cyril Penterman, that would be perfect. It now seemed as if the childish broken heart she suffered then was nothing compared to the turmoil of her thoughts and emotions now. She should be happy. She had Gervase pressing her to marry him as soon as possible, and she had her fashion warehouse. Yet it felt as though her life was a complete mess, and that nothing was going the way it should. How had she let it all happen? What on earth was she to do about any of it?

But she slept well, in spite of her unsettled mind. In the morning she rose, went to church as usual, had a quiet lunch with her parents, then the three of them went to Flora and George's for afternoon tea and to spend some time with the much-loved little ones.

It was a good thing that the butler, Greeley, showed William Hardy out the following evening, the Monday after the christenings. Left to himself, Hardy would have slammed the door with all his strength, he was so very angry. He had no words to give vent to his temper, but with a series of furious sighs and unworded sounds he reached his car, and slammed the door shut upon its inner world. He sat there in the driver's seat, his hands gripping the wheel, and wrestled with what he'd just been told.

It was beyond preposterous. It was highly improper. It completely contravened every moral and legal aspect of police work not to mention the integrity of the law. He shook his head yet again. He just couldn't believe it, although given what he'd already found out about the man, he should not have been surprised.

He leaned his forehead on the steering wheel and took a few deep breaths. Eventually he became calmer. He was still furious, yes, but the first heat of it was ebbing away, leaving him able to think in a rational manner about what he'd just been told.

She—no, *he*—it was *he* who had committed these

ridiculous and false acts. *She* was not to blame. Well, perhaps she was a little to blame—she had been far too naïve, far too trusting, and had clearly not once paused to think about what she was doing, or what she was being drawn into. The potential for harm if something had gone wrong! Anything might have happened. Leaving aside the sheer breathtaking irregularity of the event, there remained the possibility that she could have been harmed. But Hardy's rage was all against the man: legally knowledgeable, older, more experienced, and Hardy had no doubt, fully aware of the actions he was taking, and the implication of them. This was yet further proof of the uncertain nature of the man's moral integrity.

He sat there a little longer, his thoughts circling round and round in his head. He was completely unaware that Greeley was watching him from the dining room window, a troubled look on his face, and that Flora herself was peeking from behind the curtain in the drawing room, biting her lip as she realised all too late that she had said too much, and had light-heartedly confided in entirely the wrong person.

Almost half an hour after leaving the house, just as Flora had made up her mind to go out to him and bring him back into the house to talk, Hardy drove away. He reached his home and sat at the kitchen table for the rest of the evening, late into the night, pulling out a file he'd brought from work, reading and rereading, making notes, crossing them through, ripping up pages and tossing them, crumpled, into the rubbish bin in the corner of the room. He paced the floor. When it was time to go to bed, he made a fresh pot of tea and sat back down at the kitchen table, still trying to come to a decision.

He slept in the chair, waking to find a crick in his neck and ink all over his cheek. As soon as it was a decent hour to call, he drove back to the Gascoignes'. Greeley opened the door within five seconds, clearly expecting him, as was Flora who was up and dressed and waiting in her pretty little sitting room.

Hardy walked in, and without preamble said to Flora, 'Does she love him?'

Whatever Flora had been expecting, it wasn't this. 'What does that have to do with anything?' And she thought, not for the first time, how haughty she sounded, and how like her mother.

'If she loves him, if they are getting married, I'll hold my tongue. What you told me yesterday... Surely you must see what a serious breach it was? And it's not the first such breach I've discovered in the man's career. But if she loves him...'

Flora hesitated. In truth, she was not convinced of Dottie's undying affection for Gervase Parfitt. But how could she tell Hardy, of all people, about her uncertainty?

He held out his hands imploringly. 'Flora. I'm—I need to know. I don't intend to try to come between them. I don't want to make trouble. I would never hurt her. But if there's nothing serious on her side, then I have a duty to inform my superiors of what you've told me. For Parfitt, there will be a hell of a stink, and that could affect her. But as I said, what you've told me about, that's only one small breach in a whole range of... Well anyway. But you know how I feel about Dottie. I wouldn't involve her in a scandal for all the world. If she loves him, well then. I shall try to pretend our conversation yesterday never happened. But as a police officer, you must see how I stand.'

Still Flora hesitated. He threw himself down in a

chair, leaning back with his eyes closed.

She could see he'd hardly slept. He was pale; there were dark circles under his eyes. And her practised womanly eye detected he was wearing the same shirt as the day before. Either that, or all his shirts had a crinkle on the collar in exactly the same spot. This one was also blotted with ink on both cuffs. She took the chair next to him and reached out to pat his arm.

'I don't know how she feels, William, dear, and that's the honest truth. She won't discuss it with me.'

He looked surprised. 'I thought you told each other everything?'

'Yes, we did used to. We—well something happened and—you know, with the babies and everything. We just don't see quite as much of each other, so I suppose it's inevitable things change.' She looked unhappy. He was curious, longing to know what had happened, but he felt he couldn't possibly ask. Flora took pity on him.

'It was when Dottie first came back from the Midlands in the summer. My mother told Dottie something. Something that had been a secret, a painful secret. She felt she had to tell her. But... It's created something of a...' She fought for the right words. 'It shook us all up, and it's been hard to know how to go back to how things were before.'

His mind was busy. 'Is this to do with Parfitt?'

She shook her head. 'No, no it's nothing to do with Gervase.' She looked at Hardy. 'You really don't like him, do you?'

'Not at all. But I can't tell you what I think without using the kind of language unsuitable for a lady's ears.'

'George hates him with a passion and calls him all sorts of names, practically on a daily basis. Oh William, we're all so concerned that she might actually marry Gervase.'

'I must say, I'm surprised. I had assumed all the family loved him as much as Dottie does.'

Flora made up her mind to be very candid. 'I told you I didn't *know*. I'm not certain, William, but I'm not at all sure Dottie does *love* him. She enjoys his company, that's all, and he is something of a steamroller, he just seems to mow down everything in his path. But as for the rest of us, we're not especially enamoured of him. I don't know why, I just don't trust him. He's so slick and plausible. And pompous. And—well, I don't know what it is about him, I only know that I dislike him intensely.'

He had made up his mind. 'Dottie will be furious.'

'She'll get over it.'

'It could ruin him.'

'I don't care about that. I don't believe he's a good man. I don't want him to drag her into anything scandalous. And I don't want him to break her heart.'

'She won't forgive me.'

'She will, William. Just be patient and give her time. I'm afraid she'll know that I talked to you, but that can't be helped either. If there's to be a fuss, you will try to keep her out of it, won't you?'

'Of course. I don't believe she's done anything so very awful. It's he who has violated the trust placed in him. And more besides.' The clock in the hall chimed nine o'clock. He ought to be at his desk by now. 'I must go.' He bent to kiss her cheek, and she felt oddly moved by the intimate gesture.

'Goodbye, William, do take care of yourself, and come and see us often.'

He felt much lighter and happier as he left the house. His mind was made up, and come what may, he was going to do what he knew he had to do.

'What time's your train?' Dottie asked. There was no reply. She felt his lips nuzzling her ear. It tickled, and not in a good way. She pushed down her irritation, wondering when she had become such a shrew. Forcing a smile, she gave him a playful slap, nowhere near as hard as the one she really wanted to deliver. 'Gervase, stop it! Listen to me, I'm trying to ask you a question.'

'I know.' His tone was the vocal equivalent of rolling his eyes. 'That's women for you, forever chatter chatter chatter.' He gave a theatrical sigh. 'In answer to your question, it's the usual train at half past two. Can't I stay with you? I'd much rather do that.'

'Don't be silly, you know you're needed.' She kept her tone light, but in her head she was determined to make him go home to Nottinghamshire. The mere thought of him staying on was too much. She was *depending* on him going home. Although she was not at all prepared to consider why she felt that way. She pushed the feelings away with a mental shrug of the shoulders and a silent excuse: *Everything's fine. There's nothing wrong. I'm tired, that's all. I'm just so busy at the moment.*

'Well I don't know that I'm needed exactly, but I can see I'm not wanted here.' He pretended to pout, and she made herself smile, disguising another twinge of irritation. Just lately he'd started doing this. Pouting and acting like a child. She knew other couples did this kind of thing, and baby-talk and the like, but it wasn't as sweet or endearing as he seemed to think; it actually made her want to slap him. Hard. But she tried not to react too sharply. They'd had one or two disagreements lately and it had been horrid. She didn't want them to fall out over something so petty. Not when she knew she was just being beastly to him. She was just tired. And busy.

She said, 'Of course you're wanted here, but you're a very important man and I can't expect to keep you to myself.' She knew it was exactly what he liked to be told.

The very important man straightened his tie. He took her hand in his, dropping a light kiss on the back of it.

'Darling, you know I just find it so difficult to be away from you.'

'I know, but...'

'You know I love you, dearest. I wish you'd be a little kinder to me. It would be far nicer for me to go back to Nottingham with some happy memories instead of you saying, 'Stop it, Gervase,' every time I get you to myself.' He adopted what he fondly imagined was an irresistible puppy-dog gaze.

Dottie gripped her hands together, just in case she did slap him, and said firmly, 'I've told you, I'm not like that. You'll just have to...'

'I know, I know! I've just got to wait until we're married.' There was an edge to his voice. He tried again, this time in a wheedling manner. 'It's just so difficult being apart from you for two weeks at a time. I long for you, Dottie, I really do. I *ache* for you.'

She was spared the necessity of answering him; there was a soft tap on the door of the morning room, and Janet, the Mandersons' maid, said from the hall, 'Mr Gervase's cab is here, miss.'

Dottie managed to stifle her first response, '*Thank God*,' and merely smiled. Gervase cursed softly and got up to open the door.

'Thank you, Janet.' He took his hat and coat from her and began to head for the front door, which stood open. Out in the street beyond, Dottie could see a bored-looking cabbie standing by the door of his vehicle, ready for his client. She followed Gervase down the steps, felt so relieved to escape with just one more hasty kiss on the lips, then he was gone. Dottie waved, and for the first time that morning, she smiled with genuine pleasure.

Chapter Four

Two days before Christmas, Dottie looked up from her desk in the office located in the dim recesses of the warehouse to see Flora coming in, pulling off her wet hat and shaking the raindrops from her coat.

'Flora!' Dottie was on her feet and taking the coat and hat from her. The coat she draped over the back of a chair, which she placed near the fire, and the hat and gloves she put on the mantelpiece, reasoning that if hot air travelled upwards, they would surely dry. 'I didn't realise it was raining.'

Flora was already looking at the sheets strewn across the desk.

'In buckets. At least it's not cold today. So glad the weather has cheered up. Any further forward with your next lot of designs? I love the colour of this sample.'

'It's coming together. I'm hoping that, with a few late nights, we will have everything ready in time. What do you think of this peacock blue negligee set?'

'It's lovely, though I'm not sure it's really me.'

'I think it would look perfect on you. And I'm sure George would agree.'

'Oh he'd adore it, I know that. I'd better get one, we wives have to keep our husbands happy. And I'll have one in that emerald green, too; that colour does things to my eyes that reduces George to mush. Look, I know I'm a bit early but I was just so excited about going out on my own with you like we used to, and you know, being an actual *woman* again, not just a mother. But if you're not ready, I don't mind waiting.'

'I'll only be five more minutes, I promise. I need to stop working anyway, my head is swimming.' Dottie got up, 'Oh and I've just got to go and see one of the ladies. Then I'll be ready to go.' She hurried out of the room.

Flora took a seat and waited. She had never been here until Dottie had taken charge. But she'd heard that Dottie hadn't changed a thing. All that was missing from the office of *Carmichael and Jennings*, apart from Mrs Carmichael herself of course, was Mrs Carmichael's large bottle of gin.

Flora smiled. Dottie had fitted herself into the role remarkably well. In the six months since Mrs Carmichael had passed away, she had worked very hard to learn as much as she could about the business side of things. If her family had been unsure how good a businesswoman a girl of Dottie's years would prove to be—still not yet twenty-one, Flora reminded herself—then their doubts had been set aside early on. Because she seemed to manage everything: design, execution, organisation, staffing, and bringing in new clients. If not exactly effortlessly, at least Dottie's hard work and willingness to learn had eased her into the new role, and her charm had appeased most of the existing clients. Flora wondered whether it was possible Dottie's fashion warehouse might some day rival even the big, established and respected houses in Paris, London, New York and Milan. That would be an incredible achievement. Flora planned to be there by Dottie's side to support her as much as she could, and she knew their mother felt the same.

The only cloud on the horizon, apart from Gervase of course, was this new business with their Aunt Cecilia. Flora pushed away the nagging fear those thoughts brought once again. She would not—could not—lose the person she thought of as her sister. Dottie was too important to her.

And not just to her. There were their parents too. How would they feel if Dottie was wooed to Sussex by Cecilia Cowdrey? They would be devastated, Flora knew. But she hastily dismissed that alarming idea as nonsense. Dottie would never leave London and her work...

But she'll have to, a little voice said in Flora's mind, because of Gervase. She sighed. He had made it all too clear that he was keen to get engaged as quickly as possible. He would not be happy with a long engagement either, Flora suspected. He showed all the signs of a man impatient to be married. How could Dottie possibly keep both herself and Gervase happy? She couldn't possibly persuade him to leave his exalted position in the Midlands, yet it was equally impossible they should commute to and from London. How on earth was it to be managed? Flora began to have grave concerns. Not for the first time. There was something so very proprietorial in his manner towards Dottie that Flora disliked. And George said the man had indulged in some boasting of a man-to-man kind when they'd had a few drinks together. Would Gervase be a faithful husband? Was he even capable of such a thing? And how would he enjoy having a career woman for a wife? Flora was absolutely certain he would hate it. She knew in her heart he would never permit such a thing.

Dottie returned just then. 'All done! I'll just grab these and I'll be ready to go.' 'These' turned out to be the design sheets with the attached swatches. Flora helped her to stack the pages neatly, checking each one to ensure the sample of fabric and the buttons and other trimmings were all in place. In addition there were a number of rough sketches for the new children's range Dottie was still considering. The top one caught Flora's eye: a delightful christening gown in white silk and lace.

She marvelled again at how well Dottie fitted this new world. It had given her confidence, helped her develop her abilities and potentially could add considerably to her financial position. It was too much to expect her to simply give that all up, surely? Yet Flora knew that Gervase was the kind of man who would expect to be Dottie's whole world, yet she would never be the heart of his.

'What are you going to put them in? It's raining, don't forget.' Flora was putting her coat and hat back on, still horribly damp. Her gloves she shoved in her bag.

Dottie, biting her lip, looked about her. She looked anxious. 'I don't know. I don't have anything.' She looked at Flora. 'What shall I do? They won't fit into my bag, or yours.' There was the rising sound of panic in her voice. It was the sound Flora recognised in her own voice whenever she grew worried about the children. Calmly she said:

'Why don't you wrap them in brown paper? It'll keep the worst of the rain off them at least. We've only got to get to the car, and from the car to the restaurant.'

'Oh, good idea!' Dottie nodded then practically ran out of the room in search of the brown paper. It didn't take long to wrap up the sheets into a precious bundle, and they were ready to leave.

Flora's stomach rumbled. 'I'm so hungry,' she complained over her shoulder as they went out. 'Ever since I had the twins, I'm ravenous all the time.'

Dottie grinned. So often these days, Flora seemed to forget she had only had one of the babies herself, not both of them.

She said goodbye to everyone in the warehouse and wished them all a Merry Christmas and a Happy New Year. A couple of the girls came forward to hug her and to thank her for the little gifts she had left for them all.

'I can't believe I'm going to be away from the warehouse for two whole weeks. I'm a bit worried it won't be here when I get back. Two weeks seems like an awfully long time to be away.'

As they made a dash to the car, coats huddled close about them against the weather, bags and the brown paper parcel clutched under their arms, Flora said, 'I'm sure everything will be quite all right. They've got phone numbers and addresses if they need to contact you in an emergency. You've earned this holiday.' Then she pointed at the parcel Dottie cradled in her arms as she waited for Flora to open the car door for her. 'Anyway, you'll be fairly busy with those. Not such a holiday after all!'

Later, over lunch at the restaurant, once the soup dishes had been taken away, Flora leaned forward and asked, 'What time are you leaving on Friday?'

It was the first mention from either of them of Dottie's visit to the relatives in Sussex.

Dottie told her what she had planned, and after a moment's silence, Flora suddenly said, in a soft rush, 'You will come back, Dottie darling, won't you? I couldn't bear it if...'

A waiter interrupted them, his arm reaching past first Flora then Dottie to set plates of roast beef in front of them. Neither woman spoke except to say, 'Yes, please,' or 'No thank you,' to the vegetable and gravy options on offer. When he had gone, Dottie put out a hand to take Flora's.

'Don't be silly. Of course, I'll come back. Flora, I'm just going down to St Martins for a few days, to spend some time with Aunt Cecilia. That's all. I'm coming back.'

'Do you feel differently now? Now you know the truth, I mean?'

Dottie shook her head. 'No. I mean, at first it was a lot to take in. It was such a shock, and I felt rather like someone had pulled the rug out from under my entire life. I couldn't seem to understand. But that was just the shock of it. Once it had worn off, I realised that, no matter what the so-called 'truth' about my birth was, Mother and Father will always be *my* mother and father. And you...'

Out of nowhere the emotion hit her and choked her words. But it didn't matter that they were in a public place, or that both her eyes and Flora's were welling with tears, she had to continue, she had to say it in actual words. 'I know that *technically* you're my cousin, but you're so much more to me than that. You'll always be my sister, Flora. Nothing can change that, nor would I ever want it to.' She dabbed her cheeks and managed a trembly smile. 'Now for goodness' sake, let's pull ourselves together, and eat this food whilst it's hot.'

Flora did a little laugh that didn't quite work, but

they picked up their knives and forks, the tension of the recent months lifted, and they were themselves again.

A few minutes later, having disposed of three roast potatoes in rapid succession and then a Yorkshire pudding, Flora said, 'By the way, I'm afraid I've upset a Certain Person.'

'What do you mean? Who?'

'Your favourite police inspector.'

That caused Dottie to set down her knife and fork. Hoping no one else could hear the pounding of her heart, she looked at Flora steadily, and in a neutral voice she said, 'William Hardy? What could you possibly say to upset him?'

Flora said, 'He came to visit, on the Monday after the christenings. And, well, we were just chatting, you know. And then... I'm afraid I told him all about Gervase showing you the official files about that young fellow who died.'

Dottie could only stare at Flora. She couldn't eat any more of her food. Her throat felt tight and restricted. She didn't feel as though she'd ever be able to swallow anything again. She tried to speak but all she produced was a little squeak.

Flora, not appearing to notice, went on: 'And I'm afraid I also told him about how Gervase gathered everyone together for you to reveal the culprit. Just like in the mystery books.' Here Flora was on dangerous ground, as she couldn't afford to give herself away too badly. So she opted for: 'Well I suppose I thought he'd be interested.'

Dottie's cheeks flamed. She felt hot all over. After a moment she was able to say, 'Y—you told him about that?'

Reluctantly, Flora said, 'Yes dear. I'm *so* sorry. And I know I should have told you sooner, but to be honest I was worried about how you'd take it, but it's been bothering me so... Well, anyway, it didn't go at all as I expected. I didn't imagine for a moment that he would... well, I'm afraid he wasn't at all pleased. In fact he was really quite angry. I thought he'd admire the way Gervase took an interest in your ideas, but it wasn't like that at all.'

Dottie pushed her plate away. The food had turned foul to her. She couldn't even look at it. It shouldn't matter, she told herself. It didn't matter. Not in the slightest. Whatever *he* thought of her was of no interest to her. She reminded herself that Gervase was far superior to W—to Inspector Hardy in the hierarchy of the police force, and that if Gervase hadn't seen anything amiss in what had happened, there was no reason to be concerned about what W— Inspector Hardy made of it all.

Which didn't explain why she felt like crying.

Dottie took the pile of folded clothes from her mother and placed them in the suitcase. The next morning's early start meant packing the night before was essential.

Next to the suitcase was the gleaming leather briefcase that had been a Christmas gift from Flora and George. Dottie glanced at it frequently, partly from pleasure at the way it made her feel so professional, and partly with a deep, almost maternal concern that something terrible might befall the precious contents.

Janet came in with two blouses, still warm from the iron. 'That's the last two, miss.'

'Thank you,' Dottie said, but it was Mrs Manderson who took the garments, folded them carefully with the expert touch of many years' practice, and placed them into the suitcase. A small velvet bag containing jewellery items was tucked into a corner, an evening gown—not the notoriously revealing new ruby silk—was lain over the top of everything, and the lid was locked down. Then Mrs Manderson and Janet sat on the case whilst Dottie wrestled with the buckle of the strap they had put around the case for added security.

'Well that's that.' Mrs Manderson sat on the bed beside Dottie.

Janet bobbed and returned to the kitchen.

In the kitchen, preparations were underway for a fine dinner for Miss Dottie's last night before she went away. The underlying strain of those upstairs had somehow communicated itself to those downstairs and everyone felt nervous and on edge, even if they didn't exactly know why.

The young tweenie, Margie, said for the dozenth time, 'Well I don't know what all the fuss is about. Miss Dottie's only going off on a visit to her auntie for a few days. It's a shame she'll miss New Year's Eve at home though, but it's not like she's never coming back. I don't know why everyone is so upset about it. I wish *I* could go and visit *my* auntie. Miss Dottie don't know how lucky she is.'

Cook said, 'Just you shush, missy, you don't know nothing about it.' Cook remembered a day, just short of twenty-one years earlier, when her mistress had returned home from a trip away to the seaside as slim as ever, but with a new baby daughter. Cook had always wondered about that. Sometimes you had to wait a fearful long time to find out something, Cook thought. Not but they didn't all love Miss Dottie to bits. But she'd wondered about it all the same.

'But...' protested Margie.

'I said shush!' Cook said, more sharply than she

intended. Margie's face fell, her lip quivered. In a gentler voice, Cook said, 'Now just you get on with them spuds.'

Margie got on.

Mrs Manderson took Dottie's hand. 'I hope everything works out all right at St Martins. You mustn't expect too much. After all, Cecilia and you are almost strangers to one another. You mustn't expect...'

'Mother, I know. It'll be all right. You mustn't worry. I'm only going to be away for a week. Everything will be perfectly all right.'

'Well, you do have a tendency to take things far too seriously.'

Dottie leaned against her mother. She hasn't done that since she was a toddler, Lavinia thought. She smoothed Dottie's hair.

Dottie continued, 'It'll be all right. And I'll be home again next week. We'll have our own slightly late little New Year's celebration then. I'm a bit nervous about meeting my... cousins. I remember them as older and a bit serious.'

'Imogen is nine years older than you, perhaps slightly more as I seem to remember her birthday is in August. But she's the youngest. I imagine Guy must be thirty, or even thirty-one by now. Cecilia did say in a letter not too long ago that he was engaged to be married, not for the first time, but I don't think it ever came to anything. He still lives with Cecilia and Lewis.'

'But Leo's married, isn't he? The oldest boy? How old is he?'

'Oh yes, he's been married for several years. He must be about thirty-four. I can't remember his wife's name. A pale, vague sort of girl, but her father's that soap chappie who got a life peerage two or three years ago, it was all in the papers. I can't remember his name, but his firm makes the *Sudso* stuff. He and his wife adopted her when she was a baby. The wife died recently, I believe. Leo and his wife don't have any children, not so far at least.'

'And do Leo and his wife live with—er—A-Aunt Cecilia?' Dottie could have kicked herself or stumbling over the word. It was still difficult to know the best thing to say. 'My natural mother' was not only a bit of a mouthful, but felt wrong and uncomfortable somehow, like an ungrateful slap. It was easier to simply continue to refer to the woman as 'Aunt Cecilia' as she had always done. Not for the world did Dottie want to hurt the feelings of the only mother she'd known all her life.

For their whole family, life had become complicated, and something of an emotional merry-go-round since her mother's heart-breaking revelation back in the summer. But if it had been a challenge to the relationships between Dottie, Flora, Lavinia and Herbert, Dottie was determined it would ultimately bring them closer together, or at least, once they had all completely recovered from the shock, it would.

The initial sense of betrayal and of not belonging had passed quickly, leaving Dottie with the certainty that the people who had raised her and called themselves her parents, had loved her just as surely as if she had in fact been flesh of their flesh. Her sister—always close, always her best friend—was as dear as ever, perhaps more so, as it was now a relationship of conscious choice, not one merely of familial duty. Yes, they had survived and grown fonder, though the pain of discovery had not yet fully subsided. Nor the awkwardness of the current situation.

Her mother said, 'No, he and his wife have their own home. But it's in the neighbourhood. Their families were always quite close, I believe. Although I think Leo met her at a hunt ball rather than a family event.'

Dottie wrinkled her nose. She abhorred blood sports. 'What does he do? Or is he too rich to worry about such things?'

'I don't know what Leo does. Cecilia has never said. Perhaps he helps his father with the estate? I imagine it will be his one day anyhow. Lewis inherited it from his father and grandfather. It's been in the family for such a long time. Even the nearby village is named after the estate, although from what Cecilia's told me, they've sold off most of the estate to pay death duties and for various repairs and such. I don't suppose the village has actually belonged to St Martins estate for a century or more.'

'So why isn't the house called Cowdrey House, if it's always been the family home?'

'The family name used to be Martin generations ago. I think one of the daughters inherited the estate as the last of the line, and it was she who married into the Cowdrey family, but she didn't change the name of the house.'

'If Leo has taken over the estate, does that mean Uncle Lewis is a lot older than Aunt Cecilia? Or is he ill? Is he not expected to live very much longer?'

'Oh it's not that. He's five years younger than Cecilia, and she's eleven years older than me, so he must be fifty-seven or eight. But no, Lewis has always been a reckless sort of fellow, even when we were young. Obviously you won't say anything to Cecilia, but he's always been rather too fond of the drink. And gaming. Then, too, from hints she's dropped in the past, I gather he's not exactly the faithful sort. That's not the lifestyle of someone you expect to live to a ripe old age. I think Leo is running the estate more as something for the boy to do than from immediate need.'

Dottie thought for a moment, then said, 'Although Aunt Cecilia must have been unfaithful at least once, because well, here I am.' She paused, then added a little shyly, a little nervously, 'Did she never confide in you about my father?'

Her mother shook her head. 'She wouldn't say. I did ask. I always assumed he was some married man in their social circle. But I've no idea who he was.' She suddenly looked alarmed. 'Surely you won't ask her, will you?'

'Oh no,' said Dottie. 'Of course not. Unless, you know, she seems to want to talk about it. Then I might. Was it just—I don't know—a quick affair—or did she really love him? Does she still see him?'

Her mother gave an uncomfortable little laugh. 'Dearest, I've really no idea. There's nothing I can tell you. As I said, she's never confided in me. And for goodness' sake, be careful what you ask her and when. You don't want to upset everything. She can be—difficult.'

Dottie kissed her mother's cheek. 'It'll be all right,' she repeated for the umpteenth time. 'I'm only interested in going to see them all for a short visit, then I shall come home. I just want to feel I know Aunt Cecilia a little better. We might even become friends.'

Her mother's doubtful look at that didn't entirely encourage her.

The drive down was surprisingly pleasant. Although the weather at the end of December was usually horrid—as it had been at the beginning of the month, she remembered, thinking of the snow flurries on the day of the christenings—today Dottie had sunny skies all the way to Sussex. It was cooler, yes, but with the lovely new car rug over her knees—which she had to take great care to keep out of the way of the pedals—Dottie was snug and enjoyed herself immensely.

It was her first long trip on her own and when she finally arrived in the village of St Martins she felt a sense of achievement she had only had once before in her life: on the opening of her first albeit small fashion show at the warehouse at the end of September.

She pulled the car off the main road and onto the gravel drive, carefully squeezing her blue Morris Minor between the two stone pillars that stood guard at the entrance. As she slowly drove past, she noticed the pillars were topped by great stone geese, life-sized and facing each other, open beaks extended forward on aggressively thrusting necks, each bird with its wings half-raised as if about to fly at the other. The name of the place, 'St Martins House' was carved on each pillar in large letters.

She drove along the meandering gravelled drive that brought her round a huge shrubbery to an entrance courtyard where a fountain in the centre allowed a kind of passing loop in front of the house.

She halted the car, and got out, leaning back inside to grab her handbag, the hat box, and her precious briefcase. The gravel crunched under her feet as she went to the door, a single shallow step up taking her onto a colourful mosaic that formed the floor of the porch. The mosaic depicted a man in ragged clothes hiding behind something that looked like a car door but was clearly something else entirely with yet more geese, looking equally as fierce as those on the pillars, their beaks gaping threateningly. Dottie wondered if someone in the house had a fondness for the creatures.

She allowed the knocker to fall once, and waited, looking around her from under the dark porch, made darker by the rapid approach of evening. The small-paned windows were dark and secretive-looking. Grimy red bricks made up the fabric of the great barrack of a building. None of it was calculated to inspire a sense of happy arrival. She could hear the honking of geese somewhere nearby. Clearly here the birds weren't only represented in art. Away to her left, trees and shrubs seemed to crowd at the edge of what appeared to be an expanse of lawn, whilst on her right, more trees and shrubs came far closer, almost touching the walls of the house. Surely the rooms on that side must be very dark, Dottie thought.

She waited. No one came to the door. Her sense of achievement at completing the long journey, of navigating from the busy heart of London down into the green rolling hills and valleys of Sussex, began to dissipate, leaving her shivering in the shadows of the house. What should she do? She rang again but felt as though she was wasting her time. The house felt empty and hollow as it hulked before her. She felt a sudden stab of anxiety. It was the right day, wasn't it? She thought she had arrived at the right time, as her aunt—for Dottie wasn't yet ready to call her anything other than aunt—had instructed in her letter.

Dottie turned and looked about her. No one. What should she do? She began to walk back down the steps, bumping herself as her briefcase hit the corner of porch pillar. She glanced back. Perhaps someone had come to the door? But no, there was no one.

She deposited the hatbox, handbag and briefcase beside the car, blessed if she was going to carry them all the way around to the back door, especially if no one was home and she had to go away again. Go away to where, her panicking mind asked as she set off around the side of the house. What if there really was no one home?

This was ridiculous, she told herself sharply. If no one was home—but they surely would be—she would simply drive to a hotel and stay the night; she had enough money with her for such an advent, if it arose. She was regretting her refusal to listen to her father and bring their maid Janet with her. Though that had been mainly because Janet had a final fitting for her wedding gown the next day, and Dottie hadn't wanted to disrupt her plans, though she knew Janet wouldn't have minded, she had been so grateful to Dottie for paying for the gown for her as part of her wedding gift to Janet and her intended, Sergeant Frank Maple.

Thinking of Sergeant Maple sent her thoughts in William Hardy's direction, and she clamped down firmly on that. Dottie remembered seeing a little pub in the village as she drove through. Perhaps they did rooms? It'll only be for one night. 'Because if no one's here,' she said out loud, mainly to drive away her sense of loneliness, 'I shall have to go back to London in the morning.'

By the time she reached the back door, she had convinced herself she would be leaving immediately to find that pub. She found the back door closed with no light showing through the glass. Nonetheless she rapped on the glass and waited. And waited. To no avail. The house was dark and empty. The pine trees and firs that surrounded the house seemed to crowd in all round about, blocking out the light, adding to the sense of emptiness, bringing the evening in far too early.

Away to the right was a long expanse of lawn, dotted with the bulky shapes of sleepy white-plumed geese. The grass sloped down to a body of water that twinkled just beyond the trees. How lovely, she thought. On any other day... She turned back to peer through the glass of the door.

No one was here. Once again, further knocks brought no change to that situation.

Feeling dismayed, Dottie began to doubt herself, as everyone does when they arrive at the right place, at the right time, and the person expecting them is absent. She was in an area she didn't know, with only the haziest idea where the nearest inn was. It was only half past three, but it would be dark soon. Yet still she dithered. How ridiculous this was. She was tired and hungry. A few spots of rain fell from the sky that, less than half an hour earlier had been as blue and clear as a June day. The wind had got up, and she shivered again, pulling her jacket close and wishing she had worn a greatcoat and a woolly scarf.

There were some outbuildings. Perhaps she might find someone there. She hurried to take a look, turning up her jacket collar to keep the wind off as best she could. She saw a beautifully polished Morris Minor similar to her own parked in front of the double doors of the garage—surely an old carriage house—but she couldn't find a living soul. No chauffeur, no gardener, no one. Obviously everyone was still away for the Christmas holidays, presumably travelling in a different motor car.

There seemed nothing left for her to do but to go back to the car. Casting a final despairing look at the back door, then at the front door, showed nothing had changed. No one stood by either door peering out, wondering where their caller had gone. The place was desolate. It was a fine beginning to this visit to her relations.

Chapter Five

Sure enough the pub in the village had a couple of rooms they let out to visitors. The pub, called The Sheep Fold, was a sweet little white-washed, thatched-roofed affair, snuggled in under a hill as if sheltering from the oncoming bad weather. She had pulled the car off the road and into a yard that served as a sort of mews at the side of the place. The overhanging trees made it quite dark here, and her headlamps picked up the figure of a man in his middle years coming out to meet her, extending a hand to help her out of the car.

'Afternoon, miss. Brought the rain with you I see. You just get yourself inside out of the weather, miss, I'll bring your luggage in,' he told her with a broad grin. She could almost have hugged him, she was so relieved to hear a friendly voice. Once more grabbing her hatbox, handbag and briefcase, she hurried into the pub, skirting a large, well-decorated Christmas tree right inside the door. She looked back to see him lifting out her suitcase, slamming down the little luggage door, then turning back to head for the entrance, his head bent against the sudden squall. He left the suitcase by the bar, tipped his hat to thank her for the shilling she handed him, and departed.

'Good afternoon, miss. Can I help you?'

'I need a room for the night, if you have one.' Dottie gave the aproned young man behind the bar her brightest smile. He blushed.

'I'll go and find out,' he said. 'Excuse me a minute.'

Dottie looked around her. The place was almost empty, apart from a soft buzz of conversation from somewhere away to her left, behind a huge oak door that had surely been in place since well before Victoria's reign.

The young man came back. 'Er, well, I think we may be able to... Is it just for the one night?'

'I'm not certain. I was supposed to be staying with relatives. If I can't reach them, I might be going home again tomorrow.'

He turned his pink countenance away from its perusal of her face and picked up a glass-cloth. He began to wipe a wine glass. 'That's quite all right. We have a charming room facing the road, or madam might prefer a quieter room at the back of the inn?'

Madam tried not to laugh at being called madam in a pub by a boy younger than herself. Evidently he aspired to a larger, more refined establishment. Dottie told him that the room overlooking the front would be lovely, thank you, and arranged about dinner and breakfast. When he had given her a room key, she said, 'I need to make two telephone calls, I hope that's all right? You do have a telephone here?'

He told her with pride that they did indeed have a telephone. 'It was put in last year, madam. And quite private too, as it's out back by the door to the... yes, madam, we have a telephone.'

She grinned at him, leaning forward to say in a pleading tone, 'And is there any chance of a pot of tea please? I'm so cold from my journey.'

His whole face was red again. 'Certainly madam. I will arrange for tea to be sent up to your room immediately. And if madam can give me the telephone numbers, I will arrange the calls for you.'

He was sweet. After the reception—or lack of one—at St Martins House it was refreshing to meet someone so eager to please. She told him the numbers for her home in London, and St Martins House nearby. Her brief hope that the young man might hear St Martins House and say, 'Oh yes, that family is staying here at the moment due to a sudden difficulty at home...' flared and died as he looked merely politely interested but offered no comment. He said only, 'I'll let you know when the calls are through. I'm Edwards, madam. Please let me know if there is anything else at all I can do for you.'

She thanked him and went across to the stairs, hoping she had imagined that slight emphasis on 'anything else at all'. She made her way up to her room, and a few minutes later, he arrived with her suitcase and was immediately sent away again by the older woman who accompanied him. The woman brought in a tray, and setting it down, showed Dottie where the bathroom was, promising her plenty of hot water if she wanted a bath. The tray held a pot of tea, sandwiches and a cherry scone with butter and jam. It took Dottie no time at all to dispose of the lot.

Dottie was looking forward to having a hot bath once she had spoken to her parents and hopefully got through to her aunt. She opened her suitcase and got out the things for her bath, and a warm dress to change into for dinner, just to get out of the suit she'd worn all day for travelling.

An hour later, there was a knock at the door and she followed young Mr Edwards downstairs to the telephone. He went to the bar, and Dottie went to the telephone. She picked up the receiver to hear him saying, 'Your call to London, madam.' He had put on a low breathy kind of voice, perhaps hoping to sound seductive. Dottie smiled. Then she heard her mother's voice giving the phone number.

'Oh Mother! Such a mix up! Yes, yes, I got here perfectly well. No, no hitches at all. The weather was glorious, it was such a lovely run down. I didn't get lost once. Well, I did take the teeniest detour but it was all right, and only set me back a few minutes. A nice elderly farmer set me back on the right road.'

At the other end, Mrs Manderson was praising and exclaiming by turns. Dottie didn't want to listen to all that so she butted in with, 'Can you check the address for me. I went to where we thought it was and there was no one there. The place was empty. No staff, nothing. I knocked and knocked. I even tried the back door. The place was completely deserted.'

She waited for almost a minute whilst her mother went to find her address book, then came back to read it out very loudly and slowly. Dottie compared it to the directions she had written down in her diary. It was very odd, she thought. She felt utterly baffled. Her mother didn't understand it either and was convinced Dottie had gone wrong somewhere.

'But that's where I went. I'm sure I... No Mother, I'm telling you, I *did* go there. It was the right... Well the name was on the pillars at the gate. And there was only... Yes, I know but as I say, the name was on the gate, and there was only one road. Well it doesn't make any sense to me either.'

She couldn't think of an explanation for why no one

had been at her aunt's home to greet her. She had to wait whilst her mother went to fetch her father, then she had the same conversation with him. He started by telling her she must have gone to the wrong place. She defended herself as best she could, feeling irritable and worried by the time she said goodbye. She promised to come straight home again in the morning if she couldn't find her aunt's home. Resisting the urge to snap, 'I found it the first time!' Dottie said goodbye and sat on the padded leather bench to wait for the next call.

It didn't come. When she ran into the bar to query this with the young man, he told her he hadn't been able to get her connection. He was waiting to hear back from the exchange. Ten minutes later, the telephone exchange phoned him to say that there was no reply from the number given. He relayed this information to a very puzzled Dottie in his low breathy voice. She thanked him briskly and returned to her room, even more worried than before. She sat down on the window-seat to think about things.

All she could do was wait until the morning then try again. If there was no reply to the telephone, she supposed she would have to drive back to the house and see if anyone was there, before giving up altogether and driving back to London.

She had her bath. Then she dressed and went downstairs for dinner. On the way to the little private room that was used as a dining room, Dottie went into the bar. The young man was there, blushing madly when he saw her coming.

'I forgot to check,' Dottie said, 'But you did ask for the name of the residents as well as the house name when you spoke to the exchange?'

'Yes madam. Mr or Mrs Lewis Cowdrey. St Martins

House. That's right, isn't it?'

'Yes, exactly right, thank you.' Dottie bit her lip, still puzzling. 'Do you know the family at all?'

'Not really madam. The gentlemen sometimes call in here for a drink, or whatever. Mr Guy used to play darts or have a drink with his friends. But we don't see him so much these days.'

Dottie thanked him and then went in to get her dinner.

After dinner, Dottie had returned to her room to sit by the window. In summer months, it was doubtless a charming view of the road lined with cottages and gardens. But now, in the depths of winter with its short days and long nights, the window only gave onto a darkness broken here and there by a lamp glowing in a cottage. The effect was rather dreary. Mostly all Dottie could see was her own pale face, slightly strange-looking, thrown back at her from the glass. Sitting there, Dottie felt edgy and tense. Nevertheless, she tried to concentrate on the three-day-old newspaper she had found in the bar.

She couldn't shake off the feeling that she had done all this before. Just six months earlier she had sat in a hotel, admittedly an expensive hotel, located on the Yorkshire coast. The summer days had been bright and cheery long into the evening but even so, the feeling of dreary sameness endured.

Sitting here in this room in Sussex was exactly like when she had waited to tell her parents about the death of Diana, Flora's husband's sister. Dottie's hands gripped one another in her lap. When the young man tapped on her door she almost leapt out of her skin.

'Call for you, madam. The London number again.'

She hurried down the stairs in his wake, and out to

the telephone. She snatched up the receiver. 'Hello?' She had to listen hard, the noise from the bar had increased dramatically in the last hour or so.

'Dorothy dear,' her mother said without preamble, 'I think we may have committed an error here.'

'Oh dear, really?' Dottie's heart sank, if possible, even further. She huffed out a breath, making her fringe fly into the air and back down again.

'Did you manage to get through to your aunt?'

Dottie said she hadn't, that the exchange said no one was answering the call.

Her mother said, 'Of course, I noticed at the time how tattered and damp the envelope was when it arrived, but I've only just studied the post-mark.'

'But the letter said, two weeks on Thursday,' Dottie pointed out, shifting the phone to fish in her bag for the letter to herself that had been enclosed with the one to her mother. She unfolded it, scanned the contents hurriedly, and said, 'Yes, just as I thought: 'Dorothy may come to us two weeks on Thursday', that's definitely what she says.'

'Yes dear. But I thought the letter was dated the 12th. However, now I've managed to decipher the date on the envelope, and it was postmarked the 17th, so almost a week later. I borrowed your father's magnifying glass, and well, yes I think I'm right, that what I took for the 12th could just about have been 17th; the stamp is rather blurred.'

'Hmm. I see. So they weren't expecting me until...?' Dottie counted on her fingers. 'The 4th of January? Not for another week!' She leaned against the wall, closing her eyes. This only made things worse, even if it did shed some light on the matter. 'That's obviously what's happened. How aggravating.'

'It's just like Cecilia to be so unclear about things.'

'That probably accounts for me not getting any

reply when I rang earlier. Oh Mother, I can't believe I'm here a week too soon!'

'I'd have thought that at least the butler, or a maid would answer the telephone. They keep a larger staff than we do here. They're very well-to-do, and it's a much larger house.' The frown was just as clearly discernible in her mother's voice as it would be on her face if they were together.

Dottie said, 'Perhaps they closed up the house to go away for Christmas? Perhaps they took all the staff with them, and they're coming back in a day or two?'

'You're probably right, dear.' Her mother gave a sigh that came down the phone wire and prickled Dottie's ear. From the bar came the sudden sound of raucous laughter. Dottie transferred the receiver to her other ear, hoping she'd be able to block out some of the sound so her mother could hear her better. Mrs Manderson went on, 'But it's created a very inconvenient situation for you. Are you coming home again?'

'I suppose so. I don't want to stay here for a week waiting for them to come home. As it is, I'm in two minds about this whole visit.'

There was silence from the other end. Mr and Mrs Manderson and Flora had all been against the idea from the outset, thinking it would do no good for Dottie to get to know her aunt better. But they'd made no attempts to dissuade her. She knew they'd wanted to let her make her own choice.

After a pause, Mrs Manderson said in a gentle voice that was quite uncharacteristic, 'Why not wait and see how you feel about it in the morning? Telephone the Cowdreys again, or I could telephone for you from here. Who knows, they might come back late tonight or first thing in the morning. You won't lose too much time. Even if you have to come back home again, it's been a useful experience, driving there and back.'

'All right,' Dottie agreed. 'I'll phone them again in the morning. If I can't get them by lunchtime, I'll come back home again. Either way, I'll telephone to let you know what I'm doing.'

They ended the conversation with a number of cautions from Mrs Manderson that a Young Girl Staying Alone At A Country Inn was prudent to observe, including Dottie's old favourite: 'And don't forget to put a chair-back under the door handle. All too often these places use the same keys to lock all the doors, so really there is no security at all. Locking your door is not enough on its own.'

'Don't worry, Mother, I'll be careful,' Dottie said, though she had no intention whatsoever of pulling a chair across the room to try and fit the back of it under the door handle to prevent anyone from opening the door—including the maid with her morning tea.

Mrs Manderson, clearly feeling that her daughter was treating all too lightly the omnipresent dangers to single young women, then gave a final instruction, and it made Dottie giggle—this was her sister's favourite of Mrs Manderson's large repertoire of warnings:

'And remember, when you go into the room, lock your door and make sure the key is straight in the lock. There are often perverted men in these out-of-the-way places who take great pleasure in looking through keyholes in the hopes of seeing a young girl undress.'

Stifling her laughter, Dottie promised faithfully— her fingers crossed behind her back—to lock the door of her room in a manner calculated to foil all the peeping toms in Sussex. Mrs Manderson humphed, almost as if she knew her warnings were all in vain. They exchanged a few more comments then said goodnight.

Dottie immediately asked for another call to be put through to her aunt's house, but after listening to the phone ringing for almost two minutes, she was forced to conclude there was still no one at home.

She decided she would have an early night and went back upstairs. On reaching her room though, she didn't feel the least bit relaxed, so she opened her briefcase and drew out two thin ledgers along with two manila folders, one considerably thicker than the other. She was still on tenterhooks about the uncertainty and confusion of the situation regarding her visit. She'd wasted time making this journey and began to feel cross with herself. She should have been getting on with things at the warehouse. She had been a fool to come down just as she was getting to grips with the new range of clothes she was planning. It was as well she'd brought the work with her, thinking there might be odd quiet moments when she could get on with something useful, but it wasn't the same as actually being at the warehouse every day.

Taking a seat at the little table by the window, (a chair without the kind of back you could readily thrust under a door handle, being too well-padded and too low) she checked and double-checked the figures for the last month's sales, and then went on to check her business expenditure. She looked over and approved purchase orders, wages, sundry bills and other items. Then she turned back once more to the folder of new designs.

Feeling chilly, and deciding she might as well be comfortable, she carried the folder across to the bed.

She put on her nightdress and got under the bedcovers. Then she opened the folder to reveal the pleasantly thick sheaf of papers. This was the part she loved.

She plumped up her pillows behind her and stretched her feet out under the blankets. A delicious sense of anticipation seized her as she reached for the pages once more. It was a feast for the senses.

The thick foolscap paper crinkled in her hand. The sharp crack of it deepened her excitement, the sound triggering the memory of all the other times she had held these sheets of paper and gazed at their contents. Her fingers recognised the smooth cool surface of the paper; the scent of the ink teased her nose. She could smell the unique freshness of the small new pieces of fabric. Goosebumps stood out on her forearms, not just because it was four days before the close of the year, and the fire was dying down, the orange and grey of the coal peeping through the black bars of the grate. Just to hold the pages was wonderful to her. Everything else fell away and was forgotten.

If, in the early days of running the warehouse, Dottie had sometimes despaired of learning enough, and learning it quickly enough, to be able to truly honour her friend's legacy; if she had doubted she possessed the skills required, or the knowledge, or the experience that comes only with many years of work, she doubted no more. After only half a year of hard work, now as she held the new season's designs in her hand she knew she was doing the work she was made for, and she was determined to try even harder to improve and to acquire the skills necessary to perform that work to the best of her ability.

She had a brief mental image of herself in her fifties and sixties, sitting at that same desk which had been

Mrs Carmichael's, in the dimly-lit back office at the warehouse, slipping out of shoes more fashionable than comfortable, as Mrs Carmichael had often done, and thinking, 'Oh my poor feet,' and perhaps pouring herself a little glass of wine—not the gin Mrs Carmichael had been in the habit of drinking, Dottie felt sure she would never develop a taste for gin. Then, when that little ritual was done, like Mrs Carmichael, Dottie would reach for the new batch of designs.

Dottie smiled as she remembered those times she had watched Mrs Carmichael in her office, pulling off her heaps of heavy, old-fashioned but undeniably valuable jewellery and flinging it down with a crash on top of the wooden desk as if it was of no account whatsoever. Or Mrs Carmichael collapsing into her chair with a groan of relief at the end of one of their shows, or after a cocktail party held for the best customers and their friends, right there in the main hall of the warehouse, for the purpose of wooing clients to buy her latest designs. Mrs Carmichael groaning as she leaned back with her glass of gin and saying, 'My Gawd, Dot, the things we do to sell a few frocks.'

She could now perfectly understand for the first time what had kept Mrs Carmichael in her office so late at night, what had spurred her on. At that moment, Dottie felt absolutely certain that life could hold no greater pleasure for her. But Dottie was very young and didn't yet realise how much she would love her husband and her children, or the joy they would give her just by being part of her life.

When Mrs Carmichael had left the business to Dottie just six months earlier, Dottie had felt completely overwhelmed by the enormity of the task of running a fashion warehouse, one which already had a good reputation, too good a reputation to risk losing. But even before her patroness had died, Mrs Carmichael had been subtly and slowly bringing Dottie into the business one tiny step at a time. Had she lived longer, Dottie was convinced Mrs Carmichael would have increased Dottie's involvement and responsibilities still further, giving her an apprenticeship of sorts. Dottie had worked for Mrs Carmichael as a mannequin for almost five years, starting off on a casual basis during the school holidays, then working more or less full-time after that.

Mrs Carmichael had often sought Dottie's opinions about each new range being developed. She had discussed many aspects of the business both formally and over drinks in her office when everyone else had gone home. If Dottie had felt unprepared and ill-equipped to take up the reins of *Carmichael and Jennings: Exclusive Modes for Discerning Ladies*, she realised now things could have been far worse.

She'd had a great deal of help. True, some clients had shaken their heads and walked away because of the change, which had greatly worried Dottie, but there remained a small but loyal number of stalwarts, and there were already a few new clients, among them Flora and their mother, who had begun to send in their orders. Dottie had spent some time with her friend Judith Parsons, a seamstress and costumer with a famous London-based moving-pictures company, and the two of them had spent hours discussing many aspects of costuming, sewing and design, and Miss Parsons had been very obliging when Dottie had telephoned her a number of times during that first two or three months.

And now, here she was, looking through her first complete set of designs for the new range of styles for the following season. They always worked two full seasons ahead, so Dottie was looking at the designs for autumn-winter 1935 to 1936.

She took a deep breath, mentally taking a step back to try to view the designs objectively. Then she turned to the first page.

She held her breath as she looked at it. A long overcoat. Extra detailing to the shoulders, the new lapel shape. There were the buttons for fastening the coat, with extra, decorative buttons for the cuffs of the sleeves, and a belt to cinch in the garment and accentuate the waist. In many ways it was an ordinary garment. But they had sought to lift it above the utilitarian by the choice of material. Attached by dressmakers' pins to the bottom of the page were six tiny rectangles of fabric. There were two types of fabric, a heavyweight gaberdine and a wool, and for each fabric there were three colour choices: a light cream in both fabrics, a ruby red for the gaberdine, an emerald green for the wool, and again for each fabric, a navy-blue. The thread used would match the fabrics, obviously. Sample buttons had been tacked to the page with huge white cotton stitches to keep them from falling off and getting lost.

Dottie assessed the whole thing as critically as she could. It wasn't quite right. There was something wrong with the epaulettes. They were definitely too wide. She wrote a neat pencil note and a tiny sketch in the top corner of the page. She realised she was pleased overall: both with the design, and with her own ability to assess it. It had been her idea to change all the names of the garments from Mrs Carmichael's system of using women's names, and instead had created garment names from situations that her customers might relate to or aspire to. That had gone down very well with the customers currently ordering the spring-summer 1935 range. The name of the coat in this design was 'Shopping in Town'.

She turned to the next page: a rather daring negligee set the colour of mulled wine that she had named 'Christmas in Paris'. She knew it would sell in huge numbers; and it would be as popular with husbands as with their wives.

At last she slept and was rather relieved to wake in the morning unable to recall her restless dreams. She sat up in bed and looked about her, and before she'd thought about the possibility of a bath and some breakfast, there was a tap on the door, and a smiling young girl in her early teens brought in a cup of tea, and drew back the curtains to reveal a weak but welcome sun shining in at the window.

Dottie had toast and more tea in the little back room of the pub, and even as she was wiping her mouth on the napkin and wondering what to do next, she was summoned to the telephone.

She said, 'Hello?' eagerly into the receiver, expecting to hear her mother's voice. And it was—in a manner of speaking—her mother.

'This is Cecilia Cowdrey,' said an imperious voice. 'I am speaking with Miss Dorothy Manderson, am I not?'

'Yes,' Dottie said, her heart pounding. 'It's me, Aunt Cecilia.'

'I understand that you are staying at the public house in our village. I can't think why you've arrived a week early,' said the voice, still cold, still expressing no particular pleasure at speaking with her long-lost child. 'Lavinia telephoned me an hour ago and told me everything. It really is very silly, but I suppose you're young, and these things happen. In any case, you may come to us a week earlier than agreed.'

It made her sound like a paying guest rather than a relative, Dottie thought, and was on the point of thanking her, at the same rebelling at courtesy due to her aunt's tone. But the voice swept on, not waiting for Dottie to agree or venture an opinion. 'Perhaps you'll arrive this afternoon in time to join us for tea, shall we say at four o'clock?' It was phrased as a question but really it was an instruction. Without awaiting Dottie's response, Cecilia said, 'We'll see you then, Dorothy.' And the phone hummed in Dottie's ear. The line was dead.

She stayed on the bench beside the telephone in this quiet part of the pub. She felt... she felt as though she had caused annoyance and inconvenience. She felt she had put everyone out, when really it was she who had been put out. She felt unwelcome, unwanted. She felt she was most definitely not wanted. She blotted her eyes quickly and straightened her shoulders. As her m... She caught herself up, an odd flipping sensation in her stomach. She'd been about to say to herself: as her mother always said in the face of a crisis, 'Chin up, shoulders back.'

But of course, it was this woman who was really her mother. This one who had just told her what time to arrive then hung up the phone, her voice cold, and with no discernible love for her missing child.

Dottie knew it must be difficult for her m...for Aunt Cecilia. She knew that and understood it. And she had absolutely no desire to cause problems for her aunt, or to embarrass her in any way. But after all, it had been Cecilia's idea that Dottie should come and visit. Was it really so much to ask that the woman should show some warmth, some welcoming kindness? Even if the warmth was just the conventional affection of an aunt to her niece?

The young man was behind the bar already, wiping glassware again. She went across to speak to him.

'I'm afraid I'm still not quite sure if I'll need my room again tonight,' she said.

'I see.'

'I should have a better idea later on. I shall be out for the afternoon and at least part of the evening.'

'Will you require dinner, madam?'

Would she? She couldn't be certain. She hoped not. But her aunt's invitation had been vague, and the visit had not been defined by a period of time beyond arriving at four o'clock. Dottie had to say something, though.

'No,' she said, making a hasty decision. 'That's quite all right, thank you. I shall be making other arrangements. I hope it will be all right to let you know about the room later? As I said, I'm not really sure...'

'Don't worry about it, madam. If I haven't heard from you by last orders, I shall assume you've left us. I have your address for the invoice.'

'Of course. Hopefully I'll have firm plans well before last orders.'

With further thanks, she left him and returned to her room. She packed her things ready to take to her car. If she was to stay at her aunt's, she'd need her things, and if she didn't stay, then she'd be going back home anyway.

She sat by the window. What was she to do until four o'clock? It wasn't even ten o'clock now. She had six hours to wait.

Chapter Six

This time when she rang, the door was opened almost immediately. A maid stood there with a big smile on her face. She gave her name as 'Annie, miss,' and with a curtsey said, 'Welcome to St Martins House, miss. May I take your coat?'

Dottie was relieved by this pleasant welcome and most of her nerves left her.

Annie conducted her across a gloomy hall crammed with the dusty collections of several generations and into the drawing room where the family had assembled to meet her. If Dottie thought she'd have time alone with Cecilia Cowdrey to talk or at least to greet one another, she was mistaken. Dottie was perfectly accustomed to entering a room full of people, but on this occasion, it was horribly as if she'd come out onto a stage, and the audience was expecting a performance superior to any she could give. They were all looking at her.

A young man came forward, a sardonic grin on his

face. He held out his hand. 'Cousin Dottie, welcome to St Martins. We're delighted to see you. I'm your *cousin* Guy.' Taking Dottie's hand, Guy leaned to kiss her on the cheek, then drew her after him to make the rest of the introductions.

First was her aunt, Cecilia Cowdrey, looking so like Mrs Manderson, and so like Guy but her carefully controlled hair was iron-grey where Guy's was dark. Aunt Cecilia came forward to kiss Dottie's cheek with cold lips that barely touched her.

'Hello dear. My, how very like Lavinia you are.'

That surprised Dottie and threw her a little off-balance. She couldn't remember anyone ever saying that she resembled her mother physically, and in this particular case, it seemed rather an odd thing to say. There didn't appear to be anything behind the remark, yet it puzzled Dottie, as did Guy's curious emphasis on the word 'cousin'. She managed a polite smile and was then abruptly enveloped in a tight hug by her cousin Imogen, who warmly kissed Dottie on the cheek and hugged her again, in total contrast to her mother.

Looking at Imogen was a little like looking in a mirror. The similarities between herself and Imogen added to Dottie's sense of things feeling rather odd. It hadn't occurred to her there may be a familial resemblance, and it was disconcerting. Imogen was slim and tall for a woman. Her hair was dark and wavy, but a little longer than Dottie's, and her eyes too were dark. Then there was the shape of the brow, the chin. There was no doubting they were related. Imogen wore no make-up, however and the only jewellery she wore consisted of a dainty brooch of seed pearls, such as ladies of the previous generation favoured, pinned on the brown jacket that matched her skirt. She looked rather more than her twenty-nine years of age. Her skin was pale and dry-looking, with lines around the eyes and mouth. But her smile was warm, lighting up her soft dark eyes. She was clearly very excited to see Dottie, and Dottie felt very grateful for that.

'It's all my fault. You're not angry are you? Mummy says I'm a fool, but I couldn't help it, I just had to do it.'

Dottie looked at her, confused.

'It's my fault. You arriving early, I mean. You see it was me who invited you to stay. I put the note into the envelope for you. It wasn't Mummy. I didn't tell Mummy until yesterday that I'd invited you.'

The penny began to drop. Cecilia Cowdrey said in a low voice which conveyed displeasure. 'She didn't even do that right. Stupid girl. My own fault, I suppose. I shouldn't have trusted Imogen to take a letter all the way downstairs to the hall table.'

'Will you forgive me? It just seemed like too good a chance to miss. The envelope hadn't stuck down properly, so I quickly ran upstairs and wrote a note for you, inviting you to come and stay. I expect I put the wrong date. I'm so, so sorry. But I was just so excited at the idea of you coming here.'

She did indeed look wretched, Dottie thought, *and* excited. Dottie smiled.

'Of course I forgive you. I'm very glad to have come.'

Imogen gripped Dottie in another tight hug, and exclaimed, somewhat like a child, 'Oh goody! Thank you, thank you!'

She grabbed Dottie's arm and led her away from Guy and Cecilia, towards the room's two other occupants, chattering the whole time.

'It's so lovely of you not to mind. I'm so excited you're here, Dottie. It's lovely to have you here. May I call you Dottie? Or do you prefer Dorothy? Dottie? That's lovely, Such a lovely name. And this is our big brother Leo, and his lovely wife June. Oh this is *lovely*!' Imogen added as Dottie smiled and said hello to Leo and June.

Leo shook Dottie's hand rather too firmly, and gave her a tight thin smile, but said nothing, whilst his wife leaned forward with her neck, without moving her feet, and kissed the air three inches from Dottie's left ear. She too, remained silent, her pale eyes fixed unblinkingly on Dottie.

It was a lukewarm reception at best, but as the two families had maintained only a distant contact over the years, they were in effect strangers to one another. Dottie wasn't too surprised that things were awkward. Only Imogen seemed excited and happy, bouncing on her toes and clutching her hands tightly together in front of her like an eight-year-old about to go to a party. Yet, Dottie thought, she's a full nine years older than me. But it was nice to have someone on her side, so Dottie stayed close to Imogen, which seemed to excite her cousin even more. And at least now, some of the mystery of her arrival had been explained. Between the Mandersons' own mix-up and her cousin's secret invitation, it was all a lot clearer.

Cecilia directed Guy to ring for afternoon tea to be brought in, for which Dottie was very grateful. She only hoped her tummy wouldn't rumble loudly, she was so hungry after the long hours spent walking in the village or sitting at a table in the pub, looking through her designs once again.

Everyone resumed their seats and sat looking at one another. No one seemed to know what to say. She longed to say something, to make a comment about the room, but it was neither airy, nor bright, nor usefully large, but was dim because of the trees pressing up close to the house on the outside. Inside it was crowded with all manner of knick-knacks: porcelain, brass jugs and plates, china dogs, china shepherds and shepherdesses, glass fish and birds, fans and feathers, trophies, horrid tusks and antlers, and shiny-eyed dull-looking fish or stuffed birds in glass cases loaded onto half a dozen small tables. It was rather like sitting in some strange museum. How she would love to fling open a window or simply sweep all the clutter into a waste basket, just to see some clear surfaces. She stayed silent, her hands clasped in her lap, and wracked her brains to think of something to say.

Guy rang the bell and took his seat again. Whilst they waited for the tea to arrive, and after exchanging yet another smile with the fidgeting Imogen, Dottie thought, do please let the tea arrive soon, at least that will give us something to talk about. Then inspiration struck and she said, a little tentatively, 'Is Uncle Lewis at home or away on business?' As soon as she'd said it, she wondered if they would think her nosy or rude. She had an immediate sense of having done something improper.

There was a short bark of mirthless laughter from Leo. 'Where else would Father be but away "on business"?'

Guy and Imogen nodded in response to this, whilst Cecilia merely frowned at her eldest son. Dottie decided she'd better keep quiet rather than risk another out-of-place question.

The tea tray was brought in by the same maid who had answered the door. She sent a little smile in Dottie's direction then bobbed to Cecilia and left. The tea was poured by Cecilia and the cups handed round their little circle.

The tea-service was very fine. Rather too fine for a simple family tea. Dottie knew if she held an empty cup up to the light, she would be able to see through it. Eggshell porcelain. She detested such fragile china. She could immediately think of at least four men and even two ladies—as well as herself—who could not be trusted with such delicate things.

The tea was so pale it was barely tea at all. Stop being critical, she told herself, we can't all be the same. Looking up she smiled brightly at her relations.

Imogen was by Dottie's side, and she began to talk about this and that, flitting from one subject to another, as if she had to cram everything in quickly or lose her chance. But it was a good thing Imogen was a talker, because no one else seemed to have a single word to say. Dottie sipped her tea, glad of something to do.

'Do you have a beau?' Imogen asked suddenly. To Dottie it was as if the whole room crowded in to hear her answer. She felt embarrassed.

'Um, well yes, more or less. I am about to be engaged. When I'm twenty-one. So not until the end of March.'

'How lovely!' Imogen burbled. 'How did he propose to you? I expect it was terribly romantic. And I expect he's terribly handsome. *And* terribly romantic. Is he, Dottie? Is he terribly handsome? *And* romantic?'

Dottie couldn't help smiling. Imogen was like a little puppy eager to be played with. She seemed very young, and naïve.

'Yes,' Dottie said, 'he's very nice looking. And he can be romantic if I remind him.' She was trying to make a joke of it, keep things light. But no one laughed or even smiled. There was an odd tension in the room that she didn't understand, and she still had that feeling of addressing an audience in a kind of monologue.

'Gosh.' Imogen wrinkled her nose. 'I'd hate to have to remind my beau...'

'What is this young man's name?' Cecilia Cowdrey enquired, cutting across her daughter's chatter. Everyone was staring at Dottie.

'His name is Gervase Parfitt.'

Leo frowned. 'I believe I know that...'

'And what does Mr Parfitt do for a living? Or is he independently wealthy? I daresay he does not have an estate?' Cecilia again interrupted. Clearly she conceded to no one.

Dottie began to wonder if she'd fallen asleep in her bedroom at home and was dreaming this peculiar Austenesque scene. She resisted the urge to pinch herself to check she was indeed awake. Trying not to sound snippy, she said,

'His father has an estate, but Gervase works for a living. He's the Assistant Chief Constable of Derbyshire.' She could hear the defiant-sounding ring in her voice and hoped she hadn't caused offence.

Cecilia nodded, apparently finding Mr Parfitt suitable, whereas Leo snorted and said, 'Not exactly hard graft, I would imagine.'

His wife June put a restraining hand on his knee, and said, 'Leo,' in a low disapproving tone. She frowned at him, though he appeared not to notice anything. They were all still watching her.

Guy said, 'A bit out in the sticks, Derby.'

Imogen said, 'How *terribly* romantic. Are there mountains and forests in Derbyshire?'

Dottie smiled at her and was about to answer, when Leo chipped in with, 'Don't be pathetic, Imogen. Of course there aren't. It's a bloody industrial area.

Mines. Engineering. Cotton mills.'

'Really, Imogen, mountains? Forests? You are a frightful idiot.' Guy laughed at her. The others—including June and Cecilia—joined in, shaking their heads at her ignorance. Dottie felt sorry for Imogen and wondered if it was always like this. If so, perhaps that explained her need to rush everything she said. Far from being immune to a lifetime of fraternal jibes, Imogen looked as if she were about to cry.

'There is some lovely countryside,' Dottie said, feeling a desire to defend her, and to soften Leo's sarcasm. 'Rather like some parts of Sussex, I imagine. Though Gervase actually lives a few miles across the county border in Nottinghamshire. He only works in Derbyshire. It's quite a hilly area. Also close by in Nottinghamshire there is Sherwood Forest, of Robin Hood fame. Although of course, it's more like little patches of separate woodland nowadays, rather than one huge forest. And there are plenty of very high peaks. The Dales are in Derbyshire, and the Peak District is only a little further. The Heights of Abraham are very high, and from the top, you can look across the valley to see Hardwick Hall. The little town of Matlock Bath, below, looks like a child's toy from the viewing platform at the top.' Dottie felt that she could comfortably work in the tourism industry if fashion didn't work out for her.

Imogen shot her a grateful look and squeezed her hand.

'I suppose it is convenient that one can carry on a dressmaking concern wherever one lives, even in the outlying parts of the countryside,' Cecilia said, and Dottie immediately felt furious at the implied put-down. What did Cecilia Cowdrey know of it, anyway? If she had heard anything about it from Lavinia

Manderson, it wouldn't have been couched in those terms, Dottie was sure. How often would Dottie need to explain that she didn't run a mere 'dressmaking concern'?

But before Dottie could say anything rash, Cecilia added, 'Although I must admit I was surprised that Lavinia would permit you to do something so—so menial.'

Dottie's reaction must have been plain to see, for June hastily said, 'Oh how clever you must be to be able to sew. You have a very keen eye, no doubt. My sewing skills are confined mainly to a little embroidery and that sort of thing.'

Dottie simply smiled and nodded. She sipped her tea.

Guy said, 'Must save a fortune if a girl can alter her own duds.'

'Oh do you? How clever you are! I love embroidery, but I can't do clothes at all, they just don't hang right.' Imogen squeezed Dottie's hand again.

Dottie was relieved when June made a comment about the weather. From there, the conversation turned to gardening and half an hour later—a long, *long* half hour later—Imogen took Dottie upstairs to show her to her room. The group dispersed. Leo and June returned to their own home, promising to see Dottie at dinner. Guy wandered away murmuring vaguely about someone he had to see. Cecilia retired to her room with that overused excuse, letters to write. It was a relief to have a break from them. Dottie felt some of the tension leave her shoulders and neck.

'You'll be in here,' Imogen said, throwing open a door to reveal a huge room dominated by a fully draped four-poster bed. Dottie's luggage was there already, the suitcase and hatbox empty beside the dressing-table. She quickly found that all her things had been efficiently unpacked and hung up or placed in the drawers of the tall-boy. The shiny new briefcase lay, still buckled closed and locked, on the edge of a little table crammed with ornaments beside one of the two floor-to-ceiling windows. Here, as downstairs, every available surface area seemed to provide a home for an antique or collector's item. Statuettes and grimy paintings peered down at her from the walls and the top of the wardrobes; little brass and china things huddled closely together on the mantle-shelf and the shelves of the bookcase, perilously close to the edges. There was a tendency to cover furniture with draperies, too, and fringed edges hung here, there and everywhere, gathering dust, colours fading from the occasional ray of sunlight, stray loose threads dangling down in a highly aggravating fashion. As Dottie took in the scene around her, Imogen spoke from the doorway.

'I'll let you rest. Dinner's at six o'clock prompt. Mummy doesn't like to be kept waiting. But don't worry, I'll come and get you when it's time to go down. We don't dress, but if you want to have a quick wash and brush-up, there's a bathroom along the hall, and the water will be nice and hot. Oh, Dottie, it's lovely to have you here, you have no idea how lonely I get. Leo and Guy are too busy to bother with me, but now there's you. You can't know how much this means to me. I've always wanted a sister.'

She was gone. Dottie walked slowly across the room to look out of the nearest window, still inwardly puzzling over what Imogen had said.

When she said, 'I've always wanted a sister...', Dottie thought to herself. And even that, 'You have no idea how lonely I get.' Surely any company Dottie gave Imogen now would be lost again as soon as she left to return home? Of course, they'd no doubt make more effort to keep in touch once they'd got to know one another better, but even so, it seemed an odd choice of phrase.

Dottie shook herself and forced herself to concentrate on the scene before her eyes. The room looked out on the back of the house. It was fully dark now, but by the light from the downstairs windows, Dottie could make out a small rose garden with formal edging almost directly beneath her room. It ran the entire width of the back of the house, from one outcrop of trees and shrubs to another, then from the narrow strip of uninteresting paved terrace immediately outside the back windows, down to the wide, long lawn beyond. A dark mass in the middle of the grass indicated the flock of geese were still there. Now and again she heard them start up honking, as if something had disturbed them. She wondered a fox didn't get them, but then again, they were formidable birds, especially in a group.

A gap between the hedges on the far side of the rose garden allowed access to the lawn. The trees mingled with shrubs, came down on either side of it, as if a long band had been cut out of their number to lay the grass down. A little way along, the ground began to slope away out of sight. Beyond this, Dottie could see the gleam of the water, the early rising moon shining on its smooth mirror surface. On the other side of the water, there appeared to be a rise of grass and the odd tree sticking up, that was all she could distinguish.

Dottie closed the curtains and pulled off the warm comfortable coat and skirt, and went to look for a not-too-dressy evening frock. She took her time, there was no hurry.

Chapter Seven

The tap on Dottie's door preceded Imogen turning the handle, and, opening the door just a crack, she put her head through and said, 'Are you ready to go down?'

Dottie was.

She wondered if Leo and June joined the rest of the family for all meals, because there they were again in the drawing room with Guy, Aunt Cecilia, and an older man who had to be Uncle Lewis, sipping drinks and waiting for the call to the dinner table.

At least this time they didn't all fall silent and turn to stare at her as she came in, Dottie thought. She let Imogen go in front. But before she could do anything other than put a pleasant smile on her face, the butler ahemmed behind her and announced that dinner was ready.

Uncle Lewis came across the room to lead them into dinner. He held out a hand to Dottie and just touched her cheek with a conventional kiss. He smiled broadly at her, though the smile didn't seem to quite touch his eyes. Like her 'cousins', he seemed alert, watchful. But his greeting was bland enough. 'Very pleased to meet you again, Dottie. Welcome to St Martins. I hope you'll be very comfortable during your stay. Shall we go in?'

She smiled and thanked him. Then Leo said something to his father, and somehow as they all moved across the cluttered hall to the dining room, Dottie found herself walking beside Guy. At the table, he held her seat out for her, and she thanked him and sat. He gave her that odd grin again. It made her feel as though he knew something she didn't.

As he went to take his own seat, the butler and Annie began to serve everyone. There was a heavy silence whilst everyone waited for their food. Not for the first time, Dottie felt there was a certain pomp and formality in the way things were done here. But eventually they all had their meals, the staff withdrew, and dinner began.

Conversation broke out among the three men seated in a cluster at one end of the table. Their favourite topic appeared to be fishing. At the other end of the table, the ladies discussed the weather yet again with a surprising passion. Inwardly Dottie sighed.

The only interesting point during the whole of dinner was when Dottie heard her aunt speak to the butler in a low tone.

As he leaned towards her to pick up her plate, Cecilia said to him, 'By the way, Drysdale, I believe a gold snuff box has gone missing from the little rosewood table in the morning room. It's the one with the four-leaf clover design on the lid, the one that was my great-grandmother's. Kindly look into that, would you?'

He bowed and said, perfectly calmly, 'Of course, Mrs Cowdrey.'

'I told you, Mummy,' Imogen said, but Cecilia simply said:

'Shush, Imogen.'

The ladies left the dining room almost the second Cecilia Cowdrey lay aside her napkin, following her from the room one by one. How regimented it all was, Dottie thought, and how like something from an earlier generation. Her own parents at home in London had never seemed particularly relaxed or informal in their habits. Until now. The phrase 'at home' struck her deeply. St Martins could never be a home, she thought. Cluttered, dark, and far too big by modern standards. She was puzzled by how utterly different it was here to the way the Mandersons lived. How strange it was that two sisters could be so unlike one another.

As they came along the hall, Cecilia Cowdrey said to Dottie, 'Perhaps you might give me a few minutes of your time. I would like to consult you about a birthday gift for Lavinia.'

'Of course.' Dottie felt slightly puzzled. She was not aware that Cecilia was in the habit of sending a birthday gift to her sister, and in any case, the birthday, being in May, was still five months away. Then with a sinking sensation she realised this was merely a subterfuge to explain their having a private conversation. She followed her aunt into what turned out to be the morning room, just as cluttered as everywhere else, it seemed, whilst Imogen and June continued into the drawing room a little further along the hall.

'Come in and shut the door,' Cecilia said. She took a seat on one of the four sofas and indicated that

Dottie should sit opposite her. Dottie almost knocked over a small table of knick-knacks as she squeezed past it to sit down. She bent to pick up a miniature oil painting in a gold frame and put it back in its place. There was a little bare square in the dusty surface of the table. Was that where the missing snuff box had been, she wondered. Her next thought was, with so much clutter, it must be very difficult to keep track of everything.

'I thought it best to have a short talk about things,' Cecilia immediately began. She leaned forward to take a cigarette out of the box on the coffee table and lit it. She closed her eyes for a brief second as she savoured it. 'Ah that's better. It's a shame convention doesn't allow a woman to remain at the dinner table and smoke along with the men.'

'It's your dinner table,' Dottie said with a smile, aiming for a gentle joke. 'You can please yourself what you do in your own home.'

If her mother back home in London permitted such flippancy, here in rural Sussex, her aunt took a different view. She frowned at Dottie.

'That's quite obviously not suitable. Even when one doesn't have guests, the conventions must be observed.'

'Oh yes, of course,' Dottie hastened to agree. She folded her hands in her lap and waited demurely.

'I realise my sister has a different attitude to social mores, but I'm afraid I don't approve of this modern laxity. Perhaps these things are all right in London, but here they are not at all acceptable in the homes of the better families.'

Dottie again said, in her most demure tone, 'Of course.' She must remember to mind her Ps and Qs; it would not do to offend her aunt and uncle.

'Now, I think we can overlook the confusion of your

unexpected arrival.' She looked at Dottie as if half-expecting an apology. Dottie waited, wearing an attentive expression.

With a frown, Cecilia resumed, 'I assume there are things you want to ask. Though for the life of me I can't imagine what. But your aunt indicated that you had questions you wanted to ask me. Obviously, you now know that you are my natural child, and that you were adopted by my sister because it was impossible for me to keep you here. I'm sure you can see how impossible my situation was. And—I may say— twenty years ago, things were very different, such a subject could certainly not be discussed openly as we are now doing.'

Dottie didn't think this short private conversation constituted an open discussion but conceded that it surely had to be a difficult—even distressing—topic for her aunt. But now that she had the opportunity, she felt unable to voice most of the things she really wanted to know. Instinctively she knew that this woman was not as ready to be open as she stated, and Dottie struggled to think of something that seemed more or less harmless.

'My mother—I mean...'

'My sister Lavinia? The woman you always thought of as your mother?'

'Yes...' Dottie took a pull on herself. Why was she getting so emotional? She took a breath. 'She said that the day that's always been my birthday is the right one. So I was really was born on 31st of March?'

There was another quick frown from Cecilia as she leaned forward to stub out her cigarette, and immediately reached for another. Lavinia Manderson didn't smoke, and in her rather fastidious and somewhat old-fashioned way, did not really approve of women smoking, even in the privacy of their own homes. Dottie didn't much care if women smoked or didn't smoke. She didn't like the smell or the way it turned your teeth yellow, those were her own reasons for not smoking. Cecilia Cowdrey, Dottie was realising, was more particular about social conventions and doing things the right way than her younger sister, yet she smoked rather heavily. Dottie found that curious.

'Yes, yes, of course it is. Why on earth does it matter? I must admit, I'd expected some rather more searching questions from you than the date of your birth.'

Dottie felt foolish, like a silly child begging for a party or to be given praise or attention. But she needed to know who she was, and it began with her beginning. She said, 'I suppose it doesn't really matter to anyone but me. It's just that when you've always thought you were born on a certain date in a certain year, it's nice to know in the light of—recent discoveries—if those basic facts are true.'

'I see. I suppose if you put it like that. You are rather given to introspection, are you not? Not a healthy thing for a young woman. You should be thinking of others, not yourself. But you needn't worry, you're not older than you thought. There will be no knock to your vanity. To answer your question, you were born on the 31st March in 1914. You are still twenty, not twenty-one for another three months or so. The facts haven't changed a bit.'

'For me,' Dottie ventured, choosing to ignore the comment about her vanity, 'it's as if everything has changed. Everything I thought I knew is different. My mother is now my aunt, and my aunt is my mother.'

'For God's sake keep your voice down, you stupid girl! Do you think I want everyone to know all this?'

'I think they do all know,' Dottie told her. Her "aunt's" attitude helped to bolster her courage. This was not the sweet, wistful, and loving reunion of separated mother and child after all. This was an angry, resentful woman being reminded of an unpleasant episode from her past, and a young woman who was still rather afraid of someone she had always thought of as a cold, uninterested and distant relative.

I'm just one insignificant, regretful incident, nothing more, she thought. If only I'd realised this before I came, I certainly wouldn't have accepted the invitation. Then she reminded herself that the invitation had come from lonely, ridiculed Imogen, not from this brittle, chilly woman in front of Dottie now. That makes it easier, Dottie thought to herself. We have no reason to be part of each other's lives except in the normal way of distant relations. I shall be able to go home in a few days and never spare her another thought.

This braced her too. Her marshmallow heart hardened, the tears that hovered on the brink of being shed now dried.

'Somehow,' Dottie continued, 'I believe they do all know. Guy, Imogen, certainly. Perhaps even Uncle Lewis, Leo and June too. The only way they could know is if you told them. You or the man who is my father.' She took a deep breath, readying herself to ask the unaskable. 'Who is that, by the way?'

Cecilia ground out her second cigarette in the ashtray and got to her feet. She stared at Dottie with undisguised dislike.

'How dare you ask me such a thing.' Cecilia Cowdrey walked out of the room, leaving the door wide. Clearly their short, "open" discussion was at an end. They returned to the drawing room and the other ladies.

'After we've had our coffee, Guy and Imogen will give you a tour of the house,' Cecilia pronounced, taking a seat now on one of the silk-covered sofas. She patted the space beside her as she spoke, and Dottie obediently went to sit down next to her, somewhat surprised after the note their talk had ended on.

'Lovely,' Dottie replied, and she meant it. If the house was grim and cluttered, then it also intrigued her. She spared a brief moment to wonder how much it cost to heat the place during the winter, it was so sprawling. There was a constant draught on the back of her neck from the French doors behind them. Only now did Dottie notice that the other ladies all wore light drapings around them: a shawl in Imogen's case, a short silk jacket in Cecilia's and June effected a carelessly thrown scarf about her neck. Dottie realised these were not purely decorative. She also noticed the worn seams on the silk covers of the sofas, and a threadbare patch on the carpet, not quite disguised by a small rug thrown down over the top. Clearly the family were not as well off as the size of the house and their self-conscious propriety had implied.

The door of the drawing room opened, and a maid entered the room, a maid Dottie hadn't yet seen. She bore a huge tray of coffee things. Drysdale came in directly behind her to attend to the fire. Cecilia, ignoring them completely, continued to address Dottie:

'Hopefully the gentlemen will not take too long over their port and cigars. They know I expect them to return to the drawing room promptly.'

Dottie produced her smile again. Drysdale finished

with the fire, wiped his hands on a plain white cotton handkerchief, then came over to assist the maid. He handed Dottie a cup of coffee. This set, she was relieved to see, was a little more robust than the tea service of the afternoon.

'We've got a few things planned for your visit,' Imogen told her excitedly as soon as the staff had departed. This then was what her cousin had been practically bursting to tell her, Dottie was certain. 'Even though some things might have to be cancelled or rearranged.' Imogen darted a doubtful look at her mother. 'I—I'm afraid we weren't expecting you for another week.'

Dottie's cheeks felt hot at the reminder.

Imogen raced on, 'And how can we forget, it's not just the weekend, but a special weekend!'

June chipped in, 'My father always has a big party for New Year's Eve, and Leo's family always attend—after all, you're all nearly as close to Father as our own family. I'll let Father know the Cowdrey party will be bringing an extra guest this year, I'm sure that won't cause any difficulty, one guest more or less at these things makes no difference. It'll be lovely—we'll dance, there'll be lots of food, we'll all count down the seconds to midnight—it will be such fun!'

Dottie felt unaccountably depressed at the idea, but she made herself smile at June and Imogen, both sitting on the edges of their seats opposite her like eager puppies, waiting for her reaction. She thanked June, and said it was very kind of the family to include her. Inspiration came in the form of a question about June's family.

'Oh yes, Father lives about two miles over that way.' June pointed in the direction of the lake at the bottom of the hill. 'He's all alone since my mother died.'

'I'm sorry to hear that,' Dottie said, feeling sorry she'd asked. But June didn't seem especially upset. '

'Oh it's all right. She'd been ill for a while so in a way it was for the best.'

'And do you have brothers or sisters?' Dottie asked.

'No, it's just me. As a matter of fact, Father and Mother adopted me when I was a baby, they didn't actually have any children of their own. Quite a shame really.'

'How sad,' Dottie said. 'And do you and Leo have any children?'

'Not so far,' June said, and there was regret in her voice.

'Soon, I'm sure,' Dottie said.

'Follow us!' Imogen leapt up ten minutes later, grabbing Dottie's arm and hauling her along, at the same time as she grabbed Guy by his arm. Dottie couldn't help but laugh at Imogen's excitement.

Out in the hall, Imogen skipped about. 'Where shall we go first?'

Dottie watched her, amused by her childlike behaviour. Guy gave his sardonic smile, shrugged and shoved open a door behind him.

'Might as well take a look in here. You've seen the dining room and the morning room. This is the study. Or library as Mother prefers to call it. It's really more or less both, I suppose, though the rest of us just call it the study.'

'Our father doesn't use it for working anymore. Daddy's more or less handed management of the estate over to Leo,' Imogen explained.

Lucky old Leo, Dottie thought and followed them into the room.

It was comfortable, that was her first impression. Cool and relaxing after the chaotic clutter of the other rooms. A small carriage clock ticked softly on the mantelpiece, the only ornament there. Bookshelves covered one wall, the books neat in their rows, without the jumble of the rest of the house. In front of the windows a large desk had been placed, business-like and tidy, one leather chair behind it and three smaller, highly polished wooden chairs on this side. In front of the fire there was a sofa on the left and one on the right.

And that was it. No ornaments, no knick-knacks, no photos, pictures, brass animals, trays, stuffed birds or fish in glass cases, no fans, no china dogs, no elephant or rhino tusks, no silk flowers and no porcelain jugs. Nothing. Dottie found it restful.

'Daddy used to work in here, and we'd play on the floor in front of the fire,' Imogen reminisced. 'But obviously not anymore.'

'No,' Guy added grimly, 'he's far too busy elsewhere these days to be bothered with his *family*.'

Dottie shot him a surprised look. His bitter tone made her immediately want to know what he meant by that. Perhaps Imogen might tell her more when they were alone together.

The three of them returned to the hall.

'Next,' Imogen said brightly, 'we have the billiard room.' She darted a look back over her shoulder at Dottie and wrinkled her nose. 'It's really somewhere Leo and Guy could go to drink and smoke with their friends when we were growing up. It smells awful in there, goodness knows what they used to get up to.'

Dottie's senses were overwhelmed by the stench of old cigars, leather, beer and sweat. It was rather like walking into a proper public house, she thought. The billiard table stood in the middle of the room, but there was no sign of the balls or the cues, although the rack for the cues still stood, like an oddly denuded tree, near the door. There was a scoring frame on the wall, and a couple of tall seats stood in front of the French doors with an equally tall small round table, the curtains only half-closed behind them. Otherwise the place seemed half empty and held an air of neglect.

Imogen crossed the room to throw aside the curtains, unlocking and opening the doors. 'It reeks in here. Drysdale ought to open these every day to air the place. Or better still, it should be redecorated and we could get rid of the billiard table completely. No one ever comes in here anymore.'

'Well,' Guy said, taking over, closing the French doors his sister had just opened, and leading them out into the hall once again, 'the kitchen and back areas are along this corridor and through the door at the end. There's also the back door... But of course you won't need to know any of that. Except the telephone is here, if you need to telephone.'

'I would like to phone to my mother,' Dottie ventured. 'She would probably like to know that I'm actually here, after the—er—mix-up.'

'Good idea. I'll mention it to Drysdale, he can get the call put through for you,' Guy said. Then with another of his seemingly habitual shrugs and a glance around him, he said, 'Well that's it. Upstairs there's a veritable warren of bedrooms, bathrooms and quite a few rooms that are no longer used. So...'

It was clear the so-called grand tour was at an end. Dottie gave them both a brilliant smile and thanked them. She looked about her.

Her eyes took in the suits of armour that edged one side of the large entrance hall, eerie in the gloom, like people lurking just out of sight. Through the glass panes of the front door, she could see coach-lamps burning, and beyond that all was darkness.

The walls here were covered in paintings and wall-hangings of great age and considerable grime. Everything in this house seemed to be in desperate need of cleaning. Once more Dottie wondered if the family was so very well-off after all. In London they had always thought the Sussex part of the family were wealthy, living in their great, and ancient, family seat. But she was beginning to question that assumption.

On either side of the stairs that descended into the centre of the hall, there were a number of tables covered in all kinds of effects, mainly of a military type. Row upon row of tattered and moth-eaten-looking medals lay ranged on once-white linen. There were cups and trophies, ivories and other carvings. And most intriguing, she spied a little pyramid of apple-sized round objects on one of the tables.

Beside the table was something that could only be a type of cannon, smaller than the ones she had seen before in museums. Dottie realised that the pyramid on the table was formed of cannonballs, rusted and pitted with age.

'I always wanted to play with these as a child,' Guy said. 'I got into the dickens of a row when I pulled them all down once. Hell of a racket they made too, I can tell you. Mother was furious at the damage they did falling onto the wooden floor. This whole section had to be replaced. Cost a packet, I can tell you.' He indicated with a sweep of his arm a newer looking section of the decorative wooden floor. 'Of course, Father was just glad I didn't hurt myself. He said one of these landing on my foot would have crushed it.'

'Pick one up,' Imogen urged. With her right hand, she reached out and took hold of a cannonball. 'See how heavy they are!'

She passed it to Dottie, placing it in her left hand. Immediately Dottie had to support her left hand with her right. She was astonished at the weight.

'Solid iron,' Guy said. 'I think.'

'They smell wonderful,' Imogen said. 'The smell reminds me of something.'

Dottie sniffed the heavy rough cannonball. 'Is it sulphur? It smells like fireworks. Or that smell you get when you first strike a match.' Then, looking at Guy, 'Could you?'

'Oh yes, sorry.' He relieved her of the cannonball and returned it to the heap with something of a thud. He wiped his hands on his trousers. They spent a few more minutes admiring various lethal-looking daggers circled about a small shield. Guy explained:

'One of the ancestors—don't ask me which, because I've no idea—was at Culloden. On the side of the Jacobites, no less. He escaped, as they say, by the skin of his teeth, bringing these colourful mementos with him. Now over here, there are a number of muskets and some ramrods. Father loves these things as if they were his children. In fact, he may well love them more than his children.'

'Guy!' Imogen hissed, her voice lowered.

He shrugged. He moved along the hall, and showed Dottie a group of spears leaning against a wooden wall panel. The spears had rubbed the varnish off the panel, their tips rusted like the cannonballs and rough, the shafts greasy and caked with cobwebs. 'People fall over these about twice a week on average. I don't know why they can't be put in a cabinet of some sort.'

'Or better yet,' Imogen suggested, 'thrown into the lake.'

'Mother hates them,' Guy said. 'But in spite of that, she hero-worships this stuff. All the old reminders of the family's glorious past.'

'I thought these were all your father's—er—collection?' Dottie said, surprised.

'Heavens, no!' Guy laughed. 'The daggers over there, and the muskets, but that's all. The rest is all stuff from Mother's family, handed down from one generation to the next. Oh those geese, too, are Father's.'

'Our famous St Martin's geese,' Imogen said, waving a hand at some huge glass cases. The stuffed, moth-eaten looking birds stood glassy-eyed and depressed-looking in their tiny prisons, their previously white feathers now greyish and dull.

Dottie couldn't repress a shudder. 'Why exactly are there all these geese?'

'Oh that's just the legend of St Martin. The original saint chappie,' Guy said.

'It doesn't even make sense,' Imogen commented. 'I mean, the goose is supposed to be the emblem of St Martin, but in fact, he hid in a barn or something and was given away because of the noise the wretched geese made. If anything you'd think a goose was the last thing he'd want to be associated with.'

'Oh.' Dottie couldn't think of anything else to say. She stepped away from the cases quickly.

'Anyway, they are all over the place, real ones and decorative,' Guy said, 'Watch your step when you go outside, though I've never known them to go for anyone. Usually if you get too close, they hurry off in the opposite direction.'

'Don't they just fly away?' Dottie asked.

'No. Some fool had the idea of clipping their wings years ago, so they can't fly away. They're stuck here,' Guy said, and wandered over to the drawing room door, holding it open for both ladies to precede him.

Cecilia poured them more coffee.

After the long day, Dottie wanted nothing more than to sink into bed and sleep. She undressed, put on her nightgown with a warm wrap over the top, and hurried along the draughty hall to the bathroom.

When she returned, she fetched her briefcase with the designs, because tired though she was, as she had stood brushing her teeth, an idea had come to her. She knew if she didn't make a note immediately, by the morning she'd have forgotten all about it. She sat on the bed, cross-legged, and pulled out the sheets. She spread the designs out around her on the bed to find the one she needed, but at that moment there was a tap on her door and it opened. Imogen came in, a little shyly, but clearly keen for a girly chat. Dottie smiled at her.

'Is it too late?' Imogen asked. 'You must be worn out. Oh, what a lovely picture...' She held one of the sheets in her hand, and began to look at some of the others.

Dottie began to tidy the sheets away into the briefcase and said, echoing Imogen's own old-fashioned words from earlier that evening, 'So tell me Imogen, do you have a beau?'

Imogen, it turned out, was bursting to tell her about the man she loved "more than life itself". 'His name is Norris Clarke, and he has an antiques shop in Horshurst. He's such a sweet man, and he's thirty-five. He was educated at Trinity College, Dublin, on a scholarship, Dottie, he had no money but he's so very clever!'

Dottie said, perfectly sincerely, that she hoped she'd meet him soon.

Chapter Eight

'I hope you slept well, Dorothy?' Uncle Lewis asked her as soon as she sat down.

'Oh, please do call me Dottie. I prefer that, it's not quite so formal as Dorothy. Which also makes me sound about forty.' He smiled at that, and she decided she liked him. She said, 'Yes, I slept well although I heard the geese a few times.'

He pulled a face. 'I'm afraid it takes a while for visitors to get used to the racket the wretched geese make. I don't notice anymore, having been here all my life.'

Over breakfast Dottie discovered the plan was to go to Leo and June's house for lunch and tea, then everyone come back for dinner at St Martins. She politely said she was looking forward to it, though really she felt rather depressed by the prospect. And she couldn't see the sense in going there, then Leo and his wife coming back again, only to have to go home after dinner. But it seemed to be a perfectly normal arrangement for the two households. It was clearly their habit to go back and forth between the two houses all the time. Dottie wondered if the family had any other friends.

Standing by the window after the breakfast was cleared away, she looked out and could see the geese basking on the lawn in the thin winter sun. She felt sorry for them, trapped here, unable to live a normal life and migrate to warmer climes during the cold months as their instinct would prompt them to do. She shuddered, an unexpected shadow falling across her imagination as she thought of living in this miserable place for years on end. No wonder Imogen was so desperate for company.

They travelled the one mile distance to Leo and June's in two cars, Mr and Mrs Cowdrey in one, and Guy, Imogen and Dottie in Guy's car right behind them. It was the same car that she had seen parked behind the house the first day she had arrived at the house to find no one there. Odd, she thought.

Imogen was thrilled that Dottie had driven herself all the way from London.

'I should be too afraid to drive,' Imogen assured her. 'And Leo and Guy say women shouldn't be allowed to drive. I'm sure I should hit something or run someone over.'

'You'd be a rotten driver, Imogen,' Guy stated.

That prompted Dottie to say, 'You'd be fine. You'd take to it like a duck to water. I'll teach you if you like, Imogen.'

Imogen was too excited to reply. Guy just rolled his eyes. 'You'll be sorry,' he said with a laugh.

Lunch was better than she'd expected. She was placed between Guy and Imogen. And if Guy could be sarcastic, he could also be funny and entertaining.

He and Imogen kept Dottie busy for the whole meal. When lunch was over, the family returned to the drawing room, much larger and less crowded with ornaments than its counterpart at St Martins. Dottie appreciated the near-bare mantle-shelf and the notable lack of small tables.

'Come and sit by me, Dorothy,' June called to her across the room.

With a roll of the eyes and a scornful laugh, Guy had to butt in. 'For goodness' sake, June, don't call her Dorothy. She likes to be known as Dottie.'

'Oh, I'm so sorry, I didn't mean to cause offense,' June said immediately. Her tone made it all too clear that it was she who had taken offense.

Dottie couldn't see why her name should be difficult or unusual. She just smiled and said, 'Oh really, it's perfectly all right. I'm just used to being called Dottie by most people, but it really doesn't matter. My mother calls me Dorothy. Although I do rather feel as though I'm being told off when I hear my full name.' She laughed gently at her own joke, and even though Guy and Imogen joined in, it did nothing to diffuse the odd tension in the room.

June simply said, 'Your mother?' She sent a significant look in Cecilia's direction.

Dottie felt uncomfortable. She knew she was blushing. But there was no point saying anything.

'I think Dorothy is referring to my sister Lavinia.' Cecilia's tone was frosty. Clearly it was one thing to know something "privately", but quite another to mention it in front of everyone.

It was June's turn to blush. She began to stammer an apology, but Guy said, 'So, Leo, how's the fishing been lately?' And the conversation turned to fishing and to the unusually mild weather for the time of year, which had been having a beneficial effect on the men's favourite sport, it seemed.

'Mind you, there's a bad cold snap coming in from the north by the weekend, bringing heavy frost and sub-zero temperatures,' Leo said, adding, 'So that'll no doubt ruin everything. They say we could even have snow by New Year's Eve.'

'Rubbish,' Guy said. He lit another cigarette. 'This good weather will continue a while yet.'

'Guy, do take your cigarette outside. You know I don't care to breathe in your foul smoke.'

'Yes Mother.' Guy didn't roll his eyes at his mother, though Dottie thought he looked very much as if he'd like to. The three men promptly reached for their cigar cases and left the room.

Imogen began to look at some embroidery June had been working on, June pointing out to her the different stitches she'd been using. Cecilia wandered over to the window and stood looking out at the garden, apparently either deep in thought or raptly interested in what she could see of this side of a small herbaceous border.

Once again, Dottie felt excluded by her family. She remained in her seat, deep in thought.

When she had arrived she had wondered, from the odd hint or two dropped into the very first conversation, if Cecilia's children might possibly know about Dottie's parentage. Even last night, when she and Cecilia had their 'open' discussion, she had thought it likely that they did all know. Now she was completely certain. The whole family knew that she was Cecilia's illegitimate child.

How long had they known? Had they always known? Had they known even when she had visited as a small child with Flora and their parents? Had everyone always known? Everyone except her?

She supposed it didn't really matter. If Cecilia—and

Lewis—were happy to allow her to visit them, clearly everyone had long ago accepted the situation, and it was new only to herself.

Although—now she thought about it—it really was only Imogen and Uncle Lewis who seemed to be pleased to see her, and who treated her with anything like friendliness. Guy appeared to find a malicious enjoyment in the situation, Leo and June were merely socially polite, but uninterested, and her aunt—*her mother*—seemed actually to dislike her, to strongly dislike her in fact. So why had Cecilia acceded to Imogen's secretive invitation? Was she simply too polite to say that it had been a mistake?

And how did Lewis really feel about having the illegitimate—supposedly secret—daughter of his wife staying under his roof? Did he care? Did it bother him or cause him any discomfort, or embarrassment or even sorrow or, quite justifiably, anger to have this living proof of his wife's infidelity right there before his eyes?

He had been pleasant, welcoming. His anecdotes were of the dull fishing, hunting or shooting anecdotes of most men of his age and social standing. His reminiscences were those typical of the public schoolboy, featuring faceless boys and men with names such as Boffo or Chippy. He was practically a caricature of himself. But he was nice to her, she thought, and she liked him.

But he showed little affection towards his wife. Admittedly he seemed to fall in line with her wishes. Or at least, Dottie reminded herself, in front of *me*, he seems to go out of his way to please her. Who knew what happened in private, in the intimate setting of a bedroom or when visitors and children were elsewhere? But in the drawing room, morning room, or the dining room, there were no affectionate glances, no touches of the hand on Cecilia's shoulder, no kisses on her cheek. None of the small, easily overlooked displays of love that she saw at home between her parents, or Flora and George, or any of their friends who were courting or actually married.

But her mother—Lavinia Manderson—had always believed Lewis to be a philandering, gambling wastrel of a man, never at home, never spending time with his family. Perhaps that had only been in his youth, she thought. Even though he had been away for part of yesterday, she'd seen none of that side of his character, although it seemed to be there to a marked degree in his son Guy. Yet Guy and Leo had alluded once or twice to their father being frequently absent, or not having affection for his family. Why was that?

She turned her thoughts to Cecilia, still over by the window, looking out at the garden. Dottie didn't understand why on earth the woman didn't simply open the French door on the other side of the piano and go outside to get a proper look; the rain had stopped hours ago and it wasn't especially cold today, not in the sunshine.

Why did the woman do anything the way she did? Why—and Dottie was back to that enigma she couldn't find an answer to—why had she allowed Dottie to stay with them if she didn't want to spend time with her, if she didn't even like her?

A new idea occurred to Dottie now for the first time. Was it possible that Cecilia had been attacked, and that Dottie was in fact the dreadful result of that event? Was it possible that the very sight of her brought back haunting memories of that most nightmarish of situations, that without doubt, her aunt had striven to forget over the last twenty years? When she looked at Dottie, did she see the mirror image of that evil man's eyes?

Dottie exhaled, suddenly aghast at her thoughts. This was something that had never once occurred to her before. Not for one second had she thought... It seemed to make perfect sense of the whole situation. No wonder she wasn't welcome here.

'Dottie, are you all right?' Imogen called.

'Oh, er, yes. Quite all right, thank you.' Dottie felt muzzy-headed, as if she had emerged from a dream. All three ladies were watching her.

'Come and look at this lovely work June is doing for a new screen in her dressing room. She's the one who helped me with the design for the screen in my sitting room, my pride and joy.' To June, Imogen said, 'Dottie doesn't just sew, she even *designs* the clothes first.'

Dottie joined them, June moving along to make room beside her.

'I don't think I'd enjoy that. I much prefer this kind of work,' June said.

Dottie looked at the work properly for the first time, and saw it was exquisitely done, and she said so. June blushed with pleasure and became warmer. Soon they were deep in conversation about needlework of all sorts, including the layette for Flora's baby, which then had to be extended to cater for twins.

After a few minutes, Imogen said to June, 'You should see the designs Dottie's brought with her to work on. Dottie, is it just for fun, or are you planning to make all those garments for yourself? It'll take you at least a year. Probably two!'

Her sudden question caught Dottie by surprise. June's pale eyes were fixed on Dottie, and she seemed eager to hear the answer. In fact everyone was: Cecilia half-turned from the window.

Not quite sure how much detail to go into without boring everyone, Dottie began to explain about her work as a mannequin for Mrs Carmichael at *Carmichael and Jennings*, then went on to tell them that when Mrs Carmichael had been murdered—to gasps of horror from Imogen and June—in the spring, Dottie had inherited the business from her mentor, and was now in the process of putting together a collection for the season after next. And it was the samples and designs for those that she had brought with her.

'Those must be what I saw on your bed!' Imogen crowed. To June, she said, in the manner of a confession, 'I saw them last evening when I looked into Dottie's room to say goodnight. She was surrounded by all these sheets of paper with drawings of models in costumes, dresses, negligees, everything. The fabric samples were there too, so you could imagine exactly how each one would look when it was made up. It was wonderful! Will you have a revue?' Imogen began to look excited.

June shot her a puzzled look. 'What for?'

'To show everyone what they can buy, silly. To display the range. How exciting. I would love to be there to see it. Oh, I so love the designs, Dottie!'

Dottie hadn't realised Imogen had observed so much, but it couldn't possibly matter. It was only from people who worked in the garment industry that she felt a need to protect her work. One heard stories of designs being stolen and used by other warehouses or designers to their own profit. Besides, it was pleasing to know that someone had seen the designs and liked them.

Dottie smiled. 'I love them too. For me it's very exciting to go through everything and imagine the whole range coming together. Yes, there will be a show, probably with a cocktail party or something like that. That's how Mrs Carmichael always used to run things.'

'Quite the little businesswoman, aren't you?' Leo said from the French doors. His father and his brother stood slightly behind him, and it was obvious they had been there a few seconds and had heard at least some of what Imogen and Dottie had said. There was something in Leo's tone that set Dottie's teeth on edge.

'I do hope you've got some reliable fellow to keep your accounts for you, and help you with all that side of things. I hardly imagine Herbert would permit you to dabble in something that could so easily leave you deep in debt or ruin your reputation,' Cecilia said. Leo had crossed the room and stood beside her, mother and eldest son side by side, and so alike, Dottie now noticed. That same slight lift of the mouth to the left that made them look as though they were sneering at you.

Leo laughed, not a pleasant sound. 'Oh Mother, of course she has. Uncle Herbert would hardly allow a young girl of Dottie's age to actually run the business herself. I expect they just let Dottie think she's in charge, when really she's a kind of manager of the seamstress or someone. Good grief, can you imagine the mess a kid would get into handling money and placing orders? Do talk sense.' He laughed again, enjoying his own joke. Guy was laughing along with him. Uncle Lewis was watching Dottie with a kindly look, as if he knew the comments hurt her feelings, but didn't know how to stop them. Or just couldn't be bothered. This was how they all treated Imogen, Dottie realised.

And as for her aunt... Dottie didn't know quite what to make of *her* expression. It seemed almost as if she were throwing down a challenge and daring Dottie to accept it.

Dottie did accept it. She was annoyed with Leo for making her feel like a foolish child, which was how she so often felt without anyone else's help. But Leo was just a pompous idiot, she reminded herself, and she'd dealt with the likes of him before. Therefore, rather than getting on her high horse about woman's rights, she said simply, 'Oh I'm learning how to do all that, too, of course.' She turned back to June and Imogen, to see June looking at her with something like horror in her eyes. Of course, Dottie realised belatedly, Leo was June's husband. June appeared to be one of those women who derived happiness from going out of her way to let him know he was her lord and master. Beside June, Imogen was positively beaming at Dottie, which had a heartening effect.

Leo said, in a frowning voice, 'I say, that doesn't sound very sensible. I mean, a young girl dealing with business matters. You're not even of age. I'm surprised your father permits it. Or your fiancé this— this Parfitt fellow. If I were him...'

'He's not my fiancé yet,' Dottie snapped.

Into the tense atmosphere of the drawing room, June said hastily, 'Where are my manners. Dottie, do let me show you around our gardens.'

Cecilia and Lewis remained indoors, Cecilia reading a book, Lewis as always managed to find himself a newspaper to hide behind, a little like Father, Dottie thought.

June was, it turned out, an avid gardener, with a special passion for using Latin names and botanical terminology. Dottie's smile became fixed very quickly. The only thing that struck her as interesting was how Guy—the man who seemed to approach life with a sardonic grin and a shrug of the shoulders—seemed to not only hang on June's every word, but to share her passion for plants—and her knowledge.

Bored, Leo had wandered off within minutes. Guy and June continued the non-stop gardening conversation, determined that Dottie shouldn't miss a thing.

'June's plan is to create a complete collection of all the *mentha* species and their varieties as a kind of living catalogue, and of course to provide information about them, offer research and possibly a breeding and cross-breeding programme, to help other botanists and herbalists, and to give the nation a kind of definitive range as a safeguard against loss in the future.' Dottie couldn't help noticing that Guy's voice rang with pride. A stranger could be forgiven for thinking that it was *Guy*—not Leo—who was June's husband.

June smiled and clutched at his arm. 'Oh you!' She gave him a playful nudge.

So far, Dottie had seen nothing playful, or even romantic between June and Leo. This unexpected girlish laughing side of June made Dottie wonder. To Dottie, June said, 'He always makes me sound more of an expert that I am. And he's helped me a great deal in cataloguing and tracking the varieties, so really it's as much his project as mine.'

They turned to cast doting looks on some green tips on a brown twig just barely showing above the surface of the soil. Next to it was a wooden label, which Dottie could see bore some pencilled writing in a small neat hand. There was a large patch of these insignificant-seeming sprouts, each with their own label. Dottie sent Imogen a glance that begged for help.

'Mint,' Imogen whispered. 'They're all different

types of mint. With different scents and habits.'

Dottie nodded, grateful for the insight. She looked again at the almost invisible budding leaves. She couldn't imagine why anybody needed mint apart from as an occasional cough sweet or as an accompaniment to roast lamb. She adopted an interested smile, not wanting to hurt June's feelings now that she was being so pleasant. 'And—er—how many different mints do you have at the moment?' Dottie asked.

'Sixty-six.'

Dottie stared at June in complete astonishment. June took her expression the right way, fortunately, and said, 'Incredible, isn't it?'

'Yes, it certainly...'

'I owe it all to Guy, really. He's the one who has encouraged me to do it. He's the one who lets me know whenever he's tracked down the source of a new variety.'

For a moment, Dottie thought she'd said 'sauce' but then as June went on, Dottie's brain made the adjustment.

'Why, only a month ago he found out about—it's this one in here—too tender to go outside at the moment of course, but as you can see, it's really doing rather well.'

Dottie followed June into the glasshouse, feeling a perverse curiosity to see yet another small greyish-green plantlet, with yet another little wooden label.

'This isn't quite as nice as the greenhouse at St Martins, but it will do for now. My tender plants and the *menthas* seem to do all right. Of course as the weather grows warmer—God willing, in our fickle English climate—we'll need to move this little chap and his friends outside. It'll be too warm in here by then.' This was Guy speaking now, and Dottie was fascinated to see how his usual world-weary, rather cynical veneer fell away, to leave an enthusiastic, boyish young man. June's hand was still on his arm, but she addressed Dottie.

'Of course, we are madly keen on other herbs too. It's not only the *menthas* with us!' They laughed, catching each other's eye as if this had become a kind of catchphrase. Dottie was struck again by the picture they presented of being a couple. She thought if they had indeed been husband and wife, they would have been rather well-matched. As the four of them turned to leave the glasshouse, June continued, 'No, as well as the *menthas*, we love the *thymus* species too. I'd love to collect those.'

'Thyme,' Imogen said softly in Dottie's ear. 'With an H. The herb. They have tons of them as well.'

Dottie nodded.

June and Guy led them back outside and along a narrow path, turning through an archway into a walled garden. It proved to be a wide, sheltered space shaped into little round beds comprising wedge shapes, and the whole thing enclosed on all sides by low box hedges. Flowers and herbs that had already died back in more exposed ground still bloomed here in small numbers. Roses clung to the mellow red brick walls, and it was warmer, protected from any wintry weather that might batter the plants beyond the walls.

'The herb garden!' they chorused, laughing again in unison.

Dottie felt a sinking sensation. How much longer could she possibly go on? All those dull plants with their ubiquitous wooden markers. In the spring and summer, yes, she was sure it would look lovely and no doubt smell even better. But at this time of year? June and Guy looked so happy, walking and talking side by side, absolutely in their element.

Behind her, Imogen murmured, 'This will take quite a while, I'm afraid. I usually get about halfway down then either I pretend I'm feeling really cold and have to go in, or I feel faint and have to go in because of that. I can count you in, if you like?'

Dottie nodded and grinned at her, but had no time to speak, as June now took her arm and led her on, saying, 'You won't be surprised to learn that we've got quite a few of the smaller, less invasive *menthas* here, too. They're not confined just to their special herbarium. But we'll show you *that* in a minute.'

Imogen sniggered and Dottie shot her an amused look. It seemed she and her half-sister had more in common that she had at first realised.

Dottie and Imogen managed to wander off in front, bored with an extended consultation over the health of one particular specimen that to Dottie's mind was identical to all the others. Imogen, giving up all pretence of showing interest, said a hasty, 'That's it. I'm going in,' and fled.

But it was pleasant out here in the sun, Dottie thought, and who knew how many more days of good weather they were likely to have before the real winter weather came in? She walked on to the far end of the grounds where the gardens gave on to open fields, then she turned back.

At first she didn't meet anyone but then spying what she thought was a figure on the other side of a weeping willow, she turned and went over.

Guy and June were there, in each other's arms. It was obvious they had been kissing.

Guy drew back in haste, and in doing so, bumped his shoulder on the overhanging branch. He laughed, but to Dottie's ears, it sounded false.

'Gosh, Dottie, you shouldn't creep up on a chap! Oh my heart, I'm sure I'm having some sort of seizure.'

Dottie said nothing but glanced at June who was blushing furiously. Dottie waited for the expected excuse, and sure enough, June said, 'Guy was just very kindly helping me with my pricking out.'

A ridiculous lie to tell, Dottie thought, given that there were no trays of seedlings at this time of year, and in any case they were nowhere near the greenhouse. 'That is kind of him.'

'Isn't it? It's such a long, tedious job, and of course, Leo has little interest in gardening. He much prefers shooting and fishing.'

Dottie wrinkled her nose. She didn't care for those type of sports. 'Don't you like killing helpless creatures, Guy?' she asked with a smirk. Clearly he was far too busy with other things.

'I might be forced to shed blood if cornered, but only ever in self-defence. I'm a peaceable fellow otherwise.'

Leo and his parents wandered over; clearly they had got bored indoors. Dottie thought it was a good thing they hadn't arrived a minute or two earlier. Without any kind of preamble or affectionate greeting for his wife, Leo said, 'I'm starving. What time is it?'

'Then let's go in for tea,' June suggested.

Back at St Martins later that evening, half an hour before dinner, a sudden sound caused everyone to turn in the direction of the door. Imogen stood there, a jewellery box in her hand. Dottie glanced at Cecilia to see if she knew what was happening. Cecilia was on her feet.

'Imogen, child, for goodness' sake, what on earth have you done now?'

Dottie winced inwardly at Cecilia's tone.

'My pearl necklace! It's gone! It was right here this morning. I saw it when I took out my brooch.' Imogen looked on the verge of tears. Dottie wondered if this was a daily occurrence at St Martins. The men exchanged looks then laughed again.

Guy said, 'Poor Imogen. She really does just lurch from one disaster to another, doesn't she?'

'It's probably on the floor,' Lewis said and returned to his newspaper.

At this, Imogen let out a howl of mingled rage and grief, turned and fled.

Cecilia tutted and returned to her embroidery, shaking her head as if to say, 'girls today'. Lewis rustled his newspaper, commenting almost immediately to Leo that he liked Purple Emperor for the three o'clock at Newmarket the next day. Leo snorted derisively. June shook her head sadly and continued flicking through the pages of her magazine.

Guy got up and crossed the room, not to the hall door as Dottie expected but to the window. After a few seconds of gazing out into the darkness, he said, 'I might go for a quick walk before dinner. It's quite mild out considering the time of year.'

Astonished at them all, Dottie set aside the book she'd been pretending to read and went in search of Imogen.

She was lying on her bed weeping.

Dottie tapped on the open door, and, not waiting for an answer, went in. If Imogen heard her coming, she gave no indication. Dottie sat on the bed and rather shyly reached out a hand to pat her shoulder.

Immediately the older woman turned and collapsed on Dottie, weeping. Dottie couldn't think of anything to do other than to smooth Imogen's ruffled hair and murmur 'there, there' a good deal. After what felt like a very long five minutes—Dottie was staring at the clock on the mantelpiece above the roaring fire—Imogen finally took one last shuddering breath and sat up, fumbling for a handkerchief.

'What must you think of me?'

Dottie could only say, 'You're obviously very upset.'

Imogen went to her dressing table and started pulling the pins out of her hair. She combed her hair thoroughly then gradually put the pins back in again until the hair was smooth and controlled, rather like her mother's. She powdered her nose and added a thick stripe of rouge to her rather blotchy cheeks.

'Perhaps a little eyeshadow,' Dottie suggested. 'To conceal the redness from crying.'

Imogen looked alarmed. 'Oh, I never wear eyeshadow, Mummy doesn't permit it.'

Dottie didn't like to point out that Imogen was almost thirty and could surely make her own decisions. Instead she simply said, 'I'm sure she won't mind if you wear a little, under the circumstances. You can use some of mine if you like.' Without waiting for a reply, she ran to her room to fetch her make-up then hurried back to Imogen's room.

Imogen was looking excited. 'Is this what it's like for you and Flora?' she asked. 'Daring each other to do things and painting each other's faces, doing each other's hair? It must be wonderful to have such a close relationship with your sister. Oh I do wish you'd always lived with us, Dottie.'

Dottie gave her a direct look. 'You *know*, don't you?'

Imogen beamed at her. 'But of course! We've all known for ages. Leo suspected it first when you and your family visited us years ago. He spotted the likeness. For some reason he just...guessed, I suppose, and he asked Mummy, and she told him you were our half-sister. Not that she discussed it beyond that. She said it was private, and not to be talked about. It's been a kind of dreadful secret we all know but no one mentions. Leo told Guy and me immediately, of course. So we've always known. It's so exciting to have a sister, I can't tell you. Whenever we have a letter from Aunt Lavinia, I read it over and over for any news of what you've been doing. I've often pretended you came home to live with us. I know it's silly of me, but...' She turned to the mirror, closed her eyes and waiting expectantly. With gentle strokes of the tiny brush, Dottie began to apply the peacock blue eyeshadow to Imogen's fluttering eyelids. She smudged the colour into the corners of the lids and up to the hollow part of the eye socket, blending it with a little powder across the under-brow area to produce a soft, open look to the eyes. All this time she was thinking about what Imogen had said, and how Imogen behaved. Dottie didn't know how to respond to her gushing words.

But Imogen was speaking: 'I can't tell you how often I've asked Mummy to take me to London to meet you. I mean, to meet you properly, as sisters. That's why I invited you here. I was just so *desperate* to see you.'

She turned, almost knocking the eyeshadow out of Dottie's hand, and flung herself on Dottie in a suffocating embrace. Again, Dottie didn't know how to act, or what to say. She just patted Imogen's shoulder again and managed a little laugh that sounded light but not forced. Imogen sat back and allowed Dottie to finish the eyeshadow. She was thrilled with the effect and pleaded for lipstick.

'Not yet, I haven't finished your eyes,' Dottie said. 'What was it that upset you so much just now?'

Imogen reached for the jewellery box. The lid had clearly been forced open, there were scratches all around the lock, Dottie was shocked to see. The lid no longer closed properly. It had been forced open with something that had left a large dent in the lower edge of the box.

'My grandmother's pearl necklace is gone. It's been stolen. It was from Daddy's mother, not Mummy's,' she hastened to clarify.

That it was a favourite of Imogen's was obvious.

'Was anything else taken?'

Imogen shook her head. 'There wasn't much else in there to be honest. I was wearing my brooch, and there were only one or two other things, just trinkets, nothing valuable, and they're still there. In any case, it's not the monetary worth so much as the sentimental value.'

'Oh dear,' Dottie said, unable to think of something more useful to say. It was out of the question to suggest reporting it to the police. Especially if the rest of the family weren't at all concerned.

'But who'd want to do such a thing, Dottie? I know the pearl necklace wasn't the most valuable in the world, but it was quite a nice one, certainly better than anything else I've got. I wear it all the time—or did—for dinner or if we go out anywhere. I mean, it's been in my bedroom, in this drawer. I haven't left it lying around anywhere. It's been right here as always. That means someone must have come into my room and just—jemmied it open and took the necklace. But who?'

Who indeed? It was perhaps a small thing taken on its own, but combined with the other recent petty thefts that had been mentioned, in Dottie's mind it assumed a greater significance.

No sneak thief or crook would break into a house

and carry out such small thefts. No. These were
personal, malicious, *mean* acts. And such things
could only come from within the household. Not that
it had been jemmied as Imogen said. A jemmy was a
much larger tool and only used for bigger objects
such as safes and windows or doors. A screwdriver or
even a narrow-bladed strong knife or an awl would
have been used to prise the lid open when it was
found the lock didn't give way to that kind of tool.

It was incredible to think of the men of the family
carrying out these kinds of deeds although Dottie
could almost imagine Guy taking the necklace purely
to annoy his sister. Not for the first time, Dottie
reflected that Guy and Leo's behaviour to their sister
was still very much that of the nursery or
schoolroom.

But surely these incidents, individually small but
cumulatively larger, were too malicious for a mere
overgrown schoolboy prank? It didn't leave many
alternatives.

Dottie said, 'What has your mother said about the
thefts?' Because, she thought, clearly Cecilia was the
one who made all the decisions in this place.

'About the thefts? Not much. She just tells me to
look again, that I've probably just misplaced
something. Or she mentions it to Drysdale. You saw
how seriously she views the matter just now.'

'Hmm.' Dottie didn't want to say what she thought
about that. 'Have you had anyone staying in the
house recently, perhaps with young children?'

Imogen shook her head.

'Or had any staff dismissed recently, or is anyone
working out their notice, someone who might have a
grudge?'

'Not really. If we're getting rid of anyone, they just
get their week's money and go that day. They don't

work their notice.'

That didn't really help.

'Have you got rid of anyone lately?'

'A few. The maids don't stay long. And to be honest, we can't really afford them all the time. I have to help out as much as I can. Sometimes it's weeks or even months before we get a new one. Annie Vale is new, she's only been here about three weeks. She is a kind of between-maid, I suppose. She does a bit of everything.'

'Who do *you* think did it?' Dottie asked.

Imogen didn't need to think about it. She immediately said, 'Annie. Without a doubt. She's a nasty little piece, gives herself airs. I caught her last week, in front of my mirror, trying on one of my hats.'

Dottie was shocked. 'And she's still here?'

Imogen's face fell. 'Well, yes. You see, St Martins is a bit of a tricky place to get to, staff aren't all that keen to come here. But she got a warning. And was docked two shillings from her wages.'

There didn't seem to be much else to say. After a moment, as she reached into her cosmetics purse, Dottie said, 'Your colour's settled down a bit now. Let's try a bit of mascara. By the time we go down to dinner, the redness should have completely gone. Hold still and don't blink.'

She opened the little box and took out the toothbrush-like applicator and began to apply the black substance to Imogen's lashes.

When the eyes were finished, and the drastic rouge had been softened with a few swipes of a silk handkerchief, Imogen gazed at herself in the mirror, turning this way and that. Dottie fished five lipsticks out of her case, and studied them, trying to decide which colour would be best. Imogen immediately selected the pillar-box red, which didn't surprise Dottie in the least, but in the end Imogen was coaxed into playing safer with a soft, pinky-plum shade.

Finally she persuaded Imogen to allow her to try her hair in a new style, bringing soft ringlets down her cheeks, so that they softened her rather severe bun. Dottie rearranged the firm bun to sit softly and loosely at the nape instead of being tightly scrawled and skewered to the top of the head.

By the time they had finished, Imogen was transformed from a slightly gawky woman who looked every bit her twenty-nine years, perhaps a little more, to a pretty woman who could not possibly be taken for more than twenty-three or four. The change in her appearance gave Imogen a glow of confidence, or was that just the effect of having someone's attention for a little while?

They were actually on the point of going down when the door was flung open by Leo, without pausing to knock, and he said very crossly, 'Do come on, girls, we're fed up with waiting for you. Dinner has been ready for fifteen minutes.'

He whistled when he saw Imogen, then shook his head, his grin spiteful. 'You'll cop it when Mother sees you!'

'I'm almost thirty, I can wear make-up if I want to!' Imogen said, but her uncertain glance at Dottie showed her briefly gained confidence was ebbing away fast.

Her lips thinned a little on seeing her daughter, but Cecilia said nothing about Imogen's appearance, other than to remark that they had better go in to dinner. June and Guy gave Imogen a glance but again, said nothing. Lewis nodded to Imogen, practically a compliment, Dottie thought, and gave his daughter his arm. Imogen held her head high, her face relaxing into a smile. For once, dinner was a pleasant event, with gentle conversation buzzing throughout the meal. Dottie could almost relax and enjoy herself.

After dinner, Guy went over to sit on the arm of the sofa next to June. He reached into his pocket for something, saying, 'Saw this and thought you might like it, June-O.'

Dottie had a nasty suspicion in her mind as she watched him hand the small flat package to her.

Leo frowned and said, 'I don't know why you're always giving her presents. No wonder you've never got any money.' He frowned at his wife too. He looked as though he'd like to snatch the gift off her and throw it out of the window.

Lewis and Cecilia said nothing. Dottie supposed there wasn't much they could decently say in front of everyone. But Cecilia looked very put out. Her mouth was a thin compressed line, her cheeks bore slight rosy patches, and not due to a healthy glow or the uncertain application of make-up. No, it was temper. Unless Dottie was greatly mistaken, Cecilia would speak to her husband about this later, and their son too, once Leo and June had gone home.

All Imogen had to say, rather petulantly, was, 'You never buy me any presents.'

Guy seemed unperturbed by the undercurrents his generosity had caused. He went to sit in an armchair opposite June. Dottie couldn't believe he was as indifferent to the tension as he appeared: you could have cut the atmosphere in the room with a knife, she thought. Nevertheless he leaned back lazily in the chair, legs stretched out in front of him, crossed at the ankle. He gazed through half-closed eyes, and said, so very nonchalantly, 'Nonsense, Imogen, I bought you a box of fudge a week ago.' But he didn't move his eyes from June.

Leo muttered something about going out for a smoke and banged out of the room. Lewis looked like he wanted to go too, but Cecilia's hand on his arm kept him in his seat.

June had flushed a delicate pink as she took the gift. It became her. It made her seem young again. She looks my age, Dottie thought, and wondered how old she was really. She wondered at June choosing to marry Leo when Guy was still unmarried. She rather wondered at anyone *wanting* to marry Leo. Although perhaps it was as Leo had said, that Guy never had any money, had no sense of responsibility. Or because Guy was not in line to inherit an estate. From June's conversation it was clear that Leo's future fortune as the elder son was very important to her.

The package was wrapped so prettily, it had to have been done like that in a department store. Dottie couldn't imagine impatient, lazy Guy doing half as good a job. June was already smiling as her fingers slipped the ribbon off then peeled back the flowered paper to reveal a book.

'Oh thank you, Guy, dear!'

Suddenly the tension in the room seemed to disperse. Guy got up, and said, 'You're welcome, sister dear,' then fishing in his pocket for his cigar case, he added, 'I'm just going out for a smoke.'

June hopped up, planted a kiss on his cheek, her hands resting briefly on his shoulder as she did so. It was a good thing she shielded him from his mother's view, Dottie thought. For Dottie, on the opposite side of the little seating area, had seen what none of the others had: his eyes close for a single second, and the merest movement as he tilted his face towards her lips. Then he dropped his gaze, stepped apart from her as she turned to show everyone the book he'd given her. Dottie glanced back, to see him momentarily standing as if frozen. Then he turned away and went out for the cigarette that he presumably now needed.

Lewis said, 'Good idea,' and bounded after him.

The four ladies sat awkwardly together. If Dottie hadn't been present, would Cecilia have said something about Guy giving June gifts? Dottie felt her presence was a constraint on all of them. Perhaps June sensed it too, for she turned to Dottie now and said, 'Leo doesn't share my enthusiasm for gardening, sadly, although he is quite keen on art and encourages my interest in photography. He bought me a wonderful—and fearfully expensive—new camera for Christmas. I must show you. He said we ought to take a trip to Scotland in the summer so that I can take come really lovely pictures of the wonderful scenery—the lochs and mountains.'

'I'd love to go to Scotland,' Imogen said, then, and they all began to talk of holidays, and the joys and trials of travelling.

With a brief, 'May I?' Dottie picked up the gift that June had just unwrapped. The book was about alpine gardening and contained a large number of photographs, some of them beautifully in colour. On the flyleaf was the inscription, written in a surprisingly neat hand in black ink: 'To dearest June, ever yours, Guy.'

Modern young people thought nothing of calling one another 'dearest', and 'darling' all the time, like the actors they saw each week at the cinema. And it didn't mean a thing, it was just a casual endearment used for all their friends and acquaintances. Half of Dottie's friends called one another darling or sweetheart, and it had no significance beyond that of an affectionate nickname. But Guy—for all his casual, lazy, youthful ways—was ten years older than Dottie and her friends. And she assumed June as about the same sort of age as Guy. Dottie's feeling was that Guy meant every word of that dedication.

The problem was—did June reciprocate his feelings? No, Dottie told herself, the *real* problem was, did Leo know his brother was in love with his wife? Judging from his expression, she rather thought he did.

Chapter Nine

The family habitually attended church in the village and this Sunday was no exception. Dottie was glad of a break from the gloomy house as well as the tension amongst its inhabitants.

But when they arrived at the church, she was embarrassed by the way all the villagers waited outside in the drizzle and chilly breeze, until Cecilia Cowdrey led the family inside. Lewis had been called away to town on business unexpectedly. Or had he, Dottie wondered. Only when the Cowdreys had entered did the dutiful incumbents of the estate's former village follow them inside out of the weather. It was all too archaic. The curate was a Yorkshireman, and whilst he showed a proper respect for the Cowdrey family, Dottie wondered if there wasn't also a trace of amusement in his manner, as if he too felt the whole hierarchical charade was ridiculous in this day and age.

But at least they were out of the house, and no one

was arguing. Yet. Dottie fully expected a few barbed comments about Lewis's absence once they all got home again. The church was a lovely old building, typically cold inside, but with the sense of peace old buildings held. Dottie used the time to indulge in pleasant daydreams of the warehouse back home in London and her plans for it. If she slipped into a gentle doze about halfway through the service, no one seemed to notice. When the congregation stood to sing a familiar hymn to a frustratingly unfamiliar, awkward tune, Dottie awoke, surprised to find that Gervase and William were not there urging their opposing armies of geese to attack one another.

When the service was over, they hung about waiting for Cecilia to graciously acknowledge a few people, and have a short conversation with the vicar, then they returned to the house for lunch, joined as always by Leo and June. But to Dottie's relief, Leo and his wife returned to their own abode as soon as lunch was over, promising to return later for dinner, which was a special occasion as Cecilia had invited a number of guests, largely for Dottie's benefit. The rest of the afternoon was a sleepy, pleasant one. Until...

'I'd like to speak with you for a few minutes,' her aunt said at about half-past three. 'Shall we go into the morning room?'

'Of course,' said Dottie, with a sinking feeling. It was rather like being summoned to the headmistress's office at school. The morning room was less a daytime sitting room and more Cecilia's private courtroom.

'I feel the time has come to discuss your situation in greater depth,' Cecilia Cowdrey said, settling herself in a commanding position facing both the door and the rest of the room. She indicated the chair opposite her. Dottie obligingly seated herself. They were facing one another once again. Dottie could hardly see her aunt over a large vase of flowers, and with the little crowded table between them it was like surveying the opposition before going in to battle. Dottie steeled herself. She was on the point of speaking when her aunt continued. 'Now that you know the truth about your parentage, I am making certain arrangements.'

Dottie wasn't sure what to expect, but she felt on edge, convinced this could not be something she wanted to hear. Her aunt continued, 'You will of course come here to live. My husband will continue to be known to you as your uncle. I shall outwardly remain your aunt. In private, you may call me Mother, if you wish.'

After another moment of silence, her aunt directed a dissatisfied look at her. Dottie said nothing, though well aware it was intended that she should. But what could she say that would not immediately cause grave offence?

After a few more seconds, Cecilia said, 'Well? Have you nothing to say?'

Picking her words carefully, yet with an uncomfortable sense of merely postponing the inevitable, Dottie said simply, 'I'm sorry. I'm still thinking of what to say.'

'Hmm,' said Cecilia Cowdrey. She was displeased, but not able to find any actual fault in Dottie's words. She continued, 'You will of course be married from here, seeing that your fiancé is an eminent person.'

'We're not actually engaged,' Dottie clarified. 'We're just—walking out together.'

This Cecilia could object to—and did. In the iciest of tones she said, 'You are not a kitchen-maid, Dorothy.

You do not *walk out* with a gentleman. If you have been seen in public with this man, it ought to be given out immediately. Think of your reputation!'

There was so much that offended Dottie in this, that she didn't know where to begin. In her head, she'd thrown the vase of flowers on the floor and shouted, 'Only *my mother* calls me Dorothy!' For a moment she thought she'd actually done it, but a glance showed the lilies—hateful flowers—were still safely there in the centre of the table. She contented herself once more by keeping her tone mild as she said, 'As you say, he is an eminent man, and Mr Parfitt is both a respectable, and well-respected, gentleman. I'm sure my reputation is perfectly safe.'

Dottie expected an outburst of displeasure following this, but it wasn't exactly as she expected.

Cecilia gave a slight snort, and said, 'He is not quite as respectable as you seem to think, according to my husband and Leo. But he is certainly eminent. The sooner you are married the better, I'd say. For your reputation—and for his.' Her aunt got up, and crossed the room to put on the light, for the room was now almost in darkness. That done, she rang the bell. She resumed her seat. When the maid came, Cecilia ordered tea. The maid bobbed and departed. Cecilia turned towards Dottie, hands slightly outstretched as if in appeal.

'These are my wishes, Dorothy. I know it's difficult for you to think of me as your parent, and I'm fully aware that it will take you a few days to get used to being here. But you have all the time in the world to come to terms with this, but it's not as though you are a child any longer. We'll send to London for the rest of your things, of course. Once you have some familiar belongings about you, you'll feel more at home.'

This time Dottie couldn't help herself. 'But—I'm here on a *visit*,' she said, explaining what had previously seemed obvious. 'I'm only here for a short while. You invited me to visit, or rather Imogen did, and I came. But not to stay. I can't possibly stay.'

Her aunt was affronted. Of course. Dottie had known she would be. She had instinctively known from the moment they met that she would have to choose her words carefully, that offense was always just a few syllables away, and her aunt was ready to view every comment as an attack. Inwardly Dottie sighed. They were about to have a row. She knew it. After what her aunt had already said, Dottie wondered if thoroughly offending her aunt might be the only way she would be able to return to London.

The door opened. The young maid, Win, who'd woken Dottie that morning, came in now with a massive tray. Dottie jumped up to hold the heavy door open as it seemed about to bump the girl and send everything flying. Her aunt frowned but said nothing.

The maid, her back slightly to Mrs Cowdrey as she handed Dottie a cup, mouthed thank you and winked at her. She took up the teapot, ready to pour, but Mrs Cowdrey dismissed her. As soon as the door closed behind her, Cecilia said, 'Dorothy, it's not appropriate for someone of your standing to hold a door for a servant. Kindly refrain from demeaning yourself thus.'

Mrs Cowdrey poured Dottie's tea, handed her lemon, which Dottie declined, and Cecilia frowned again when Dottie added milk to her cup.

'Clearly there are a great many differences between the way my sister and *that man* have brought you up, and the way you should have been brought up in this household. I shall endeavour to overlook some of your lighter failings, and concentrate on those which will prevent you making a success as your future husband's hostess.'

Dottie hadn't paid attention to anything Cecilia said after 'that man', which she supposed was her aunt's own special way of referring to Herbert Manderson, whom Dottie had always thought of—and still thought of—as an absolute sweetheart.

She sipped her tea. It was very hot. But not as hot as her temper. Her aunt was talking—still—but Dottie heard nothing of what she said. After consulting her own feelings again, she decided to throw caution to the wind. She set down her cup, and said, rather bluntly, 'How do you plan to explain suddenly taking me into your household? What do you think my parents will have to say about this? Surely you can't possibly imagine they will agree? Even if they did—which they won't—I have no intention of agreeing to your plans. Leaving aside the fact that I shall be of full age in a few months, you cannot genuinely expect me to uproot my life, turn my back on my beloved family, and my work, and settle down here in this household.'

Her aunt stared at her in disbelief. For once she seemed to have nothing to say.

'Who was my father? And don't bother to say you won't tell me. I have a right to know.' Dottie had blurted it out before she even knew what she was going to say. The question seemed to hang there for a second, rather like something unpleasant neither woman could look away from. Cecilia Cowdrey was icily indignant.

'We do not speak of such...'

'Really?' Dottie challenged. 'You seem to feel able to speak of anything that suits you. You make all these demands. You insult me, my family and the way they brought me up. Well, now it's I who have something to demand. Tell me who my father is.' She was appalled at her own temerity, but couldn't help feeling a sense of triumph too, and she was on tenterhooks to hear her aunt's response. She was confident her aunt would answer. Until...

Cecilia Cowdrey was on her feet, outrage making her rigid and pale. 'I certainly shall not discuss...' She was walking towards the door.

Dottie actually laughed at that. And could have laughed again at the sheer astonishment on her aunt's face. Had no one ever stood up to her before? She said, 'I'm afraid that won't work with me. I must insist that you are open and honest with me. I'm perfectly content to return home tonight if you prefer to keep silent. In any case, I shall be returning to London on the 2nd of January. I'm afraid I have to get back to work then. I had only expected to stay for a week.'

She felt quite proud of this little speech. She had no intention of staying at St Martins longer than a day or two more. The visit was a disaster. It had been a mistake to come. Her life was in London. But she needed information. Her aunt was certainly not going to have things all her own way. Cecilia fixed her with a look of sheer hatred.

The door was opening. Cecilia, with her back to the door now, said, 'How dare you! How dare you come here and make these threats against me!'

The door closed again, and whoever it was, probably a servant, Dottie thought, had evidently decided to come back later.

Dottie glanced at her aunt now and felt dismayed.

Cecilia Cowdrey, grey-faced and breathing heavily, clutched the back of the nearest chair so tightly, her knuckles turned white. Dottie was afraid her aunt was about to faint.

'Aunt Cecilia!' Dottie said at once, going forward, stretching her hand out. 'Don't upset yourself. I only want to know the truth.'

Her aunt took a breath, then stepped back from Dottie, saying, 'No!' Her hand was outstretched as if to fend Dottie off. She took another breath. Then in a low voice, as if afraid someone should overhear her, she said, 'I admit you have a right to know. I suppose I didn't really expect you to leave Lavinia and... But I just need...' She halted. With an attempt to get back her earlier haughtiness she added, 'I shall think about what you've said. And now, I am going to lie down for a while before our guests arrive for dinner. I have rather a bad headache.'

Everything seemed more or less normal, Dottie thought, looking around the dinner table. There was a jolly buzz of conversation. The food was excellent as always. Her aunt appeared at ease and in a good mood, and although she and Dottie had exchanged few words since their "discussion" earlier, her aunt didn't appear to be resentful or annoyed with her. Lewis had returned from his brief business trip. Leo and June were chatting happily with a laughing plump young woman and a tall thin young man; Dottie had already forgotten their names, but the young man was a friend of Leo's, and the woman was the man's fiancée.

Across the table, Imogen sat beside June's father, Sir Stanley Sissons, the *Sudso* soap king, who was regaling Imogen with a very long anecdote that sounded more than a little dull. Imogen smiled and nodded at appropriate intervals, and the gentleman seemed to be enjoying himself. He frequently glanced across the table at Dottie. Dottie, encountering his look, smiled back. She made herself a silent promise to talk to him after dinner, to give Imogen a break.

Once dinner was over everyone made their way to the drawing room, and within a few minutes, other guests began to arrive, invited for evening drinks. The room grew hot and noisy.

Dottie was on the point of keeping her promise to entertain Sir Stanley, but saw that he was busy talking to Cecilia. Dottie heard her name being called, and saw Imogen beaming at her. Beside Imogen was a young fellow who could only be Norris Clarke, Imogen's beloved.

'Dottie, may I present Mr Norris Clarke. Norris, this is Dottie Manderson, the *cousin* I've been telling you about.'

Dottie wasn't sure if she imagined the slight inflection on the word cousin. No doubt Imogen had already explained their precise relationship privately. Norris came forward eagerly and pumped her arm with enthusiasm, telling her several times he was delighted. His hand was warm and plump, rather like the rest of him, she thought, and all in all he was rather like a cherub come to life: plump, smiling, curly-haired and rosy-cheeked. His eyes held mischief until they lit on Imogen, when his look became one of undisguised male passion.

He was perfect for Imogen, Dottie thought. If she had not already known he was in his mid-thirties, she would have taken him for her own age—his roundness made him seem school-boyish and cheeky. Yes, she thought, Imogen would have a jolly life with him, and if it could start soon enough, before Imogen was too much older, that life would be filled with plump, rosy-cheeked mischief-filled children too, and Imogen would have the family she craved. Dottie felt more than ever that she had to support Imogen in her quest for a life of her own.

'I'm so pleased to meet you, Mr Clarke,' Dottie said, grinning at him.

He waved politeness away. 'Oh please, do call me Norris. I've heard so much about you from my dear—er—from Miss Cowdrey.'

'I understand you've been helping Imogen restore the old screen in her sitting room.'

That it was a topic close to his heart was obvious by his beaming response. 'Oh yes. I say, Imogen, do you think anyone would mind if we went up to take a look?' Before Imogen could answer, he was looking back at Dottie again, saying, 'I left Imo—Miss Cowdrey some homework the other day, and I'd like to see how she got on with it.'

'You're going to love it,' Imogen told him as they reached the hall. She hugged his arm. He grinned back at her. 'I'm sure I shall.' They gazed into each other's eyes for a few long seconds. Dottie felt somewhat *de trop*. He led the way upstairs, clearly perfectly at home in the house.

As they followed him up the stairs—Dottie averting her eyes from his ample buttocks—Imogen grabbed her arm in a tight grip and whispered rather loudly, 'I badgered Daddy to invite him. Isn't he a perfect pet?'

Dottie almost laughed at the amount of adoration Imogen managed to cram into a whisper. She nodded. 'He's very sweet, and perfect for you.'

Imogen was pink again, and just had time to say very softly, 'Oh do you really think so?'

Norris was already holding the door open, and both ladies went into the room ahead of him.

They spent a good half hour admiring the screen. Dottie was surprised by how tense Imogen was about it. Was she really so anxious that Dottie should admire their handiwork and approve? Norris stood beside the screen, leaning on the top with his elbow, as if he were both holding it up and presenting it. After a moment Dottie realised he seemed proprietorial. As he explained everything they'd done—the removal of the old fabric, the repairs to the wooden frame, the varnishing of it, followed by the search for the perfect new covering fabric, then how Imogen had embroidered and decorated it before Norris had tacked it all into place, and the further embellishments he had left her to do in the two weeks since he had been to the house—Dottie couldn't shake off her sense that something was not quite right, and that his stance, though not unusual, seemed odd in some way she couldn't quite figure out. It felt all wrong, and she had an odd urge to leave, as if she'd stumbled into something too private for outsiders. His smile hadn't changed, but there was something in his eyes, something calculating and wary. She had the sudden thought that perhaps he was not so sweet and charming after all.

'What's the back of the screen like?' she asked, unable to listen to any further details about the project, and desperate to move the conversation along. It was beginning to be a bit like the herb garden tour.

He glanced at the back of the screen, sent the briefest of looks towards Imogen then with a broad smile that didn't touch his eyes, he said to Dottie, 'Oh it's still just plain and dull at the moment. We haven't quite got to that yet. Perhaps in a few weeks, we'll have something worth looking at.'

He was lying, she thought. But why on earth would he do that?

'But as you can see, the front of the screen is glorious, thanks to Imogen's delightful work. Really her embroidery is exquisite, and far superior to the original work.'

Imogen blushed and smiled. She suggested they ought to go back down to join the others. Her arm went through Dottie's and she led Dottie to the door. On the threshold, Dottie peeked back. She saw that Norris was still by the screen. She had the impression he was looking hard at something on the back, leaning to look more closely. Seeing Dottie had glanced his way, he straightened up and gave a beaming smile, and said, 'Oh yes, of course. I quite forgot the time. It was so good of your father to invite me, Imogen.'

Dottie was pleased to note that he didn't persist in calling her Miss Cowdrey when they were away from the rest of the family. He continued, 'We'd better hurry, I don't want to cause offence by being absent.'

He turned his relentless smile on Imogen. Somehow he and she managed to get ahead of Dottie on the stairs, their hands almost, but not quite, touching. Then at the bottom of the stairs, Imogen did actually pat his shoulder and Dottie heard her murmur, 'It'll be all right,' as he straightened his tie and brushed imaginary fluff from his sleeve.

Poor Norris, Dottie thought. She realised the cause of his odd behaviour. He's nervous of my aunt. Doubtless she's made it clear she has no plans to marry her daughter to an antiques dealer. She understood too that her uncle Lewis had probably not consulted his wife before inviting Mr Clarke.

But then again, Dottie thought, Imogen has some money of her own, and she's of age. Surely she can make her own choice of a marriage partner?

They went into the drawing room just as Guy and Leo were going outside for their usual smoke. They barely even glanced at Norris, whilst, in the drawing room, Cecilia Cowdrey's nod and curt 'Good evening' to Norris was most telling.

It was a long evening, though a pleasant one, and Dottie enjoyed herself immensely, having plenty of people about her eager for conversation, and without even having to work at it, she found she had two new customers for her ladies' wear. But her heart sank when she glanced over her shoulder to see Cecilia approaching for the first time since their conversation earlier that day.

Never given to frequent smiles, her aunt's expression was practically a frown as she said, 'I hope you've had a pleasant evening, Dorothy?'

'Oh yes, very pleasant thank you. I've met some delightful people.'

Her aunt inclined her head graciously, as if that had entirely been her doing. Which, Dottie had to concede, it had been, seeing that Cecilia was the hostess and had invited the guests.

'Dorothy, I've now spoken with Sir Stanley and he is perfectly happy to invite you to the New Year's Eve Ball at his home...'

'Oh that's wonderful!' Imogen, coming up behind them, squealed with excitement, bouncing up and down on her toes. Beside Imogen, and arm in arm with her husband, June beamed happily whilst Leo smiled his polite, cold social smile.

'Imogen,' Cecilia snapped, at the same time trying to keep her voice down to avoid attracting attention. 'Kindly do not behave as if you were still in the nursery.'

Imogen looked chastened. Looking around the room, Dottie wondered where Norris was. She soon spotted him, standing with Sir Stanley. They appeared to be discussing one of the paintings on the far wall. If Norris could gain Sir Stanley's seal of approval, Dottie thought, that would go a long way to making him more acceptable to the Cowdreys.

June said, 'I knew it would all be fine, no one cares about too much formality these days.'

Unless you're a Cowdrey, Dottie thought, but said nothing.

'It will be lovely to have you there for the ball, Dottie. My father adores having young people around him. He gets quite lonely these days, the poor old thing. The New Year's Eve Ball is *the* big event of his social calendar. He's done it for so many years, it's become something of a tradition locally. Father's got another reason to celebrate this New Year,' she added, and leaning closer, she dropped her voice dramatically, even though there was no one else close enough to hear a word. 'But he's keeping it a secret. I've absolutely no idea what it is, but the old darling has been practically bursting with excitement since yesterday.'

Dottie smiled again and said, 'How interesting!' Inwardly she wondered, are all families as odd as this one of mine? What secret on earth could an older gentleman possibly keep that he would be bursting to tell everyone?

'My dear June, I really don't think your father would like us to be discussing these private matters...' Cecilia cautioned with a frown, but June simply waved a dismissive hand in Cecilia's direction and said:

'Oh Dottie's all right. She's family. I'm sure Father wouldn't mind a bit.'

Dottie's interest was definitely piqued. She waited in silence until June, her eyes excited, her lips smiling, a tiny bubble of moisture in the corner of her mouth, was unable to hold back any longer.

She said gleefully, 'He's going to make an

announcement. I'm sure of it. I know I shouldn't expect anything, but he's dropped so many hints lately. And, well, the last time anything like this happened, it was a big announcement about bringing Leo into the family business, and now...' She clapped her hands, bouncing up and down on her toes, not unlike Imogen. Her voice was almost a squeal. 'Ooh I just know it's to do with Leo taking over!' She sent Dottie a quick glance that implied a confidence, and said, 'I don't know if you know, but Father is the owner of *Sudso Ezee Soap Suds*? That's what he got his knighthood for: services to British industry. Not to mention bolstering the party funds, of course.' She grinned without concern at this small indiscretion. 'Anyway, he's almost sixty now, and he has talked about retiring for a while, and I'm convinced he's finally made up his mind to do it. He's going to put Leo in charge of everything, as chairman of the board, and who knows, that could lead to a knighthood for Leo too, *Sudso*'s become so well respected, and obviously it's a household name. Oh I know it's wrong of me to speculate, but really, it's so exciting!'

Dottie was slightly disappointed. She had no idea what she'd expected, but it had been more momentous than this. She failed to see why June was so excited: it didn't sound as though there was anything solid to base her speculation on, although possibly June's own knowledge of her father meant that she was able to read between the lines. Dottie tried to sound pleased.

'How wonderful...'

'My mother passed away two years ago,' June said. 'Now Father has no one else but Leo and me. And as I say, Father is getting on a bit, sadly. For the last year or two he has heavily depended on Leo's help with business matters. Father has not been in the best of health since his heart attack two years ago. In fact I suppose we are lucky to still have him with us. But he's not getting any younger, and so he's got to leave it all someday to Leo or any children we might have. We shall have to wait and see, but something tells me... But the evening will be wonderful. We always have such fun at the New Year's Eve Ball. And it will be lovely to have you there with us, Dottie, dear.'

Chapter Ten

At nine o'clock the next morning, Cecilia Cowdrey set aside her dainty teacup with the air of a business mogul coming down to brass tacks. She looked at Dottie. Dottie, finishing her slice of toast, had a familiar, sinking feeling. Clearly the day was not going to get off to a good start, but at least she hadn't been summoned to the morning room.

'I know your invitation to stay with us was a rather impromptu affair. However, seeing that my daughter was so keen to meet you, I decided to go along with it. It offered the chance of gaining the support of a girl of Imogen's own age to make her see reason.'

Dottie's polite house-guest smile froze on her face. Without moving her head, she could see Imogen's ashen face. Tears were already starting to well up in Imogen's eyes. Lewis remained stubbornly behind his newspaper.

'I don't really think...'

'Surely,' interrupted her aunt, 'it's perfectly clear

that a young woman of good family needs to be prudent in the area of matchmaking. It's obvious. I'm sure you'll agree, that a girl like Imogen can't just throw herself away on some—' her aunt wrestled for a moment with various adjectives and discarded them all. 'On some—*antiques dealer.*'

Heavens above, Dottie thought to herself, instead of an ordinary family breakfast, it's become like a drawing room comedy from the nineteenth century. *Antiques dealer* had clearly become a synonym in Cecilia Cowdrey's mind for all words meaning reprehensible, inferior, inadequate, unsuitable, and even, Dottie thought, poor. Dottie's sympathy for her half-sister grew.

Imogen's tears overflowed. 'Mother...' she pleaded, her hand reaching out to rest on Cecilia's arm. It was shaken off with no patience at all.

'For goodness' sake, Imogen, have some decorum, do! Go and pull yourself together and don't come down until you can behave properly.'

Imogen fled from the room, a sob escaping her on the threshold. As the door closed behind her they could all hear her crying as she went to her room.

Dottie felt wretched for her. She said, 'She obviously loves him very much.'

This brought a derisive snort from Guy. It was all Dottie could do not to roll her eyes.

'That's hardly the point,' Mrs Cowdrey said. 'These girls...'

Dottie couldn't let that go. 'At almost thirty, Imogen is hardly a girl. It's not as though she's sixteen and wants to run off with the first young fellow who's flirted with her.'

There was a frosty silence.

'Hear, hear,' said Guy, but with a malice that showed he was only interested in stoking the fire. He added, 'Although, actually this Clarke chap *is* the first fellow that's ever flirted with poor old Imogen.'

'It's completely impossible,' Cecilia said. 'Anyone can see that.'

'Oh absolutely,' said Guy. 'From the point of view of status alone, it's all wrong. He lives in a flat above the shop. I mean, the chap doesn't even earn enough to keep a decent roof over their heads.'

'He's not even *English*,' Cecilia added, lowering her voice as though speaking about something coarse and unpleasant, something that wasn't at all suited to dining room conversation. 'He's from *Dublin*.'

'A beautiful city. And don't forget, I've met him,' Dottie couldn't hold back from saying. 'He's very nice. And he cares for her a great deal.'

The temperature in the room decreased by several degrees.

In for a penny, in for a pound, thought Dottie. I might as well do what I can for Imogen. 'He's very polite, and respectful, and he wouldn't dream of taking advantage of her. When they get married, they will live in the flat above the shop. It's got four rooms, overlooks the market square in Horshurst and he has a woman in twice a week to clean. It will be perfect for them. It would be such a good match. Imogen loves music, and art, so they've got that in common, plus she has a little money of her own. With that, and his earnings from the shop and a small annuity from his grandmother, they won't be so very badly off. It will be good for her to have her own home and the chance of a family of her own.'

She paused to look around at their stony faces. Only from her Uncle Lewis did she detect any kind of sympathy. But even though he was the only one who could help, he chose not to speak. Recklessly Dottie decided she may as well go the whole way.

'He cares for her very much, and she cares for him. I think you should encourage the match.'

'Oh bravo!' Guy laughed, clapping his hands. 'The town mouse has spoken!'

Dottie could have cheerfully slapped him.

His mother said, 'Shut up, Guy.' Cecilia then turned back to Dottie. 'I would have thought it was clear that I expected you to support me in this matter.' Her voice was low and cold. It was worse than being shouted at. Dottie's cheeks burned with embarrassment. Cecilia continued: 'I would have expected you to display a modicum of family feeling. I have to say, I'm bitterly disappointed by your ridiculous suggestions, and by your behaviour in general. I can see my only option is to speak to Clarke himself, and tell him to leave my daughter alone or I shall do my very best to ruin him.'

With that, Cecilia Cowdrey got to her feet, said a terse, 'I'm going upstairs to lie down. I'm not to be disturbed.' She left the room, shutting the door very carefully and quietly.

Dottie took a breath. There was a stunned silence that suggested this was not part of Cecilia Cowdrey's regular routine.

Guy laughed loudly and said, 'Well, well, Dottie-Dot, you *are* a naughty girl. Bet she's glad she got rid of you to Auntie Lavinia now.'

'Shut up, you idiot,' said his father.

Guy said something to do with seeing a man about a dog, and left.

Dottie sat back, a little appalled at the turn the day had already taken. She began to dread the rest of it. But in the morning, she could say she was ready to go home. She was certain no one other than Imogen would miss her. She left the table and went into the drawing room, forgetting about her uncle behind his paper.

She sat in a corner of one of the sofas and stared into space. Could she possibly leave right now? That was what she wanted to do. It would only take her ten minutes to pack, after all.

A hand appeared in front of her face, holding a glass of sherry. 'You look like you need this, Dottie.'

She looked up in surprise at her uncle but accepted the drink. He took the seat beside her. He gulped his sherry down in one go. Dottie sipped hers and shuddered.

'Ghastly stuff, I know. Fancy something stronger?' He actually smiled at her, and she could see the shadow of the handsome young man he had once been. She smiled back but shook her head.

'I don't think I'd better. It's not even half past nine.'

'Hmm. Hope you don't mind if I indulge.' He fetched himself a glass of whisky, and rejoined her on the sofa. 'Well, Dottie, welcome to the family, my dear! After a scene like that, you know now that you really belong. It's why we all drink so much.' He toasted her with his glass then sank the drink in one. With a sigh of satisfaction, he set the glass down. 'That's good stuff.' He looked back at her. 'Is this how you imagined it would be?'

The question caught her off-guard. His look was direct, and almost for the first time since she'd arrived, she thought she'd encountered a human being.

She half-turned in her seat, leaning her elbow on the back of the sofa. 'No. Not a bit. Though I don't really know what I did expect.'

'Must have been a shock for you, finding out, especially after all this time.'

This time his words didn't surprise her, she had been half-expecting them. She felt as though she could tell him anything, and it would be quite all right. With perfect candour, she said, 'Yes. It was the worst moment of my life, and I've seen several deaths.' There was a silence before she added, 'But I thought I was coming here as your niece, and that everything else was still a secret that only I and Aunt Cecilia shared.'

His low laugh was sardonic. 'No, Dottie, my dear, we all know. I've known since the beginning. The children have known for a long time. You see...' He got up and crossed the room to fetch the decanter, returning with it and pouring himself another glass. 'You see, my dear wife and I have not been—close— for many years. Not since Imogen was born. My wife's choice, not mine. And now...' he shrugged, resigned. 'I loved her once. I actually thought, back in the early days, that we would be one of those couples one hears about, blissfully happy for the rest of their lives, a perpetual love story.' He drank the glass of whisky in one rapid swallow, as before. He set the glass down and leaned back into the sofa cushions, staring into space. 'But I was foolish. We were never really as close as I'd thought, as I'd hoped. I was merely—suitable. Horrible word.'

Dottie had no idea what to say. She sipped her sherry and grimaced. He took it from her with a smile.

'Don't drink it if you don't want it, dear. Anyway,' he continued. 'I'm digressing. The thing is, I recognised the signs. I'd seen my wife when she was expecting all three of my children, so I knew. I'd half-wondered a couple of times if she was seeing someone in secret. To be honest, I didn't mind too much. I'm sure this will shock you, but I also saw— still see—someone. I've been seeing her for more than twenty years.' His expression softened, his smile was gentle. 'Her name's Maria. She—she is different. She gives me... Well I know it's a cliché, but when I'm with her, I'm a different person, a much nicer person. A much *younger* person. I like myself with her, and she's so easy to be with: gentle, relaxing, undemanding, kind. She's an artist so I think the arrangement suits her as much as myself. She likes the time we have apart; it enables her to get on with her work. I'm just telling you this to explain about Cecilia. I wasn't angry, or jealous. I was just glad for her. I thought she'd found someone she truly loved, and I expected her to ask for a divorce so she could marry this fellow. Especially once I realised she was pregnant. But the subject was never raised, she never said anything, not so much as a word, and so like a fool I also said nothing. I just assumed at some point she'd ask me to pretend to be the child's father.'

'But she didn't?'

'No, Dottie. She never spoke to me about it. She still hasn't. And yet somehow everyone seems to know. Back then, one day over breakfast, she said, 'I've been invited to Margate to spend some time with Lavinia and the little one. Poor Lavinia's had this nasty bronchitis everyone's been getting, and she's been ordered to the coast for a few months' rest. You don't mind, do you?' What else could I say but, no, of course I don't mind. She was gone for a little over three months, from the middle of January to the last week in April. I got the odd post-card, what a marvellous time they were having and so on, and how well Lavinia was recovering, and a bit about the arrival of a surprise baby Cecilia hadn't realised Lavinia was expecting. My wife wrote to the children. They were all away at school, of course.'

Dottie nodded. Of course. In many ways, her arrival couldn't have been better timed.

'She came back so slim, refreshed, and talked endlessly about how well she felt, how rested, what a lovely time they'd had, and so on. Told me all about Lavinia's new baby daughter, how surprised and happy everyone was, how pretty the little thing was. And all along, I knew. We never spoke about it, but I knew.' He poured himself yet another whisky, but this time he sipped it meditatively. 'I was just glad the poor little beggar was—sorry, *you*—were going to be brought up by Lavinia. A damned good woman, Lavinia.' His hand was shaking as he set the glass on the table, still more than half of the measure intact. Without looking at her, he said, 'Did you have a happy childhood?'

Through sudden hot tears, Dottie said, 'Yes, very happy.'

He squeezed her hand. 'I'm glad, my dear.' He held out his handkerchief to her. 'Always thought the world of Lavinia. And Herbie. Excellent people. The kind you always want on your side in a scrape.'

She couldn't speak, and simply nodded.

He sipped his whisky, then said, 'I was at school with Herbert. Herbie, we used to call him, though Lavinia didn't like that. A good fellow. When you go home, ask him to tell you about the time we almost burned down the cricket pavilion. Lord, I don't believe we could have been more than thirteen or fourteen.' He smiled at the memory.

Dottie said, 'Who was my father?' She'd blurted it out without even knowing what she was going to say. The words seemed to echo, to hang in the air.

He sighed. 'I can't tell you. I suspect, but I don't actually know. And it's not my place to tell you, in any case.'

'Please don't tell me there were too many for her to know which one...'

'Oh my God, no, my dear! There was just one special man, I'm sure of it. Someone we've seen a good deal of over the years, always in our social circle for one reason and another. Cecilia and he were always close, but he was married to someone else, as was she of course, and then—well, there were objections from a social point of view.'

'He wasn't good enough for her, you mean? Or she wasn't good enough for him?' Dottie couldn't help the bitter edge to her voice. She'd wanted this information, and now—so close to the truth—she couldn't quite decide how she felt.

Lewis shot her a look. 'The former.'

'So he wasn't good enough for her. You obviously do know who it was. What was his name?'

He hesitated. 'Look, it's better you ask Cecilia. In any case, as I say, they were both married. No one wanted a scandal.'

'I have asked her. She won't tell me. She doesn't even like me,' Dottie pointed out. 'Especially not after this morning.'

'Ask her again, you never know. Give her a day or two to calm down, and you might have a chance to talk to her again.'

He sat forward on the edge of the sofa, and she knew the conversation was at an end. 'Well I need to do a few things in my study.'

He paused at the door, looking back to say, 'By the way, I agree with you about Imogen and this chap Clarke. They would be good for one another.'

'Then why on earth don't you say so?'

He shrugged. 'It's no use with Cecilia. She doesn't listen. Really, she just doesn't want Imogen to leave her. She's afraid of being alone. And with Clarke, you know how it is, he's not really one of us, is he? But for Imogen's sake I invite him to the house for this and that. Not that Cecilia approves.'

'Well,' Dottie said with some vinegar to her voice, 'If she lets Imogen marry Norris, there'd soon be grandchildren to keep Cecilia busy. Not to mention Guy, and any children he might have if he marries, and there's Leo and June. They might have children in time. There's no reason for Cecilia to feel alone.'

He nodded vaguely. 'Very true. Well, I'll see you in a little while, my dear.' He closed the door behind him. Dottie waited a few moments then went upstairs. She was relieved that she met no one on the way.

Norris Clarke had been invited for lunch by Lewis Cowdrey, and Imogen's excitement at her beloved coming to the house an unprecedented two days in a row had been quickly squashed by her mother. Though Imogen was still distressed about the scene over breakfast, Dottie couldn't help feeling the situation could have been better handled.

'Things could have been worse. Your mother could have told Drysdale to turn Norris away at the door,' Dottie pointed out. 'You ought to have reminded your father to mention it to her sooner than this morning.'

'But what if she speaks to him, tells him he mustn't see me anymore? She thinks he's not good enough for me.'

'Norris won't take any notice even if she does warn him off. But you really must stand up to her.'

But Imogen was almost in tears. Even before Dottie finished speaking, she was shaking her head. Her shoulders slumped in defeat, her whole demeanour was that of someone completely broken down and hopeless, making her look far smaller and more fragile than she actually was.

'No, Dottie, I can't. I just can't. I know I'm a goose,

but Dottie, I can't do the things you do.'

'What things? What things do I do?'

'Well, you know. You go here and there on your own. You travel. You drive a car. And you have a career. That's so terribly exciting—and so brave and I—I don't know, I just think it's so *bold* of you. And you've got your wonderful beau—handsome, wealthy, influential. You'll be *the* society hostess of Derbyshire when you're married.'

That was something Dottie didn't want to think about. 'I don't know about that. In any case, although he works in Derbyshire, he actually lives over the county border in Nottinghamshire. And I'm quite sure he already entertains; he isn't going to be relying on me to do it all. There are lots of county families. I'm sure they are all far more elegant and experienced in entertaining than I am.'

Imogen's lack of confidence must be contagious, Dottie thought. She was beginning to feel rather anxious now, 'And as for my career, well, I sort of fell into that by accident. I had no idea poor Mrs Carmichael had left the business to me in her will, and I'm afraid I'm likely to make a fearful mess of things. Most of the time I feel like I hardly know what I'm doing. So it's not really exciting or fun, it's just rather worrying and exhausting.'

But Imogen was hanging on her words like an eager puppy, not in the least discouraged.

'But the designs! And you know—everything else— paying the bills, ordering the stock, managing the girls, making all those decisions. Talking to clients. All of that—I could never do any of it.' Her face fell even more. The corners of her mouth turned down. 'I—can't even get Norris,' she whispered. A tear rolled down her nose.

They were back to the beginning again. Dottie

quashed her impatience. She said, 'You need to stand up to your mother. You need to say, 'Mother, I'm very sorry, but I'm in love with Norris, and he's in love with me. And we're both of age, so you can't stop us. I'd rather have your blessing, but if you won't give it, that won't stop me.' Then you and Norris run away, get married and open a new antiques' shop somewhere else. You could help him with his business—yes, Imogen, *you*. You could pay the bills, order the stock, manage staff, or talk to clients. It would be no different than talking to a new acquaintance invited to dinner. You, Imogen. *You* can do this.'

Imogen stared at her as if she'd just witnessed the impossible. 'Golly.'

'You could go anywhere together. You could go to London, or Bournemouth. Derbyshire. Anywhere. You could have your lovely little antiques business, with a cosy little flat above it, or a house somewhere. And your mother will just have to like it or lump it. It could be wonderful. But you'll never have it if you sit here saying 'I can't...' all the time.'

'Oh, Dottie, I c-can't...' Imogen was screwing her handkerchief into a tight damp ball. 'I just...'

'Then you'll be an old maid with a broken heart, and so will Norris,' Dottie said heartlessly, determined to make Imogen understand. 'You'll be miserable and alone and it will be all your own fault. And your mother will get everything her own way. You'll be her slave until you die. Or rather, until she dies,' Dottie corrected herself. She looked at Imogen, and couldn't believe she still dithered, not seeming convinced. Why did Imogen seem to think only other people deserved to have their own life?

'If I said any of that to my mother—to *our* mother— she'd be absolutely livid and go all 'get thee to a nunnery' on me. Honestly Dottie, I'm sure you're the only one she'd listen to. Would you please, please, please speak to her about Norris and I?'

Dottie's heart sank. Somehow she'd known all along that this was coming, yet she still felt as though she'd been ambushed. In spite of knowing it was the last thing she could bear to do, for some reason she said, 'I'll try. But I can't promise anything. I really don't think she'll listen to me. But, if you really want me to, I'll try.'

Imogen sat up, excitedly clapping her hands like a small child. 'Oh, I knew you would! Thank you, thank you, thank you!'

'Norris!' Pink-faced and practically giggling with excitement, Imogen hurried to greet him. He kissed her cheek, but his look was so intense, Dottie thought, that given the opportunity she had no doubt at all that he would have caught Imogen into his arms and kissed her on the lips. The gentleman was certainly in love.

Flustered but glowing with happiness, Imogen stepped back, patting her hair and straightening the sensible cardigan she wore. The garment was in Dottie's opinion at least three decades too old and two sizes too big for Imogen. But better that she should be comfortable and as confident as she could be in something too old, than to put her in something modern and youthful that would leave her on edge.

Cecilia treated Norris to a slight frown but mercifully said nothing. She led her guests and her family into the dining room. Norris whispered to Dottie, 'I think she's warming to me.' He had a twinkle in his eye. Dottie smiled. He had a rogueish sense of humour, she thought. Why on earth didn't he just arrive one night at Imogen's bedroom window with a ladder and take her away?

After lunch it was a relief to take advantage of the dry, sunny afternoon to walk down to the lake.

Leo, always pompous and self-important, strode on ahead of everyone, his wife clinging to his arm and clearly struggling to keep up with his pace. Behind them were Lewis and Guy. Cecilia was not with them, having gone upstairs to rest immediately lunch was over. She had expressed the intention of joining them again for afternoon tea.

Dottie was left to bring up the rear with Imogen and Norris, walking side by side but so close they may as well have held hands. Dottie felt impatient with them. For goodness' sake, she thought, this isn't the nineteenth century. No one could possibly object to a little hand-holding.

Out loud, she said, mildly, 'I can't think why the two of you don't just run off together and get married. It's not as though anyone can stop you, you're both of full age. Why waste time hoping Aunt Cecilia will change her mind?'

They both halted and stared at her. Imogen looked horrified.

'It's all right, no one's listening. Anyway, they're too far ahead.' Dottie indicated the backs of the two men, deep in conversation.

'We can't run away!' Norris protested.

'Why not?' There was a note of challenge in Dottie's voice. So much for concealing her impatience, she thought. The other two seemed uncomfortable. They exchanged a look.

Imogen said, 'Well, to start with, there's Norris's business to consider. Remember this morning Mother said she would make sure he's ruined if he continues his attentions.' She was looking thoroughly upset.

'I assume Guy told you she said that. She was upset, Imogen. I'm sure she didn't mean it. If she did, then why would she allow Norris to come to lunch?' Dottie said. 'She can't disapprove of him so completely if she invites him to the house.'

'You know Daddy invited him. I begged him to. I thought if Mother could get to know Norris a little better...'

Dottie felt exasperated. 'Again, why would your father do that if he disapproved of Norris?'

'Norris's father is an old friend of Daddy's, so Daddy likes to invite Norris. Besides, Daddy enjoys annoying Mummy. So that's his main reason for doing anything.'

It's ridiculous, Dottie thought. And said so out loud, adding, 'Not to be rude, Imogen, but really you ought to get married soon. If—you know—you want to have children.'

'But Mummy...' Imogen persisted. 'And Norris's business.'

Dottie sighed. With a patience she didn't really feel, she said, 'Norris, do you own your shop and flat, or rent it?'

'Er—no, Miss—er—Dottie, I rent it.'

'Then you can take your belongings, your stock and your business, everything—and move somewhere else. You can have a business wherever you want—Worthing, Hastings, Reigate, anywhere. And *you*, Imogen, can get your savings out of the bank, and take it, and go with Norris, get married and live happily ever after. You don't need to do all this silly mooning about and fretting your life away and waiting for someone's permission.'

She wished she hadn't said 'silly', but fortunately they didn't seem to take it amiss. To Dottie it was a perfectly simple situation, and surely if they truly loved each other, it was the obvious solution. In time, Aunt Cecilia would come round. She would have to if she wanted to know her grandchildren. If not, well, surely happiness away from her family was better for Imogen than unhappiness with them?

Norris and Imogen looked at each other. With great daring, Imogen took his hand and held it tight. They walked on.

Dottie felt she'd said enough. Now it was up to them.

The wreath lay on the bench in the greenhouse behind the rose garden. Anyone standing nearby might have caught the fresh earthy fragrance of the soft rosemary stalks twined about the raffia with columbine and campion. The observer's eye would certainly have seen the delicate sprigs of new bronze fennel, pulled up from their position in the greenhouse; or the winter aconites, their bright yellow blooms so welcome in the cold months, along with the deceptively soft-looking young nettle leaves, and the violas, past their best now at the close of the year, but still dotted here and there in sheltered places about the grounds where they were protected from the few mild frosts that had so far visited.

It was careful work, neat, precise. It would hold together come what may. And when at last it was held up for examination, it was important that no one should miss the tiny scrap of ruby satin just that minute so painstakingly placed amongst the twisted stems.

People passed by the greenhouse, chatting and laughing. They didn't come inside. They walked on without seeing the wreath or wondering who it might be for. Beyond the enclosed world of the greenhouse, the geese honked and flapped their tortured wings.

They ended up separating and reforming into other groups during the course of the walk. When Dottie finally returned to the house, it was in the company of Leo and Lewis. Not a happy stroll back, as they continued another of their seemingly endless discussions about fishing. Without pausing they made their way to the drawing room, where afternoon tea was about to be served.

Norris and Imogen wandered in, still hand in hand, and looking radiantly happy.

It was another ten minutes before June came in with Cecilia, stating they had met in the garden when June was admiring the last few chrysanthemums still lingering on from the autumn. They seemed tired of each other's company, which didn't especially surprise Dottie. June, appearing out of sorts, went to sit beside her husband immediately, dropping her capacious handbag down by the side of the chair as if it had been weighing her down.

Through the window, Dottie spotted Guy ambling along, coming from the front of the estate, whistling casually, his hands thrust deep into his pockets. If anything, his very easiness made Dottie more suspicious than if he'd been behaving furtively. But as he came in and greeted everyone with his usual wry good humour, nothing seemed out of the ordinary.

She went upstairs to take off her coat, gloves and outdoor shoes just as the first tray was brought into the drawing room. Passing the hall mirror, she noticed she needed to try and tame her hair; even with her hat holding it down, it had been fluffed up by the breeze to a shocking degree and was beginning to resemble a dandelion clock, she thought.

As she entered her bedroom, something hard

scraped under her shoe. Stooping to pick it up, she saw it was the bright steel of a dressmaker's pin. She frowned, puzzling. How it had come to be there? What a good thing she'd still had her outdoor shoes on, and had not stepped on it in bare feet. She placed the pin on the mantelpiece out of the way.

Her glance drifted about the room. If she'd been a dog, she would have said her hackles rose. As it was, she shivered. She felt the goosebumps prickle out on her arms. She'd known this feeling once before: when her parents' house had been burgled.

Someone had been in her room.

She caught sight of the little briefcase she'd left on the side table in front of the window. Anxiety gripped her, a cold hard hand about her heart. She rushed across and grabbed the case.

It was unlocked, open, and empty. Save for one more dressmaker's pin caught in the seam, her briefcase was completely empty. All her designs were gone.

Chapter Eleven

She looked everywhere. She even looked in all the impossible places as one does when something valuable is missing. When she went downstairs in a few minutes, she would be able to say, perfectly honestly, that she had looked everywhere.

She threw back the bedclothes, pulled aside the pillows. Nothing. She then pulled back the other end of the bedclothes where they overhung the bottom of the bed. She knelt to look underneath the bed. All she found was a hair pin and a handkerchief—not even one of hers—then she crawled across the floor to peer under the chest of drawers, under the dressing-table, the chair, behind the floor-length curtains that hung at both windows.

She searched all the drawers—even though she'd never put the designs inside any of them. She pulled the chest out from the wall to look behind it. She took the drawers out one by one to check the designs hadn't fallen behind one of them. She searched the wardrobe. She got the key out of her handbag and hauled her big suitcase out of the wardrobe. She already knew it was empty from the light hollow feel of it, but nevertheless she unlocked it and checked inside. It was still empty. As was her hat box.

She sat back on her heels and gazed around the room for somewhere she had overlooked. There was nothing else to do but admit it. The designs were gone. All she had left were the two pins. She stifled a panicking sob and perched on the foot of the bed. She had to think about this rationally. She pressed her hand to her forehead. She would not let herself think about the consequences of not finding those designs.

They had been taken. This much was obvious. They might very possibly have been disposed of by accident, such as something being spilt on them, or some other damage occurring that the person who caused it—one of the maids, perhaps—felt they had to hide or cover up what had happened. So perhaps they had taken the designs—here she took a deep breath—and disposed of them. Or perhaps they had simply taken the papers thinking they were rubbish.

Following that train of thought, she hurried to the fireplace, but it was clean, and neatly set for use later in the evening when it was colder.

But in order for them to have been taken, even by accident, the person would have had to look inside the case, where she'd put them. She bit her lip. Had she put them back in the case after looking at them the night before last? She couldn't remember. She thought she had, but she couldn't swear to it... In any event, she had clearly not remembered to lock the case.

Dottie looked about her bleakly.

She thought she *had* put them away. She could

picture herself doing exactly that. Only... what if she hadn't?

She shook her head. No, she *had* put them away. Therefore they had been taken—stolen—and the person who had taken them had done so either by accident, which she couldn't see happening, or out of malice, purely to hurt her. Or because in some way they thought that the designs could be turned to profit.

Dottie flattered herself that her design ideas had been quite good for a beginner, but they were hardly the sort of thing that could be of value to a really professional fashion warehouse with their whole team of designers and dressmakers.

She had to tell someone. There was a chance—a very small chance—that they might still be able to catch the perpetrator and get the designs back. Or they might be lying in the ash can outside with little damage other than a bit of ash on them. With another pull on her emotions, holding her head up and putting her shoulders back, Dottie forced herself to walk calmly down the stairs to the drawing room.

Imogen looked up as Dottie came in, but no one else noticed her.

She halted in the doorway and said, 'I'm sorry to bother everyone, but I'd just like to say that my designs are missing from my room, and that if anyone has taken them—by accident, I'm sure—I would be grateful if they could return them straight away.'

Everyone turned to stare at her. They looked bewildered. It was impossible to say whether there was any guilty face amongst the group. Not that she actually thought it was one of them, of course.

Lewis actually laughed and said, 'You probably just

mislaid them. You girls...'

Glad she'd anticipated someone saying just such a thing, Dottie said, 'I've searched the room thoroughly. They are definitely gone.'

Imogen, her face stricken, said, 'Oh Dottie! How terrible. See Mummy, I told you these thefts should be taken seriously. First the pearl earrings that were my grandmother's, then Daddy's cigar case, and the snuff box, and then my pearl necklace. Now Dottie's designs have gone missing!'

Cecilia said, 'Nonsense,' in that same brisk way Mrs Manderson had. Dottie spared a bit of her brain to wonder if they'd both got it from *their* mother. Cecilia set down her cup and saucer with rather a jarring chink and went from the room.

Guy said, 'I'm sorry, I really don't understand. What is it, exactly, that's gone missing?'

'Some pictures Dottie had drawn, you know dresses and what not,' Lewis said, and he didn't bother to disguise his boredom with the subject.

'Pictures?' Guy sounded none the wiser.

'Designs. Professional designs for my new range of ladies' wear. A whole stack of forty foolscap pages. With fabric samples attached.' She knew she sounded angry now, but she was upset. What was wrong with these people and their complete lack of interest in anyone but themselves?

Imogen came to put her arm about her shoulder. 'Don't worry, Dottie, I'm sure we'll get them back.'

Cecilia returned, saying, 'Well I couldn't find them in Dorothy's room, so if she did bring these drawings with her, I imagine she must have left them somewhere. But really, Dorothy, it's a bit much to be so put out. Surely you can just draw them again if you can't find them when you get home? Or think up something new to draw.'

Guy said, 'I thought you just did a spot of dressmaking?'

Dottie didn't answer; she was choking back a sudden burst of anger at Cecilia's tone. She took a deep breath, and completely without thought, blurted out, 'I'm sorry, but if they are not back in my room by the time we return from the ball tonight, I shall have no choice but to inform the police.'

For the first time, June spoke, and her tone held an edge of amusement. 'Surely there's no need for that, Dottie. Do be reasonable. Come, dear, I'll have another look with you. I'm sure they're just hidden away somewhere.'

Dottie was adamant. 'They're gone. I've already searched for them. And if Aunt Cecilia can't find them either, then I don't see what you think you...'

'Dorothy, I'm not having my servants upset by the arrival of a police constable. If you like, I'll ask them discreetly if they've seen anything. Really, that's as far as I'm prepared to go,' Cecilia said. 'But before I do, I think you should go and telephone to your mother and ask her to have a look for the wretched things. I don't want you to look silly in front of everyone by making a huge fuss about them here, only to find they are under your pillow when you get home.'

'I brought them with me,' Dottie insisted. 'Imogen has seen them. I showed them to her.' She glanced at Imogen who nodded in confirmation.

'Oh yes,' she said immediately. 'Dottie showed me all her lovely designs, they were terribly good. She's terribly clever.'

Cecilia gave a theatrical sigh, got up and went to ring the bell. After a minute, the door opened, and the butler entered.

'Yes ma'am?'

'Drysdale, please ask downstairs and see if anyone has seen anything of Miss Manderson's dress designs, will you? She seems to have put them down somewhere. There are about twenty or thirty sheets of paper with pictures of outfits on them, and bits of dress material held on with pins.'

'Very good, ma'am.'

That accomplished, Cecilia Cowdrey seemed to feel she'd done all she could. She went to the door.

'Well, it's time to get dressed. I shall see you all later. Remember not to be late, please, the cars are booked for seven o'clock prompt.'

As soon as the door closed behind her, the three men went back to talking about politics, and Imogen asked June if she thought she should enhance her hair colour.

'Oh no, not at all, Imogen,' June said without hesitating. 'Enhanced hair is so brassy. Men might think you're *fast*.' She dropped her voice on this last word. She added, speaking to her husband, 'Leo, dearest, we really ought to be getting back. I have to dress, you know, and I need to look my best for tonight.' She grabbed her bulky, unattractive handbag and moved past Dottie to the door.

Dottie left the room. She didn't trust herself to stay another moment. Why didn't anyone care? Why didn't they seem to feel that this latest theft ought to be investigated—along with the earlier ones—and the culprit discovered? In any case, for whatever reason, they just didn't care about what the loss of her designs meant for Dottie herself. What was wrong with these awful, awful people?

She went back up to her room, not bothering to turn on the lights, but made her way across the dark space to the chair by the furthest window. She sank down into it and sobbed on the padded arm with frustration.

A few minutes of crying, though, served its purpose: she recovered from the initial shock of discovering that her designs were missing, and her aunt's—and her aunt's family's—indifference to that. She pulled herself together. She got up to close the curtains.

She grabbed her wrap and went along to the bathroom. Whatever the other shortcomings of the house, there was always plenty of hot water. She filled the bath and wallowed in it, letting the warmth seep into her chilled body. She relaxed. When the water began to cool, she got out and rubbed her body vigorously with the towel until her skin sang.

She went back along the chilly corridor to her room and found that during her absence the maid had been in and lit the fire. The bedroom was deliciously toasty. The crackle of the flames on the logs made a comforting sound, and the soft scent of the burning wood was pleasant and homely.

Dottie drew her evening gown from the wardrobe and observed it with satisfaction. It was constructed of a delicate midnight-blue lace over a plain shift of fuchsia pink silk-satin. There was a band of fuchsia pink silk draping across the top of the bodice to tie in a bow on the right shoulder. The dress fitted close over the bosom, waist and hips then flared out gently from mid-thigh—Dottie being a young woman who loved to dance. It was one of her own creations, she loved it with a passion, and this would be its first public appearance.

For a moment her courage wobbled. The little taunting voice inside asked her why she thought she should wear such a thing, and who she thought she was, trying to make dresses. Leo was right, said the spiteful voice, girls had no business in business. Then it reminded her that a mere matter of days after bringing them home from her office, she had already managed to lose her entire collection of new designs—just like an amateur—and how would she ever recover from that?

'Nonsense,' said Dottie, though with not quite as much confidence as her mother said it. 'Fiddlesticks,' she added for good measure, and felt a little better.

She got her underwear, slip and best silk stockings ready. Her high-heeled silver dance shoes, freshly wiped to deal with a minor scuff on the toe of the left one, had been returned by the maid, and placed neatly beside the bed. Dottie got out her evening wrap—a winter one in heavy navy silk lined with fine wool—and placed it ready to just pick up as she left the room to go downstairs. And she would take her tiny silver evening purse. Earrings, necklace and bracelets, the perfect complements to her dress, were ready on the dressing table.

Still warm from her bath, Dottie went to the window, and opened it to lean out and breathe in the early evening air. It was definitely colder. Icy crystals of frost already gilded the path below her, and the window frame, though it was barely six o'clock. It seemed that the mild weather was finally over. The geese grumbled ill-naturedly and huddled together on straw under a large wooden shelter at the side of the walled rose garden; the glass roof of the greenhouse just showing as a dark shape above the rose garden wall. The New Year was arriving with a change of weather and a fierce reminder that spring was still many weeks away.

She closed the window and went to the dressing table and began to get ready for the evening ahead.

The New Year's Eve ball was in full swing, and

Dottie had been listening to Sir Stanley Sissons for easily twenty minutes. He appeared to have singled her out to entertain. Perhaps her aunt had asked him to make Dottie feel welcome? He had been talking about June and Leo. It was clear he hoped for grandchildren. He talked and talked, often patting her hand that was tucked through his arm as they meandered about the crowded room, nodding to this person or that.

He was a nice man, if rather old-fashioned in his views about women. It seemed clear to Dottie that he didn't usually have much of an audience. She heard all about how he started his business with just a shilling in his pocket, and then he told her about his collection of old weapons. And his stuffed animal trophies.

On hearing that Dottie didn't hunt, shoot or fish, he said, 'I suppose you're one of those liberals. All bleeding hearts and wanting to look after everyone.' But he smiled as he said it.

She grinned. 'I'm afraid I am, Sir Stanley, that's what happens when you give the vote to the fair sex.' She said it with her tongue in her cheek, and he laughed with delight.

'Don't mind telling you, I joined the campaign trail to support m'wife. She ran for parliament, y'know.'

That did surprise Dottie. 'I didn't know that. Was she elected?'

'Oh yes,' he said, as if surprised she should even ask. 'Yes, she always achieved everything she set her mind to. She was a very determined woman. That's how she hooked me, y'know.'

'Marvellous,' Dottie said. 'You must have been so proud of her.'

'I was.' He looked sad. Dottie patted his arm.

'You must have loved her very much.'

'Not half as much as she deserved, I'm ashamed to say. Wonderful thing, hindsight, but I'm afraid it always comes that little bit too late.' He gave a great sigh, then took Dottie's empty glass. 'Let's get you another.' He smiled at her, and his eyes were somewhat over-bright. 'Soon be time for the count-down to midnight. Then, as you know, I've got a special announcement to make.'

But when he crossed the room to the drinks table, he was immediately drawn into conversation with some other gentlemen. Dottie looked about her. She felt a little like the proverbial fish out of water: everyone knew everyone here, and she only knew her family. The guests were all chatting in groups, but Dottie was all on her own.

As midnight approached, Sir Stanley's butler brought a gong into the midst of the dance-floor then struck it two or three times to get everyone's attention. The sight of it brought back everything from the previous New Year, slamming Dottie suddenly with a weight of painful memories.

Sir Stanley, bidding everyone to charge their glasses, pulled out a stopwatch, ready to count down to the hour.

On his signal, the guests joined in with deafening enthusiasm.

'Ten.'

Dottie looked about her, her eyes blurring as mental images presented themselves. Every guest had their eyes fixed on their host. She felt alone.

'Nine.'

She remembered the previous New Year's Eve, at George's parents' house.

'Eight.'

She and George's sister Diana had brought the radio into the hall and turned it up so everyone could hear the chimes live from Big Ben.

'Seven.'

Diana, who had talked that evening of having babies as a woman's sacred duty to her husband.

'Six.'

Diana, who had been secretly having an affair with a married—then murdered—man.

'Five.'

Diana, who had told the police, told William Hardy, about her predicament.

'Four.'

Diana, who had been sent away by her parents to have her child in shame.

'Three'

Diana, whom Dottie had found too late, half-starved in a filthy hotel, punishing herself for her guilt.

'Two.'

Diana, too weak for childbirth, who had died as soon as her baby daughter was born.

'One! Happy New Year!'

The guests were a drunken mob all about her. They screamed with laughter and shouted with delight, pushing and shoving and falling all over the place. Tears streamed down Dottie's face as she fought to tear herself from the past, and repeat the words of the present. But the excitement of the occasion had gone, leaving her feeling cold and empty now. It was all so pointless. She set her glass aside untouched, turning to push her way through the bodies and into the coolness of the hall. She ran up the stairs to the ladies' cloakroom, and leaned against the closed door, fighting to compose herself.

She got her breath back, and bit by bit pulled herself together. She went to the basin and splashed some water onto her face, blotting her burning cheeks and neck with the towel. She had the face of a ghost; her make-up was mostly on the towel. But it couldn't be helped. She had a lipstick in her bag and added a little of that, and gently tried to slap a little colour back into her cheeks. A few more minutes looking out of the window at the cold glistening stars and the frost-laced garden, then she went back downstairs.

The dancing was in full swing. Norris and Imogen went by in each other's arms, Imogen looking ecstatically happy. Dottie hadn't even noticed Norris was there until now.

Leo went by with June, both looking bored. Guy danced with a young blonde woman, but his frequent glances in June's direction told their own story. Dottie went to the drinks table and asked for a sweet white wine.

Before she could taste it, the glass was taken out of her hand and placed back on the table.

'Sorry I neglected you, m'dear. I believe the honour would be mine,' said Sir Stanley Sissons, and without further ado, he swept her onto the floor. In spite of his age, he turned out to be no mean dancer. He regaled her with hilarious anecdotes of a misspent youth, pointing out a few childhood co-conspirators who were there that evening, presumably having grown in wisdom and good sense by now. Dottie felt calmer; her spirits lifted.

When the dance ended, Sir Stanley signalled to his butler once more and the gong was sounded.

'My dear ladies and gentlemen, friends, family and cohorts! I have something to announce, a very exciting piece of news to share with you all. As some of you will no doubt be aware, I shall be sixty-one in a month's time...'

There were cheers and shouts of, 'He don't look a

day over eighty' and 'Don't you mean *seventy*-one, you old fool?' from a man who looked ninety if he was a day.

This then was the big announcement June had been expecting. Dottie looked around and found her and Leo, coming towards the front of the crowd. June's eyes were avidly fixed on her father, and she gripped Leo's arm in what had to be a painful pinching hold.

'Now, now!' admonished Sir Stanley with beaming good humour. 'As I was saying, I shall soon be sixty-one. You might think a fellow was beyond being surprised when he got to such a great age. But I have been surprised, charmed and delighted to discover something I had previously only hoped for. It appears that at the ripe old age of sixty-one, I have become a father.'

Dottie thought June looked puzzled now. Dottie herself wondered what Sir Stanley was getting at. It certainly didn't sound like a retirement speech. But then...

'I would like to introduce you all to my daughter, long lost to me but now restored...'

Dottie saw it all as if in slow-motion. And then, just as he was about to speak, she knew what he was going to say. The room seemed to be swirling. As he continued to address the room, everyone turned to look at her. He held out his hand to her.

'Dottie, my dear, do join me up here. Ladies and gentlemen, Miss Dorothy 'Dottie' Manderson. My daughter.'

The deafening applause died eventually, and the band struck up a waltz. Sir Stanley escorted Dottie, still dazed, to the centre of the floor and after a few moments other couples began to dance. Dottie could hardly focus on moving her feet in time to the music, and yet she was aware of Lewis and Cecilia going by, and on the other side of the dancefloor they encountered Leo and June, deep in conversation but June sent her a dazzling smile as the couples passed one another.

It felt completely unreal. Dottie looked at Sir Stanley.

She hadn't expected to see tears in his eyes. She had thought only of her own feelings. The sense of shock was not all hers, she saw now. He smiled at her, but for once seemed at a total loss for words. She didn't know what to say either. She tried to smile back and was only partially successful. A moment later he guided them off the dancefloor, and making a path through the throng, he opened a door and invited her into a small room lined with books.

'Let's sit down and have a chat, shall we?'

There was a roaring fire, though Dottie had never felt so hot in her life. But the sofa looked comfortable, and she was relieved to be away from the noise of the ball.

Sir Stanley looked at her. 'Well.'

She nodded. 'I have no idea what to say.'

'I must apologise for making that announcement. As soon as I saw your face, I realised you didn't know. I'm so sorry, dear, I thought Cecilia... But there, she always did go her own way, regardless of the feelings of others. When we spoke earlier, I thought you knew then. But now I see...'

'I'm afraid I had no idea. But I can see why Cecilia told you. I've rather badgered her about it since I arrived. I just wish I had been prepared. I must have looked like a rabbit in the headlights.' She was still fighting for composure. But he seemed to sense it, and simply smiled at her, and took a seat opposite her.

'It was very wrong of her not to tell you.'

'Or you,' Dottie said. 'All these years... Did you have no idea?'

'Oh I knew there had been a child. Later. She told me she gave the child up for adoption. She—she didn't want to think about things or talk about things. But at the time, I knew nothing. I had ended things, you see, a few months before you were born. She felt abandoned and angry, no doubt. I pointed out we were both married, we had made our decisions and had to, so to speak, lump it. I felt it was wrong to continue to see one another—in that—er—in that way. If she had told me, things would have been very different. In fact, she only told me two days ago. It was—a shock—but a wonderful one. She said she would speak with you, but... But there we are, as I said, Cecilia... she can be very stubborn, very proud. I'm afraid we never did truly stick to our vows to return to our spouses.'

'But you love her? Still?' Dottie realised it was a bold thing to say. Would he be offended? She did so hope not. She needed to be able to discuss the situation fully and frankly.

But he nodded, and gave a rueful smile. 'I have always loved her. That might surprise you. She hasn't always been so cold. When we were young...' His expression grew wistful. 'She loved to dance. And she used to sing and play the piano. Years ago it was the thing we did in the evenings, at one another's houses, after dinner parties, that sort of thing. Oh she was lovely. She bewitched me when I was still in my teens, and I never truly had eyes for anyone else. Her parents separated us. I was not 'one of us', as the landed gentry say. Not good enough for her. Well, it broke my heart but we carried on secretly, until she married that idiot Cowdrey.'

'And you married too...'

He nodded. 'Yes my dear Evelyn. I—I'm afraid I treated her very shabbily. I loved her too, though not enough to say no to Cecilia. It was a different kind of love I had for Evelyn. She was so patient, so kind. She knew all along, of course. She forgave me a hundred times. The number of times I told her it was over and that I would be a faithful husband.' He shook his head at the memory, then sighed. 'What must you think of me, Dottie my dear? To find out that some philandering old rogue is your father. Carrying on with another woman all these years... And to have it announced to the world before anyone so much as thought of telling you. I'm so sorry, dear.'

'It's quite all right.' Dottie meant it too. Just to know... that was enough. And if he had been weak, all too fallibly human, well, she could understand that.

He held out a hand to her, gripping her tightly, his other hand closing over the top.

'My dear young lady, my dear...' His eyes were full of tears again. He couldn't go on. Dottie's lip trembled. It astonished her that she felt so emotional when she hardly knew the man. She felt a connection that she couldn't describe.

He got to his feet. 'Excuse me, my dear.'

She thought he was indicating they should return to the ball. But no, as she stood up, he enveloped her in a hug, and murmured, 'My dearest child, I still can't believe it. After all these years. I really am such a lucky man.'

He stepped back to look at her. There were no words. He drew a gigantic handkerchief from his trouser pocket and blew his nose vigorously. More composed, he pulled her hand through his arm, and said, 'Cecilia has been telling me all about you. About your fashion warehouse. It seems you have something of an entrepreneurial spirit. Perhaps you have inherited that from me. Well, well, I'd like to think so. Thank the Lord you didn't get my nose.' He turned to show her his profile. She saw now he did indeed have a prominent nose. He gave her a grin. She laughed.

'It's a very distinguished nose.'

'Ha ha, very kind, my dear. I realise this has been a shock for you, but for myself, I'm delighted, utterly delighted.' He beamed down at her again, his eyes still misty with emotion. 'Dottie dear, I don't want to take over your life. I know you have people who love you, whom you consider your parents, and that's only to be expected. I'm so very glad you have them. I couldn't bear to think you had been alone or unhappy. I shan't try to come between you and your parents. But may I ask for the chance to get to know you? I come up to London from time to time on business—if you would honour me by dining with me. As the father of a beloved adopted daughter, I know how deep these relationships go. June is as dear to me as if she were my own, and I'm certain the Mandersons feel the same about you. But may I have the chance of knowing you better?'

'Of course,' Dottie said. It seemed the only thing she could say, yet she meant it. She wanted to get to know him. If this man had been despised by Cecilia Cowdrey's family for his low origins, she found him sincere and compassionate. He seemed like a nice man. She wanted to know him better.

'Now then, perhaps we should go back to the ball, eh? Time for a few more dances before we all pack off to our beds. June promised me a waltz. And I'm afraid this revelation has been something of a shock to her, too.'

'She knew something was happening,' Dottie said. 'She said that you seemed to have something on your mind.'

'She's a good girl, my little Junie,' Sir Stanley said. 'She will be thrilled with the news.'

Dottie couldn't help but wonder. Especially in view of what June had expected Sir Stanley to say, Dottie had a feeling that June would not receive the news with unalloyed pleasure.

She was pleasantly surprised. June took the news far better than Dottie had expected. Leo seemed more astonished than June, though Dottie couldn't help but feel he must have had an inkling. After all, he'd known for years that Dottie was his half-sister. Surely he must have considered who her father might be once or twice in all that time? But he invited Dottie to dance, and left Sir Stanley and June to have their waltz and to talk.

By the time they all said goodnight—a little after three o'clock—and drove back to St Martins, Imogen still chattering nineteen to the dozen about everything, Dottie's spirits had lifted.

It was a New Year. No more sorrow, she thought, no more sadness. She had the answers she had come to Sussex to find. She could go back to London knowing who she was and where she had come from. Time for a new start. Time to be happy.

But it was not Gervase's face that came to mind with those words.

Chapter Twelve

Dottie was stirring in her bed when a panting young woman tapped on the door and came in with a tea-tray.

'I hope you don't mind miss, but if you could wait a little bit for your bath? 'Cos I've been told to tell you there's no 'ot water. Cook's had the devil's own job to get the stove going this morning. We've been boiling kettles for over an hour. If you can hold on another half an hour, I don't doubt it'll be fixed by then, or so Cook says. Oh, and the missus sent word for everyone to have breakfast in bed as it's still jolly chilly in the morning room and the dining room, and besides which, I doubt no one will want to get up too early after having a late night last night.'

Belatedly the maid remembered a quick bob.

Dottie sat up in bed. 'Happy New Year,' she said to the maid. 'I'd love a cup of tea. I don't think I want anything to eat just yet. And I definitely don't want a bath, it's freezing this morning!'

'Happy New Year to you too miss. Yes, miss, there's the heaviest frost you ever saw. Just like snow it is. And that don't bode well for the New Year, do it? Shall I make up your fire? It'll only take me a jiffy.' As she did this, she set the tea-tray down on the bedside table and went across to open the curtains. A grey sky appeared through a window rimed with frost.

'Thank you, er—I don't know your name?'

'I'm Norma, miss. Norma Maxted.' Norma moved across to the fireplace and began to get things started.

'Norma. Thank you. What happened to Win who was here yesterday and the day before?'

'Oh miss, she's been let go.' Norma turned big eyes on Dottie. Dottie was surprised.

'Let go? You mean she's been sacked?

Norma nodded. 'Right after breakfast yesterday. And begging your pardon miss, I shall too if I don't crack on.'

'Oh of course Norma, don't let me keep you. Look, while you're here, I suppose you haven't seen some items I'm missing. I know it's not very likely.' Dottie described the missing design sheets. Norma's eyes were round with interest until it seemed to dawn on her that Dottie might suspect her of theft.

'I never saw them,' she said stoutly, 'Nor have I been in this room before, apart from when I helped Win get it ready for you, before you got here. I never touched them, miss, I swear on my grandma's life.'

'I'm sure you didn't, Norma. I just wondered if anyone had said anything about finding them and not knowing what they were.' Dottie was anxious that Norma didn't feel accused. 'I know this sounds a bit silly, but you haven't seen anyone waiting in my room, have you. They might have looked as though they were waiting to talk to me.'

Norma shook her head. Dottie thought it was curious that the other maid had been 'let go'. She wondered if there was a reason for that. She'd seemed a pleasant, competent young woman from the little Dottie had seen of her.

It was just one more item to add to the list of things that didn't seem to quite make sense.

Dottie drank her tea, then washed in cold water, dressed hurriedly and went downstairs. She decided she would be calm and philosophical about the designs. It was quite likely that when she got back to London and discussed things with the seamstresses, they would be able to replace most of the designs quite quickly. If some special detail or other was missing, well, she would just have to put it down to experience and remember in future to always have the designs copied. Or perhaps, she thought with a laugh, she could hire someone from Scotland Yard to guard them for her. A mental image of William Hardy in his shirt sleeves, his collar open, came to mind.

She had an odd sense of deja-vu when she entered the drawing room, warmer than the morning room that morning. Everyone was there and sitting in the same places as the previous day. Did they always sit in the same places? They all looked up as she came into the room, and there was a definite tension. Was it to do with Sir Stanley's announcement, she wondered?

Her aunt spoke straight away. 'Dorothy, I've spoken to the servants about your pictures. It took a while to get them to understand to what I was referring, but then they all—practically as one—told me they'd seen Win with them. I'm sorry, but it seems that Win mistook your pictures for scrap paper and—well, dear, I'm afraid she put them in the furnace. It's a nuisance, I know, but hopefully you'll be able to get them all done again. In the meantime, even though it was a pure mishap, I've given Win her week's pay and sent her packing. I can't have servants in my house making mistakes of that kind. So there it is, Dorothy, unfortunate, but at last the case is closed, so to speak. I thought you'd like to know.'

Dottie didn't believe her aunt for a moment, and not just because her aunt had called her 'dear', suspicious in itself. But she simply nodded gravely and said, 'What a nuisance. Thank you for letting me know.'

Cecilia seemed satisfied by that, and she was clearly relieved that Dottie had taken it so well. The conversation became general and light, no one mentioned the ball at all, and Dottie only listened with half an ear until Imogen came to sit beside her and ask her about the hair rinse she had been thinking of using. Did Dottie think June was right and that men would think she was 'fast' if she used one?

Leo and June came to lunch as usual. Dottie wondered how they could all stand it; they seemed to live so much in each other's pockets. After lunch, the younger generation all went for the usual walk in the grounds. The days blurred into one another, she thought, each day's activity the mirror of the one before. Was it just because she was there, or did they always live this way?

Dottie wondered if she should speak to June in private, or even with Leo. There had been so far no mention of the ball, Sir Stanley's announcement or the new shift in their relationship. She felt uncomfortable about it and wondered that June could act completely as normal. She treated Dottie no different to usual.

They set off down the sloping lawn to look at the lake. Here and there geese dotted the grass, their heads tucked under their wings. Imogen was careful to give the geese a very wide berth.

'They won't hurt you, Imogen, don't be such a baby,' June said, pulling her scarf closer about her neck. 'How cold it's suddenly turned today! It's been so mild until now. I'd hoped the mild weather would continue a little longer. I do so hate the winter, don't you, Dottie?'

'Actually, I quite like it,' Dottie said. 'I love to put on my warm jumpers and coats, and wrap up to go outside. I do hope we get a really good fall of snow this winter. Last year it went into mush almost straight away.'

'What a child you are, Dottie. Snow!' June said with a giggle, taking the spite out of her words.

'Snow is the very worst kind of weather,' Leo pronounced.

Dottie privately thought he acted as though he was at least twenty years older than he really was. Only an old fuddy-duddy would complain about snow in winter.

'Oh, but it's so pretty when it covers all the trees and fields!' June protested. 'Not that I like to go out in it. I like to look at the snowy scene from indoors.'

'Leo and I used to have fun on our toboggan. Then we had snowball fights too, before he got so old and pompous,' Guy said, grinning at her. Dottie thought it was nice to see him sober.

'Oh, that's so dangerous,' June scolded. Guy was not swayed.

'Nonsense. Healthy outdoor fun. A bit of rough and tumbling never hurt anyone.'

'Leo fell and broke his arm two years ago, so it can be quite dangerous really, Guy.'

Guy, his collar turned up against the weather, turned to grin at Dottie. He rolled his eyes. 'Should make him take more water with it.' His breath frosted the air in front of his face.

It was all said good-naturedly. For once the spiteful sniping seemed to have stopped.

'That's why these trees have so many red berries this year. It's nature's way, to provide food for the animal kingdom when the weather worsens. So it's a portent, warning of harsh weather to come.'

'Now that's just rubbish, Leo,' Imogen said with some scorn. 'The proliferation of berries is due to the mild spring weather and a good pollination of the flowers. That's what causes a good crop of berries. It's not some dire omen by mother nature predicting disaster!'

Pleased that Imogen had stood up to him for once, Dottie noted that Leo seemed irritated by his sister's contradiction, and not for the first time she realised that he really liked to be seen to be the wiser, older brother, the authoritative one. But he said nothing, though his lips set in a firm straight line, rather like his mother's did when she was offended, and he turned back to look down at the path.

Guy gave Imogen a playful punch on the shoulder, and they shared a laugh. June was hanging back, and once again, Dottie wondered if she was torn between her desire to act like the good little wife, and the desire to just put her arm through Guy's and enjoy herself. Leo, his hands thrust deep in his pockets, marched off back up the slope, calling over his shoulder, 'I'm frozen. I'm going in.'

The remaining four of them turned back towards the house, but walking in a leisurely manner, they made no effort to catch him up.

As her cousins chatted and bickered gently, Dottie looked around. If she squinted, she could almost turn the scene of fading flowers and grassy slopes with their heavy coating of frost into a snowscape. The white of the frost on the grass, the grey-brown of the branches and trunks of trees and shrubs, and the bright contrast of the red berries, now being gobbled by magpies indeed made a beautiful scene. As they approached slowly, a magpie flew to a branch overhanging the path. Another joined it, squawking for its share of the fruit. Some berries fell with a splat onto the path, red juice leaking onto the frost and making a tiny lurid puddle of crimson.

'Such jealous creatures,' June commented, 'they always want what belongs to someone else.'

At the sound of her voice, the birds took to the air, scattering still more berries to the ground, creating a burst of blood-like juice across the silvered paving stones. Down on the grass behind them, the geese brayed and honked.

It was early evening. Outside on the terrace, Imogen shivered. Not that it was cold, but the trees with their long shadows stretching forth like dark grasping fingers made her feel cold and afraid. Last night, Norris had promised to take her away from here. It was an alluring thought. Did animals in the zoo feel like this? The door of the cage just barely ajar, and such a small, small movement would push it wide enough to slip out and be gone. She was tired of waiting. She wanted to go to Norris now.

She hugged herself and thought longingly of the wrap she had left on the back of the sofa. But she wanted to stay outside as long as possible. Then:

'Imogen, what on earth are you doing out there?

We're going in to dinner, and I need you to fetch a handkerchief from my room. I think I left it on the dressing table, next to my jewellery box.'

'Yes Mummy, of course,' Imogen called, her voice devoid of any indication of her reluctance to enter the house. She turned and went obediently in, shutting the door on her thoughts and the terrace.

'What a fearful bore you are, Imogen,' Guy drawled. He laughed, and leaned to light his cigarette from Leo's match. Their mother was already by the door, on her way to the dining room. The two men caught each other's eye and laughed at their sister, just as they had since boyhood. Imogen said nothing. She never said anything. She crossed the room to the hall. She counted the steps as she always did. Twelve, then the first turn, six more, then another six, then twelve. Thirty-six. She counted the steps from the head of the stairs to her mother's door. Thirty-seven. That was seventy-three so far. Then across the room to the dressing table. Twenty-two. That made ninety-five. There was no handkerchief on the dressing table's beautifully polished surface. She pulled out the top drawer to reach for a new one. The envelope surprised her. She took that, and a handkerchief.

It was another forty-nine steps to her own room. Which made—she wrinkled her nose as she added the two numbers in her head—one hundred and thirty-four. No, one hundred and *forty*-four. She opened the envelope. She drew out its contents, and when she saw what she had in her hand, she gasped. It only took a few seconds for her to make up her mind. She put the envelope under her mattress for now; she would put it away safely later. She went back to the top of the stairs. Her heart was pounding, but she ignored it. Ignored her shaking hand. She must focus on the steps. Another fifty-one, that made it one hundred and ninety-five. She began to go downstairs again. She went slowly, counting under her breath as she went. By the time she reached the bottom, and said to herself, 'Two hundred and thirty-one,' she was calmer.

She slipped past the staff who were serving the meal, held out the handkerchief to her mother who took it, saying only, 'You were quite an age. I can't think why it takes you so long to do the least little thing.'

Imogen slipped into her seat without a word.

At bedtime, Imogen followed Dottie to her room, clearly wanting to talk. Inwardly Dottie sighed. She'd been looking forward to the quiet of her room as a refuge from everyone else, but Imogen needed a friendly ear and some sympathy—two things she got precious little of from her family.

'What if I can't get Mummy to change her mind about Norris? I'll be on the shelf, a spinster, living with my parents until they die and I'm left all alone.'

It was a miserable picture, Dottie had to admit, and a cold hand seemed to close over her heart. It must be the secret fear of so many single women, she thought, herself included. Everywhere you went, every book, newspaper or magazine you read, every radio programme, every film at the cinema shouted the same message of the ideal life for a woman: married. Wasn't it every woman's hope to have her own home, her own family, and to know love?

She reminded herself that she had Gervase. The cold hand did not leave her. To Imogen, in a bright voice, she said, 'You won't be alone, you won't be a spinster, you have a dear man who loves you. Nothing can change that unless you let it.'

Imogen stared at her. 'That's so true...' Her

whispered words came out slowly, as if they were still being revealed to her. 'That's...' She got up. Her face bore an expression of wonder that gave Dottie terrible misgivings. Now what have I done, she thought.

Newly decisive, Imogen said, 'I'll telephone Norris now. I'll tell him I want to meet him tomorrow at our usual place. I'll bring him into the house, we can talk to Mummy, make her see reason. If she gets to know him a little better, she will see how wonderful he is. I'll talk to Daddy, he might be able to...'

Not sure what to say to this, yet not wanting to snatch away Imogen's hope or dash her new strategy, Dottie said, 'Your father seems to think you and Norris are well-suited. He might be able to help you with your mother.' She almost felt like crossing her fingers behind her back as she said that, because if there was one thing she'd observed of Lewis Cowdrey it was that he was an unusually passive man. She added, 'Norris and Sir Stanley seem to get on well. I should think *he* could put in a good word to your mother. She seems to respect his judgement.'

Imogen's eyes were glassy, her attention only half on what Dottie said, the other half inventing dream scenarios of her wedding to Norris and picturing herself dancing with him in the moonlight, her long flowing gown swirling about her, the heady scent of roses filling the air. 'Yes!' she said, but not to Dottie. 'Yes, we *are* well-suited. He *is* a dear man. He *does* love me. Yes, that is what I must do.'

She turned to Dottie, seeing her properly now, and kissed her on both cheeks, gripping her hands far too tightly. 'Oh thank you! You've made me see what must be done!'

She hurried to the door, opened it, and before disappearing through the gap, she shot Dottie one last radiant smile. 'Thank you!' And she was gone.

Oh dear, Dottie thought, still sitting on the edge of the bed. Have I done something good or something truly awful? She waited for a moment, but heard no sound. Whether or not Imogen went downstairs to telephone to Norris, she couldn't tell. She was glad Imogen was no longer sunk in despair, but it was alarming to see her veer so far in the opposite direction. She worried her cousin would do something too impetuous, something all too likely to trigger another painful scene between Imogen, Norris and Cecilia within the next few hours.

She got ready for bed and waited in her room. She didn't hear Imogen come back upstairs. She went to the door and opened it. She looked out. She couldn't see or hear anyone or anything. On an impulse she went along to the top of the stairs. There was a light on downstairs in the hall, and as she leaned forward, she could see the light was on in the back hall too. Perhaps Imogen was still telephoning.

Dottie hesitated. She couldn't see or hear anyone. She decided to go down and see if Imogen was there. Perhaps it wasn't too late to urge her to be patient and hold back from phoning right now. It would probably be better to wait until morning before doing anything.

But there was no one in the back hall, where the light was switched on. The telephone receiver was in its rest. Dottie shivered. A strong draught was blowing in from the back door along the little corridor that led to the kitchen. If the back door was open, was Norris already here? Or had Imogen gone outside to meet him in the rose garden as she often did?

On Dottie's right was the door to the morning room. A slip of light showed at the bottom of the door, illuminating the wooden floor boards and the tips of Dottie's slippers. She heard a soft murmur of voices. She couldn't quite remember, but she had a feeling there was a telephone extension in that room. That must be where Imogen was, then.

She was about to turn and go back upstairs when, from the morning room, Cecilia's voice shocked her, ringing out with, 'That's the end of it. I'll have nothing more to do with you. It's a disgraceful way to carry on, and I'm ashamed to call you my child! There's nothing more I have to say to you; I've already said all I have to say. I want you out of this house first thing tomorrow.'

There was a soft murmuring response. Dottie was frozen to the spot, her hand on the wooden panelling of the wall beside the door. Never had she heard such rage in her aunt's voice, or such venom. It shook Dottie, and her first instinct was to get away. She hesitated. How could anyone talk to timid Imogen like that?

Her aunt's voice rose again, and it was shaking with anger. 'Oh really? You don't care what I think? Well, you shall care! I'm leaving you nothing in my will. You are never to come to this house again, or to contact your siblings. As far as I'm concerned, you are dead to me. I will no longer support you. For the first time in your life you will have to find your own way, you'll get nothing from me. Nothing!'

Surely her aunt couldn't be talking to Imogen with such fury? At this, Dottie turned and scurried away from the door, in case someone should open it, and she should be caught there. Coming into the main hall, she bumped into one of the staff, a woman, in her rush.

'Do excuse me,' Dottie said, and ran up the stairs to her room.

Her ears were burning with embarrassment at having listened at the door. But as soon as she had heard her aunt's voice, it was as though she became rooted to the spot. Poor Imogen—to have such words directed at her by her own mother. Dottie shook her head. Imogen would be in a terrible state when she came back to her room.

Taking off her slippers and her wrap, she began to get into bed, half-expecting at any moment to hear a tap on her door, a distraught Imogen running in to fling herself into Dottie's arms, sobbing. Dottie waited for half an hour, but Imogen didn't come.

She didn't know what to do. Her mind was still on what she'd overheard, and the astonishing, almost horrifying fury of her aunt.

She got into bed and picked up her book. Ten minutes later she realised she'd read the same paragraph several times and not taken it in. She kept looking up, her head cocked on one side, listening. She pushed the covers back and sat on the edge of the bed.

Perhaps Imogen was too upset to come and talk to her? Or she might have assumed Dottie would be asleep by now. Had she gone straight to her room to cry herself to sleep? Outside the geese were making a fearful racket. Presumably they had been startled by something. Dottie felt sure she would never get used to the noise they made.

After a few more minutes, Dottie went to her bedroom door, opened it and looked out. The hallway beyond was in darkness. No light was coming up from the hall. She hesitated for a moment. Then she tiptoed along to Imogen's room and tapped on the door.

The air was cold. After a cold day, the temperature had dropped still lower. It felt truly wintry for the first time that season, and Dottie couldn't help but remember all the late-summer flowers in June's beloved garden, clinging to their fading splendour. The heavy frost would be the end of them. Dottie shivered and wished she'd thought to put on her warm wrap. And her slippers.

There was no response to her tap on the door. Carefully and quietly, Dottie opened the door and put her head round it. Keeping her voice low, afraid of attracting attention, she asked,

'Imogen? It's Dottie. Are you all right?'

There was no response. She stepped inside the room and pushed the door almost closed. She didn't want to put the light on, that seemed like an intrusion. If Imogen was red-eyed and weeping, she would not welcome the glaring light. Dottie listened.

The wind on this side of the house was louder, and with the geese still complaining, it was difficult to be sure, but she thought she could just make out the sound of Imogen breathing. Dottie called out again, very softly. Still no reply. Was it possible that Imogen was already asleep? More likely, she just couldn't face anyone after what had happened. She softly called Imogen's name again, but there was still nothing. Dottie withdrew and returned to her room.

She stood in the darkness looking out of the window. She could see the treetops thrashing in the wind. Certainly it was far stronger now. Dark clouds fairly tore across the sky, driven onward by what was rapidly becoming a gale. Things fell over on the terrace below her; thin branches rattled against the window. Looking at the lawn beyond the terrace, she could see it was light and almost glowing. Icy crystals of frost covered it. It seemed the late-arriving winter was going to be as unforgiving and harsh as the weather experts had predicted.

Dottie reached behind her to pull the counterpane about her shoulders. She stayed by the window, thinking. If Imogen had come upstairs as soon as Dottie had left—and let's face it, Dottie thought, no one's going to wait around to be yelled at even more after what Cecilia had already said—then it was *just* about possible that Imogen had fallen asleep after a really good, exhausting cry in the three-quarters of an hour or so that had elapsed since Dottie had run back upstairs. Just. Which was all to the good, as it meant that Imogen would be well-rested for what would doubtless be an uncomfortable family breakfast in the morning.

Dottie was dismayed at the unwelcome prospect of seeing everyone at the breakfast table. She'd better get to bed, or she'd oversleep. The last thing she wanted was to be on the receiving end of her aunt's wrath—again. As she took half a step back to push back the curtains and go to bed, she thought for a moment she saw a figure on the edge of the drive, to one side of the house, amongst the rhododendrons. She paused and looked again.

Yes, there was definitely someone. But all she could make out was the pale shape of the face, and a vague dark outline of a shoulder and an arm, mostly hidden by the tall shrubs. Was it Imogen? She couldn't tell. She couldn't even make out whether it was a man or woman.

As she watched the shape moved and was gone, melting away as a shadow in the night. After a moment she heard a door banging shut somewhere downstairs.

Chapter Thirteen

It was marginally warmer just here. The little outcrop of trees on this side of the sloping lawn sheltered the spot from the wind, and she could almost forget it was midwinter. The early morning sun threaded weak pale rays through the clouds and lit up the space all around her. A willow tree on the verge of the water had dabbled its long fronds into the water and now they were stranded, locked into the ice that the night had brought.

Dottie seated herself on the stone corner of the pavilion platform. She closed her eyes and tipped her face to the sun, longing to feel warmth on her skin. The small stone structure of the pavilion, a fashionable homage to the Greek style so popular for the last thirty or forty years, guarded her back like a watchdog as she turned to look into her deepest thoughts.

One more day. One more day and she could return to her home, her parents—truly, they were her parents, not because that was how she had always thought of them, but because now, with the knowledge of everything that had taken place—or as much as she'd ever know, she saw the real love they had given her—they had taken her in, clothed, fed and housed her, they had schooled her and paid her bills.

But more than that, they had filled her life with love. They had sat with her overnight during her childhood illnesses, they had bathed and soothed her grazed knees, wiped her tears, held her when monsters haunted her dreams. She remembered both her parents lying on the carpet with her and Flora to do jigsaw puzzles or drawings or to build castles out of wooden blocks. She had a fleeting memory of clattering about the house in her mother's shoes, of draping herself with ropes of beads and hats and scarves, she and Flora together, running about the house laughing, her mother and the cook and maid running after them, then standing perfectly still in her father's study whilst he took a photograph to capture that moment. Neither she nor Flora had been capable of keeping still for the requisite amount of time, and the resulting photo was somewhat blurred, yet still held its place in one of her mother's albums.

They had loved her every bit as much as they loved Flora, she saw that now. Even when she had been sick, fractious, teething, naughty, and during the awful, fidgety, hurrying adolescent years of sulks and door-slamming.

How many times had she and Flora rolled their eyes at their mother, or complained to one another behind her back? How many times had they grumbled over her strictures and her attempts to train them to be decent, hard-working, responsible young women? Or her attempts to help them to meet nice eligible men with whom to spend their lives?

She had to bite her lip. She didn't want to cry, not here, not now. Later when she was in her room, perhaps. Or when she got *home*. If only she were there now... More to the point, if only she had never come. Far better to have remained in ignorance of her origins and enjoyed what she had. Though now, she had to admit, she saw more clearly exactly what she did have.

The wind seemed to be growing stronger. It whipped up tiny waves in the middle of the lake where the ice did not reach. The wind whipped at Dottie's skirt too; she had to hold it about her legs. It sniped at her face, nipping her ears and cheeks, causing tears to start in her smarting eyes. But she wasn't ready to return to the house. What a shame she couldn't stay out here until lunchtime, she thought, but it was far too cold. She got to her feet. Going down the last bit of slope to the bank of the lake, she began to walk slowly along, still thinking about parents and children.

Beyond the willow, there were a few more trees, some with their branches bending towards the water. There were several fallen branches, ice-frosted and lining the water with their old limbs. Last summer's reeds stood up like the frozen masts of shipwrecks, and here and there some autumn leaves cling about their bases, black now after weeks in the water.

Further ahead, there was something that wasn't a branch or a reed moving gently in the ice that was weakening under the coaxing sunlight. There was an odd heaviness in the way the whatever-it-was moved so slowly, low down in the water. Dottie hurried towards it. She almost laughed. Her imagination! Given free rein, for the moment she had thought she saw something terribly melodramatic, a corpse or something, struggling to raise itself above the water, to make itself known to her.

'Ridiculous,' she told herself out loud. But she couldn't pull her attention away, and for a moment she felt no surprise, no shock, as a hand, yes, most definitely a human hand, was raised briefly above the rippling icy water then was gone again from sight.

Another gust of wind, and Dottie ran now. There, not twenty feet away from her, a face stared at her.

The hand bobbed on the water again, and now she saw some of the plants from the lake had got caught between the fingers, drowned flowers and assorted leaves, and the face, half-covered by the wet dark hair slickly plastered about it, turned and turned again, buffeted by the rising wind across the water, and the eyes, sightless though wide open, looked at her.

It was her Aunt Cecilia.

Hysteria rose in her throat and was gulped back. She sprang towards the water, pausing only to kick off her shoes before wading in. The water was deathly cold, but she hadn't far to go. She *had* to reach the body, yet even as she grabbed at it, missed then grabbed again, she was gasping from the cold, sobbing over and over again, 'It's too late, oh it's too late.'

The water deepened too quickly, and only three yards from the bank she was up to her chest. Another two big steps and she managed to catch at the body and found she held an arm, stiff and heavy. She turned back to the land, slowly hauling the body with her, its submerged weight pulling her back.

She lost her footing on the muddy bank and slid on her knees back into the water. Her hands were too numb to hold onto the arm. The body slipped from her and began to drift. She couldn't get a purchase on the bank. She snatched at dry stalks of reeds and finally, finally she managed to inch her way up onto the grass, somehow dragging the corpse behind her. She fell on her face on the unyielding ground, gasping with exhaustion, retching from the water she'd swallowed, and the sight of the dead, staring eyes.

The head—the face—seemed perfectly normal, unmarked, undamaged, the eyes staring with mild enquiry, the brows raised in that characteristic way, the lips were as near white as Dottie had ever seen. But the back of the head was broken in like an eggshell, the bone poking white through the tangled mass of dark hair and flowers. There was no blood. That made it terrible. So clean, so bare.

Dottie threw herself onto her feet but only made it to the treeline. She vomited on the weeds and grasses and old, brown ferns that grew there. Above the sound of her disgracing herself she heard someone speaking, someone shouting. She used her sleeve to wipe her mouth, and shrank back onto the grass, shivering and weak. The wind dropped again, the sun reappeared from behind a cloud, but its fragile warmth did nothing to relieve the chill that shook Dottie now.

Hands seized her roughly and dragged her to her feet. And a man—was it Guy or Leo?—said, 'My God! What have you done?' Then Imogen began to scream and scream and scream.

A slap like a shot cut the air, and Imogen fell into hiccupping silence, her scream cut off short yet still seeming to hang in the air. Dottie couldn't stop hearing it. Imogen's fingertips went to the white mark of Leo's hand across her mouth and cheek, her eyes staring with shock. Then she began to weep softly, saying over and over again, 'Mummy, oh Mummy.' Oblivious to the mud and water that immediately began to soak into her dress, she sank to the ground.

Guy grabbed Dottie's arms more tightly and turned her towards the house, beginning to force her forward as if he was frog-marching a prisoner. This was further enhanced by Leo calling, 'Lock her in the downstairs cloakroom, then telephone to the police right away.'

Dottie pulled herself free, protesting. Leo crouched beside his sister, murmuring to her words Dottie couldn't make out. His hand was on Imogen's shoulder. June's hands covered her face in horror. Dottie, unable to ignore meaningless details, noticed that the hem of his jacket dipped in and out of the mud with all his movements. Beside him lay the tangle of flowers that had been in Cecilia's hands, and now Dottie saw they were tied together in the shape of a wreath, the uppermost plants matted with dirt, the underlying ones wilted from the icy water. Something about this snagged at Dottie's mind, but as she spoke Leo's name, put her hand out to him, he reared up on his feet, turning on her rapidly, his fists bunched in a threatening manner. She leapt back, certain he was about to hit her, but he only spoke to his brother:

'Get that filthy bitch away from our sister. Lock her up. Throw away the key for all I care.'

He turned back to Imogen, putting his arms around her in the first ever display of tenderness Dottie had witnessed between the members of this family. Guy dragged her away.

'This is ludicrous, Guy, I couldn't possibly do such an awful thing. Let me go at once!' she said as soon as they were a little distance from the others. She fought to try to get his hand off her. He simply tightened his grip.

'I'm sorry, old girl, but Leo's right. We've got to keep you under lock and key until the police get here. If it was up to me...'

'It *is* up to you, Guy! Do you honestly think I killed your mother?'

She saw now that he was white as a sheet. She tried again to shake off his hold on her. But even in his state of shock, he refused to let her go. Gently she said, 'Guy, I'm so sorry about... But you do know I would never...'

He hesitated. She felt he almost believed her. He glanced over his shoulder down the slope to where Leo and Imogen were talking, sitting side by side on the grass some twenty feet from their mother's body. Imogen was wiping her skirt with something white, presumably Leo's handkerchief. June had her hand on Leo's shoulder but she was looking this way.

'*If* it were up to me,' Guy repeated, 'I'd let you go and good luck to you. Perhaps you'd get away. Possibly you'd even get abroad somewhere and never be caught. Frankly, I don't much care. Whatever they do to you, it won't bring my mother back.'

His words stopped the shivering of her body from the cold and shock. She felt stone dead inside. For a few seconds she'd almost thought he was on her side... Yanking her arm again, he pulled her around the side of the house and in at the door that opened onto the kitchen corridor. On reaching the cloakroom, he pushed her inside, then turned the key in the lock. She heard his steps going away, then his voice, presumably issuing orders to the staff, or telling them what had happened. She heard a cry of shock from one of the women. Dottie tried the door.

Yes, he had locked it. The keyhole was empty, he had taken the key away with him.

She was shivering again. Her wet clothes stuck to her, reeking of silt and rotting vegetation. It was dim in the cloakroom; the stone floor and rough, white-washed plaster walls were bare and added to the damp air. She felt like weeping, but instead she washed her face and hands, rinsed her mouth at the sink, then tidied her hair as best she could with cold water and no mirror. She took up a position leaning against the sink, her arms folded across her chest for the small amount of warmth it gave her, and she waited.

It was the best part of an hour before the door was unlocked and a strange male voice said, 'Miss Dorothy Manderson, I am arresting you for the wilful murder of Mrs Cecilia Cowdrey.'

It was almost two o'clock before Leo Cowdrey, with a sigh, said to his wife, brother and father, 'I suppose I'd better telephone Aunt Lavinia. She will need to know what's happened.'

'I'll go up and see if Imogen needs anything,' June said and left the room.

The three men looked at one another. There was a long silence. Finally, Lewis Cowdrey got to his feet. 'I'm going to my study.'

As the door closed behind him, Guy gave a short bitter laugh. 'Leaving us to fend for ourselves as always.'

Leo frowned. 'Tell me why you did it.'

'What? Did what?' Guy stared at him.

'You had to have done it. It couldn't have been Imogen, and...'

'It might. It might have been Imogen. Or Clarke. Either of them could have done it. They had a colossal falling out with Mother recently; she disapproved so much of them seeing one another.'

Leo shook his head. 'From what I can gather, pretty much everyone fell out with Mother yesterday. Yourself and Father included. Only June and I...'

June returned to the room. 'She's asleep, and there's a maid sitting with her, so that's all right, the poor girl.' She looked from Leo to Guy then back to Leo. 'Are you two having a row?'

Guy nodded. He went to pour himself another drink. June frowned at him and said, 'Guy, dear, are you sure you should? The police could come back at any moment to ask us some more questions. You don't want them to think you've got a guilty conscience to numb with drink.'

'I've just lost my mother,' he snapped. 'What could be more natural than to want to get slammed and forget all about it?' He swigged his drink in one go and poured another, bringing the bottle back with him.

Leo left the room.

Guy went to sit beside June. He put an arm about her. 'Leo's just asked me why I did it,' he told her. 'I can't believe he thinks I would do such a thing. My own brother, accusing me of murder!'

She patted his knee. 'Don't worry about it, he's just upset. He doesn't really believe it. He's just trying to make sense of it all.'

'That's just it. He doesn't seem upset. He's just as cold and controlled as always. I think he really believes...'

'Nonsense, dear.' She turned and kissed him.

Guy leaned his head on her shoulder for a moment. Softly he said, 'How much longer is this going to go on, June? When are we going to tell Leo the truth? I can't keep this up...'

She patted his knee again. 'Shh. It will be soon, I promise. Not long to wait now.' She pushed him aside as he turned to kiss her again. 'No more, he'll be coming back shortly.' She moved to a seat further away.

Two minutes later Leo returned to the room and sat down heavily, his face gloomy. He grabbed Guy's drink and swallowed it.

'Well that's done.'

'How did they take it?'

'How do you think they took it, Guy? I'd just phoned them to say our mother was dead and their daughter had been arrested for murder.'

'I don't see that it's our fault. I mean, we just told the police what we'd seen,' June pointed out.

Leo said, 'I don't think the Mandersons will see it that way. They'll be here as soon as they can. Aunt Lavinia says she expects us to show them every hospitality.'

Guy and June exchanged looks. 'They're staying here? But...'

'My dear, they'd hardly stay at The Sheep Fold, would they? Do be sensible, June. I had no choice but to agree. I'll tell Drysdale to expect them for dinner. No idea how long it will take them to motor down from Town. At least an hour I should think.'

'I'd say easily two, especially if they have to make a stop. And don't forget it'll be dark by four o'clock,' Guy said.

'True. They'll be here for dinner then. I don't particularly want to see them, but it should be all right if it's just for dinner. They won't be thrilled to hear it was us who told the police we suspected Dottie. June, we'll leave as soon as we've finished eating. We can say we're distressed and it's been a long day.'

'All perfectly true,' June agreed, 'and understandable.'

'I've been thinking,' Guy said. 'I think you're right, Leo. This Clarke chappie of Imogen's. He's clearly the most likely suspect. Perhaps we should put the police onto him? After all, he was here late last night, so he could easily...? I'm not sure it could really have been Dottie, you know, I mean she's just a girl. I'm pretty sure she wouldn't have tried so hard to help Mother if she'd been the one who...'

'That was just a blind,' Leo said. 'She may be just a girl, but she's got brains. And a temper.'

'I haven't seen any...'

'It's there if you look for it. Her fake smile, the way she looks every time Mother tells her...' Leo caught himself up. 'The way she looked every time Mother told her what she expected. She's a little rebel. Doesn't like being told how to behave, like all these modern young girls. Wants everything her own way. Stubborn. And she must be pretty hard, she's in business for herself, so she probably thought that with Mother out of the way she'd come into some money. Like I say, she's exactly the sort of person that just cracks and lashes out.'

'Sadly, yes,' June said, shaking her head. 'She does seem the most likely suspect. Or she could have been working with Imogen's fellow. They could have been in it together, they'd both benefit, after all. Although I'm not sure about Norris Clarke, he always seems such a genial character.'

'Until it comes to business,' Guy said. 'He's another one who can be quite determined from what I hear. He doesn't give way, you know. Knows how to stick to his guns and drive a bargain. Knows what he wants and gets it. Plus, he was on the spot, so...'

June looked worried. 'I never knew that. He always

seems so good-humoured. Perhaps your mother was right, and he's not suitable for Imogen after all.'

'You say he was here last night?' Leo asked.

Guy nodded. 'He's here every night. He waits in the rose garden for Imogen to slip outside after dinner. Or, well, just lately with Dottie here, I think it's been near enough bedtime before Imogen gets away. It's supposed to be a secret, but I've known for some time. I'd had a few drinks, last night, and... well, what with one thing and another, I'm afraid I let it slip to Mother...'

'What?' Leo said. He sank back against the cushions. 'Can't you see, this definitely makes him a suspect? What if Mother went out there last night to confront the pair of them? If the police hear about this, they will soon let Dottie go. I only hope they don't come for Imogen.'

'We'll need to let them know about Clarke. I'm pretty sure they'll go for it. Anyway, it doesn't much matter which of them the police suspect so long as it isn't one of us,' Guy pointed out. The others nodded.

'Absolutely,' Leo said.

Chapter Fourteen

Mr Manderson looked at the telephone receiver, hanging useless in his hand, the buzzing of the empty line filling the tiny space. He could hardly believe what he'd just heard. He replaced the receiver crookedly, his mind not on what he was doing, then returned to the morning room where his wife— uncharacteristically flustered and impatient—waited to hear his report.

As soon as he came into the room, she said:

'What did Gervase say? I imagine he was every bit as shocked as we were.' Only now did she notice that he was deep in thought, moving like an automaton. 'Herbert?'

'What? Oh yes. Yes, he was very shocked.'

'I hope he didn't swear too much, it shows a deplorable lack of self-restraint.'

Herbert smiled at this. He was attending, but there was still something in his expression that told her he was preoccupied. 'In that case, dearest, all you need to know is that he was extremely unrestrained.'

'Humpf.'

That sound alone said it all. He'd known it for the best part of twenty-six years. It meant she strongly disapproved but knew there was nothing she could do about whatever had happened.

Lavinia Manderson changed tack. 'Is he phoning Sussex police immediately, or is he driving straight down there?'

Her husband said nothing. He took a seat on the sofa. She plonked down next to him in a manner she herself usually described as boisterous and unladylike, for example when her daughters did it.

'Herbert? Is Gervase sending someone, or is he going down himself? No doubt he knows someone who can get Dorothy released at once.'

'He may well know several people who could do that,' Herbert said, giving himself a little shake in an attempt to formulate his thoughts and bring himself back to the present moment. 'But he won't be calling any of them.'

She put a hand on his arm. 'He's going himself! Oh Herbert, thank goodness! We'll see him there, then, and the three of us will be able to get to the bottom of this nonsense. We shall be such a comfort to poor Dottie. She must be terrified, the poor child.'

She sat back. After a moment something in her husband's odd manner seemed to get through her bubble of relief. She leaned towards him, peering into his troubled face. She put a hand on his chest.

'Herbert? Darling, what is it? What's worrying you? I'm sure everything will be all right now.'

'Lavinia,' he said, and his voice held a warning note. He took her hand, held it briefly to his lips, kissing the fingertips as he had been wont to do in their courting days. The gesture pulled at her heart. This time it didn't reassure or comfort her. She felt cold and afraid.

'Herbert, what is it? What don't you want to tell me?'

He took a deep breath, held it, then let it out slowly. 'Lavinia, dearest,' he said again. 'Gervase is not intending to call anyone to intervene in Dottie's case. Nor is he planning to go to her aid. His words to me—those few I can repeat in front of a lady—were to the effect that a man of his position cannot be seen publicly to have any connection with a person accused of murder, and he advised us to do as much as we can for her in terms of legal counsel. He asked that we keep him informed.'

Lavinia Manderson was shocked into silence. Something that rarely happened. Herbert watched his wife's face as she registered this information, analysed it, and her emotions found their response.

'The bastard!' she said with vitriol. Herbert Manderson blinked in surprise. He had only known his wife to use such language on two previous occasions in the last twenty-six years. He wisely said nothing, although in his head, he thought admiringly, she always was a game gal.

'Keep him informed?' Disgust fell from her lips. 'Keep him *informed*? And this is all the help the girl can expect from the man who wants to be her husband?'

She fell silent again, and sank back against the sofa cushions, leaning into his arm. Herbert nodded and patted her shoulder, dropped a kiss on her forehead.

'I know, my love, I know. I feel the same.'

'Surely he doesn't actually believe she could have done this terrible thing?'

Herbert shrugged, and shook his head. 'I have no idea. He didn't say anything to specifically indicate either way.'

'I hate him now,' she said, sounding a little surprised. Again, her husband could only nod and agree. 'He is truly the worst son-in-law we could have almost had,' she added.

'If I ever lay eyes on him again, I shall call him out,' Herbert said.

Through tears, Lavinia said, 'That's very sweet, but don't be silly, dear.' She took the handkerchief he offered her and wiped her eyes. 'Oh dear. Oh Herbert, I can't believe it.' She sighed. 'What on earth shall we tell Dottie?'

She sat up, patted his arm one last time, and said, with the air of someone with a new plan of action, 'You should ring Monty right away, tell him what's happened. I'm sure he'll help us, he's a good sort, and has always had a soft spot for Dottie.'

'Right. Whilst I'm doing that, could you and Janet pack, then get Cook to put together some food and a flask of tea or something for the journey. We'll be away for at least a few days. Don't know exactly how long, but we can telephone when we know more, of course. After I've spoken to Monty, I'm going to ring George and Flora and tell them what's happened, then there's someone else I want to try and get hold of.'

Lavinia's brow furrowed. 'Who?'

'William Hardy.'

'You'd better call him first.'

The Mandersons talked of little else all the way to Sussex. By the time they arrived at St Martins village, they had come to one conclusion and one only: They were determined to do everything in their power to make Dottie realise that her choice of Gervase Parfitt as her future partner in life was a bad one.

'And it shouldn't be too difficult,' said Mr Manderson, changing gear to cope with the road's steep incline. 'She may be romantic like all girls her age, but she's no fool. She will take as dim a view of this abandonment as we do.'

'How I wish I'd encouraged her more with William Hardy. Florence was right. He is so much more suitable. He may not have a fortune, but that's irrelevant in this case.'

'Definitely. With his ability and his commitment to his work, he will rise very quickly through the ranks. He already has his own home.'

'And he is *so* very good-looking,' said Mrs Manderson with a wistful sigh. Her husband shot her a suspicious glance. She was gazing out of the window in a dreamy manner. 'He has such nice hair and eyes. And he has a sense of mischief about him. That Parfitt fellow is too pompous and... oh I don't know... Herbert, he's just so *middle-aged*. Too old for Dottie.'

Mr Manderson was in complete agreement. It made him smile to hear the once much-adored Gervase Parfitt, Assistant Chief Constable of Derbyshire, referred to dismissively as 'that Parfitt fellow'.

The Assistant Chief Constable of Derbyshire sat at his desk. He had turned his seat so that he could look out across the fields and hedgerows. If only the department was located in the centre of the little town of Ripley, that would have been far more to his taste: to be able to look out at his domain and feel a proud sense of ownership, to gaze benignly upon the bustling streets and the market place. But here they were in this out-of-the-way spot, from the point of view of the citizens of the town, very much out of sight and out of mind. Admittedly, he thought, it was easier to get through the traffic to reach his office in the mornings.

He sipped the tea, freshly brewed and brought to him by the comforting motherly figure of Mrs Holcombe, his secretary. Generally Gervase Parfitt didn't approve of lady secretaries. However it was becoming quite the thing now for respectable widows or spinsters who needed to support themselves to undertake these administrative positions formerly filled by men. He was aware that the Chief Constable was keen to be seen as a champion of progress and modernity.

That Holcombe was efficient was beyond doubt, although Parfitt regretted that she was not both younger and prettier. But doubtless it was a good thing to keep his mind on his work when he was at the office. And on seeing her, he thought, no one could possibly suspect anything untoward. She had the attitude of a mother hen, and was very good at keeping unexpected or undesirable visitors away.

Heaven knows, I need some peace and quiet so I can think, he reminded himself. He was feeling very distracted at the moment. Furthermore, he was really very annoyed. This latest scrape of Dottie's was the limit. He could scarcely believe she'd do something so ridiculous as to get herself mixed up in a murder case—of her natural mother too, of all things. The scandal if it were ever to get out! He'd never live that down. He'd be ruined. She really had absolutely no regard whatsoever for his position, or how difficult she had made things for him.

He'd pandered to her during the summer. It had suited him to take her up: she was *very* pretty, and had—usually—a sweet, pleasing manner. She was delectably youthful. She had good breeding, and for the most part knew how to behave—or so he'd thought until this latest escapade—and even though he was almost certain that she knew about him and Margaret, and knew that the child, Simon, was his, she'd never challenged him on it outright. No, she would turn a blind eye when required. Though not necessarily without a certain amount of fuss, at least in the beginning. She was a little too moralistic, that was her trouble. One of many faults, he admitted now.

To himself he could acknowledge that women were his weakness. As a rule, he managed to keep things discreet—apart from Margaret, the stupid girl—but he knew Dottie would not be pleased if she ever found out about the others. It annoyed him that she was likely to be rather puritanical about it if she had so much as half a clue about what he got up to. But after all, what did she expect when, even though he would be giving out their engagement in a matter of months—as soon as she was twenty-one at the end of March—she still denied him and kept him at arms' length. Very well then, she would have to learn to accept him as he was. She had only herself to blame if a man was forced to seek solace elsewhere.

Though that wasn't working out too well for him either at the moment. He sent a brief frown in the direction of the letter on his desk. Another annoyance he would have to deal with. When would anything go smoothly for him? All these little but aggravating bumps in the road to his ultimate destiny: Chief Constable and a knighthood. This was just another little bother for him to sort out quickly, before things became unpleasant. Another thing to keep from Dottie until after they were safely married.

He had known Dottie was one of these bluestocking types, of course, but it was only after a courtship of some months he began to realise that today's bluestockings certainly didn't seem to have the same clinging, affectionate natures of women ten or twenty years ago.

A case in point: not content with being the fiancée of an important man, she was forcing him to indulge her ludicrous aspirations in business: this idiotic pretence at being a dress saleswoman. Surely she knew she was too young and naïve for any kind of proper business? Besides, the thought of girls running businesses... well it *was* ludicrous. And how on earth did she think she could keep it up from her new home with him once they were married? Besides which she'd be busy entertaining his guests, and of course, bringing up his children. He'd been patient long enough. It was time to put his foot down. After all, they were about to become engaged.

Gervase Parfitt sighed. All that was only going to happen if Dottie survived her current predicament unscathed. If there was even the merest whiff of guilt, of wrongdoing of any kind, he would of course be forced to think of his own career and the impact such a connection could have upon it. After all, he'd never be Chief Constable, or achieve a lordship or a seat in parliament with a wife who had been suspected of murder. How very like Dottie to get into this sort of hole. Did she really have the maturity to be the wife of a man of his importance? Yes, she was pretty enough to charm his guests, but could he really see her at the opposite end of the table from him, at some crucial dinner party, saying the right thing to eminent politicians or nobility? Or would she feel compelled to point out certain social injustices or spout the propaganda of some women's political group? The thing with Dottie was, she never knew when to just sit back and let the men settle things. He sighed. But she was so... alluring. Not that it was a blind bit of good if she kept saying 'No, Gervase,' in that virtuous manner. He was not accustomed to listening to the word 'No'.

He sipped his tea again. His eyes caught sight of a small boy playing with a dog and a stick. He smiled at the scene of happy innocence. He had had a dog at that age. Rollo. What a time they'd had, walking, swimming in the river, chasing rabbits and squirrels. If someone had told him back then that one day, he would be the Assistant Chief Constable—and that was only the start of the illustrious career he envisioned for himself—he'd have laughed in their faces. And the things he'd had to do to get where he was...

He took another sip of his now-cold tea, grimaced and set it aside. Well, some damned illegitimate young wench wasn't going to ruin his chances, his mind was made up on that score.

It was almost a relief to be taken upstairs to be interviewed again. She asked the warder to let her go to the outhouse but was told she had to wait. She'd had nothing to drink since the early morning cup of tea the maid brought to her in her room at St Martins. It was now, she guessed about three o'clock in the afternoon, if not a little later. There was still some daylight to be glimpsed through the skylight as they made their way along the corridor.

Halfway up the stairs, she stumbled, suddenly light-headed, but the warder's grip merely tightened on her arm and forced her onward. The pain helped her to pull her woolly thoughts together.

The police sergeant she had seen before was waiting for them. He opened the door of the miserable little room where they had questioned her earlier. On the other side of the table, the inspector didn't look up from his notes. She reminded herself that William Hardy had once told her this was just a ploy to unnerve suspects and make them talk. If so, it was working excellently. But what could she tell them she hadn't already said?

'Take a seat, Miss Manderson,' the sergeant said kindly. As if she had a choice. The warder shoved her onto the chair and cuffed her to its arm. That done, the warder took up her position just inside the door, as if on sentry-duty. Which, Dottie thought, perhaps she was. Dottie tried not to giggle as a line from a children's poem came to her: *They're changing guards at Buckingham Palace, Christopher Robin went down with Alice.* Oh dear, she thought, I feel as though I'm tipsy. Her head swam and the room seemed to be tipping to one side. *A soldier's life is terrible hard, says Alice.*

'Why did you do it, Dorothy?' the inspector bellowed at her, slamming his fists on the tabletop.

Dottie practically leapt out of her skin. If she hadn't been cuffed to the chair, she certainly would have fallen on the floor. She jolted and bit her lip. The salt-and-rust taste of blood filled her mouth; she could feel it coating her teeth and seeping between her lips, running down her chin.

'My name is Miss Manderson,' she told him, lifting her bloody chin and straightening her spine as best she could when cuffed to the low right hand chair arm. The note of defiance only caused the inspector to laugh, however. Then he suddenly slammed his palm down on the desk again, and this time even the sergeant jumped. The inspector's carefully ordered papers floated to the floor. The sergeant got onto his knees to gather them together and handed them up, a page at a time, the sheets sticking this way and that and doubled over. The inspector snatched them and hurriedly set them straight once more before him.

'Your name is whatever I say it is, young lady,' the inspector snapped at her.

It was such an idiotic thing to say, Dottie stopped being afraid and smiled at this. 'You can't simply rename me, inspector.'

'I can do...' He paused to get his temper under control, finishing in a calmer tone. 'I can do whatever I wish, and I will keep you here until I get some straight answers. So, I ask you again, why did you kill your *mother*, Mrs Cecilia Cowdrey?'

'I didn't,' Dottie said. She noticed that one of his pages was still upside down, and she had a brief moment to read some of what it contained.

She looked up, surprised. 'I noticed the plants too. I thought they seemed to be wound together in a kind of wreath.'

The sergeant looked puzzled, and for a moment so did the inspector. 'What on earth...?' Then Dottie saw understanding come into his eyes. 'How dare you read my confidential reports, Miss Manderson, these are official documents.'

She didn't waste time trying to apologise. He carried on: 'And seeing that it was you who actually made the wreath with your own murderous hands, I've no doubt it appeared wreath-like to you. Why did you do it, that's all I'm interested in.'

'I...'

He leaned forward, folding his hands on top of his confidential papers. 'I'm an important man, young lady. I can help you if you help me. Or I can hinder you, which will cost you your neck. Now, which is it to be?' He smiled now, and she knew it had pleased him to watch her blanch. It was hardly a surprise that she was shocked. His reference to death by hanging had frightened her. It brought home the truth of her situation: this was no laughable mix-up that could all be sorted out with a chat over a cup of tea, or fixed with a phone call to the right person. If she wasn't able to convince this man in front of her that she was innocent, then what chance would she stand with a judge and jury? Especially in this area, far from home, where the Cowdrey name was respected, and had been so for decades.

She felt faint. She leaned forward as far as the cuffs permitted. In a voice barely above a whisper, she said, 'Please, you've got to believe me. I didn't kill my aunt.'

'Your mother, you mean.'

'Well, yes, she was really my mother, but I only found that out recently. Until then, I'd always thought she was my aunt.'

'How did it make you feel to know she had cut you out of her will? That she left all her money to your half-brothers?'

Dottie tried to shrug. The cuffs clanked and jolted her wrists. 'It doesn't concern me over much. I've never even thought about it before. I have a small income from a grandmother, and a business, and I shall come into some money when I am twenty-five or marry. It's plenty for what I need. I live with my parents, my *adoptive parents*,' she carefully amended, 'and they are very generous and support me financially.' And in every other respect, she mentally added. 'So I don't need money.'

He gave a disbelieving laugh. 'Do I look like I came down in the last shower? Do you expect me to believe that a girl of your age has her own business? Or that money doesn't matter to you? Why, certainly,' he leaned back, sending a glance in the direction of the sergeant first, and then the warder. He exchanged a witty smile with them. 'Certainly, if you say you have *plenty* of money, then obviously you'd have no need of a share of your mother's assets and estate which total almost ten thousand pounds. My goodness, why didn't you just say so, I could have let you go at lunchtime. If only I'd realised you have no need of money.'

The warder laughed outright at this, and the sergeant, though looking less sure of himself, smiled and said, 'Yes sir, if only we'd known.'

'No really, I didn't mean...'

'Pulling my leg are you? Think us mere coppers don't know anything?' He got to his feet, anger and disgust in his small features and his sneering mouth. He went to the door, saying over his shoulder, 'Lock her up again. Perhaps a night in our finest accommodation will help her to remember her manners. I've no doubt that by this time tomorrow she'll feel like telling us the truth for a change.' He left.

Dottie knew she had tears in her eyes, tears of frustration as well as from the pain from the warder hauling her to her feet so roughly and pulling her to the door. The sergeant looked sorry for her, but the warder felt no pity as she ignored Dottie's pleas for a drink of water and the use of the outhouse.

The key grated in the lock, and with a last jeering look, the warder thrust her into the gloomy cell and slammed the door behind her.

Chapter Fifteen

William Hardy arrived an hour before the Mandersons, driving down in one of Scotland Yard's brand-new fast cars and making no stops. He even broke the speed limit on three occasions in his grim determination to reach Sussex as soon as humanly possible.

He went straight to the village pub to find out about a room. He was in luck, and took one of their rooms, dumped his hastily packed weekend case then drove immediately to the police station five miles away in Horshurst. On arrival he showed his identity papers and demanded to see the senior officer. A few minutes later, Sergeant Palmer, looking wary, came to meet him and conduct him to the inspector's office.

The sergeant's look of dismay told Hardy everything he needed to know. It was just as he'd hoped. The arrival of an inspector from Scotland Yard would shake up the local men. Hardy was glad he'd taken ten precious minutes to quickly see his superiors and get this visit put on an official footing. At first they had quibbled, but he had been able to persuade them of it's being in Scotland Yard's interest to oversee this little provincial murder. It had been a great help when he explained that Miss Manderson, apart from being a friend of his, was also on the point of announcing her engagement to none other than the Assistant Chief Constable of Derbyshire; the Yard had their own reasons for being interested in him.

But very soon, Hardy was struggling to hold on to his temper. It immediately became all too clear there was no real reason for holding Miss Manderson other than to look as though they had achieved something. Inspector Woolley was being defensive and unhelpful.

'This is my patch,' he said, exactly as Hardy had expected. 'And I know these people better than you do. I'd thank you to remember too, that I have at least twenty years' experience on you, and this is not my first murder investigation.'

'No indeed,' chipped in the sergeant with a fair amount of malicious pleasure. 'We've had easily four murders this last ten years alone.'

Hardy confined his reaction to a raising of the eyebrows. 'It's my eighth. In as many months.' He didn't trust himself to say more. 'I'd like to see your case notes, and the medical report.'

'This isn't London. This is not the sinkhole of depravity you appear to think. We're a nice quiet part of Sussex. This is just some sordid little local matter that we've already dealt with. You're just wasting everybody's time.'

'I must insist...'

The inspector cut Hardy off. 'We, and our coroner,

are perfectly capable of assessing whether or not
someone has drowned, or hung themselves, or
tripped over the cat and fallen down the stairs. We're
not backward here, you know, just because we're not
a big city full of wet-behind-the-ears young coppers
from some fancy college out to make a name for
themselves.'

'I want your case notes right now,' Hardy said.
'Along with witness statements, the pathologist's
report and anything else you have.'

The inspector nodded at Sergeant Palmer who went
to fetch the file and handed it to Hardy. The sergeant
looked at him. It was clear the young fellow from
London was furious, but it seemed the angrier he got,
the quieter he became. And he wasted no time on
bluster or being defensive, unlike the sergeant's own
inspector who thought he'd be heard all the more for
shouting louder. The sergeant felt a dawning respect
for this new chap, even if he did seem rather young.

'And,' Hardy added, 'I want to see the corpse. That
is not a request. I expect you to cooperate fully with
Scotland Yard, or my superiors will contact yours to
find out why.'

Settling himself in a chair, Hardy opened the case
file and began to read.

Sergeant Palmer felt secure in sitting back to enjoy
the scene that he knew was about to unfold. After all,
he'd only been following orders, and on at least two
occasions had voiced his own admittedly tentative
doubts about the likelihood of Miss Manderson being
the guilty party, and the wisdom of keeping her
locked up.

It was only about four minutes later that Hardy
said, 'Why didn't you at least interview Miss
Manderson at the same time as the other suspects at
the house?'

'We interviewed her here at the station,' the inspector said with exaggerated patience.

'Yes, but only after you'd arrested her for murder. Why didn't you interview the other suspects?'

'Because we already had our murderer. The rest of them wasn't suspects. They were witnesses, and I don't like your tone.'

Hardy shrugged away the inspector's concerns about his tone. He said, 'Has she spoken to her parents? Or a local solicitor?'

'When I'm good and ready, she can call someone. She can call whoever she likes. No doubt her family have got some tame chap in their pay, they're that sort. I shall have her family informed in the morning, if I remember.'

For tuppence, Hardy would have been on his feet, hauling Woolley over the table. Instead he took a steadying breath. Adjusted his tie. He counted to ten, then to twenty just to make sure. Then, certain he could trust his temper, he said, 'Luckily for you, Mr Leo Cowdrey informed them at lunch-time. They will be arriving shortly. And kindly tell Miss Manderson that her solicitor is on his way and should be with her by eleven o'clock tonight at the latest.'

There was an angry silence. Then Inspector Woolley said through gritted teeth, 'Now just you look here. I'm not having any lawyer coming down here in the middle of the night talking to my suspects. *And*, I'm not having you coming down here, some glory-boy from Scotland Yard, telling me how to do my job. I'm running this investigation, and I say, we get her back up here, and question her over and over until we get her to confess, that's what we need to do.'

'No.' Hardy got to his feet. 'No. You're going to conduct this investigation the correct way. My way. I am taking charge, with this authority from Scotland Yard. And you will kindly inform Miss Manderson that her solicitor is on his way. He will arrive late, no doubt, but that can't be helped since you chose not to notify Miss Manderson's family of her arrest and you denied her early access to legal advice. I'd like to point out that she is not of full age. Now I wish to speak with Miss Manderson. You will have her taken to the interview room, and you will have a pot of tea sent in for both of us. And I expect to see biscuits. I've had nothing to eat since breakfast.'

Without waiting for a response, he gathered up the case notes and left, shutting the door very firmly behind him.

Dottie sat on the hard bench and made up her mind she would be here a while. She couldn't give way now. To keep her nerves steady and her eyes dry, she fixed her attention on the cell itself.

First, she measured with her eyes the length and breadth. About eight feet by six or seven, she decided. More or less the size of the small staff cloakroom off the scullery passage at home. Then she looked at the way the two benches were attached to the wall—presumably so no one could pick them up and throw them at anyone else, the immense, terrifying female warder for example, or another inmate.

She glanced at, then quickly away from, the other two women in the cell. She wondered vaguely if one could catch fleas from being in prison. She had been so itchy since her arrival. She scraped at a spot just behind her knee. Then, itchy again, she risked a further covert look at them from behind her hand as she scratched her temple.

The woman on the other bench was hunched up

against the wall, concealed beneath a huge ragged shawl, apparently asleep. Her shoes—holed and heelless—lay beneath the bench, one resting on top of the other. One bare grubby foot poked out from under a skirt or some other dark voluminous garment.

On the opposite end of Dottie's bench, the other woman leered at her, open-mouthed and gaptoothed. She was a red-faced greasy-looking creature in what appeared to be just her underclothes—and none too clean either—with a blanket wrapped around her. She was clearly amused at the idea of a well-to-do young lady in jail with a couple of 'women of ill repute'. She looked strong and aggressive. Her bare arms, poking out from under the blanket in spite of the chill, were muscular and solid. Dottie felt a knot of anxiety in the pit of her stomach.

It seemed a lifetime later that the outer door opened, very slightly thinning the darkness with a little grey light from the corridor beyond. Before the warder—a woman of almost six feet in height, and not much less in girth—had even begun to unlock the gate, she was bellowing orders at them. Dottie's two companions took little notice; it was Dottie she'd come for.

'Manley, get up. You've got a gentleman caller.'

The red-faced woman along Dottie's bench laughed.

The 'sleeping' woman called out, 'And not for the first time, neither!' then cackled at her own wit. So not asleep after all. The cackling gave way to a paroxysm of coughing and hacking that made Dottie feel ill.

Dottie approached the bars with caution, then seeing they were all laughing at her timidity, she straightened her back and lifted her chin.

'It's Manderson, thank you very much. Not Manley.'

But they only laughed harder. Dottie bit her lip. She would not cry. She wouldn't give any of them the satisfaction.

The warder pinioned her by the arm and chivvied her out into the draughty corridor, pausing to handcuff her. The corridor was almost as dark as the cell, and Dottie was slow to see where she was to go or understand what the warder wanted her to do. As a result, she got slapped twice by the warder, who clearly believed in the adage that actions spoke louder than words.

A door on the right was thrown open, and Dottie was thrust, blinking, into a room brightly lit by an electric light hanging low over the table. A figure across the room rose, but with the light in her eyes it was half a minute before she found the chair and sat down. Then she looked across the table into the eyes of Inspector Hardy.

It was so unexpected. It broke her composure entirely. The tears ran down her face, and with no handkerchief to check them, the prison uniform rapidly became spotted with damp patches.

Hardy was aware of a rage greater than anything he'd ever felt in his life. He glared at the warder.

'Get those handcuffs off her at once! Then get out. This is a private interview.'

The warder threw the keys onto the table and giving him a filthy look, banged out of the room.

He came around the table to unlock the cuffs. It concerned him to see bruises on Dottie's wrists, and it made him feel ten times worse when she said very quietly, 'Oh no, those aren't from just now, those are from yesterday when they first brought me in.'

He removed the handcuffs and threw them down on the table with a bang. He had to do that, or he would have taken each wrist in his hand, stroked each bruise then kissed it. He forced himself to get his temper and his emotions under control. The loud noise of the handcuffs falling onto the table helped, as did the swift action of it, though not by much. He took a deep breath, resumed his seat, and, not knowing what else to do, began to shuffle his papers.

When he glanced up, her lovely hazel eyes, with the dark smudges beneath them, were resting on his face. She'd stopped crying but tears streaked her cheeks. He was dismayed by how pale and fragile she looked. He looked down at his papers again, then cleared his throat.

'So, it seems you're being charged with murder.'

'Yes,' said Dottie Manderson. She couldn't think of anything else to add.

'William! Have you seen her?' Mrs Manderson launched herself at him as soon as she spotted him entering the crowded bar of The Sheep Fold. He hid his surprise at her tight hug, putting it down to concern over her daughter.

He shook hands with Mr Manderson. 'How do you do, Mrs Manderson, Mr Manderson. Yes, Mrs Manderson, I've seen her. I've just come from the police station in Horshurst where they are holding her pending charges. She seems well, and in fair spirits, all things considered. Of course, I need hardly add, she says she is innocent.'

'Of course she is,' Mrs Manderson said with impatience. She was peeling off her gloves to look in her bag for something. She drew out a tiny diary and used the pencil that came with it to write a brief note, then she tore out the page and handed it to William. 'That's the telephone number for St Martins house. In case you need to reach us. We were hoping to catch you to find out what you know. We guessed you would probably be taking a room here, it's so handy. Have you eaten, William dear?'

William glanced at the paper and put it away in his wallet for safekeeping. 'Er—no, I haven't eaten—sorry, what do you mean? You're staying at the Cowdreys' place?'

'You sound surprised,' Mrs Manderson said. They moved to a vacant table and clearing it of the worst of the bottles and tankards, Mr Manderson wiped the filthy surface with his handkerchief. He held out a chair for his wife, then he took the seat next to her. Mrs Manderson continued, 'I'm sure it's the least they can do, to put us up for a few days, after all the trouble they've caused. They can't possibly object to me coming to offer my condolences. And where else should we stay but in the home of my deceased sister?'

'Oh, er, absolutely.' Hardy said.

Mr Manderson said, 'Do you know if the police have any other suspects?'

Hardy shook his head. 'As far as I can tell, they haven't even considered the possibility of someone else carrying out the crime. I'm afraid her cousins are unanimous that Dottie is the one responsible.'

'But...?' Mrs Manderson shook her head, trying to make sense of this.

'Why are they saying that?' Mr Manderson demanded. 'It can't possibly be true. What are they trying to hide?'

'One of them must have done it,' his wife said. 'As soon as we get there, I shall ask them what they think they're up to.' She seemed very determined. And she was—Hardy could attest—formidable when she took a view on any matter.

'I'd ask you not to confront anyone, Mrs Manderson. You could very possibly be staying under the same roof as a murderer, and I urge you in the strongest terms to reconsider.'

She sent him a look that told him her mind was made up. Consoling himself that the regular police presence at St Martins should afford them protection, coupled with the fact that she was not alone but had her husband with her, Hardy wisely decided to drop the subject. He said, 'I'd like to ask you a few questions, if I may, Mrs Manderson.'

If Lavinia Manderson was startled, like a true lady she gave no sign, saying simply, 'But of course, Inspector Hardy. I'm always happy to help.'

The fact that she'd called him 'Inspector Hardy' and not the recent 'William, dear' showed that she sensed he had switched roles to his official capacity, and in a way that made things a little easier for both of them.

He was parched but he couldn't risk a pint of beer, no matter how tempting, on an empty stomach. He wondered if the landlord would be able to offer him some food. But it would have to wait. He looked at her and said, 'I'm afraid some of the questions are of a rather private nature. They may seem impertinent.'

She smiled then and was transformed into the image of an older Dottie. It seemed almost impossible to accept that they were not really mother and daughter. 'I quite understand. I hope I will be able to help you.' She glanced at her husband, who put an arm about her shoulders, moving forward to kiss her cheek. As he did so, his wife leaned into his shoulder, briefly closing her eyes at his caress.

It struck William as a poignant private moment between two people who had loved each other for a long time. Just such a relationship as he had always hoped for. He didn't feel he was intruding, but he dropped his gaze to his notebook as he felt a sudden lump in his throat. He was annoyed with himself for feeling emotional. As he fumbled for his pen he thought, we should all hope to be so lucky in our choice of a spouse.

He cleared his throat. 'I understand that you recently revealed to your daughter Dottie—I mean, Dorothy—that she is in fact the natural daughter of Cecilia Cowdrey, your late sister.'

'It's all right, William, I know that everyone else calls her Dottie. I have no objection to your doing so.' She smiled again, then said, 'Er—yes—that's quite correct. Many years ago, my sister had told me she was expecting a child that wasn't her husband's, and had begged me for help.' She paused, biting her lip just as both Flora and Dottie were wont to do. 'It might have been the age-gap between us, but we hadn't ever really been close, you understand, but I suppose she had nowhere else to turn.' She hesitated.

Hardy had never seen her uncertain before. Just as he would do with any other nervous witness, he gave her an encouraging smile. In a gentle tone he said, 'And of course, because she was your only sister, you wanted to help.'

'Y-yes. We already had our little daughter Flora. She was almost three years old. Due to complications when she was born, I was told by my doctor I wouldn't be able to have any more children. And certainly up to that point, that had appeared to be the case. But I so wanted...' She broke off, tears threatening. Herbert passed her his handkerchief, and it was he who continued:

'We discussed it and decided to offer to adopt the child. Lavinia wrote to her sister to suggest how it might all be managed. They planned to stay at the coast for a few months, and, in the fullness of time, Lavinia came home with our new baby daughter, and Cecilia returned to her husband and the three children she had with him.'

There was a prolonged pause. Hardy sensed the most difficult part—and the most private—was over and the rest might be easier. He made a few quick notes. Glancing up, he saw that Lavinia Manderson was composed once more.

'But neither of your daughters knew that they weren't actually sisters? Dottie didn't know about her true parentage?'

'No, William, dear. Oh, sorry, *Inspector Hardy*,' Mrs Manderson said. 'We had always felt it should remain a secret for Cecilia's sake, although I must admit, in a way I didn't want Dottie to ever know I wasn't truly her mother. When you are older, William, and you become a father, you will realise just how deeply you can love a child and how you want them to love you every bit as deeply in return.' More tears threatened, and her hand on her husband's sleeve gripped so tightly that the knuckles were almost white. With an effort she continued. 'It was never discussed with either of the girls.'

Hardy nodded and made more notes. Not that he needed them, but it was to give Mrs Manderson a short breathing space. 'So when did you tell Dottie?'

'It was when she returned from being away in the summer. She was so upset about the damage it had done to people's lives, keeping secrets of that kind. I—I just felt I had to tell her. But I was so afraid of losing her.'

'I imagine she was very upset,' William said. It was an understatement of colossal dimensions. But he was red in the face, embarrassed, and all too acutely aware of his own role in the damage those secrets had caused. Mrs Manderson was looking down at her hands, playing with the plain gold band of her wedding ring, turning it and turning it. She nodded.

As she did so, a tear ran down her cheek and dripped onto her dress. She made use of her husband's handkerchief once more.

'She was devastated, as you can imagine,' Herbert Manderson said. 'And of course, we'd to tell Flora, but she'd just that evening given birth to Freddie—er—and Diana of course.' He blushed at that point.

William smiled slightly, one of the few people who knew the truth about that blessed event. 'Naturally,' he said.

'It was a few weeks before we were all able to calm down and realise that it made very little real difference,' Herbert Manderson continued, 'Or, I should say, that it *ought* to make very little difference. Because of course, it's one thing to know something with your head, but it's a very different fish altogether to convince yourself deep inside that things are still the same. I'm afraid it was something of a difficult time for all of us.'

'How I wish now I had kept the truth to myself. If I had known the impact... Then none of this would have happened. But it seemed so important that she shouldn't be lied to anymore.'

'Mrs Manderson, I don't think you should blame yourself. You did what you thought was best at the time. Personally, I'm convinced that Dottie didn't kill your sister because of it.'

She shot him a vexed look, and very much like her old self, said waspishly, 'For goodness' sake, William! Of course she didn't kill my sister. That is a ludicrous suggestion. What I meant was, someone else has used this private family situation to further their own interests. I want to know who benefits from my sister's death.'

Taking the reproof in good part, he said, 'So do I, Mrs Manderson. And I shall do my very best to find that out.'

He snapped the elastic back around his notebook, placed the book and pen back in his jacket pocket. Then he asked, 'By the way, did your sister ever confide in you the identity of Dottie's father?'

If she was startled by this question, once again, Lavinia Manderson didn't reveal it. But she turned away from him, busying herself with her gloves and bag. 'No, Inspector, I'm afraid she refused to discuss it with me. But I believe Dottie hoped to find that out.'

He nodded, got to his feet and shook Mr Manderson's hand. 'Well thank you both for your time. I'll keep you informed as things progress. In the meantime, I know you'll be relieved to hear that you can visit Dottie any time between nine o'clock and eleven o'clock tomorrow morning, although Inspector Woolley has agreed to allow Sir Montague to consult with Dottie tonight as her legal representative.'

Lavinia Manderson once again hugged him warmly, tears in her eyes as she thanked him for this bit of good news. Herbert shook William's hand, and clapped him on the shoulder, calling him a 'good man' and saying 'jolly good show' a couple of times.

Chapter Sixteen

He was supposed to be working. The reports and witness statements lay scattered across the bed. On the little side-table was a tray with a pot of tea, chicken sandwiches and a generous slab of cherry cake, kindly provided by the pub's landlady half an hour ago yet still untouched.

The flower-sprigged china reminded him suddenly of his grandmother. He remembered a dozen afternoon teas with her when he had a day out from his prep school. He must have been eight or nine years old. She had spoiled him rotten, her only grandson at that point. A fleeting memory of her smile, her scent, roses and face powder. Her soft hugs and the sad look as she waved him off again. He remembered sobbing and begging to be allowed to stay. The sense of nostalgia that washed over him was almost too painful to permit the memories. He shook his head. If he ever had a child, boy or girl, they wouldn't go to boarding school. Having experienced the sense of loss, of separation for himself, he could never do such a thing to his own child.

He really should be working.

Nevertheless, he stayed where he was. He'd let the top window right down to sit behind the lower sash, and he leaned on the frame, looking out into the darkness, his chin propped on his arm. The weather was mild again after the sudden cold snap over New Year, the fresh winter air refreshing after the close confines of the police station in Horshurst. He stayed as he was for another half an hour, going back over his conversation with Dottie at Horshurst police station.

It was clear she was frightened. Given the situation she was in, that was understandable. The colour was gone from her cheeks, she looked anxious, nervous. She'd been upset on first seeing him. That too was understandable; she had been shocked by his arrival, and no doubt the memory of all the things that had happened between them during the previous year. He'd been upset too; he had needed to fight to control himself.

Yet once she'd composed herself, she was lucid and convincing. Not that he'd needed convincing: he knew she could never commit a murder. She might shout. She might even slap a fellow who got out of hand. But she'd never commit such a terrible crime as murder. She'd faced him across the desk, her chin up, her shoulders back, and looked him right in the eye as she'd answered his questions.

He had been annoyed with himself for feeling proud of her courage. But not every well-to-do young woman who found herself facing a night in prison would be so composed. But to begin with, he had no right to feel proud of her. She was her own person, not some creation or protégé of his to be applauded and praised. And he had no rights where she was concerned—there was no 'us', he had to keep reminding himself she was with Parfitt now. But even so... It was so hard to tear his heart away... If only things were different. He fell back into his daydream.

At last he checked his watch—almost ten o'clock—and was shocked by how much time had gone by. He turned from the window, giving himself a mental shake. He really must get on. He hoped Monty would arrive shortly and spare him some time before he went to see Dottie.

He drank half a cup of cold tea straight down in one, and ate half of a chicken sandwich. Eating made him aware of just how hungry he was. He finished the rest of the sandwich in record time, then still standing by the table, wolfed down the cherry cake as if he were again that ravenous eight-year-old. He wiped his fingers on his handkerchief, topped up his cup and went to sit on the bed. He took up the first witness statement and began to read.

'I am Imogen Cowdrey. I am twenty-nine years of age, and I am a single woman. I live at St Martins Manor House, in St Martins village, Sussex. On the evening of Tuesday 1st January, I was at home in the drawing room. My mother and father were there, and there were also my two brothers, Guy and Leo, my brother Leo's wife June, and my cousin Dottie, Miss Dorothy Manderson, who is visiting us at the moment...'

'Monty! I'm so relieved...' Dottie could have hugged Montague Montague when she saw him seated at that same table in the now perfectly familiar interview room. She wanted to say more but couldn't quite manage to get the words out. Even Monty seemed overcome, which given that he was almost fifty and had been a lawyer for many years was quite something. He leapt to his feet nimbly in spite of his generous proportions and took her hand in both of his. He ignored the warning looks from the warder who had stationed herself by the door once again.

'My dear Miss Dottie. What a thing. I came as soon as I could. I can only spare you until the weekend, I'm afraid, as I'm already committed to another case, but I'm absolutely certain that will be ample time. This is a preposterous situation, m'dear, truly preposterous.'

They sat. He put his monocle firmly in place and scrutinised her. 'And are you quite all right, m'dear?'

'I've been better, of course,' she admitted. 'But I understand my parents have arrived, and of course I've already seen W—Inspector Hardy, and now you...'

'Ah yes, Inspector Hardy. I've met him a few times now, professionally and through your parents. A very personable young fellow. I must say, we at *Montague, Phillips and Ardlui* find him a wee bit formidable, there's something of the terrier about him that makes us all worry what he's going to dig up next. Unless he's on our side, of course, then well, we count our blessings.'

'Oh yes,' Dottie said. She looked down at her hands. 'Inspector Hardy has been—er—very—'

'Indeed.' Monty's eyes twinkled at her. He clearly believed her confusion to be of a tender nature. He ahemmed delicately and turned his attention to the papers in front of him. After a moment he said, 'Well of course this is all ridiculous. I'm sure we can get all this thrown out by the local magistrate almost straight away. Looks as though the police simply fixed on you from the outset and looked no further.

Negligible, circumstantial evidence, pure supposition. Nothing to give us any real worries.' He pocketed his monocle behind the neatly presented silk handkerchief and looked at Dottie once more. 'Hardy said that he thought you may have been mistreated?' He shot a glance at the warder, who noticeably paled.

'Oh—er—well, not really. They've been a bit—firm— with me, but no one's actually—hit me or anything.'

'Hmm.' He didn't sound satisfied by that, but he let it go. 'Now, m'dear, I'm afraid you'll be going back to your cell tonight. But I shall speak to the magistrate first thing in the morning, and I'm confident we can have you released very soon. So keep your chin up, Dottie m'dear, and try to get what rest you can. You've seen your parents, haven't you?'

'Oh no, I couldn't see them.'

He looked annoyed. 'What? This is insupportable. You're not even of age.' He glared at the warder. 'See to it your inspector remedies that error immediately, or I will have something to say about it to my friend, the Home Secretary.'

The warder nodded, gulped and said, 'V—very good, s-sir.'

'There you are then,' he said with a beaming smile at Dottie. She smiled back. She was immensely reassured by his certainty. At last she had the feeling that everything was going to be all right. 'Thank you, Monty.'

'Good, good.' He got to his feet and gathered up the papers. 'Look m'dear, I'm going to leave now. But I shall see you in the morning. I'm loath to leave you here, but there's nothing for it tonight, I'm afraid.'

'It's quite all right, Monty. Just—thank you so much for coming all this way. It's very good of you.'

'Not at all m'dear.' He just touched her shoulder,

smiled and then the warder closed the door behind him. She seemed to not quite know what to do about Dottie. After a moment's thought she said to Dottie, 'Stay there.'

As if I have any choice, Dottie thought once again. The warder left the room, leaving the door ajar. A pleasant breeze wafted in, but on it came the tantalising smell of bacon. Dottie's stomach rumbled. She had only eaten two pieces of dry bread since breakfast.

Ten minutes later, the door opened but this time it was Inspector Woolley.

'I just thought I'd pop by and let you know,' he said in a light tone, then he thrust his face close to Dottie's, his breath stale and stinking of beer and cigarettes, 'I don't appreciate being told how to do my job, and I don't appreciate being told who can visit my prisoners at all hours of the day and blasted night!' He gestured to the warder who was waiting in the doorway. 'Take her back to the cells.' He turned on his heel and left.

The warder unlocked Dottie's cuffs from the chair and led her back to the cells. The whole time, Dottie had a sense that the woman wanted to say something, but she never spoke a word, completing the short journey in silence. She was less rough than before, Dottie noticed. That was at least something. The warder held the cell door open and waited for Dottie to go inside, instead of shoving her in as before and slamming the door almost on her.

Dottie huddled on her bench once again, shivering. It was a relief that the other two occupants were either asleep or pretending to be asleep. If they had jeered at her now... But the only sounds were the rain and the soft sound of her fellow inmates' breathing.

She had hoped the inspector might accede to

Monty's demands and allow the Mandersons to visit her. The disappointment was worse for coming on top of the brief flare of hope.

But she comforted herself that she wouldn't be here for much longer. It was chilly and damp in the cell, the air was stale, but if Monty was right—and she trusted him utterly—this would be her only night in the cell and in the morning she would be a free woman once more. She felt excited at the prospect, but a little afraid. What if Monty couldn't persuade the magistrate? What if there was some kind of evidence that looked more convincing?

No. She must hope for the best. This time tomorrow she would be with her family again, and she would be sleeping in a proper bed. And before she went to bed, she would have a hot bath. And before that she would have a lovely hot dinner.

Dottie fell asleep on her bench dreaming of the bath she would have, with the bubbles, the fluffy towels and her own clean clothes to put on afterwards. Oh it would be such bliss.

Although it was almost half past eleven by this time, Monty and Hardy spent half an hour talking about Dottie's case in a slightly less noisy corner of the pub, the raucous laughs and scraping of benches and chairs covering their conversation which was almost as private as if they had been in Sir Montague's own chambers at Lincolns Inn.

They ordered food: steak and kidney pudding, a sea of rich gravy rippling across heaped fluffy mashed potatoes, and their conversation stopped being just about work and became far more pleasant. Half a glass of beer to wash that down, and Hardy began to relax for the first time that day. The pub was empty now, the landlord had locked the doors, and everything was quiet.

Monty hadn't known Hardy had been up at Oxford studying law, before his father's illness and early death made earning a living essential. Monty had been a close personal friend of several of Hardy's tutors. They exchanged anecdotes and memories.

Over the rum baba dessert, they talked more generally. Hardy was surprised to find himself letting his guard down, telling Monty about his family. Monty condoled with him on the loss of his mother the previous year, and heard all about the married sister, and the young sister who was courting, and the younger brother still at Repton. By the time they had finished their coffee, they were firm friends; Hardy felt as though he'd known Monty for years.

'Did you know that Dottie—Miss Manderson, I mean—was not the Mandersons' own daughter?' He felt able to ask such a question now. Monty had lit a cigar and was reclining in his chair, completely relaxed after the meal.

'No.' Monty shook his head. 'I never had the slightest suspicion. If not for this current crisis, I doubt anyone would have ever guessed she was not their own delightful child. There's never been the slightest indication, to my knowledge.'

'Hmm.' Hardy sank back in his seat, staring up at the ceiling, lost in thought.

'Back to work?' Monty asked.

'Sorry?' Hardy blinked at him. The food had made him start to feel drowsy. He shook himself and sat upright. It wouldn't do, to fall asleep like this. 'Oh yes, work. Yes, I'm thinking about this wretched affair again. I'm anxious to get Miss Manderson out of that jail cell.'

'I feel dreadful, actually,' Monty said. 'I promised Dottie I'd have her out of there first thing in the morning. But when I left her just now, that idiot Woolley told me the coroner's inquest was planned for nine o'clock. I'd assumed it would be later in the week. But with everyone busy with that, the poor child will probably have to stay there a little longer than I'd hoped.'

'I shall be at the inquest. It's going to be in the church hall just along the road,' Hardy told him. 'What I don't understand is, why did Mrs Cowdrey's children all declare that they actually saw D—er—Miss Manderson killing their mother when it had to be perfectly clear that she was doing no such thing?'

'It's all right to call her Dottie,' Monty said with a paternal smile, 'I shan't think it a liberty in the least. Well, it seems clear there was an obvious motive for them to do that.'

'Yes. In any case, it's difficult to see that anyone but one of the family could have a motive,' Hardy said.

Monty nodded. 'Exactly. One of them—if not all of them—must have some guilty knowledge. They know something. Perhaps not everything. But something.'

Hardy sighed. 'And it was easier to let the relative stranger take the blame. Perhaps they didn't even mean for her to be kept in custody, let alone actually charged. But I find it hard to believe they would have really risked so much. Just imagine if she *had* been convicted.'

'It doesn't bear thinking about,' Monty agreed, looking closely at Hardy and wondering if the young fellow liked Dottie as much as he suspected. Monty had heard the odd rumour, of course. Herbert Manderson had even confided his hopes of a match before the year was out. But yet...

'What do you know of this Parfitt fellow?' Monty asked suddenly, impulsively.

Hardy's response was that of an angry, jealous

lover, Monty decided. Hardy said, 'He's an out-and-out bastard. Rotten to the core: rotten, plausible, pompous, relies on people being awed by his importance—of which he never fails to inform everyone he meets—and he loves the sound of his own voice. Treats Dottie like some kind of pretty accessory to his own ego.'

Monty winced. 'Ouch. And I presume those are just his good qualities? So apart from hating the man, do you know anything to his discredit?' His eyes were sharp over the glowing tip of his cigar.

'I might.'

The two other women were released in the morning. Dottie was surprised how lonely and afraid she felt in the cell without them, and how vulnerable, considering she had been quite nervous of them while they were there with her. The night had dragged. The cell had been cold yet airless, and she had sat rigid on the bench, scratching now and again: she was certain either the cell or one of the women had fleas, and these were looking for fresh meat. No wonder people confessed to all sorts of things they hadn't done, Dottie thought, I've never felt so miserable or alone.

Early in the morning, she was once again summoned to the interview room upstairs. Inspector Woolley, flanked by Palmer and the warder, came in and the inspector sat opposite her. Hope flared in Dottie's chest once again. She held her breath to hear what he was going to say. Would she be released? Was she free?

'Tell me again why you came to visit your aunt—or should I say—your mother.'

Her hopes plummeted to the floor. So they weren't letting her go after all. She daren't think what that might mean. For the umpteenth time, she went back to the previous summer and told him all about her mother's revelations, and the subsequent invitation to go down and spend a few days in the house to the near stranger she had always thought of as her Aunt Cecilia. She explained about the mix-up over the date she should arrive, and that the invitation had actually come secretly from Imogen, and her aunt had not heard about it until the day Dottie arrived and found no one at home.

The inspector kept interrupting, or jeering at her, and firing questions at her, clearly trying to confuse her or make her contradict herself. She was almost in tears of frustration when, he angrily grabbed his papers and got up to leave. The warder came forward to unlock Dottie's cuffs and was about to take her back to the cell, when Woolley, pausing in the doorway for effect, said casually:

'By the way, you'd best stay put. You've got visitors.' He turned to the warder, 'Come with me, I need a quick word. Palmer, stay here and keep an eye on our guest.'

As soon as the other two had left the room, Sergeant Palmer came over to unlock the handcuffs. He said gruffly, 'He's going to the coroner's inquest in a minute. He should be gone a while. But you never know, so behave yourself, or you'll get us both into trouble.'

Dottie thanked him profusely and massaged her bruised wrists. There was a sound outside and a single rap on the door. A constable let someone into the room.

It was her mother and father. Dottie's heart swelled with emotion. 'Mother! Father!'

The police sergeant, soft-hearted but wary of his boss, took Dottie's arm and pulled her away to the table and chairs. 'Now then, miss, I need you to sit down here and stay put. Otherwise, I'll have to ask these people to leave.'

'Of course,' Dottie said.

Her mother, dabbing her eyes, drew out the seat opposite her and sat. Her father, looking as if he wanted to punch someone, remained standing.

'I'll leave you to talk in private, but I'll be right outside the door.' The sergeant patted Dottie's shoulder. The kindly twinkle in his eyes glittered suspiciously brighter than usual. 'I can only let you have five minutes, mind, not a minute more, so be quick. If the inspector comes back and sees you out of them cuffs, we'll all be for it.'

They thanked him. The door banged behind him, and Dottie heard the sound of the key turning in the lock, less terrifying now that she wasn't alone.

They looked at each other.

'Well, Dottie,' said Mrs Manderson, and to Dottie's mind that seemed to sum up this impossible situation perfectly.

'Thank you for coming, I'm so grateful,' Dottie began but her voice croaked on the last word and she fell silent.

'Silly girl, of course we came.' Lavinia Manderson said it briskly, afraid her anxiety would betray itself too much. She was here to comfort and encourage, as well as to talk to Dottie about what had—or hadn't— happened. 'I'm only sorry we didn't get here sooner. We didn't hear anything about it until lunchtime, when Leo telephoned.'

Her mother's brisk tone, so normal, so *her*, was reassuring. When Dottie spoke next, her voice was perfectly steady. 'Did you manage to speak to Gervase?'

Her mother pressed her lips together so tightly the

skin around them blanched. Her hands gripped the edge of the table. She leaned forward. 'Oh my dear, I'm afraid his manner was rather odd. Your father and I are not at all happy.'

Dottie's brow furrowed. She looked from one to the other. 'Why? What did he say?'

'Well, we explained what had happened, or rather your father did—it was he who spoke to Gervase. Gervase said a few choice words, apparently, which I suppose is hardly a surprise given the circumstances, and gentlemen do seem to use expletives when surprised or upset. But then he said, 'Please keep me informed.''

Dottie stared at her. 'He said what?'

''Please keep me informed.' Then he rang off. Gervase, not your father. Didn't he, Herbert?'

'Absolutely he did, the...'

Dottie shook her head, bewildered. 'What on earth?'

'Your father was furious. I even had to speak to him about his language. I have to say, Gervase has gone down a good deal in our estimation. I had hoped he'd leave at once to join us here.'

Dottie had been hoping the same thing, although of course she'd been quite sharp with him when she'd last seen him. All the same... Could he possibly still be sulking over her refusal to further their intimacy? 'He's not coming? At all? Not even at the weekend? I mean, I know that he's busy, but all the same...'

Her mother shook her head. 'We rang him again this morning. We thought it would be a good plan to give him overnight to consider things. He thanked us, and once again asked us to let him know what was happening.'

Dottie stared at her mother. Her parents stared back.

'So Gervase is not coming?'

'No, Dorothy, dear, he is not coming.'

'Surely he can't think I actually did this? He couldn't possibly believe me capable of such a terrible thing?'

Her mother shook her head but made no reply. Dottie, her voice rising with emotion, cried out, 'You and Father don't think that, do you? You *know* I would never...'

'Of course not...' Her father was moving forward, but wary of the sergeant outside, took the other seat opposite her and held her hand in his. 'Of course not, my love,' he said again, softly.

'Calm down, Dorothy, darling,' her mother said, gently but firmly, casting a look at the door. 'We don't think any such thing. And Monty is going to prove it. Along with Inspector Hardy, of course.' She couldn't help slanting a quick glance at Dottie's face, though it was hard to tell if her daughter had heard her. 'Now dear, are you getting enough rest? I know it can't be easy, but you must try. And make sure you eat properly. You need to keep your strength up, as I'm afraid it may be a day or two yet.'

Dottie nodded. 'Yes, I realise that. Monty said something about seeing the local magistrate, but I can't imagine they would just let me walk out without someone else to put in my place. I'll be all right. Especially now that you're here. Mother, I'm so sorry about Aunt Cecilia...'

Her mother bowed her head and took a moment before she said, 'It's very sad. I hope the police will stop wasting time with this ridiculous case against you and get on and find the real killer.'

'Where are you staying?'

'At the house. I insisted on staying. Lewis wasn't happy about it, but that's too bad. Imogen has been in a state, as you can imagine, poor child, so I'm glad we're there to take care of her. But we've seen almost nothing of Lewis and Guy. Something of a blessing.'

'But Mother, surely one of them must be Aunt Cecilia's killer? It had to be one of them. I don't want you to stay at St Martins, you'll be putting yourself in danger!'

'Nonsense, Dorothy. In any case, I have your father with me, at least for the next few days. He's got to go back to London with Monty at the weekend, of course. But it won't have been a member of her own family who did that to Cecilia. It's clearly the work of some madman or passing tramp who attacked her.'

'That's what people always say, but it's silly.' Dottie reflected that if passing tramps did half of the murders they were accused of carrying out, they'd be very busy people indeed. She consoled herself that it would only be for a few nights and that the police were surely carefully watching the household.

The door opened. The sergeant came in, a jangling bunch of keys in his hands.

'Time's up, everyone.'

They had a quick hug, whilst the sergeant protested, 'Come on now, the inspector will be back in a minute. He'll have my guts for garters if we get caught. Let's get these cuffs back on you, missy.'

'Tell Imogen how sorry I am about her mother, and tell her I didn't do it, of course. You will look after her, won't you?' Dottie was saying as she was led away. 'She must be devastated.'

Her parents assured her they would take care of everything, and reminded her to eat and take some rest, her mother adding, 'We'll come and see you again later today, or tomorrow.'

Dottie was returned to her cell. The cell door slammed shut and the key turned in the lock.

Monty arrived a little later, and told her about the inquest.

'My dear Dottie, I didn't realise they were having it so soon,' he said. 'Or I would never have got your hopes up last night about being released in the morning. I'm so sorry, but I believe it might be another twenty-four hours.'

'Oh that's all right,' Dottie said, trying to sound as if it didn't matter a bit.

'The local chappie wanted to have you put down as the murderer, but luckily the coroner overruled him in the light of Inspector Hardy's submission that the case warranted looking into in greater depth. Of course it helped that the pathologist stated that he found almost no water in the lungs of the deceased, so she had been dead before she went into the water, and that death was caused by a heavy blow to the temple some hours prior to her body being taken out of the water assumed. So there we are. More time to investigate the case, and I have an appointment later to speak with the magistrate.'

Dottie nodded, taking all this in.

Monty said, 'Hardy said you told him about seeing someone outside the night your aunt was killed?'

'Yes, I did see someone, but couldn't make out enough to tell who it was. It was really only a blur of a face amongst the trees. I couldn't even tell if it was a man or a woman.'

'That's all right, dear. And what time was that?'

She wrinkled her nose up. 'Let me see. About half past eleven? Perhaps a little later. I went upstairs about half-past ten. Imogen came to my room to talk. She went downstairs again. At least, I assume she did. Then I went down too, to try and catch her.'

'To suggest she didn't telephone this Mr Clarke after all, Hardy seemed to think?'

'That's right. Then I heard the arguing coming from the morning room and I went back upstairs. I waited for a while, thinking Imogen might come to my room and when she didn't, I went along to hers.'

'But she was asleep?'

'I think so, yes.'

'You think so?'

'I didn't check,' she said. 'I stood just inside her door and listened. It was dark so I couldn't see her in the bed, but I called her name and there was no response. I assumed she was sleeping. I thought I could hear her breathing, but I'm not certain. I just assumed she was there.'

Monty looked pleased, as if she'd given him something useful.

'I'm almost sure she was there,' Dottie said. She didn't want to think what it might mean if Imogen had not been in her room.

In the cells it was dark, but not silent. Beyond the now-familiar walls of Dottie's tiny room were voices and banging, and the occasional shout or sound of laughing. Next door, the drunk who had been brought in an hour earlier was on his fourth chorus of Onward Christian Soldiers, which he was alternating with a slightly muddled version of The Old Rugged Cross. Clearly, Dottie thought, he had been under the care of the Salvation Army at some point. And doubtless would be again.

But within the four walls where Dottie was confined all alone on her bench, there was a sense of peace. Now that she was no longer anxious about her own welfare, she was using the solitude to think.

Mrs Christie, who had taken the world by storm with her detective novels during recent years, had created an odd little gentleman investigator who advocated the employment of what he famously termed 'the little grey cells': the brain cells that held all the information about a crime and that could, given sufficient opportunity, solve the crime simply by examining and thinking about that stored information.

Dottie wriggled her shoulders as she attempted to reach an itch in the middle of her back. That minor problem dealt with, she settled again into her corner and tried to discover what her own little grey cells knew.

At first she thought that she knew precious little. But after some moments it occurred to her that she knew the people of the 'case'. She began to think about each person involved or affected by Cecilia Cowdrey. She ticked them off on her fingers.

There were the staff, of course. Drysdale and the cook had been with the Cowdreys for a number of years, whereas the maids came and went with regularity, with greater emphasis on the 'went', and often were either not paid or were kept waiting for their money. That the staff were overworked was beyond doubt, but they were probably not treated any worse than most others.

But could any of them really gain anything by killing their mistress? Dottie couldn't see that anything other than lashing out in a blind rage would be likely. Surely no one who had only worked at St Martins for a matter of mere weeks or months would be bothered enough about the place to lash out in a rage? In Dottie's limited experience, these days, staff had more choice of employment and a great advantage over the many employers who offered work. Most staff would just shrug their shoulders, say something unflattering, and move on, usually to a factory or large business where the money was better and the working day shorter.

The touted murderous insanity, of lashing out in a blind rage, was only in books, or almost only in books, Dottie thought. Most people needed a real, pressing reason for killing someone. And as Mrs Christie's books showed, murder was almost always done by someone close to the victim. You had to really know someone to feel that the only way out of a situation was to kill them.

Which really only left the family.

It was one thing to know this with your mind, a completely different sensation to know it with your heart. A member of the family. Someone so close to Cecilia she had held them in her arms as a baby, or as a loved one. Someone who had sat with her at her table, who had taken a cup of tea from her, or a coffee in the drawing room. Who had walked in her home or gardens.

This realisation filled her with fear for a moment. That kind of person—the kind who knew you yet nurtured a deep hatred, deep enough to plot and carry out your murder—that was a person who would stop at nothing, who cared not a jot for your life, your well-being, who strove to achieve their aims no matter who had to suffer—that was someone truly terrifying. In the dark cell, Dottie shivered.

She pulled the threadbare, fuzzy blanket over her and up to her shoulders. It smelled of dog, a fact that still puzzled her, and was horribly itchy, but it was all there was, and she was too cold to be proud. Warmer now, she continued the horrifying thread of her thoughts.

It was awful to remember that her aunt was dead. Her aunt. Her mother, really. No longer moving about her home, conversing with her friends and family, making decisions about meals or who to entertain.

I never did get to know her properly, and I shall never be able to think of her with affection, Dottie thought. Certainly she had no affection for me. But I'm sorry she's dead. She didn't deserve to die. No one deserves to die like that. She hadn't wanted Dottie to visit, that had been all Imogen's doing. Poor Imogen, Dottie thought. How was she coping with all that had happened? Dottie could only hope that Guy, Leo and Lewis, and her own parents of course, were comforting Imogen.

Cecilia had not welcomed her, and definitely had not welcomed her curiosity, her ability to defend herself from criticism and to even hand some criticism back. Yet after her own peculiar fashion, she had allowed Dottie into the family home and had tried to entertain her. She had even tried to make Dottie stay there.

'But why?' Dottie asked the darkness.

The slot in the cell door opened and the fierce warder's voice said, 'You all right, Manley?'

'Yes, thank you.'

'Good.' The slot was closed with a snap.

Dottie sighed. The warder had been a little kinder since Inspector Hardy arrived. She hadn't shoved or pulled, shouted at Dottie or slapped her. But even though the warder knew her name wasn't Manley, she persisted in calling her that. Why did people do such things?

Why had her aunt resented her so much yet attempted to make her stay? She'd said she wanted Dottie to keep Imogen company, and to pressure Imogen into doing what Cecilia wanted, particularly in regard to keeping her away from Norris. She'd wanted Dottie as an ally. She wanted to control her daughter—or daughters—and keep them at home.

But why, when she took no pleasure in their company, in their achievements or happiness? What was this urge to control?

Out of nowhere Dottie had a mental image of the geese that sat on the grass at St Martins. Controlled. Unable to do what geese naturally do and fly away to warmer climes in the winter, not able to move to other grazing or roosting places. Completely controlled and living an artificial life. The geese who had given away St Martin's hiding place, according to legend. A constant reminder of how they had failed him. It was Imogen who had told Dottie about that.

What did Imogen remind Cecilia of? An unhappy marriage? The old triumph of snobbery and desire for status over true love and mutual care? Was it a punishment to Cecilia to see her daughter's face every day and remember how she had compromised her heart and taken the man who had her parent's approval, rather than the man who offered her devotion?

Could there be a financial motive behind Cecilia's death? Surely if anything, Cecilia had been the one gaining material benefits, not the other way round. Unless she was heavily insured, of course, Dottie suddenly thought. After all, St Martin's estate appeared to be failing and falling into debt; repairs could not be carried out. Staff were not paid. Dottie made a mental note to ask William to look into that aspect of the murder.

That Lewis had been able to give Cecilia the grand feudal home she had so craved seemed little enough reason to marry someone. How had she been able to turn her back on the love of the man she had wanted all those years ago? What about more recently as the place began to fall apart around their ears? Had Cecilia resented St Martins as a millstone around their necks?

If Cecilia had been so unhappy with Lewis, Dottie did not understand why she was so against Imogen following her heart and marrying Norris. Was it really only a question of his lack of money and coming from the wrong background?

The wrong background had meant nothing to Cecilia when she had been a young woman in love with Stanley Sissons, a mere soap manufacturer. Had it been the addition of a knighthood that overcame her objections? Or the financial success? Or just the death of her parents? It was true, Dottie thought, that her aunt seemed to have set great store by status and tradition.

But after resisting and refusing to tell Dottie—or over the years, Lavinia—the identity of Dottie's father, suddenly—*very* suddenly—Cecilia had had a change of heart and brought about the meeting of Dottie and Sir Stanley. Why had she done that? What had changed her mind? Or had she merely given in to what had perhaps seemed the inevitable?

Why had Cecilia and Lewis not simply divorced, Dottie wondered. Divorce would not have materially affected either of them, plus it was so easy to obtain these days. And becoming almost commonplace, it lacked some of the intense social stigma it had always had. A divorce would have meant Lewis could have gone to the woman he loved, and Cecilia could have finally been with the man she had rejected so many years ago. Her parents were dead. Sir Stanley's wife had died. There appeared to be no further reason not to follow their hearts. That would have the advantage of placing Cecilia in the elevated social position she appeared to crave, as well as financially benefitting her.

How could Cecilia do the same thing to her own

daughter as was done to her, refusing her the hand of the man she loved merely on the grounds of social class? It was entirely due to Cecilia that Imogen, at almost thirty years of age, had no viable candidates for romance. If only Cecilia had got down off her high horse and allowed Norris Clarke to court her daughter. Though now, with Cecilia's death, the way was surely clear for Imogen and Norris to marry?

It occurred to Dottie now for the first time that her own mother had been something of a rebel to marry the notoriously once-penniless Herbert Manderson. Had her parents forbidden her Herbert, just as they had forbidden Cecilia to allow Sir Stanley to pursue her? At some point there must have been a painful scene in which Lavinia told her parents she had no intention of settling on a man for whom she had no love. Dottie felt sure she would do the same, risking comfort and security for a man who had few material advantages but who loved her devotedly.

Unbidden, William Hardy's face came to mind, stopping her thoughts and her little grey cells in their tracks.

Chapter Seventeen

Dottie awoke quite suddenly and felt wide awake. In the cell it was almost dark, but it might be any time between three in the afternoon and ten o'clock in the morning—the long winter nights were even longer when you were below ground-level. The only light coming into the cell was a glimmer of electric light through the tiny slot in the door whenever the warder checked on her. Checking for what, Dottie wondered. Did the woman really think she would catch Dottie in the middle of a daring escape, digging a tunnel or filing through the bars of the little slot window up by the ceiling at street level?

Dottie sat hunched on the bench under a thin scratchy blanket. Her back ached and she had a crick in her neck. The space at the end of the bench that ran into the corner was a premium spot and highly sought-after by inmates, affording as it did a more comfortable prop for the head and back. Dottie, having the cell to herself for the second night, had taken over this position, planning to get the most sleep she could before her earnestly prayed for release in the morning.

Now though, she got to her feet and stretched. She tried a few movements she vaguely recalled from gym as a schoolgirl. The stretching helped to relieve her aches and pains and boosted her spirits.

She felt cheerful. She knew that beyond the confines of her cell, her parents, Monty and of course William were all doing everything they could to get her out of prison and clear her name. She hoped that her release was almost at hand, and that nothing would stop Inspector Woolley from releasing her today. She relaxed as much as she could, grabbing a second blanket from the other bench to drape over her lower half. She wouldn't let herself think about fleas, or the odd doggy smell of the blankets. Instead she began to think about what had happened to her aunt.

As soon as she turned her mind to the problem, one name sprang to it immediately. And every time she shook it away, it came back, insistently, intruding on her thoughts again and again.

Imogen.

Dottie felt a knot in the pit of her stomach. It couldn't be timid, childish, scared-of-her-own-shadow Imogen. It just couldn't. Dottie closed her eyes tight against the darkness, as if trying to turn away from her terrible doubts.

Imogen...

...who had wanted to be free to marry the man she loved.

...who had been the butt of teasing and ridicule her whole life. The endless ridicule that had gone unchecked by an indifferent father and a mother who only wanted blind obedience and service from her daughter.

...who wanted to have a free, independent life, that she had only glimpsed from afar until Dottie had arrived, younger, yet independent, courting, free to marry whom she pleased, enjoying all the advantages of a happy social life and a warm, loving family.

...who was thwarted at every turn, and who, when she finally found the courage to stand up for herself, found that her hopes were dashed to pieces by the very person who should have wanted to promote her happiness: her mother.

Had Imogen really been in her room that night? Had Dottie simply imagined the soft sound of breathing in the darkness? What had been the reason for the cold draught of air in the back hallway? Had someone gone out? Or had someone come in? Who had stood outside in the dark, their face the only sign that someone was there?

'Oh dear Lord,' Dottie whispered, 'please don't let it have been Imogen.'

But who else could it have been? Guy and Leo, like their father, were free of the unfair restraints applied to the daughter of the house.

'And they care not a jot for what other people think,' Dottie reminded herself. Leo had his own home, his career, his wife. Lewis, she knew from his own mouth, had his other, illicit, relationship and his heart was beyond Cecilia's power to crush or control. Guy—surely his happy-go-lucky approach to life cushioned him well, and then there were his feelings for June, which no doubt kept him far too busy to be worrying about his mother's attitude to him or her desire to control those around her.

The only other person Dottie could ascribe even an inkling of a motive to was Norris. His motives were, she supposed, broadly the same as Imogen's, though seemed less pressing. He already had his own home and business, after all. But...

Imogen.

All Dottie's reasoning and thoughts seemed to return her again and again to her cousin. Her half-sister, she reminded herself. Shrugging her anxieties about Imogen aside, she thought about the rest of the family again.

What about Guy? He seemed to embody so many weak indulgences, yet his devotion to his brother's wife seemed able to transform him into a completely new man. Exactly what Lewis had said about his own involvement with another woman, she recalled. Would Guy—would June—act on their feelings? How could this work yet ensure everyone's happiness? Would Guy be content to just see the woman he loved in snatched guilty moments, as Lewis had done for years?

What were June's own intentions? Was she merely fanning the flames of her own ego by surrounding herself with adoring men? Not that Leo seemed to be especially attentive or inclined to romance as far as Dottie had been able to tell. He seemed bored, cynical and uninterested. Rather like his father, Dottie thought, and immediately wondered if Leo was likely to have an interest elsewhere. Another thing to ask William to look into. Yet who knew what passions might lurk unseen? Or perhaps in the privacy of their own home Leo might sweep his wife off her feet with romantic yearning, sweet kisses and complete devotion?

Dottie exhaled heavily, and felt her hair rise and fall. It seemed something of a stretch to picture Leo and June being lovey-dovey and passionate towards one another, but you never knew. It seemed far more likely that their relationship mirrored that of Lewis and Cecilia, and that Leo did indeed have a mistress somewhere, a woman who... What was it Lewis had said? A woman who made him feel like a different, nicer person; that he liked himself when he was with her.

She shook her head. It all seemed such a waste. Such a long waste of long years. So much misery, heartache and lying. It was all so sad. She didn't want to think about it anymore.

Who was it that had accused her first? She had wracked her brain since yesterday but still couldn't be sure.

She had been trying to help her aunt, then she had been overtaken by the nausea and shock of what had happened. She'd wanted to get back to the house, but knew she only had time to make a dash into the trees. As soon as she finished being sick, and wiped her face on her wet jacket, someone had grabbed her roughly—a man—Leo? Or Guy? And someone, a man again—had said something like, 'What have you done?'

But had it been Leo or Guy who had said that? She couldn't remember. She had felt faint and ill; it had all been happening too fast; one moment she was alone, struggling to drag her aunt's body from the freezing water, the next everyone was there. Or at least, the 'cousins': Imogen, Guy, Leo and June. They had been shouting, and Imogen had been screaming, someone had slapped her. Leo—yes it had certainly been Leo who had slapped Imogen's face and stopped her screaming.

The men's voices were quite similar, but Dottie had a feeling it had been Leo who had shouted at her, 'What have you done?'

Then Imogen had gone to her mother's body, practically falling down by her side, and Guy had grabbed Dottie, hauling her back to the house to lock her in the cloakroom. Yes, she thought she was right about that. Leo had shouted at her, and Guy had taken her away.

Guy had said, 'If it were up to me, I'd let you go and good luck to you.' That also made her think it had been Leo who had said, 'What have you done?'

Had the others all agreed with him and accused her? Or had any of them said anything to protest her innocence? Imogen? June? No she was sure they hadn't. They'd said and done nothing to help her, all their thoughts had been centred on Cecilia.

Leo had crouched beside Imogen, putting his arm around her as she knelt on the ground. He'd done something else. But what was it? It nagged at her now, just at the fringes of her memory where she couldn't quite get at it. He'd been crouching down, his jacket dipping in the mud, then he'd turned on her so fast, flying at her in a rage, and she'd been afraid of him.

But of course the wreath had been there. Or part of it. She'd been distracted by that, it seemed so odd. She'd been looking at the plants there on the ground beside her aunt's body, then Leo had...

She shook her head. It wouldn't come. Best not to try and force it. It would no doubt come back to her when she was thinking about something else.

All night long, her thoughts ran around and around this same track.

As soon as breakfast was over, Hardy went to St Martin's house with Sergeant Palmer.

When Lewis Cowdrey stalked into the room, easily outstripping the sergeant, it was clear from his demeanour that Hardy's assessment had been correct. Hardy's condolences and introduction were waved away with impatience. Cowdrey's response to Hardy's opening questions were clipped and sarcastic. His lifted chin gave the man the air of someone who quite literally looks down his nose at the world.

Then Hardy said, 'On the day that Miss Manderson first came to the house, there was no one at home. Why was that?'

'How the hell should I know? No doubt got herself into a muddle, the way these girls do.'

'Hmm,' was Hardy's only response. He forced himself to ignore his urge to defend her.

'Did you know she was arriving that day, sir?' Palmer asked.

Cowdrey had barely even noticed the sergeant sitting in a corner of the room. Now he saw him looking his way, his pencil poised over his notebook for Cowdrey's response.

'Can't recall. Perhaps I did, I can't remember what day it was. My wife deals—used to deal—with all that.'

Hardy felt for the man then. After all, he had just lost his wife, which was the very reason for the visit from the police, and at least some of his manner had to be disguised grief. Cowdrey dropped his gaze to the floor, and his jaw tightened.

'Of course,' Hardy said in a gentle tone. 'I think most men leave social details to their wives. Not really our thing, is it?'

There was a non-committal huff from Lewis Cowdrey. But he regarded Hardy now with a marginally pleasanter eye. Hardy said, 'If I might jog your memory, it was the day you and your family went to spend the afternoon and evening at the home of your elder son and his wife, I believe, and the day before Miss Manderson arrived to stay here.'

'Ah yes. I remember now.' He sounded rather like a sulky schoolboy admitting breaking a window with his catapult.

Hardy nodded. 'How far away is Mr and Mrs Leo Cowdrey's home?'

'Matter of a mile or so. Perhaps not quite so much.'

'Did you walk there? Not a very nice walk this time of year, I imagine, though in the summer, it would be quite pleasant.'

'No, we went by car.'

'Did you all go in one car?'

'Took two cars. I drove mine, and Guy drove his.'

'I see. And did your younger son travel alone, or did he take someone in his car with him?'

It was a mild enough question, but Cowdrey was angry again, and in a belligerent voice, said, 'What do you mean by that? What are you trying to say?'

Quietly, Hardy said, 'I just wondered if your daughter travelled with you and your late wife, or if she went with her brother.'

Mollified, and clearly feeling foolish, Cowdrey said, 'I see. Er—she went with us, I seem to recall.'

'Thank you. These small details can sometimes be useful.' Hardy made a note on his paper. Cowdrey couldn't see it, but it said, *remember to get a new notebook*. 'At what time did you return home from your son's house?'

'Let me see,' Cowdrey said slowly, looking up at the ceiling, pondering. 'We left at—about five past ten, I suppose. Got home—I'd say about twenty past. Thereabouts, anyway, it's difficult to be precise.'

'Of course,' Hardy said smoothly. The hairs on his forearms prickled. As Cowdrey said that last part, he'd looked right into Hardy's face and smiled. Up to that point, Hardy had been inclined to believe his story, but this sudden smile, along with his assumed vagueness, and the way his focus fixed in such a calculated way on Hardy as he said it, all of this came together in Hardy's mind as proof the man was lying. They had not all got home at twenty minutes past ten on that evening.

Nevertheless, he thanked Mr Cowdrey for giving up his time, and for so graciously allowing the police the use of his study. The two men stood, shook hands across the desk, and Sergeant Palmer walked Lewis Cowdrey to the door.

The door closed behind him; they heard his footsteps go along the corridor, and then Palmer said, 'I think he's telling porkie-pies.'

'Yes, sergeant, so do I,' Hardy said. 'But why? What really happened?'

'It's come to my attention, Mr Cowdrey, that you were actually in the house the day Miss Manderson arrived, but you elected not to open the door to her.'

'What makes you think that?' Guy was angry, caught off-guard.

'Miss Manderson saw your car at the back of the house when she went that way to try to find someone to let them know she was here. And your father has told me you took two cars to your brother's home that day.'

'What's that got to do with you? Or my mother's death?'

Hardy said nothing. In the long silence that stretched between them, he took the opportunity of observing a few details about Guy Cowdrey. Self-assured, yes, and arrogant as the sons of wealthy families all too often were. No doubt I'd have turned out the same, he thought then, and almost laughed. Losing everything had changed him, and privately he thought it was for the better. He wondered if the rest of his friends and family would agree. Bringing his thoughts back to the interview and the man in front of him, he decided that he couldn't see any familial resemblance between this man and Dottie. Guy Cowdrey was only of average height, whereas Dottie was quite tall for a woman, and probably just an inch or so shorter than Guy. Guy had light brown hair, his eyes had grey irises and rather red, watery whites that suggested too much alcohol or too many late nights, or both. There was nothing of Dottie in him, Hardy concluded.

Guy Cowdrey broke the silence at last, and he was irritated by feeling compelled to do so. 'If you must know, I was upstairs, and I didn't hear anyone knock at the door. The butler and the rest of the staff were not back from their Christmas holidays until the following morning, and I simply forgot to listen for the arrival of any visitors.'

'Does that include the arrival of your cousin whom you hadn't seen for a number of years and who had been invited to stay at the house for New Year? The same cousin whom you knew in fact to be your half-sister? Yet you felt no curiosity about her, and her visit—an unusual and remarkable event—simply slipped from your mind?'

'Well to start with, she wasn't invited for New Year, but for the week after. The stupid girl came on the wrong day,' Guy retorted.

'True,' Hardy said mildly, hiding his annoyance at hearing her called a stupid girl. 'So you weren't expecting anyone that afternoon.'

It wasn't exactly a question but Guy Cowdrey chose to answer it anyway. 'No one.'

Hardy was looking at his papers, and without looking up, he said, still in that deceptively mild tone, 'And when you say you were in an upper room of the house, I suppose you mean your bedroom?'

Cowdrey fidgeted. He ran a hand through his hair. 'Well, yes.'

'In spite of saying you expected no one, can I assume that you were not alone, that you did in fact already have a visitor with you?' Hardy knew he was being blunt, but he was fed up with the polite tip-toeing around that seemed to form the greater part of his job.

Cowdrey flushed, and hesitated. Hardy attempted a man-of-the-world laugh. As if they were two friends at the same club, and both understood what was going on. Cowdrey relaxed visibly.

'Well, yes,' he said again, but this time he didn't sound half so defensive.

Hardy nodded then added, 'And what would the lady's name be?'

Cowdrey shot him a look that said he felt betrayed by Hardy's assumed comradeship going off so quickly. 'What?'

'I need to know the lady's name, so that...' Hardy began, but before he could finish, Guy Cowdrey, leaning forward on the edge of the chair, said with undisguised hostility:

'I'm not saying another word.' He got up and left the room.

Hardy sighed and sat back. Clearly he wasn't the right type to wheedle information out of a well-to-do young man. But he knew someone who quite possibly might be able to obtain all the answers he needed. Not that it was entirely ethical—or legal—to involve someone else, but...

'That went well,' Sergeant Palmer commented from his corner.

'When I want your opinion, sergeant...'

'I know, I know. You'll tell me what it is.'

Hardy sighed again. 'I admit I could have handled that better.'

'Perhaps that Miss Manderson can get something out of him? Once she's released, of course.' Palmer slanted a sly look at Hardy.

Hardy refused to take the bait, simply looking at his list. 'Right Leo Cowdrey next I think. You can drive.'

Chapter Eighteen

As they drove to the home of Leo and June Cowdrey, Hardy said, 'Tell me about the family.'

Sergeant Palmer, his eyes fixed on the twisting road ahead, replied, 'Not much to tell. Reputed to be as poor as church mice, not that you'd know it from the way they carry on. The late Mrs Cowdrey was known as a haughty one, not given to charity work or the usual welfare interests these well-to-do ladies have. As far as she was concerned, the good Lord had made poor folks to graft, and it wasn't nothing to do with her if they couldn't feed their kids or pay their rent in the wintertime. The daughter—Miss Imogen, I mean—not the one we've got in the cells...' He spared a glance at Hardy's thin-lipped expression and added hastily, 'Sorry sir, meaning no disrespect. I forgot she was a friend of yours. Anyway, Miss Imogen, she's known for being a dried-up old stick, ready for the shelf, if not actually on it. I doubt if she was ever young, that one. Mind you, she was always very much third place to her brothers. Feel a bit sorry for her, myself. I did hear a whisper she was carrying on with a chappie who runs an antiques shop in Horshurst. Don't know if it's true, though. Knowing her parents, I doubt someone like that would be a good enough catch, even if she is knocking on thirty. I should think mater and pater would put the kibosh on anyone 'unsuitable'.'

Hardy filed that away in his memory to find out more about it later. 'And the rest?'

Palmer slammed the brakes on, jerking them both forward in their seats. Hardy steadied himself with a hand on the dashboard. Palmer dropped the window down to hurl abuse at a shepherd whose sheep were all over the road. They had no choice but to wait for the man to send his dog to guide the sheep into a gateway fifty yards ahead. 'As for the men. Lewis Cowdrey and young Guy are well-known for their exploits away from home. They sail quite close to the wind, but they've never got caught for anything too serious.'

'What kind of exploits?'

'Women of ill repute and gambling mostly. Guy likes a flutter on the horses, and the dogs. And cards. And you know, that posh-folk game, with the wheel and that. Goes up to Town to some club there.'

'Roulette?'

'That's the one. And his father plays cards: poker, blackjack, all of the above really. If Guy is the chip, Lewis is the old block he came off. They both go to their old boys' clubs, get plenty of drink inside them, get a bit rowdy. Both been banged up overnight for causing a ruckus a couple of times, but always out the next morning with a fine.'

'Do they lose enough for it to cause them trouble?'

'Not that I've ever heard. As I say, usually it's

something fairly small, up before the beak, a small fine and home they go. But as they have got money troubles, I'd say even a small loss could be hard to manage.'

'I thought Lewis Cowdrey *was* the beak?'

The sergeant allowed the car to gently roll forward now as the shepherd, sending a rude gesture in their direction, followed his dog and the sheep into the field and barred the gate behind them. Then they were able to build up speed and head off again. The sergeant replied, 'He used to be our local beak, yes, but not anymore. It didn't give him any authority in London, though I daresay all those nobs look out for each other anyhow.'

'I imagine so. And the older son, Leo?'

'Well it's a funny thing. He's never been in trouble, never caused any mischief. He's his mother's son, all right. He stays quietly at home and minds his own business. Yet you'd be hard-pressed to find a soul around here with a good word to say about him. He's—he's got a nasty side to him—I can't put it better than that. One of those 'You don't know who I am' types, always telling you about the names he knows.'

Hardy grunted. 'Hmm I know a few of those. Clearly you don't like him.'

'Well,' Palmer said with a laugh and a wink in Hardy's direction. 'He don't like me neither. Punched him on the nose when I was eight years old.'

'You did?' Hardy laughed. 'Good Lord, why?'

'He broke my best conker. It was a twelver—I cried all night about that, I did. And his nose has never looked the same. His father came down and threatened my father, said if he didn't keep me under control, he'd have us out of our cottage. But that's the only time I ever remember him doing something like that. Lewis Cowdrey was a good landlord, otherwise.'

'Leo must have had a jolly good conker to break your twelver.'

'Kept his hand over it, didn't he? It was only as it swung, I saw it was a stone. Too late then. Cheating little git. I'll never forgive him for that.'

It was clear from Leo Cowdrey's disdainful look that he hadn't forgotten that punch on the nose. He scowled at Palmer, though he said nothing. Palmer smirked at Hardy behind Cowdrey's back and went to sit on a hard chair slightly apart from the group of sofas. He took out his notebook, and licked his pencil lead, as June began to fuss about tea.

Hardy started with a few pleasantries. As commonly occurred when he was interviewing people of the higher social classes, his own cultured accent set them at ease and gave him a useful advantage over the working-class policemen that usually investigated crime. Even so, it was clear Leo Cowdrey wanted him to get to the point.

'I'm a very busy man, inspector, and I'm expecting the eminent barrister Sir Montague Montague K.C. for coffee this evening. Usually I invite my guests to dinner, but under the circumstances, it's only right to observe the decencies of mourning, so we shall just enjoy coffee and cigars.'

Odd, thought Hardy. Did status trump associates or did Cowdrey not know that Monty was here to defend Dottie, not to prosecute her? He said, 'Very trying for you, sir, having to rearrange your plans. I'm very sorry about your mother.'

'Yes, well, to be honest, this isn't helping matters. You people already have my cousin in custody, so I fail to understand why you come here asking damfool questions. It's a bit much.'

Hardy's impression of Leo was of a slightly plump, ineffectual man, full of bluster, and looking older than his years. His hair was heavily peppered with grey, slightly thinning on the crown, whilst his forehead and the area around his mouth showed a trace of lines. Hardy tried not to stare at the slightly crooked nose. He felt it right to ask, 'May I ask, why you're so certain Miss Manderson did this?'

'What?' Leo Cowdrey looked startled, as did his wife. 'Well of course she did. Who else could it have been?'

'That's what I intend to find out,' Hardy said pleasantly. 'I just thought it rather surprising that you were so quick to conclude Miss Manderson was the guilty party.'

'Well of course it was her,' Cowdrey repeated, his tone growing belligerent, defensive. 'We caught her actually in the act. There wasn't anyone else it could have been. I'd hardly suspect my own sister, or my brother, would I, inspector?'

'I suppose not. Although of course, we now know that Miss Manderson is also your sister.'

If Leo Cowdrey was surprised this information was known to the police, he refrained from saying so. Instead, he corrected coldly, '*Half*-sister, inspector, that's all she is. Half-sister. I don't wish to discuss such a private matter any further. It's completely scandalous.'

'I'd be grateful if you'd take me through the afternoon and evening of the twenty-seventh of December. I understand your family came to spend the afternoon and evening with you. If you could just go through anything you remember from that day.'

'But... don't you mean the night before my mother was killed? Surely that's the relevant time?'

'Humour me, Mr Cowdrey,' Hardy said with a

smile. Leo Cowdrey flushed with annoyance. His wife darted him a frightened glance.

'Why is Scotland Yard so interested in our little crime?' Cowdrey demanded abruptly.

'I've been asked to assist in the enquiry.' Hardy wasn't going to allow Cowdrey to rile him or divert him until he was ready. Out of the corner of his eye, he saw Palmer looking somewhat alarmed.

'You're rather young to be an inspector, aren't you? I've a good mind to check your credentials. I'll certainly be lodging a complaint with my MP, Algernon Epps, who is a close personal friend of mine, and I shall also be discussing this matter with Sir Montague Montague this evening, and I shall inform him of your offensive line of questioning and your blatant disregard for the accepted line of enquiry.'

'That's an excellent idea, sir,' Hardy said, leaning back in his seat. 'Please, do give my regards to Monty when you see him, I've met him several times socially in London, he's a delightful fellow. You must ask him to tell you about his father's pocket-watch, it's an interesting story. He and I dined together last night at the pub in the village, as we are both staying there at the moment. As you no doubt realise, he is providing Miss Manderson with legal advice. He is another person who utterly believes in your cousin's innocence. I'm sure he's looking forward to discussing the case with you. Now, perhaps you could just answer the question.'

The room was still. There was a sudden chill over the inhabitants. Monty, always professional, would of course do no such thing, but Cowdrey failed to realise that. Sergeant Palmer bent low over his notebook to hide his broad grin. June Cowdrey looked at William Hardy with eyes rounded in astonishment.

Eventually Leo Cowdrey deigned to give Hardy a terse outline of that day's events. It was unenlightening. Hardy doubted the truth of some of it. With an inward sigh he realised he would have to come back here too and talk to yet another Cowdrey for a second time.

Hardy asked, 'Did your mother have any money or property of her own?'

Cowdrey said she had, adding, 'I've no idea exactly how much. We've never talked of it.'

'Do you believe it could be a substantial amount? Enough to present a strong temptation to someone?'

'I very much doubt it, Inspector.'

'Did you ever hear your mother say that she was thinking of leaving any or all of her money or property to Miss Manderson?'

'No.'

Hardy looked at Cowdrey. His jaw was set in a mulish manner. Clearly there would be no new information from this quarter. He had intended to ask other questions, but all at once he knew it was a waste of time. He'd get nothing further out of Cowdrey or his mouse-like wife today. He'd find out a bit more then come back, in the hope that Cowdrey would be better disposed towards helping the police next time.

Hardy got to his feet. Sergeant Palmer glanced up, surprised, and quickly gathered up his pencil and notepad to cram into his pocket, fumbling with the button.

Hardy held out a hand to Cowdrey who stared at it as if it were a slug in his salad bowl. Hardy dropped his hand back by his side. 'Well, thank you, sir, for your—er—' He couldn't exactly say cooperation, so left the sentence hanging.

At the door he turned back to say, 'Enjoy your

evening with Monty. He partnered me at bridge once at the Mandersons'. We won. Jolly decent chap.' Leaving the Cowdreys staring after him, he walked out.

Sergeant Palmer with a malicious twinkle in his eye as he anticipated sharing the scene with his colleagues back at the station, said to Leo and June, 'Good day to you, sir, ma'am.' He shut the door behind him as he left.

Later that afternoon, Inspector Hardy and Sergeant Palmer crossed the grassy slope and came down, slipping and sliding on the frosty surface, to the edge of the lake. A cold breeze blew in across the water and pinched at their noses and throats whenever they tried to breathe in. Their breath clouded the air in front of them like an apparition. A more suitable spot for seeing such things couldn't be dreamed up, Hardy thought. The sky was low and grey, the water was grey, the very air seemed to hang like a shroud about them, cold, threatening and eerie. The geese that huddled under the trees for shelter seemed spooked into silence. No birds sang in the grey naked trees. The sooner they saw what they had to see and got back into the warm, the better.

Palmer took Hardy to the muddied, debris-strewn spot. 'That's where Miss Manderson pulled Cecilia Cowdrey out of the water and was apprehended by her cousins. She said she was trying to rescue her aunt. You'll already know this, but they maintained she'd been in the act of drowning her aunt when they came along, and she was just trying to wriggle out of it by saying she was helping.'

She must have been chilled to the bone, Hardy thought. And how like Dottie to throw caution to the wind and try to help someone. He had never known her to turn aside from anyone who needed her. Apart from me, his mind told him before he could stop it. He squashed the thought and forced his brain to think about the crime.

Some ice still drifted on the surface of the water, but he had no way of knowing whether there was more ice now than when the body had been discovered. He could only hope it wouldn't make much of a difference. The bank was churned up, there were heel marks of a woman's shoes on the grass, and whole footprints in the boggier part of the mud that went down to the water. The frost had acted on the tracks and marks, freezing it all quite efficiently.

'What are those?' Hardy pointed at some stems and petals in the mud.

'Oh those are the weeds we found. You remember the corpse had what we at first thought was some kind of wreath on it? When we took a closer look, it turned out to be more like just a tangle of stems and leaves, just some weeds caught up on the lady's arm. I did wonder if she fell into the water and got herself all caught up in weeds and that was what drowned her.'

Hardy bent for a closer look. He made out the mauve and white face of a small flower. 'Well that's not a water plant, surely? Isn't that something people grow in their gardens? My mother used to have those.' He frowned. 'It seems rather odd. Get them picked up, will you, and put them in a bag. I'd like a closer look at them at the police station later.'

'We've got the wreath sir, still in an evidence bag if you want to take a look at it.'

'I will, later on. Meanwhile, let's have as many of these as we can get.'

'Yes sir.' Palmer produced a paper sack from his

jacket pocket and began to carefully extract the plant matter from the mud. It took him a few minutes. Hardy held the bag for him. When they were done, Palmer closed down the top of the bag and put it under his arm, taking care not to press it too firmly. Hardy found nothing more of interest at the scene. They looked about them.

'You can't be seen from the house, just here,' the sergeant pointed out. Hardy turned to look back up the slope. It was true. The steeply inclining lawn coupled with the little stand of trees and bushes formed a kind of natural wall to cut this part of the lake off from the view of the house. Very nice and private. He could see the windows of the upper floors, but not the lower.

He set off back up the slope. When he reached the top, he paused and looked first down to the lake, then behind him back towards the house.

'It slopes down a little this side too,' he called to Palmer.

'That's because this bit we're standing on was designed to be useful as well as pretty,' Palmer said. 'The lake is actually artificial. They dug out tons of rock and dirt, and piled it all up at either end to create a dam, and they grassed it over to make it nice for the ladies in their long frocks to walk on. They widened the river that was already here to make a pretty lake for the posh folks to admire. The river always used to burst its banks in the spring due to the heavy rains coming down off the hills. And one year, it got right up here, so they decided to be extra cautious and add in a kind of gully all the way round, so the slope does a double dip, and that stops the house getting flooded even during the worst downpours.'

Hardy nodded, appreciative of the common-sense

approach of the construction.

'They have boating parties and music evenings, and all sorts in the summer. I've heard they has little orchestras coming along the lake in boats lit up with lanterns for all the nice ladies and gentlemen to ooh and ahh at.'

'Very nice,' Hardy said with a grin.

'Of course, us ordinary people don't get invited.'

'Not until there's a murder...' Hardy replied grimly. He stood and looked in every direction again, until he felt he knew the layout thoroughly. After a while, he said, 'Nice work for a young woman, bringing a dead body down here on her own, in the dead of a frosty winter night, up this side and down the other, and getting it into the water, leaving no trace at all, then getting herself back to the house again. Quite a way.'

He sent a straight look at the sergeant who had the grace to look away and look down at his shuffling feet. But then Palmer seemed to have a brainwave. 'I bet there's a wheelbarrow in the potting shed, I think, sir. If so, the guilty person might have used that.'

'Do we know if Miss Manderson knows of either the existence of this possible wheelbarrow or the location of the possible shed?'

'No sir, we don't. But a place of this size, you could lay a pretty safe bet on there being a wheelbarrow somewhere.'

'True.' Hardy turned to walk back down to the side of the lake. He walked along the perimeter, checking the edges of the water. He halted after a minute and crouched down to look at the mud that ran from the treeline right into the water and beyond. There were deep footmarks in the mud, some going towards the water, and into it and some going away from it, up into the trees. The water was clear enough just to see the holes, indistinct and large, beneath the surface.

'Can't tell anything from those,' the sergeant commented. 'Although they look so big they could even be a man's.'

'Exactly,' Hardy said.

'Does Miss Manderson have unusually large feet, sir?' Palmer asked with a grin. His accompanying wink seemed to suggest that Hardy knew her very intimately indeed.

From anyone else, this would have been disrespectful at the very least, and Hardy would have been angered by it, but working together closely, Palmer had grown on him. Hardy couldn't help returning the grin.

With perfect honesty he said, 'I have to admit, I've never paid much attention to her feet.'

The sergeant gave a snort of laughter. He shook his head in mock maidenly disapproval. 'You young fellows are all the same, only interested in one thing. Or I should say, two things.'

Hardy smiled again, then went back to his perusal of the footprints. He crouched down to look at them again, measuring the marks roughly with his hands. At least a size ten, if not eleven or even twelve. Far too big to be a woman's. He straightened up. 'I don't like it,' he said. 'And I'm sure you'll think it's just because a friend of mine is accused of murder. But really, Palmer, can you picture her doing it?'

'Nervous type, is she? I can't imagine any young woman coming out here at night and sloshing about in the mud and ice like we've been having lately. My sister would probably scream the place down if she heard a fox or an owl or anything. Or them geese. Town girl.'

'I wouldn't say Miss Manderson was of a nervous

disposition especially. And she is an intelligent woman. But my thought is, there are easier ways to kill someone, especially if you wanted to make it look like an accident or even a suicide.'

'You'd need gloves and a wheelbarrow, some good strong muscles, sturdy boots, a warm coat and nerves of steel to carry out a crime in this way.'

'These grooves here and here could be made by a wheel, for example the kind of wheel you might find on a wheelbarrow. What do you think, Sergeant?'

'I think that's exactly what they look like, sir.' Palmer put his fingers into the mud. About two inches or so wide, and this must be a foot long. The ground's harder there and there's no trace. Might be worth tracking all the way back up the hill. We might be able to find more wheel marks.' The sergeant paused to think, then added, 'Inspector Hardy, sir, I asked this question before of my own inspector, but he was determined it was her what done it, and said there was no point in trying to mess up the case, as that was the defence's job. But I'm asking again, do *you* think we should be looking for a man?'

'Anything's possible. A man would certainly find the whole thing a lot easier to accomplish. Also men, if they are interested in outdoor pursuits such as fishing or hiking, can far more easily explain mud or water on their boots or clothing.' Hardy wiped his hands on his handkerchief. 'To be honest, I don't much care who did it, so long as I can prove it and get Miss Manderson out of that prison cell.'

Palmer clapped him on the shoulder in a companionable manner. 'I heard she was affianced to some big-wig up North.'

Hardy sighed. 'Yes, I'm afraid she is. Or as good as.'

'He hasn't exactly raced down here to be by her side, has he? Sir,' Palmer added as a hasty afterthought.

'No, Palmer, he hasn't. I'd say it's a classic example of keeping his professional hands lily-white.'

'Then he don't deserve her, sir.'

'Hmm. Unfortunately that's not for me to say.' Hardy had no intention of continuing that line of thought. 'Right let's go back to the house. I want to talk to the staff again. Then I want to time how long it would take someone to get from the house to here with a body, with or without a wheelbarrow. But first, let's see if you're right, and there *is* a potting shed.'

The potting shed was tucked away behind a jutting wall in a sheltered corner of the garden just beyond the rose garden. They followed the wheel marks practically to the shed door. Hardy was satisfied they were tracing, backwards, the route taken by the killer. The weight of the body in the wheelbarrow had formed a nice deep trail on the soft ground.

The gardener produced the key from his pocket, picking it out from a mess of grimy, bristly string, several toffees, a book of matches, a battered pouch of tobacco, and a walnut in its shell. He stooped to retrieve two pennies and a sixpence from the ground.

'Is that the only key?'

The gardener thought long and hard. Eventually he admitted it was not.

'Where is the other key kept?' Sergeant Palmer asked. 'Or keys? How many others are there?'

With great reluctance, as if betraying a strict confidence, the gardener told them there was definitely only another one key, he would stake his life on it, and that he thought it might hang on a nail just inside the back door by the kitchen.

Hardy and Palmer exchanged a grin at this. The gardener pushed the key into the lock and turned it easily. The door swung outwards, revealing a neat, orderly array of tools and gardening paraphernalia. It was probably the neatest shed Hardy had ever seen. There in the centre of the floor with its handles towards them, was a large wheelbarrow.

'Thanks very much, we'll take it from here,' Palmer said and almost thrust the gardener out of the doorway.

Palmer and Hardy squeezed inside the shed and shut the door, only to discover it wouldn't stay closed without being locked.

Hardy said, 'Well that's that.'

Palmer couldn't deny the truth of that, adding, 'If you'd just used it and brought it back, you'd put it in nose first, just like this, with the handles facing the door.'

'Exactly, And look—that mark could be blood. We'll need to get someone out to take a proper look. Just move it out a bit, would you? Don't touch the handles.'

That was a tall order, Palmer thought, given the lack of space, but after a bit of puffing and cursing, he managed to back the wheelbarrow out onto the path without using the handles.

Sure enough, there was the dark damp patch Hardy had noticed, all down the inside, quite near to the top. A tentative dab at it came away brown and sticky. Hardy sniffed it. Even after the passage of several days, there was still the tang of blood.

'So we can be more or less certain that this was used to transport the body.'

'There's mud and grass on the wheel and on the rests at the back,' Palmer said. They both looked the barrow over carefully, then turned their attention to the shed itself. A little mud had fallen onto the floor. This Palmer carefully trapped in his handkerchief and dropped into an envelope. He labelled it neatly and stored it in his pocket.

There were a couple of sturdy looking trowels. But to their disappointment, they were perfectly clean. If either of them had been used to deliver the deadly blow, they showed no sign.

'Palmer, tell our chaps to be on the lookout for anything out of the ordinary. You never know. We need to find the weapon if we possibly can.'

'He might have thrown it into the lake, sir.'

Hardy sighed. 'I'm afraid that's all too likely. And if he did, I'm not convinced we'll ever find it.'

A few more minutes and Hardy decided there was nothing else of interest. He left Palmer to wait for the expert to come out from Horshurst, and went back to the house to make the phone call.

Next, he intended to have that word with the staff.

Chapter Nineteen

'Thank you all for sparing me some more of your time. I wanted to tell you that I am now certain that Mrs Cowdrey died in the late hours of the evening before she was discovered by Miss Manderson.'

His words were greeted with silence. He wasn't entirely surprised. He looked at them. Mr and Mrs Manderson, side by side, composed, alert, giving him their full attention. Imogen, her hands restlessly fiddling with something in her lap, her face pale, her large eyes fixed on him. Lewis, as pale as his daughter, but keeping all emotion, all movement locked away, his arms folded and rigid across his chest, his eyes staring at some part of the floor. Guy, looking uncomfortable, and as if he was working through what Hardy had just said, puzzling it over in his mind, glancing from one to another of the people around him. Leo, an expression of bullishness on his face, one knee crossed over the other, his arms stretching along the back of the sofa as if claiming the whole seat for himself, though his wife perched beside him. It was Leo who spoke.

'I don't know why you're accusing us of making this up, sergeant. All we said was that we thought Dottie had killed our mother. It's up to you to investigate and find out if that was what happened. We can only tell you what we saw.'

Inspector Hardy knew Leo had called him sergeant deliberately. It didn't matter. Let the man flex his muscles if it made him feel better. Hardy said:

'Of course, sir. Which is why I came here to let you know that Mrs Cowdrey died the previous evening from a blow to the head.'

'From what, exactly?' Leo Cowdrey demanded. His lip curled in a sneer.

'I don't know as yet.'

'Well I suggest you get on with it, sergeant, and stop wasting our time. My wife and I are going home now, we've had quite enough or one day.'

'Very well, sir. I'd just like to add that Miss Manderson will be released from prison either this evening or tomorrow morning.'

No one said anything. Not that there was much they could say, Hardy thought, with Dottie's parents sitting right there. Lewis Cowdrey gave a nod and got to his feet. It was clear he was showing Hardy out. At least he made the effort to be civil.

'Well thank you, Inspector. Please let us know if you discover anything more.'

Hardy nodded, smiled briefly at the Mandersons, and left the room. He didn't go far. Just along the hall to the study.

But only an hour later, Hardy and Lewis Cowdrey faced one another again, this time across the desk. Hardy felt they were making little progress. Lewis

Cowdrey was undeniably hostile, and although Hardy knew that people grieved in different ways, it seemed to him that Cowdrey was not so much grieving for the loss of his wife, than annoyed with her for causing him inconvenience and unwelcome attention.

With a change of tack, Hardy said, 'I understand there have been a number of petty thefts of late?'

Cowdrey was surprised. But he answered easily enough. 'Yes, but I'm sure it's nothing. How is this relevant to my wife's death?'

Hardy shifted in his seat. 'I'm not certain that it is. I just want to have all the facts. Any odd occurrence within the household recently may be relevant in a manner we don't yet understand. I'd be grateful if you could add a little more.'

'Well, there have been I suppose three or four petty thefts. Small, unimportant things have been taken, nothing particularly valuable. To be honest, I gave it little thought at first. I assumed that my daughter had simply been careless with her earrings and put them down somewhere then forgotten where. I gave little attention to the matter.'

As with most things that concerned his daughter, Hardy imagined. Hardy said, 'Excuse me interrupting, Mr Cowdrey, but when was this?'

Cowdrey frowned as he tried to recall. He leaned back in his seat, fiddling with a pencil. His posture had relaxed, and he was no longer hostile or defensive. Perhaps Hardy might get something out of him after all.

'About a month ago, I suppose. She last had the earrings at the dinner for my son Leo's birthday. That would have been on 28th November.'

Hardy nodded and made a brief note in his book. 'I see. Thank you, do go on.'

'As I say, I gave the matter little thought. But then, about a week or so later, I couldn't find my cigar case. I knew I'd put it on the table in my dressing room when I undressed before bed. There were a number of items: a handkerchief, my signet ring, a pocket watch.' He thought for a moment. 'I think there could have been a small book of matches. I don't know what else, that's all that comes to mind right now. Anyhow, the next morning, Drysdale asked me if I had left the cigar case on the table as usual, because he couldn't find it.'

'He didn't help you the night before?'

Cowdrey looked sheepish. 'Er no. Must admit, we'd had a few jars, Guy and I, and stayed up rather late after everyone else had gone to bed, setting the world to rights and so forth, as you do. Didn't think it right to keep old Drysdale waiting, so about one in the morning, I told him he could go, that I wouldn't need him anymore that night.'

Hardy managed not to smile. It surprised him that Drysdale still remained in Mr Cowdrey's service if he was the kind of employer who thought it perfectly all right to keep his manservant waiting until one in the morning to see if he was needed. Clearly Cowdrey paid well.

'Anyway, I went up with him to check, but the cigar case wasn't there. Everything else was still where I left it but not the cigar case. I have to admit, knowing that I was a bit under the weather the night before, I merely assumed I'd dropped it somewhere, under a chair or something, and that it would reappear. But it still hasn't turned up. I've had to order another. The staff told me they've looked everywhere they could think of, and I told them they'd better damn well look again. Which they did, but...' He raised his hands and let them fall in a 'what can you do' manner.

'Did you search the terrace?' Hardy asked, mainly to keep the conversation trickling along.

'Oh yes. My wife is not keen on gentlemen smoking in the drawing room, which was where we ended up, so we had to haul ourselves out to the terrace during the evening whenever we wanted to smoke.' He gave Hardy a matey grin. 'Not that we bothered once she'd gone up, you understand, though we left the door slightly ajar to disperse the smoke.'

'Even in winter?'

Cowdrey shot him a look. For a moment Hardy thought he'd annoyed the man, but Lewis Cowdrey just smiled and said, 'Ah well, it was so mild that last week of December. In fact, right up until the night my wife died, it could have been early autumn rather than midwinter. Very pleasant that evening. Besides,' he added, 'it's easier to do that than to risk an argument with my...' His own words trapped him, and he stopped mid-sentence. His face fell, and he fumbled in his pocket for a packet of cigarettes and a match-book. He drew one out with trembling fingers, put it between his lips and lit it. He took a couple of long drags, then said, 'At least, it *was* easier than risking an argument with my wife.'

There was a silence, then after a few moments he said, 'Of course, if we'd been dining with friends, usually the ladies would leave us, and we chaps could have a chat and a laugh, we'd have port or brandy, and it was always perfectly easy to just pop out onto the terrace for a few minutes' breath of air along with a cigar. It was never really a nuisance, I just used to make a fuss sometimes, no idea why.'

'I understand,' Hardy said, 'And were there any other incidents?'

'Well, about a week or so ago, I think it was either Christmas Eve or Christmas Day—they were here for both—there was June's bracelet. Don't ask me to describe it because I didn't take any notice of it at the time. But what she said was, she took it off to wash her hands, then came out of the cloakroom and left it behind on the side of the basin. She rang up for it the next morning, and Drysdale went to check, but it wasn't there. June made quite a fuss, as a matter of fact. As far as I recall, she said it was a family heirloom. I promised to speak to the staff about it.'

'And did you?'

'Not right away, no.' Cowdrey looked sheepish again. 'No, I must admit I thought the woman had left it at home all the time, or something like that. She is very stupid, even for a woman. And there was a snuff-box or some such taken from the morning room.' He sighed, thought for a minute, then: 'Oh yes and Imogen lost a pearl necklace last week. She made a fearful fuss about that.'

'Anything else?'

'Yes, Dottie—Miss Manderson—missed her drawings. I had all the staff in my study, and I told them straight I wouldn't stand for petty thefts. I asked that the items be returned immediately.'

'And were they?'

'Not so far as I'm aware.'

'Didn't you think of reporting the matter?'

'No. Didn't seem terribly important, plus, you know, didn't want to get caught up in a police investigation.' He had the grace to look slightly ashamed.

Imogen came back into the house. It was a bare minute before midnight, and frost peppered her hair.

Guy, pausing at the foot of the stairs, said, 'Where on earth...? Have you been outside all this time? And without an overcoat? My word, Imogen, you'd better hop upstairs and get yourself into a scalding hot bath before you catch your death.'

Without a word she went right by him and into the billiard room. She shut the door. Guy hesitated. Should he just quickly go and check that she was all right? She was acting damned queer, even for Imogen. But he shook his head and continued up the stairs to his room. His thoughts quickly drifted elsewhere. How much longer...?

In the billiard room, Imogen pulled back the curtains. She hauled one of the tall seats right up to the glass of the French doors and perched herself there as if on watch. Yet even now, she knew it was a waste of time. It was over. She stared out into the night, desperate for any sign.

Ten minutes later she couldn't sit still any longer and went to put on her coat. She took a torch from the kitchen and went back outside. She would wait until he came. He had to come. He just had to.

Hardy had only been asleep for half an hour or so when the pounding on his door woke him so abruptly that he fell off the narrow lumpy mattress and onto the floor. Stumbling to the door, he threw it open, ready to give whoever was there an earful. Then he saw it was the landlord, there to summon him to the telephone.

'What's happened?' Hardy asked the second he picked up the receiver.

'You've got to come. We've—I can hardly believe I'm saying this...' Guy Cowdrey took a breath. 'We've just found Norris Clarke dead in the grounds.'

At the other end of the line, in the study at St Martins, Guy sank back in the chair and closed his eyes. He shook his head. 'What's happened to us?' His voice was almost inaudible.

'I'll be there in a couple of minutes. I'll meet you at the front door, and you can show me the way.' Hardy hung up the phone.

He was as good as his word. When he arrived at the house, the front door was open and Guy Cowdrey stood there waiting for him.

'Don't you want to ask me questions?' Guy came forward.

'Perhaps you could show me where the body is first.'

'Of course. It's this way,' Guy said and led Hardy around the side of the house.

As they went Guy told Hardy what little he could. Hardy heard that Norris Clarke was in the habit of meeting Imogen for a secret rendezvous two or three times a week. Usually they met in the rose garden, but if the weather was overcast, he waited under the better cover of the trees at the edge of the lawn. Imogen had waited for him in the rose garden as agreed, but when he had failed to show up, she had gone looking for him amongst the rhododendrons, beech and chestnut trees. There she had quite literally stumbled over his body, it being a cloudy, moonless night. Her hysterics had woken Lewis Cowdrey who had in turn woken the staff, his son, and the Mandersons.

They went through the drizzle in the direction of the rose garden, along its slightly overgrown and muddy path to the lawn, and slipping slightly on the wet sloping grass, across to something oddly hunched at the foot of a small chestnut tree surrounded by rhododendrons. The something proved to be the body of Norris Clarke.

Hardy dug in his greatcoat pocket for his electric torch. He stayed where he was for a moment, checking the condition of the ground near the body.

Finally he turned his attention to the body itself. At that point he could have kicked himself for failing to do the most obvious thing first. Because the light from his torch showed him that Norris Clarke's chest was moving.

'For God's sake, get an ambulance. He's still alive!'

Without hesitating, Guy turned and ran for the house.

Once Norris had been removed to the hospital, police constables carried out a search of the immediate vicinity, and as soon as it was light, would extend this search to conduct a sweep of the entire estate. As yet, no weapon had been found, but Hardy did not expect to find anything, and especially not during the hours of darkness, with what was now a persistent rain falling. He now knew, though, that they were looking for something solid and slightly curved, a handle or club of some sort would be his guess. Now he had to deliver to the household the news that Clarke was still—just barely—alive.

Three hours later, Hardy finished the bacon and eggs and steaming mug of tea the Cowdrey's cook had provided him with by way of breakfast, and thanked her with real gratitude, 'That's the best bacon I've had in twenty years.'

Unconcerned by his rank of police inspector, the blushing cook flapped a grimy oven glove at him and told him he was a caution. He grinned and bid her goodbye for now.

A minute later he was sitting behind the desk in the study. He glanced through his notes. Not much to go on so far. He had no serious concerns about the residents of St Martins House. No one had seen anything much to tell him—and this didn't particularly surprise him. If there was a perfect time of year to commit a violent attack, it had to be in the middle of the night, in the middle of the country, in midwinter.

He sighed. It was still rather early to expect Imogen Cowdrey to be back from the hospital, and that was really all he was waiting for. Mr and Mrs Manderson had taken her in their car. The early report from the doctor who had attended to Clarke was not an encouraging one.

'In conclusion, Inspector,' Montague Montague said, taking his monocle and polishing with a large pink handkerchief, 'It's time to put up or shut up, as they say in the common parlance. Let Miss Manderson go. Whilst I realise she was a useful suspect for you, and represented the kudos of an early conclusion to this sad affair, you and you alone will be the one to be vilified in the press for your victimisation of a young, and *very* photogenic woman. It will of course, destroy your career. But on the other hand, you may feel it's better to go out on a high note. However I can assure you that your lovely wife, Mrs Woolley—or Beatrice, as she kindly permitted me to call her—is very much looking forward to spending her later years in a delightful holiday villa at Hopton-on-Sea with her sister and brother-in-law, and she will not welcome a notorious husband who will be the talk of the East coast. Quite a temperamental lady, your dear Beatrice,' Monty said with the suggestion of a wink at Dottie. 'I imagine she has some theatrical blood. A temper like that can be trying to live with on a daily basis, of course, but such fire, such passion is only to be admired in such a lovely lady.'

Inspector Woolley stared at the papers in front of him on the desk. His foot beat a tattoo on the floor.

His hand trembled a little. It was a full two minutes before anyone said anything. The clock ticked loudly. Dottie gnawed her lip, hardly able to keep her seat. William Hardy and Sergeant Palmer exchanged a smile and nod. Montague Montague, satisfied his monocle was perfectly clean, replaced it, folded his arms and leaned back in his seat, fixing his gaze on the inspector.

Yet still the inspector hesitated. Very softly, M'dear Monty said, 'Don't make me run to the magistrate again. Think how badly it will reflect on you, man.'

Inspector Woolley seemed to give himself a little shake, rather like a dog coming in from the rain. Then, appearing to return to reality, he scooped up his papers in a decisive manner, and cleared his throat vigorously.

'Miss Manderson, during a routine review of my evidence and case notes, I find that there is insufficient cause to suspect you of this crime. Therefore I am happy to tell you that the police no longer consider you a suspect in the death of Mrs Cecilia Cowdrey and that, as a consequence, you are free to leave. I am sorry for any inconvenience. I wish you a pleasant journey home. Good day to you.'

He stood up, feeling he'd made the best hand of it he could. At least old Monty now knew he wasn't the only one who could make a pretty speech.

The inspector headed for the door, halting whilst Sergeant Palmer belatedly opened it for him. As he went out, the inspector thought, bloody Hopton-on-Sea. How Bea did go on about it. Mind you, the fishing wasn't bad over that way. He went to telephone his superiors.

Hardy came forward smiling. He held out his hand to shake Dottie's, but she mistook him and went into his arms, hugging him tightly. Almost immediately she remembered they weren't alone. Or in love, she had to remind herself of that too. She stepped back awkwardly and turned to smile at Sergeant Palmer and Monty.

'Thank you so much! I really didn't think...' She felt herself getting emotional and made herself shush.

M'dear Monty gave her a peck on the cheek. 'I'm only glad I was able to help, m'dear.'

The sergeant said, 'Well miss, if you'll come with me, we have your belongings, and your mother is here with a change of clothes for you. The clothes you had on when you arrived are still in the evidence safe.' He wrinkled his nose. 'Plus, you know, they're a bit smelly from the lake.'

Dottie didn't care. Feeling almost lighter than air, she followed Monty outside, glancing back over her shoulder to see Hardy dip his head and turn away.

An hour later, lunch was over and they were bidding Monty and Mr Manderson goodbye outside the pub. Mr Manderson had already apologised a dozen times for having to leave them. But he had business in London, and it was convenient for him to take Monty back with him as Monty had his own commitments.

'Now remember,' Monty said for the third time, 'if you need me again, just call. I can be back down here in next to no time. I'm in court for most of tomorrow, but then after that I'm free until I'm due to leave for Paris next Thursday.'

Dottie kissed his cheek and thanked him yet again for all his help. Monty bent over Lavinia Manderson's hand, then Mr Manderson said goodbye to his family, kissing his wife's cheek, shaking Hardy's hand, and after a tight hug and whispering, 'Take care, sweetheart,' to his daughter,

Herbert along with Monty got into the Manderson's car and drove away, on their journey back to London.

Dottie and her mother headed off to St Martins house courtesy of Palmer and a police car.

Dottie's first thought was to have a bath. And to change her clothes again. She was convinced the fresh ones her mother had brought her already smelled prisony. She had to change. She and her mother went down at a little after four o'clock,

Everyone looked up as they came into the room. In fact they all looked up, then away, then back again, this time in astonishment.

'Dottie!' Guy was the first to seize the opportunity. He leapt to his feet and rushed over, hugging Dottie and kissing her cheek. 'How wonderful!'

Lewis added, 'Let you out, have they? About time too. You're lucky they didn't hang you. Bunch of plodding fools.'

To Dottie's amazement, her mother simply said, 'Oh do shut up, Lewis. We don't want to hear such things.' She swept across the room to the little table, poured herself a cup of tea, then sat next to Imogen who was staring, her mouth hanging open. 'Do ring for more hot water, Imogen,' Mrs Manderson said, 'There isn't much left in the pot.' Imogen hastily complied. 'Dorothy, dear, do sit down,' Mrs Manderson added.

With a sense of walking in a dream, Dottie made her feet obey her, and found she was sitting on the other side of Imogen.

'Mother told me about Norris. How is he, Imogen? Is there any news?' Dottie asked Imogen, taking her hand.

Imogen smiled bravely. 'He's all right, I suppose. I mean they said there's nothing much they can do. It's just a question of waiting. Oh he looks awful, Dottie, his face is so bruised and cut.'

'We've got to hope for the best, dear,' said Mrs Manderson.

Guy came over with plates and offered them various sandwiches. 'Frightfully good to have you back, old girl. I hope they weren't too rough with you. Never thought you'd done it myself.'

Dottie stared at him, almost unable to believe what she was hearing. She still bore the bruises on her upper arm from when he'd marched her up to the house and put her in the cloakroom. But she said nothing, leaving him to his lies.

'Oh no!' Imogen piped up, 'we never for a single moment thought you'd done...'

'For God's sake!' Leo roared. He got up so quickly his wife spilt her tea. 'Come along June, we're leaving. I'm not sitting here like this, taking tea with my mother's murderess!'

The door opened, the maid entered, in response to the ring of the bell, and Mrs Manderson asked her for fresh tea to be brought up. She bobbed to Mrs Manderson and left.

Leo stormed from the room. With a tiny handkerchief, June dabbed apologetically at the damp patch on the sofa caused by her spilt tea. At his repeated, 'June!' she jolted, shot them a smile, grabbed her bag and scuttled from the room.

Mrs Manderson just tsked and shook her head. Dottie was amazed by her mother's poise.

Lewis said he would take his tea in his study, that he had something to see to. Guy and the three ladies remained in the drawing room.

Imogen immediately said, 'So what happened?'

'Our friend from Scotland Yard came down here to take over the investigation. The local fellow isn't very happy about it, but he has the backing of some high-ranking officials in the police force,' Dottie's mother said.

'Do you mean Dottie's beau, Gervase? Oh, I'd love to meet him.'

'Erm...' Dottie didn't know how to respond to that. Once again, Imogen was like a little girl pleading for a present. Dottie hated to disappoint her. But her mother spoke:

'The Assistant Chief Constable of Derbyshire, as I'm sure you realise, has been kept informed regarding recent circumstances. But of course he cannot put his personal concerns ahead of his duty, nor has he any jurisdiction here, whereas local police officers are bound to cooperate fully with an officer from Scotland Yard. Inspector Hardy is not only an excellent officer, he is also a very dear friend of our family.'

'Oh!' Imogen's eyes were round with excitement. Even Guy looked mildly interested.

'I remember he was the one who cracked those dinner party robberies a few months back. It was in the newspapers. He called here to ask us some questions. He's younger than I expected.'

Dottie didn't really want to discuss William Hardy any further. Or Gervase if it came to it. She sipped her tea and wracked her brain to think of something to say to steer the conversation away.

Guy got up to carry over the cake-stand. The ladies made their selections. He set the stand down and chose one for himself, and taking half of it in one enormous bite, he said, 'Good thing you know people, Dottie. I shudder to think what might have happened.'

'I'm afraid the investigation is still ongoing,' Dottie said. 'And Inspector Hardy will be coming out to

speak to us all again after dinner. I'm to ask everyone
to stay at home this evening.'

Guy looked alarmed, as did Imogen. Guy said, 'Well
I hope he won't be late, or keep us too long, I've an
appointment at nine o'clock, and I can't miss it.'

Dottie was fairly sure he meant 'assignation', but
she said nothing.

Mrs Manderson said, 'I'm sure Inspector Hardy
won't mind talking to you first, Guy. That shouldn't
ruin your plans.'

The door opened and the maid came in with a fresh
pot of tea.

'William!'

She had almost forgotten he was coming to the
house again. She had gone to the morning room for a
few minutes' solitude. Unlike her, he wasn't caught
off-guard. He grinned at her.

'William? Surely you mean Inspector Hardy?'

She blushed, but he smiled and said, 'Not that I
mind at all. How are you, Miss Manderson?'

His voice was gentle, the 'Miss Manderson' said
completely without irony. She felt suddenly
overwhelmed. Again. Tears prickled, and she turned
to the left then the right, flustered and unsure what
to do or say, unable to escape.

She didn't hear him move. His arms came about
her. She fell against his chest and sobbed. After a few
minutes, a white neatly pressed handkerchief
appeared in front of her. As she wiped her face and
blew her nose, she became aware his hand was
stroking her back. It was warm and reassuring. For a
few more seconds she leaned against him, her eyes
shut.

But it wouldn't do. She had to pull herself together.
She blew her nose again vigorously and blotted her

cheeks.

'I'm so sorry I keep doing this. It's all been rather... I'll let you have it back as soon as it's been washed,' she promised.

He laughed softly. 'It's all right. It can join your collection.'

She managed a little rueful laugh. 'I do have several of them now. I promise I really will make sure you get them back.'

Rather awkwardly they stepped apart. Dottie pulled out a chair and sat down at the table.

William remained standing. He said, 'Please don't bother about it. Anyway, how are you? I hope there aren't any lasting effects from your incarceration. It must be a relief to be out.'

'It is rather,' she admitted. 'I don't know how criminals stick it. It's the boredom as much as anything. Just sitting there all day.'

He nodded. 'So I've heard.' He didn't really know what else to say, so he said, 'Sergeant Maple sends his regards.' Maple had done no such thing, though no doubt he would have, given the opportunity.

'That's very kind of him,' she said. 'Please thank him for me next time you see him.'

'I will.' This was inane, he thought, this pointless exchange, when only a few moments ago she'd been in his arms, and he'd wanted nothing more than to kiss her. Why in Heaven's name hadn't he done exactly that? Perhaps because he doubted such a thing would be welcomed by her. It was a comfort to know they were friends again. Or at least, almost friends. An idea came to him—a real life-saver. With relief he used it now, 'I understand you've had some property stolen since you've been staying here?'

'Yes.' She went on to describe the designs and the attached samples. She went into quite a bit of detail, and he heard the ring of pride in her voice as she spoke. He was impressed.

'How is the business doing?'

'Oh you know,' she said. She gave a little shrug then she smiled again. Her smile was lovely—he'd always thought that. Not as lovely as her eyes, but almost. 'A few people took their business elsewhere after Mrs Carmichael...' She didn't want to say it.

He understood. 'Yes...'

'Well, there was a bit of a slump during the first few months. And several of the mannequins left, and one of the seamstresses. But I've got some ideas, and I've been learning as much as I can. This new range would have helped to bring in new clients, which obviously means more money.' She looked troubled. 'Now though, I'm not so sure. It will be quite a lot of work to put together a replacement range. No doubt we'll remember most of it, but I'm rather worried about the odd little detail we could forget—those are the things that matter, and that make a difference. And I've got to wait until I get back to London, so obviously the whole thing's up in the air, and I feel rather anxious about it. One thing's for sure, I shall never again take the only copies we have of an entire new range. So that's something useful I've learned from all this, anyway. I just want to get back...' Her voice wobbled but she steadied herself again.

He was even more impressed. 'Of course,' he said, 'I'm hoping it won't take too much longer to get this little problem sorted out, then you can be on your way back home.'

'My aunt's death is a little problem?' she asked, her eyes narrowing.

He could have kicked himself. 'No,' he said hastily. 'Of course not. I'm so sorry. Er...' he took out his notebook, saying, 'Ah yes, quite an obvious thing, but

I almost forgot. Is the new collection valuable, would you say? Well, not the range, of course, that doesn't exist yet. The designs themselves, I mean.'

She seemed surprised. She thought for a moment. 'Well, if I was a famous designer, they could be valuable. They'd be highly sought-after within the fashion world. But as it is—an unknown designer with an almost unknown fashion house—probably not valuable at all. It's more the nuisance factor than the actual value.'

'But what if someone were to offer your designs to another fashion house? Would the receiving people pay serious money for your ideas?'

'I wouldn't have thought so,' she said. 'But I can't be certain. I suppose it's just barely possible. Some of them were uncommonly good, though I say it myself.' She grinned at him, laughing at herself as much as anything.

'All right, well let me know if anything else comes to mind.' He didn't want to leave, but he had no further excuse to stay. He looked at her. She smiled, a little uncertainly. He couldn't resist it, he just had to lean forward and kiss her cheek before leaving the room. And it wasn't just a quick, socially acceptable peck, either. His lips touched her skin with the softest of caresses, his eyes closing. He inhaled her scent, light, floral. His fingers longed to twine in her hair, then to hold her in his arms. He wanted so badly to really kiss her.

Instead he stepped back, made a play of putting the strap around his notebook, the cap on his pen and both of these items into the inner pocket of his jacket. He cleared his throat. 'Well, good afternoon, Miss Manderson. I'm so glad we managed to get you out of prison. I'm afraid I must go along to the study now, got a few things to write up.'

She put a hand out to touch his arm. 'William.'

'What is it?' He almost said, darling. For a brief second he thought he had said it, but then he heard his words on the air as if delayed by some seconds and realised he had not said it after all. He forced himself to concentrate.

'I think I know who killed Aunt Cecilia. And attacked Norris.'

He nodded and chose his words carefully, not wanting to offend her, but needing to make it clear she was not a police officer. He said, 'Any information you can give me will of course, be very welcome. But I as I said just now, I must ask you not to tackle or confront anyone with any suspicions you may have.'

'I know Flora told you about what happened last summer,' Dottie said. 'She said you were very angry...'

He nodded. 'Well yes, I was. Not with you, Dottie, d—er—but with him. With Parfitt. He ought not to have allowed it.'

'I see.' She dropped her gaze, fidgeting with her bracelet.

'It's not because you're a woman,' he said. 'It was completely unethical. But more than that, he could have been placing you in grave danger. It was also highly illegal. It's exactly the kind of thing that could completely wreck a conviction; a trial could be overturned, and a guilty person could be acquitted because of some illegal aspect of the process. As a police officer, I'm not allowed...'

'It's all right, William, I understand.'

He wasn't convinced. But he said, 'All right, you'd better tell me your suspicions.'

She told him. It took her twenty minutes, and he was surprised to find her thoughts chimed with his, though perhaps not for exactly the same reasons.

When she'd finished, he said, 'Thank you. But you realise you can't say anything to anyone about this? Things nee dot go through official channels. I need to make sure my evidence is sufficient to give the prosecution their case.'

'Of course.' She frowned at him. 'William...'

'Is there something else you wanted to tell me?'

'Actually it's more that there's something I need to show you. Come upstairs.'

At the top of the stairs she went first to her own room to fetch something, then she led the way to Imogen's sitting room, knowing Imogen had gone to take a bath.

'We need to be quick,' she said barely above a whisper. He nodded.

Chapter Twenty

Dottie lay suddenly sharp awake in the darkness and for a moment fought to remember where she was. 'Oh yes,' she thought, 'I'm back at St Martins, I'm no longer a suspect.' For a brief, wonderful moment she felt relief. The weight of suspicion had left her.

But. Who had that burden moved onto? Who was the one who had committed the terrible act? Alarm filled her. It might be someone still in the house. It might be—anyone. Someone she knew. Someone who was here now, under this very same roof.

Dottie sat up in her bed and put out a hand to turn on the light.

There was a soft tap on the door. Imogen peeped round the door. Softly she asked, 'Is it all right to come in?'

'Yes,' Dottie said. She glanced at the travelling clock she had brought with her. It showed that it was two o'clock in the morning. 'Of course. Something woke me. I don't know what. Can't you sleep?'

Imogen looked as though she hadn't slept in a week. Dottie was shocked by how pale and thin she had become. The worry about Norris was taking its toll. She was hunched up in some kind of odd garment, rather like...

'Imogen? Are you wearing Norris's pyjama jacket?'

'Hush!' Imogen was blushing, and looking around as if someone might hear. She looked down at it, buttoned loosely over her nightgown. She touched the soft cotton. 'You won't tell, will you?'

Trying not to laugh, Dottie solemnly swore not to tell a soul.

'It's just... sitting beside him for the last two days in the hospital, not knowing if he would live or die... It's been so awful.' She sighed. 'I've never been to his flat, of course. But I know where it is—I've visited the shop two or three times. That's how we met. I—well, I took something in to see if I could sell it.'

Dottie nodded. She had already worked this out for herself, but she said nothing.

Imogen continued: 'Anyway I was looking in his trouser pockets for a handkerchief. I'd been upset. I found the door key. Then when the matron came and told me it was time for me to leave, I didn't feel like coming home. You weren't out of prison yet, and I couldn't bear the thought of coming back to Daddy and Guy. In any case they were just as likely to be out. And Aunt Lavinia is a bit—scary.' She shot an apologetic look at Dottie, who just smiled. Grown men were scared of her mother so it was no surprise a meek woman like Imogen was too.

'Go on,' Dottie said. 'You went to Norris's flat.'

'I expect you think it's very silly of me. But it helped me to feel as though he was with me. I'm so frightened I'm going to lose him.'

'You might as well get into bed,' Dottie said,

throwing aside the covers on the far side. 'It's much too chilly to be out of bed.'

It was a simple friendly gesture, but it was almost too much for Imogen. She started to cry. Dottie hugged her and provided a more-or-less clean handkerchief.

'The doctor has told me his chances are not very good. He told me to prepare myself for the worst.' Imogen's voice was muffled and despairing. Dottie felt a sudden hot anger go through her. What was wrong with the doctor? Why couldn't the stupid fellow give someone so very anxious as Imogen a little hope?

'I've a good mind to send my mother in to the hospital in the morning to yell at that doctor,' Dottie said. 'How dare he say things like that to you! Of course Norris is going to be all right. We've got to be patient. And brave.'

'Do you really think so? Oh Dottie, if I lose him...'

'You won't. You really won't. After all you've been through, you two deserve some happiness.'

There was a long hiccupping silence from Imogen. Presently Dottie began to think of going back to sleep. She would tell Imogen she could stay if she wanted.

But abruptly, out of the darkness, in a clear and perfectly audible voice, Imogen said, 'As a matter of fact I came in here because I wanted to confess to you. I've done something really terribly wicked, and that's why I'm worried about Norris. You see, I don't deserve to be happy, I'm a wicked person. I've been bottling it up and I just feel as though I can't go on any more pretending to be a decent person.'

Dottie turned to stare in Imogen's direction. There was a slight metallic clinking sound from where Imogen sat. Dottie looked. Imogen was laying things out on the counterpane. Small things. Shiny things for the most part that took the small flame of the candle and shone it back at them. They were the items that had been stolen. The things Dottie had already secretly shown to William.

'Imogen, are you telling me you are the thief?'

Imogen's eyes welled up again. She hung her head. 'I am. I am the thief. Oh Dottie, I'm so ashamed. I just can't go on.' She picked up a small dagger with a jewelled handle.

'No!' Dottie yelped, on the point of lunging to save Imogen from herself. Then she realised Imogen was holding it out to show her. Dottie took a breath, and more calmly said, 'But why did you do it?'

'I wanted to sell them. I wanted some money. I thought if Norris could sell some of the items for me, we'd have enough money to run away together.'

Dottie put out a hand to pick up the snuff-box. 'The one from the morning room?'

Imogen nodded. 'That's not even the worst part. Oh Dottie, I did something so terrible, you'll never forgive me.' Her voice wobbled.

Dottie said, as gently as she could, 'I know about the designs, Imogen. I found them this morning. I've already showed the hiding place to Inspector Hardy.'

'How did you...?' Imogen's jaw dropped.

'It's simple really. Norris was behaving so oddly when you both showed me the screen. I mean, he was really keen for me to see it, but then as soon as we got upstairs, he began to be so odd. When I thought about it later, I realised he hadn't wanted me to look at the back of the screen. And then it all made sense.'

'I've been hiding things inside, between the front cover and the back cover, the layers of fabric made a kind of pocket. But I was careless. I left part of my pearl necklace sticking out. I was in a rush, you see.

Then as soon as we went upstairs, he just glanced down and saw it right away. We had to get you out of the room so we could put it right. He said he thought you might notice. I didn't realise that you understood what it meant. And then later... Oh Dottie. I took your designs!'

Imogen hopped out of bed and ran from the room. Dottie wondered if she should go after Imogen. If she was upset... But after another moment, Imogen returned, carrying the little pile of papers that Dottie immediately recognised.

Imogen handed the papers to Dottie, who held them close to her, relief and joy almost overwhelming her.

'Imogen! Thank you! You can't possibly know what it means to have them safely back again.'

'But you knew where they were.' Imogen shook her head. 'I don't understand why you didn't just take them back. Or tell my father... or... or something.'

'I wanted to wait and see what happened. Just knowing they were safe was enough. More or less.'

'I'm so sorry. I should never...'

'It's all right. Forget about it. I've got them back, that's what matters. Now, are you getting back into bed, or are you going to stand there in Norris's pyjamas and freeze?'

Imogen got into bed. Dottie blew out the candle.

'Do you think I'll be sent to prison?' Imogen asked in a small voice.

Dottie burst out laughing.

William arrived before breakfast was over, eager to consult with Dottie, telling himself it was purely a need to clarify something for the case, not a personal call at all.

'Right then, here we are.' He pulled the sheet out of

the stack to read it. 'So it says here that there were some weeds found, and some other sort of flowers. Sergeant Palmer and I found some small bits of flowers and stems still down by the lake where you pulled your aunt out of the water. Strictly speaking they should have been collected up as evidence, but it seems the local inspector felt it wasn't necessary to have all of them. He told me he authorised the gathering of some of the plants, but that he felt there was little reason to believe they had anything to do with your aunt's death. Er—let me see...' He glanced down the sheet of paper to the part he needed. 'Oh yes. There's pansies...'

'That's for thoughts,' Dottie said without thinking.

He looked at her, frowning. But she knew all his looks, recognised all his moods. His frown was a frown of deep contemplation as he considered something, not one of irritation or annoyance.

'What d'you mean?'

'That's the quote, isn't it? Ophelia. 'There's rosemary, that's for remembrance; pray, love, remember; and there is pansies, that's for thoughts...' Tut, tut. Don't you know your Shakespeare, William?' She darted him a cheeky smile as she said it. Her eyes twinkled at him.

His heart did an odd little flip and he had to glance away quickly. But he nodded slowly, still mulling it over. 'Not as well as I thought, clearly. Ophelia? From the play *Hamlet*? You'll have to remind me about Ophelia, I'm afraid.'

'She died. She'd gone mad with grief and went to pick flowers. I was never sure if she fell into the water by accident or if she deliberately drowned herself. But before that, when she went mad, she was trying to give flowers to soldiers. And she says, 'There is pansies, that's for thoughts'.'

'She died? In water? Drowned?'

'Yes, she drowned. William, you really are a terrible scholar. I'm sure your English master would be ashamed of you.'

He grinned. 'No doubt. But you say she wasn't murdered? Ophelia, I mean.'

She shook her head. 'No, it was either suicide, which I think is everyone's favourite, or she fell into the water by accident.' She paused. 'Could Aunt Cecilia...?'

'I'm afraid not. It's pretty clear she was killed by a blow to the head. I'm sorry. Can you remember seeing these when you pulled Cecilia out of the water?'

'Yes.' She bit her lip. The memory of it made her feel ill, but it was there, and it was vivid. 'She was holding them clasped to her front. Or rather, they were sort of wrapped around her hands, tangled in her fingers.'

'Tangled in her fingers?'

She thought for a moment. 'It rather reminded me of school. Of playing cat's cradle. You know, that thing girls do with wool or string.'

He nodded. 'I know. Yes, I remember Eleanor doing it.'

'It was as if the weeds or flowers or whatever they were had been deliberately wrapped around her fingers. I mean, if you're holding flowers, a small bunch say, you don't twine them round each other, or bend them all round your fingers, do you?'

He smiled. 'I don't recall ever holding flowers, but no, I should imagine not. But was she actually holding them? Or are you saying they were used to tie her hands together? Surely it's possible they just wrapped themselves around her in the water?'

She was on the point of shrugging, of saying she

didn't know, that he needed to speak to the police's expert in these matters. And there was something nagging at her she just couldn't quite... Another thought struck her, and instead she said, 'But why would these be in the water? They're not water plants. And they don't grow on the bank. Especially not this time of year. So how did they get there?'

He shook his head. 'That's only one of many things I don't know.'

'I think they were wound around her fingers. When I first saw it, I thought...' She halted, thinking.

'Go on. What did you think, Dottie?'

She glanced up and met his eyes watching her. She stared at him, wondering. Would it be completely wrong of her to throw herself into his arms right at that moment? She wanted to so much. His eyes seemed to darken. His pupils grew larger. She knew he felt the same.

'You're engaged,' he said softly.

'I'm not,' she said. 'It's not being given out until I'm twenty-one. Not until 31st of March.'

'Even so, he thinks of you as his fiancée. In any case...'

'Yes, yes, of course,' she said impatiently. Anything to prevent him from seeing just how much she wanted him to declare his feelings, to sweep her off her feet, and all the rest of it. 'Sorry. Back to business.'

'Yes...'

She was irritated by his reluctant tone. After all, he'd been the one to remind her of Gervase, of their 'understanding'. Now he didn't want to drop it. Men! Who knew how they thought and why?

'What did you think, Dottie?'

She was deep in thought. He waited, outwardly patient, inwardly he was kicking himself for a fool.

Why had he to bring her boyfriend into the matter? Well, he knew why, he admitted to himself. He had wanted to see how she looked when he mentioned her being engaged to Parfitt. It surprised him to see that, quite the opposite to his expectation that she would light up at the mere mention of the man's name, she actually looked depressed by it. Yet when she looked into his own eyes, he could see her expression immediately soften. What was he to make of that? Was Flora right, and Dottie's heart did not in fact belong to Gervase Parfitt at all? Did he have the courage to challenge her?

She stared at him. She'd forgotten what they had been talking about.

'When you saw the weeds tangled around Mrs Cowdrey's fingers?'

'Ah yes. It was nothing really, just, as we were saying... I thought they looked as though they'd been deliberately wrapped around her fingers. It was like a kind of bouquet, if rather ragged, or a wreath, or something. It looked...*meant*.'

'Plants do have meanings, don't they?'

'That isn't exactly what I was getting at, though. I was saying, I suppose, that it looked intentional, deliberate.'

He nodded. 'I understand. But also, in old wives' tales, or old sentimental romances and such, plants have meanings, like jealousy or admiration. Don't they? They are symbolic. That's what you meant about the pansies, isn't it?'

She was looking doubtful. He began to think he'd completely misunderstood what she had said. But then she said, 'Yes that's true. But were these symbolic? I'm not really sure. I didn't take time to notice particularly how they were arranged. I mean, it all happened so quickly, and I just couldn't believe that Aunt Cecilia was dead. And I was frozen, I'd just jumped into the lake like a complete idiot instead of going for help, not thinking how cold the water would be. Not realising of course that she was already beyond help. Then the others arrived, and everyone started shouting that I'd done it, that I'd killed my aunt.'

He nodded. 'That is what makes me think that one of them did it.'

She stared at him.

'Well surely you've thought about it too, Dottie? Realistically, it seems most likely to have been one of them. I mean, who else could it have been?'

'Yes but...'

'I'm certain that one of them then attempted to kill Norris Clarke to cover their tracks. It seems likely he saw something. Perhaps he even tried a spot of blackmail. Until he wakes up, we just don't know. And that's *if* he wakes up. But if he saw something, it seems safe to assume the killer realised, and went after him. And who better placed than a member of the family? More specifically, someone living in this very house.'

She was gnawing on her lip, thinking about what he'd said. But she didn't seem to disagree.

'Be careful Dottie,' he warned her softly. 'Don't discuss anything with anyone. I'm worried about your safety. I didn't want you to stay here, but when I mentioned it to your mother...'

She gave him a wobbly smile. 'I expect she said something like 'nonsense'.'

He laughed. 'Yes, that's exactly what she said. So don't take any risks, please. And if you think of anything, anything at all, no matter how small or seemingly irrelevant, let me know straight away. Even if it's the middle of the night. I certainly won't mind if you keep me up all night. I mean...' Too late, he heard the double-entendre. But she just smiled.

'Thank you, William.'

'I might want to talk to you again about these flowers. That's an idea that intrigues me.' He shrugged. 'I just don't know if it's relevant.' He looked at his watch. 'I'd better go.'

They were on the way to the front door when Drysdale hurried after them.

'Excuse me, inspector. There's a call from the hospital.'

Dottie's heart was in her mouth as she rushed after Hardy and saw him snatch up the receiver.

'Hello? Yes, this is Inspector Hardy. Ah, Doctor... Yes. Yes? I see. Absolutely, yes. I see. I see. Yes. Quite. Yes of course. Well thank you.'

It was, she thought, the least informative conversation she'd ever heard. But he didn't look grave. Or did he? He could be so hard to read sometimes. He hung up the receiver and looked at her.

'What is it?'

He said nothing.

'Oh William! What...?' She was afraid to ask.

'Norris Clarke woke up ten minutes ago. The doctor says I can go and speak to him for five minutes at the most.'

She almost hugged him. She folded her arms. 'Oh that's wonderful! I must go and tell Imogen! Will you ask the doctor to let her see him? She's been beside herself.'

'Of course. Bring her down after lunch. I'm sure they won't mind letting her see him for five minutes.'

She beamed at him. 'Thank you!' She turned and ran upstairs to wake Imogen.

It was later that afternoon that he returned to the house and asked to see her again. Hardy was holding an envelope. Going over to the nearest coffee table and pushing a host of tiny ornaments and detritus out of the way, he tipped the contents of the envelope onto a dirty lace-edged cotton mat.

Dottie came to look. 'The bits of the wreath?'

'Yes. I've got more of them if you'd like to see them. You might call this a representative sample. I'm afraid some of the plants aren't in a very good condition. I suppose we weren't sure either of the best way to preserve them, or even if there was any need to do so. Could you take a look, tell me any that you recognise?'

She immediately grabbed something and held it up.

'This is a sample from one of my designs! Not that it looks like it now, poor thing. It was ruby satin. Now it's a dingy brownish scrap.'

He took it and placed it in a small envelope and wrote on the front.

Dottie poked amongst the rather dry stems, trying to extract some more or less intact flower heads, badly crumpled and faded, and some of the different types of leaves she could make out.

'These two bits are definitely the pansies you've already mentioned. These little bits look like...' She raised a piece to her nose and sniffed. 'Yes, that's rosemary. It's still quite fresh.'

'Does it come from the gardens here?' He was leaning back, watching her closely, looking very definitely at her, not at the plant samples on the table. His arms were folded across his chest and he leaned against almost the only bare patch of wall in the room.

She frowned, trying to remember. 'I'm not sure. I

can't remember seeing any. I know it's stupid but I think I'll have to actually go outside and look. Shall I make a list? Then I can check for each plant and let you know if I find it?'

He came forward now, reaching into his pocket. 'It's all right. I'll write it down in my notebook. We'll go out together if you like. It would be a help to have you with me, but I don't like to ask you to do all the work. So what have we got? Pansies, yes? And rosemary?'

She confirmed those two, and examining the samples, added, 'This white one is some sort of daisy, like you see in pastures, the tall sort. I remember dancing in a field of daisies and buttercups. I must have been about four I suppose. We'd gone somewhere, and Flora and I wandered off to explore.' She was smiling at the memory. Then glanced up and caught his eye. 'I don't remember anything other than the sublime joy of being surrounded by all these tall flowers, almost as tall as I was. I thought I was a fairy princess.' She shook herself, brought herself back to the world of now. 'This daisy—it's odd, the colours are very bright but it's completely dry...Oh! Of course. This must be from the display in the drawing room. As you go in, the two big urns of dried flowers. I believe there are daisies amongst those.'

She was moving, on the point of leaving the room to check, but he said, 'Shall we look in a minute? Let's finish these first.'

'Of course.' She went back to the coffee table. 'Let me see. Well these two are some sort of herbs. They've got fancy leaves and a strong scent. But I'm afraid I don't... June might know. Or Guy. They are herbs experts.' Seeing his surprise, she quickly told him about the book Guy had given June, and about the lengthy tour she had endured of June's herb beds.

Hardy made notes in his notebook on a separate page. 'Something else to check,' he said cryptically.

'And—ow! Yes, this one is a nettle! So not a herb really.' She sucked her stung finger.

'Didn't they used to be used for something years ago? Something to do with cheese? Or dyes?'

She shook her head. 'No idea. I can't really help you. William, I think you'd be better off with June.'

'I might speak with her later. Anything else?'

'Not really. This is one of those woodland spring or early summer plants. It looks vaguely pinkish. Is it campion, or something?'

He shrugged.

She said, 'The thing is, these don't all come out at the same time, and certainly not in December and January. Perhaps they are all from the dried flower arrangement? Anyway, that's all I can really tell you.'

He snapped his notebook shut and put it away. She helped him scoop up the plant pieces and put them back into the envelope.

'Thank you.'

She smiled. 'It's quite all right.'

'Let's go and look at those dried flowers.' He stepped aside to allow her to go in front of him and enjoyed watching her figure as she crossed the hall to the drawing room.

The urns contained an identical assortment of grasses mainly with just one or two flowers. Some of the grasses were painted with silvery paint to give them a more ornamental look, Dottie supposed. Amongst the displays there were also some thin branches from a fir tree, with tiny cones still present here and there, also painted silver.

They identified the daisies but that was all. It was disappointing. Outside, the weather had turned, and rain lashed the windows.

'It looks as though our tour of the grounds will have to wait.'

He sighed. 'I suppose so.'

'Just a minute,' she said and ran upstairs. When she came down, she held out a book to him. He took it, puzzled, and looked at the title. 'Hamlet?'

'The Ophelia connection, remember? It's the one from Imogen's room last night. She's been reading it lately. And quoting from it. Her favourite part is the 'get thee to a nunnery' bit that Hamlet says to Ophelia. I think it struck a chord with Imogen. Because she feels that she's 'on the shelf'.'

'Hmm.'

'The thing is, Imogen told me last night that she is the thief.'

'We already knew that,' he pointed out.

'Yes, but now she's confessed. And given me my designs back, which I am incredibly grateful for.'

'Oh Dottie, I'm so glad about that,' he said. 'But why is this significant?'

'Someone wanted to make it look as though the wreath was made by Imogen. That's why it had the bit of fabric sample from one of my design sheets.'

'That odd bit of brownish stuff?'

She smiled. He wouldn't say that if he saw the garment made up, she thought. She would quite like to see his face when he saw it made up. And on someone. Herself, perhaps. How would the cool Inspector Hardy look then, when he saw her in a ruby red satin nightgown? She shook her head slightly, made herself concentrate.

'Imogen knows quite a lot about plants. I know that because when Guy and June showed us their herb collection, she explained some things to me.'

'Yes?'

'So, she was the thief. She is a bit over-excitable, emotional even. She desperately wanted to meet me and sent a secret invitation. She's been so unhappy about her affair with Norris.'

'And? You think someone wanted her to look as though she was depressed? Suicidal?'

'Well I think someone wanted to make it look as though she was the killer. Or maybe to hint at her being deranged.'

He frowned. 'I don't know...'

'Look at the inscription. I think that tells us quite a lot, don't you?'

He opened the book and looked at the flyleaf.

Chapter Twenty-one

'Gathering us all together in one room, inspector? Do you aspire to being immortalised in detective fiction some day?' Guy sneered as he took his seat.

From the opposite end of the sofa, Lewis said, 'Everyone knows police colleges use Mrs Christie's novels as a blueprint for their training programmes.'

They laughed. It had a sarcastic ring to it. Leo, not to be outdone by his younger brother or his father, chipped in with: 'I hope he's not going to make us all sit in a train. That seems to have become the norm these days, but my wife suffers terribly from motion sickness.' He placed a hand on June's knee and smiled at her. Dottie realised that was the first time she'd witnessed any kind of affectionate contact between them. Not that June appeared to welcome her husband's touch. Rather, June crossed her legs and leaned away from Leo, a somewhat fixed smile in place.

June was tense, her whole small frame was rigidly

held in check, her face half in shadow due to the position of the lamp behind her. Dottie felt an unexpected flash of sympathy for her half-sister. There was a difficult scene ahead. Imogen was also on edge, her arms tightly folded. The men coped with banter and silly quips, the women with silent control and tight-lipped patience.

Hardy wisely chose to ignore all these jibes. He brought an upright chair over from its place against the wall and set it on the edge of the circle and sat down. He had his notebook in his hand and was about to address them. At a nod from Hardy, Sergeant Palmer closed the door and stationed himself in front of it, practically at attention.

I don't have a guilty conscience, Dottie thought, but even so this feels very ominous. She looked at William. His stare was blank and impersonal, fully concentrated on his work, leaving him with no energy for flirtatious glances. She would have been greatly reassured by a wink from him at this point, but nothing so unprofessional was forthcoming.

Inspector Hardy cleared his throat. 'Thank you all once again for sparing me some time this afternoon. I'd like to explain why I asked you here.'

'For God's sake,' Leo said, his tone pure sarcasm. He sent a glance around the room, inviting everyone to agree with him. 'Is he actually going to do one of those tedious theatrical recaps, telling us all the stuff we either already know, or don't give a fig about? As if he's been very clever and solved a riddle that none of us mere mortals could fathom. Hardy, this really isn't amusing any longer.'

'Sit down, Mr Cowdrey.' Hardy didn't bother to soften his tone to something more polite. Sergeant Palmer took a menacing single step forward.

Leo, somewhat taken aback, sat. The tension in the

room palpably increased.

Hardy had a moment of self-doubt. Perhaps this was a rather melodramatic way to do things. But better to say it all just once, to everyone, than to attempt to convey all the information multiple times and risk forgetting something vital. His moment of self-doubt passed. The audience were unaware it had even existed. He began.

'You are all aware that Mrs Cecilia Cowdrey was killed on the night of the first of January by a heavy blow to the temple. She was later taken in the gardener's wheelbarrow down to the lake and put into the water, where her body was discovered at about half past ten the following morning by Miss Manderson.' His eyes flicked onto her for the barest second and away again. In that time he noticed she was looking, as always, heartbreakingly lovely.

'Miss Manderson jumped into the freezing water to attempt to haul Mrs Cowdrey's body out onto the bank in the hopes that she may still be saved. However, unfortunately, life was extinct. Whilst Miss Manderson was doing this, her cousins—or should I say, half-siblings—came along and even though it was doubtless perfectly clear what Miss Manderson was attempting to do, they accused her of the murder of Mrs Cowdrey. Mr Guy Cowdrey took Miss Manderson back to the house and locked her in a cloakroom then summoned the police.'

He paused here. Another brief glance around the room showed that whilst Leo, Imogen, Mrs Manderson and Dottie were watching him attentively, Guy, June and Lewis were all looking elsewhere. Guy was staring into the fireplace watching the flames silently devouring the logs. Lewis was gazing out of the window, and June was focussed on her hands that fidgeted in her lap with the lace edge of her handkerchief. Once or twice she shot Hardy an anxious look then glanced away.

'As you know Miss Manderson was then arrested on suspicion of murder and placed in a holding cell until such time as the police had sufficient evidence to proceed against her. That is where I came into the case. I may say that I know Miss Manderson and her family quite well, and that I was absolutely convinced of her innocence even before I arrived. But I pride myself on my professionalism and try to never allow personal feelings to prevent me from carrying out a very thorough investigation of all the facts. To do so would be highly unethical and in violation of police procedure.'

Dottie was stunned by this. It had never occurred to her that he would actually investigate her as a possible suspect. She felt cold and afraid, even though she knew he was certain of her innocence. She felt she had come all too close to complete disaster. All eyes were on her. Dottie looked back at them, feeling afraid. This was horrible. She felt she had to try to explain, yet what could she say?

And then he winked at her. The tension left her; she relaxed back against the sofa cushions, her eyes fixed on him. His mouth formed the ghost of a smile. He looked down at his notebook.

'It was clear from my interviews of all of you, and from reading the witness statements, that there had been a great tension between Miss Manderson and her aunt. They did not seem to see eye to eye on any subject. They argued on two or three occasions and relations between them could be said to be strained. Mrs Cowdrey seemed not to enjoy Miss Manderson's visit at all, yet she wanted her to remain at St Martins indefinitely.' He paused and consulted his notes.

'These things seemed completely at odds. Why

allow her to come and visit, but take no pleasure in her company? And why then attempt to persuade or demand that Miss Manderson leave London and make her home permanently at St Martins when she appeared to detest everything about her? Mrs Cowdrey stated that she expected Miss Manderson's support against Miss Cowdrey's desire to marry Mr Clarke, with whom she was in love. Additionally, D—er—Miss Manderson was to provide companionship for Miss Cowdrey and help her to forget Mr Clarke. But this does not appear to be sufficient reason to have someone under your roof when the two of you just don't like one another, and there is no legal or familial sense of responsibility to do so.'

'Why did Miss Manderson accept the invitation in the first place? That at least appears to be simple enough to answer. Miss Manderson wanted to get to know her natural mother with whom to that point she had only a distant aunt-and-niece relationship. But was that all? A brief look into Miss Manderson's business affairs immediately revealed a small financial deficit which potentially could increase and leave Miss Manderson drastically out of pocket.'

'Bloody women in business,' Leo said.

His father nodded.

William felt terrible about what he'd just said, and a glance at both Dottie and her mother showed that they were equally unhappy about it. Dottie's cheeks were burning with embarrassment. She folded her arms and refused to look at him. Inwardly he sighed. He'd have to apologise for this later.

'On the face of it, it appeared at least vaguely possible that Miss Manderson had a financial motive for her visit to St Martins. A member of staff told the police they had heard Mrs Cowdrey arguing in the morning room the night she died. And not for the first time. It was known that Mrs Cowdrey and Miss Manderson had agreed that the visit should be concluded as soon as possible. In fact, on the morning Miss Manderson discovered Mrs Cowdrey's dead body, she had already made up her mind to leave the following day.'

'Oh no!' wailed Imogen, clutching at Dottie. Dottie patted Imogen's arm and turned a furious look on William. Forcing himself to ignore her, he continued.

'Of course from the outset the visit went awry. Miss Manderson arrived on the wrong day, a full week earlier than expected. But even so, the house was not empty when she knocked on the front door. Someone was there, upstairs, and deliberately ignored her knock. Miss Manderson therefore went to the village pub for the night, had telephone conversations with her mother in London, who, very late that evening, was finally able to reach her sister and inform her of Miss Manderson's arrival. At that point it came to light that Mrs Cowdrey had not invited Miss Manderson to stay at all, but in fact the invitation had been sent by Miss Cowdrey disguised as coming from her mother.

'Why was Miss Cowdrey so keen for her "cousin" to visit? Her own life was one of duty and misery. She was the butt of everyone's jokes, ridiculed, never taken seriously, treated unkindly on a daily basis by her parents and her siblings. Perhaps she thought it would be interesting to create some tension or mischief in the house, by inviting the illegitimate daughter of her mother?'

'Oh no, I didn't. I really didn't!' Imogen was on her feet, tears threatening, her lip trembling. She threw her hands out to her family. 'Tell him I would never do such a thing!'

Guy shrugged. Lewis looked away.

Leo frowned. 'Imogen please,' he said. 'Sit down and stop making a fool of yourself.'

Dottie felt revolted by them. As Imogen fell back into her chair, Dottie hugged her.

'It's all right, he's just talking about possibilities. aren't you? Inspector?' Dottie added. She gave him an angry look.

'Please calm yourself, Miss Cowdrey. I'd like to continue if I may.' His tone was gentle and Imogen appeared reassured.

'Damn well hurry it up, man.' It was Leo again, still angry, still prickly.

'Miss Cowdrey is known to be in love with Mr Clarke, but her family deeply disapproved of this, especially Mrs Cowdrey. So much so, she actually paid Mr Clarke a substantial sum of money to leave her daughter alone. Isn't that true, Miss Cowdrey?'

Tears spilled down Imogen's face. She nodded, unable to speak.

'You waited for him to meet you as usual in the rose garden on the night of his attack, but he didn't arrive, did he?'

Imogen shook her head.

'Or did he?' Hardy asked softly. 'As we now know, he had been attacked, and left for dead amongst the trees at the edge of the lawn. Perhaps you did meet him after all.'

Imogen was sobbing now.

Dottie was furious. 'William! Stop it! You can't possibly believe that Imogen would actually attack Norris. She loves him.'

'People have attacked those they love. People can lie and manipulate, and conceal their true feelings, indeed their true natures. Miss Cowdrey lied and manipulated. Or people can bottle things up until they can't hold back any longer, and then they lash out in a fit of rage. Miss Cowdrey has also shown that she is emotional and has a tendency to act on impulse. In fact it seems clear that someone intended to capitalise on that by suggesting that Miss Cowdrey was mentally unstable.'

'Now look here!' Lewis was on his feet in defence of his daughter. But he subsided equally as quickly, quelled by a single look from the inspector.

'And you sir. Mr Cowdrey—a downtrodden husband, no longer the head of your household but despised and undermined at every turn by your wife.'

'It didn't touch me. Not at all. It was water off a duck's back,' Lewis insisted, leaning back appearing relaxed and without a worry in the world.

'Didn't touch you?' Hardy quirked an eyebrow at him. Ticking the points off on his fingers, he said, 'One, your wife was unfaithful to you and had a child by another man. Two, she lorded it over you in your ancestral home, and refusing to contribute a penny of her own money to assist you in repairing your home, even though it is in dire need of maintenance. Three, she treated you with ridicule and disrespect in front of your friends, family and acquaintances. Four, she invited her illegitimate child here to stay under your roof, parading her guilt in front of you without remorse or shame. You have a remarkable collection of antique weapons. Perhaps you simply tired of the whole charade and took one up and killed her with it.'

A stunned silence fell on the room. They looked at Lewis. He was pale, but still composed. He shook his head, even attempted a smile.

'Not at all. I was immune to my wife's behaviour. I knew about Dottie, had always known. And having met her, found her to be a delightful and charming young woman, a breath of fresh air. As to the rest, my wife was well aware of my lengthy involvement with my mistress, as were my children. My love for Maria is something I've barely troubled to hide. And I may say, that is why my wife's infidelity and coldness towards me could not touch me. With regards to this house, I am in the habit of leaving it to my son Leo to deal with. I don't care if this revolting millstone stands or falls. It can crumble into the dust for all I care.'

Dottie almost felt like cheering at this speech. If Hardy was surprised at how neatly he was rebutted he said nothing, merely nodding and saying, 'Ah yes, your son Leo.'

Leo immediately sat up straight. 'Oh it's my turn is it? I wondered when you'd get round to me. Now look here...'

'With Mrs Cowdrey out of the way, Leo Cowdrey stood to inherit a neat little sum. Not enough to make him a millionaire perhaps. No. Doubtless he is relying on his father-in-law's demise to do that, after all Sir Stanley Sissons is a wealthy man. But the money Cecilia Cowdrey left would certainly be enough to carry out the most pressing repairs to St Martins. The roof, for example. It's widely known how much Leo loves the estate, and his strong sense of duty and honour have made him work hard to do what he can to manage the estate, as well as becoming Sir Stanley Sissons's right hand man over the last few years.'

'You shall be hearing from my solicitor,' Leo said tersely. He was on his feet and heading for the door. 'Out of my way, Palmer.'

'Don't make me bop you on the nose again, Cowdrey,' Palmer warned.

'Calm down Mr Cowdrey, please. Kindly resume your seat. Should you wish to make a formal complaint, you will of course be entirely free to do so once I've finished.'

For a full minute Leo Cowdrey and William Hardy faced one another, Leo sizing the inspector up. His intake of breath signalled his decision to back down. Not that he did so graciously. Still muttering under his breath, he returned to his place on the sofa. Dottie only caught a couple of rude words and the phrase, 'jumped up little nobody'.

'But Leo Cowdrey did not kill his mother,' Hardy continued as if nothing had happened. Dottie looked at him. She was impressed, in spite of her ruffled pride, at the way he was laying it all out before them. 'Leo is as passive as his father. Additionally, his position as the independent eldest son with his own home makes him almost impervious to the actions of both of his parents. Also, his confidence in his father-in-law's regard for him has convinced him that he has only to wait patiently to reap his reward from that quarter. But if Leo Cowdrey had little motive or taste for murder, then I had to ask myself if the same held true for his brother Guy.'

There was a slight pause. No one spoke. Even Guy, Dottie noted, was as enthralled as if he listened to a radio play about someone wholly unrelated to himself. Hardy turned the page of his notebook. He looked around at his audience. All eyes were on him, and he was completely at ease.

'Guy Cowdrey is in many ways the image of his father: selfish, uninterested in his family, showing little inclination for work or for the estate that supports him. He has had a string of fines related to drunkenness, has been bound over twice for assault, again drink-related, and is suspected of drug-taking and illegal gambling. He owes a considerable amount of money as a result of his addition to playing poker.

A problem that would be eased by the sudden acquisition of a lump sum. Again, he'd hardly be set up for the rest of his life. But the money would be very welcome all the same. Of course, it could be argued that with the Cowdrey estate paying his day to day living expenses, and giving nothing in return, Guy Cowdrey actually already is set up for life.'

'Oh come on!' Guy jeered. He looked around, seeking support from his family. No one spoke. No one moved.

'Things have been quite difficult lately, however. Haven't they, Mr Cowdrey? It was in fact you who argued with your mother that night, and not Miss Manderson as was originally believed.'

Guy was on his feet. 'No, please. I must insist we discuss this in private. It's not at all what you think. I really must insist...'

'You don't want it to come out?' Hardy suggested.

Guy's face was white, his forehead dotted with perspiration. In almost a whisper, he said, 'Please, Inspector. Please. I'm begging you, don't say another word about this...'

Hardy could almost feel sorry for the man. Everyone was looking from Guy to Hardy and back again, trying to work out what was going on. Dottie knew exactly what Hardy was about to say. Her heart was in her mouth. Beside her, Imogen was holding her breath; she looked terrified.

Palmer came over to encourage Guy to take his seat. With another, 'Please, inspector.' Guy sat down, and as Hardy began to speak, he hid his face in his hands.

'Mrs Cowdrey had made a discovery. And it was going to change your life. She had told you to leave the house immediately because she was so angry about this discovery. She wanted nothing more to do with you. Told you to never return or contact your family again.'

Guy shoulders heaved. Only now did Dottie realise he was actually weeping into his hands.

Leo frowned. 'What the hell...?'

June said, 'Really inspector, this is blatant bullying. I'm sure it's not legal. There can be no need at all for all of this.'

'Oh but there is, Mrs Cowdrey,' Hardy said softly. 'Because what your mother-in-law had found out was that her son Guy and yourself had been having an affair.'

Silence fell on the room. Dottie felt as though time stood still. Several clocks in the room hammered out the seconds. Leo gaped at Hardy, unable to take it in. Suddenly, June was on her feet.

'How dare you!' She raised a hand to slap Hardy's face, but he easily caught her wrist and put her back into her seat. For a moment everything was still. Then the guilty sound of Guy's weeping caught his brother's attention.

Leo looked at his wife. He gasped, a ragged, hastily-gulped inward breath.

'You bitch,' he said. He didn't even shout it.

She blustered. 'But Leo, darling, you can't possibly believe this rubbish! It's a filthy lie.'

But Guy's shaking shoulders, the tears leaking between his fingers told the truth. Leo looked as though he was reliving every moment in his mind: the gardening; the walks; the odd disappearances; the easy teasing conversations between his wife and his brother. The gifts.

Leo was on his feet before anyone was ready for it, hauling Guy off the sofa and pounding a fist into Guy's face.

Hardy, Palmer and Lewis Cowdrey ran forward to separate the men. It was several minutes before it was safe to let Leo go. He collapsed finally, slumping against the back of the sofa.

Mrs Manderson crossed the room to pour Leo and Guy a brandy. Both took it and downed it in one. Lewis looked disappointed not to get a drink and went to fetch his own.

Mrs Manderson, sitting neatly on the sofa beside Dottie once more, said, 'Do continue, Inspector.'

Hardy immediately said, 'But Guy Cowdrey did not kill his mother.'

Everyone looked at him in surprise. Even Guy looked bewildered, Dottie thought.

Hardy said, 'No he didn't. He didn't care in the slightest for anything his mother or this estate had to offer him. All he cared about was June Cowdrey. And she had money enough for both of them. Or would have, on her father's death. Then they could go off into the sunset together, scouring the world for rare and exotic herbs. That was all he wanted. And if it was hard to wait to be together, well at last he had their assignations to look forward to. They met regularly. They were here together on the day that Miss Manderson arrived and knocked on the front door one week early.'

'I don't understand, inspector. If you're saying none of us killed my wife, then who on earth is the murderer?' Lewis frowned.

'It must have been some passing madman,' Imogen said.

'Or Norris Clarke,' Leo said. 'I've been saying all along he's a rum sort.'

Before Imogen could react to that, June said, 'Or the person who's been behind all the thefts lately.'

'Ah yes,' said Hardy with the suggestion of a smile. 'The thief of St Martins. It's true that the thief could have had a motive for killing Mrs Cowdrey.' He looked at Imogen.

She was pale. Her hands clasped one another tightly. Her whole frame was tense and expectant, as if she waited for an axe to fall. Dottie put out a hand to cover Imogen's.

'She could have,' Hardy emphasised. 'But she didn't.'

'She? You mean Imogen? You're saying *Imogen* stole all those things?' Lewis frowned at his daughter. 'I can hardly believe it. Why would she do such a thing? Imogen?'

She was perfectly composed as she said, 'To run away, of course. I wanted to run away. And then when I met Norris, and he was so kind to me and paid attention to me, it was him I wanted to run away with. Anything to get away from all of you.'

Dottie said, 'I wondered if the wreath was your work. The wreath of flowers that were wrapped around your mother's fingers. I'm sorry to say that I suspected you at that point. I knew that you had the book of Shakespeare's Hamlet in your room, I'd seen it on your shelf. You had quoted from it earlier when you said, 'get thee to a nunnery'. That's what Hamlet says to Ophelia.

'Then you see, you seemed to know so much about plants. You explained a few things to me when Guy and June showed me around the herb garden. Then there was the gardening twine that had been used to tie the wreath. Leo found it beside your mother's body when he bent to comfort you. He saw it was the same as their twine, although I don't imagine twine varies a great deal from one place to another. But Leo saw it and worried that it might look bad, I suppose. So he took it, and I imagine he probably burnt it or something.' She shot a look at Leo, but he was looking at the floor and didn't speak.

'Another thing was that Imogen was deeply unhappy, and we could say that her mother stood between Imogen and her happiness with Norris. So that was another reason I suspected her. Perhaps she had been so desperate she had lashed out. There was also the scrap of fabric that was caught up in the wreath. It was a sample from one of my designs. As we now know, Imogen stole my designs, so she could have put the sample amongst the flowers of the wreath to implicate me.' Dottie paused for a moment, then went on, 'But then—we looked inside the copy of Hamlet and saw the inscription. 'To June, with love always, Guy'. It didn't necessarily follow that if Imogen had stolen the missing things, she was also the person who had killed her mother. I could imagine her lashing out in a panic, or if distraught, but not laying in wait in the dark to bludgeon someone. Imogen had the opportunity to kill her mother, and the motive.'

'But she didn't do it,' Hardy repeated. 'As we now know.'

'No, she didn't,' Dottie said. 'In prison I had plenty of time to think. I thought about the thefts. And how several of them were Imogen's own things. Then it occurred to me that if there was somewhere to hide small, potentially valuable items, where they would go unnoticed, then the screen had to be one of the best options. Imogen stole the items and hid them in the back of the screen that Norris was helping her to restore. Between the front cover and the back, it's essentially a hollow box, wide and shallow. Perfect for small items. When I got out of prison, I went into Imogen's sitting room whilst she was at the hospital with Norris. Later, I took Inspector Hardy in there to show him what I'd found. I'd found the things straight away hidden in the screen, at the bottom.

Part of the cover was only pinned. It seemed clear. She would take things from time to time, and would give them to Norris to sell them in his shop.'

'Even your designs?' Lewis asked. There was a little spite in his question. Dottie wondered if he wanted to embitter her against Imogen. Like Guy's, his character had a malicious side. But it couldn't happen, Dottie knew, because she refused to allow herself to be bitter about it.

'Yes,' she said simply. 'Even my designs.'

'Oh Dottie!'

'It's all right, Imogen. You know it's quite all right. Though I've no idea how you hoped to get any money for those.'

Imogen gave a rueful smile. 'I didn't even think about that.'

Hardy said, 'Because Miss Cowdrey's only plan was to escape, she had no real reason, no *pressing* reason to kill her mother.'

'But what about the money you said my wife gave Clarke to pay him off? Surely that ruined Imogen's plans. I'd say that gave her a big enough motive all right.' Lewis seemed to think he'd put one over the inspector. But had he really meant to implicate his own daughter in her mother's death? Dottie could only hope either the brandy or the situation had made him overlook the possible impact of what he had just said.

Hardy just smiled. 'It's true Miss Cowdrey was in despair over Clarke failing to arrive for their meeting. But she knew nothing of the money that had changed hands. She only found that out when he regained consciousness. At the time, she merely thought that Mr Clarke had tired of her and abandoned her. She was distraught and after keeping watch for him from the old billiard room to no avail, she went outside to look for him. And found him, though he was unconscious, mercifully, and not dead as she thought.'

'But were you in your room the night of your mother's death?' Dottie asked. 'After you went downstairs to telephone Norris? I waited to see if you would come back up, and then I went down to try and find you. I heard the argument in the morning room and came away. I went to your room, but—I wasn't sure—were you there? Were you asleep? I'd seen someone outside, but I couldn't tell who it was. I thought it must be Norris, but...'

'I went into the billiard room. I put a lamp by the French doors so Norris would know to come over to be let in. It was far too cold to be outside. I thought it would be nice to be inside for once.' She looked embarrassed. From that, Dottie assumed that Norris had indeed come into the house that night.

Imogen continued, 'The money was from my mother. I found an envelope in her drawer when I was looking for a handkerchief. There was a cheque there, made out for a thousand pounds, from the account of Sir Stanley. She must have planned to pay the cheque in, against the one she gave Norris. He told me about the money this morning. He took it from my mother. He said he thought it was about time my family gave me something, and it may as well be money. My dowry, he called it. He went to the bank and cashed the cheque, then he went to the jeweller's and bought me an engagement ring. He rang up a hotel in Paignton and booked us into a room for a two-week stay. It was going to be our honeymoon. Lastly, he went to the registrar and arranged a marriage license. We're to be married tomorrow morning at ten o'clock. But instead of at the town hall in Horshurst, it will be at the hospital.

He's not quite well enough to leave yet. As soon as he is well enough, we shall go to Paignton for our honeymoon. I've spoken to the people who run the hotel and they've been very understanding. And when we come back, we shall live in the flat over the shop. I love him, I intend to be happy, and to live my own life. Nothing any of you can say shall stop me.'

A stunned silence greeted Imogen's speech. Dottie wanted to clap and cheer. Lewis came over and kissed her cheek.

'I'm very happy for you, my dear. Many congratulations.'

'Will you give me away?' Imogen asked him. Dottie saw the regret in his eyes and knew before he answered what he was going to say.

'I'm sorry, Imogen. I can't. I've been a rotten father to you, I know. But I've rather gone off the sacred estate of matrimony. I intend to go to Maria as soon as possible. I shan't come back. Leo, I will sign everything over to you legally and finally, and I will step aside. I can't stand this place for another minute, and it's the least you deserve.'

Leo was on his feet, all bluster and alarm. 'But Father... I mean, really, no I don't want...'

Lewis smiled and clapped his son on the shoulder. 'I'm sorry my dear boy, but I'm through with it all. And you don't need me. You've been nominally in charge of everything for several years now. Rather like Imogen, I've decided to go and live my own life with the one I love. In fact, why wait? I think I shall leave now.'

'Er, sir...?' Palmer shot a look of alarm at Hardy.

'You can't keep me here, inspector. You know perfectly well I didn't kill my wife. I'm leaving.' Lewis looked ill, Dottie thought, and immensely weary. He had no energy left for his children. His shoulders slumped, his feet shuffled. Thirty-five years of lies hung on his neck like a weight he could no longer support.

Hardy nodded to Palmer. 'It's all right. Let him go.'

Palmer opened the door and let Lewis go out into the hall, Palmer followed, presumably to unlock the front door, Dottie thought.

'But I don't understand,' Leo repeated. 'Then who did kill my mother?

Hardy was about to reply, but June beat him to it.

'Oh Leo. You really are very slow sometimes. I did it. I killed her.'

Even though Dottie had known what was coming, it was shocking to hear June say it out loud.

Leo stared uncomprehendingly. 'You?'

'Of course. Oh, not on purpose.' She gave a careless little laugh. They might have been discussing some mix-up at the post office. 'I'd never have done that.'

'Then why?'

'I thought she was Dottie. Pure and simple. Imagine my horror the next morning when I realised the truth. Although the chance of getting her hanged for the murder almost came off. It was a stroke of genius to suggest to you that she'd been trying to kill your mother instead of saving her. You really got the bit between your teeth, didn't you, Leo dear? Oh, it almost worked.' To Dottie she sounded wistful.

'But why?' Leo persisted.

'Oh she can tell you,' June said with a nod at Dottie. 'I'm not in the mood for this foolishness any more. She thinks she's so clever, let her tell you all about it.'

Everyone looked at Dottie.

'She was standing near the back door. She'd come to the house to kill me. She refused to allow me to get in her way. June had plans for Leo to succeed to her father's business empire, and hopefully gain a title.

Not to mention St Martins as well, when Lewis was gone. She no doubt thought they could in a few short years unite both estates and practically become nobility. Certainly, she aspired to great wealth and influence. She craved status and to feel important. Obviously having been to the house almost daily for years, she knew how to get in, the best way to move around the house without being seen. She didn't even have to make her way upstairs.

'But she thought the same as the staff: she heard arguing coming from the morning room, and thought it was me in there with Cecilia. It was well-known in the family that Cecilia and I had been arguing. When Cecilia said, 'I want you out of this house first thing tomorrow,' and the door opened, someone came out into the darkness of the hall. I suppose it must have seemed like the perfect chance to get rid of me.'

'We still haven't found the murder weapon,' Hardy said. 'I am fairly certain it was thrown into the lake at the same time the body of Mrs Cowdrey was disposed of.'

Dottie shot him an embarrassed look. He stared at her. 'I think you'll find it was probably this,' she said, and pulled a small heavy object from behind the cushion of the sofa where she was sitting. She held it out to him. He took it, almost dropped it, not seeing what it was and finding it heavier than he'd expected.

'A cannonball?' He was more than a little surprised.

She sent him an apologetic look. 'I meant to tell you. But it was when we got the phone call to say Norris was awake. Everything else went out of my mind. But if you look at the tablecloth the cannonballs are resting on, you can see a patch that is sort of rusty and brown right where this one was. I think the patch was made by water and blood from the cannonball. I suppose June tried to wash the blood off but it left a little puddle on the tablecloth which is still slightly damp. It's quite hard to properly dry rusty iron...'

He looked at her still. Torn between a desire to laugh at his own stupidity, or her sweet cleverness, or to feel irritated that she had seen something he had missed, or that she was now telling everyone what had happened, the very thing he had criticised Gervase Parfitt for allowing. He couldn't think of anything else to say other than, 'Thank you. Perhaps you'd continue?'

She thought for a moment, then said, 'Well as soon as the door opened, June was ready. She'd grabbed the cannonball from the heap and planned to simply lash out. It was heavy enough that very little actual force was needed. But of course, it wasn't me who came out but Cecilia. We're roughly the same height and build. Our hair was similarly styled, and in the dark...' Dottie shrugged.

Leo stared at his wife, appalled. 'You killed my mother.'

She ignored him, going to stand by Guy's side.

Hardy said to June, 'Luckily for you, the person Mrs Cowdrey was arguing with was her son, your lover Guy. He saw you and helped you get the body out of the house.'

'Oh he went to pieces, poor lamb,' June said, reaching up a hand to stroke Guy's cheek. 'I had to keep telling him to move, to do something useful. He just stood there, frozen to the spot. I remembered there was a wheelbarrow in the potting shed. I knew where the shed key was kept. I told Guy to bring his mother's corpse to the back door, whilst I went out for the wheelbarrow.'

'I knew the door was open,' Dottie said, 'I could feel the draught coming into the hall. But I thought it was either Imogen going out or Norris coming in. I never dreamt...'

'Was Mother actually dead at that point?' Leo asked, his voice rasping with emotion. 'Did you even bother to check, Guy?'

'Yes. Of course I checked. What do you take me for? She was already dead. Otherwise I should never have gone along with it.'

'As it was,' Hardy said, 'your decision to go along with it almost cost Norris Clarke his life. I presume he saw you wheeling the body to the potting shed.'

'Coming back from the greenhouse, as a matter of fact. Not me, June. With that damned wreath,' Guy admitted. 'That was stupid. I almost caved when I was waiting for her to fetch it. She was gone so long, and I was breaking out in a cold sweat, convinced I'd get caught. I was almost on the point of phoning the police then. I wish to God I had.'

'The wreath was a dramatic flair that was perhaps a step too far,' June said, but with a careless shrug, as if it was of no real account. 'But at the time, it seemed perfect. I knew Imogen made the wreath; it was supposed to be for Christmas, but Cecilia didn't like it. It seemed like the perfect finishing touch to anyone going into the water. I just had to add to it the bit of fabric I found on the floor upstairs. I guessed it was from one of Dottie's designs. Another little detail that seemed perfect, but was perhaps a bit too much. It had all gone so well, even if I'd ended up with the wrong corpse on my hands. I'd actually started thinking that it could turn out better this way. Cecilia was such a difficult woman. But then of course, Norris got in the way...' She shook her head sorrowfully.

Guy said, 'June didn't even know Clarke used to wait around out there for Imogen. When June found out, well...' He paused, then added, 'I didn't realise she'd attacked him as well. I thought she was just going to pay him off. Thought he'd see it as his chance to get Imogen away.'

'You idiot,' June said, shaking her head. 'But no, Norris was an unforeseen problem that had to be dealt with. I hadn't realised he lurked outside to see Imogen. How pathetic. Although Norris didn't really know what he'd seen, or he would have gone straight to the police. I went out there to him, right up to him and he wasn't at all suspicious. He just asked me what I was doing there. He thought I had a message from Imogen. I walked right up to him, then crash...'

Dottie gasped. Imogen turned her head away in horror.

June actually laughed. 'He went down like a sack of potatoes. Sadly though, I didn't do quite such a good job with him as I did with Cecilia.' She looked genuinely annoyed at that.

Perhaps she *was* mad, Dottie thought.

'But why, June?'

'Oh Imogen, really? Because he saw me, of course. You're such a goose.'

'Better a goose than a murderer. I mean, why did you kill my mother—why did you want to kill Dottie? You hardly know her.'

'And yet she managed to ruin my life, all the same.'

'By being the real flesh-and-blood daughter of your adoptive father,' Dottie stated.

'Exactly. His bastard child. Taking away *my* heritage, destroying *my* future plans.'

'It wouldn't have made any difference, June. Sir Stanley told me that he loved you as if you were his own child. He had no plans to disinherit you.'

June stared. Her face had gone an odd greyish colour. 'Yes, he would...'

'No,' Dottie said firmly. 'He wouldn't. He told me he'd like to settle a lump sum on me now to help me with my business. But he had no intention of changing his will. Besides, I didn't want him to, we had only just met and barely knew each other, and I told him I thought it was right that you should be his heiress as he'd always intended.' After a moment she couldn't resist adding, 'So it was all for nothing. You had no reason to kill me—or Aunt Cecilia. You did it all for nothing.'

With a howl of rage, June launched herself at Dottie. The men rushed forward to pull her away, then Guy suddenly yelled:

'Everyone, stop!'

They froze, seeing that he now held a gun in his hand.

'Where did he...?' Dottie asked.

'Everybody stand perfectly still. June, my darling, come. Let's go. We can get away now.'

'We can rush him,' Hardy called to Palmer, who nodded.

'Oh William, no!' Dottie shrieked, stepping forward.

'Stay where you are!' Guy and June began to back away. The hall beyond was in total darkness, and as the policemen rushed at them, June grabbed at something hidden from view behind the door frame.

There was a blast. Spears and suits of armour fell and tangled to form a hurdle across the doorway. Tables and shelving splintered. Muskets subsided into the wreckage, tearing down a pennant and a standard. Cannonballs crashed and rolled. Shields toppled and spun like coins on the wooden floorboards. The men fought their way through the heavy iron and wood to reach the front door.

Guy and June were already out of the house, their feet smashing the gravel.

In just a few more seconds, Hardy reached the front door, racing round the side of the house to cannon straight into Guy's fist. Hardy went down and Palmer fell over the top of him.

At that moment, June tore past them in Guy's Morris Minor, leaving Guy standing there, bellowing after her, a look of disbelief on his face. Everyone crowded outside. Hardy and Palmer helped each other up. Dottie reached for Hardy, alarmed to see the blood pouring from his nose.

If they thought June would head out of the park to the village street to get away, they were mistaken. She drove at full pelt down the hilly lawn and into the lake, the car slamming into the freezing water and disappearing almost at once beneath the heavy black surface.

Guy sank to his knees sobbing. The gun fell from his hand to the gravel and Dottie saw it was just another broken relic from the past, snatched from a shelf of curios.

The geese on the lawn flapped their mutilated wings and honked in indignation at the disturbance.

Chapter Twenty-two

It was two hours before the police finished taking statements.

William, looking exhausted and grim, came over to where Dottie and her mother were standing by the window, watching the search lights being erected to continue the attempt to retrieve June's body from the submerged car. He stood there a few moments with them, then said, 'By the way, I'm driving back to London tomorrow as soon as the funeral is over. If Miss Cowdrey and Mr Clarke are borrowing Dottie's car for a while, can I give you a lift?'

Lavinia Manderson exchanged a questioning look with her daughter. Dottie nodded. Mrs Manderson said, 'Thank you, William, dear, that would be very kind. I must admit I wasn't looking forward to going back by train.'

'I'm sorry I spoke so much when you were trying to tell everyone who had done the murder.'

He gave her a wry smile. 'I'm beginning to see how

it happened to Parfitt. But thank you. You were insightful and very intelligent, and I was grateful for your assistance.'

'Glad to be able to help. Will you come to Imogen's wedding tomorrow morning?' Dottie asked, keen to change the subject and get his eyes off her.

He shook his head. 'I'm afraid I can't. There's still so much paperwork to be done before I can leave, and I promised Sergeant Palmer I'd buy him a pint.'

'Don't drink too much, Inspector,' she cautioned, her eyes teasing him. 'Remember you've got to drive us back to London.'

'So I have. Poor old Palmer will have to wait—or settle for a pot of tea.'

They made arrangements for the next day, and he said goodnight, hesitating in the hall. They looked at one another. Dottie bit her lip, then after another moment, held out her hand.

'Well, goodnight, William. I'll see you tomorrow at twelve. It will be such a relief to get away from here.'

He nodded, turned and left, hunching his coat closer about him, holding onto his hat as the sudden breeze snatched at it. Dottie closed the door, and sighed.

The funeral of Cecilia Cowdrey at nine o'clock the next morning was attended by only six people: Imogen, Leo, Dottie and her mother, with Inspector Hardy on one side and Sir Stanley on the other. The curate said the requisite words over the coffin, and it was lowered into the ground. The mourners cast their flowers and handfuls of soil onto the lid, and with another prayer, were glad to walk away. It felt like an empty end to a life.

They turned away from the graveside, Dottie with her arm through Imogen's. Mrs Manderson was talking to Sir Stanley. Dottie thought the events of the last twenty-four hours had aged him dreadfully. Leo hovered nearby; the two men seemed to be supporting each other. Dottie was glad of that. Sir Stanley's car waited to drive him home after the service; Dottie said goodbye to him, promising to write often, and he vowed to visit her in a few weeks. She hugged the old man, really sorry to see him so grief-stricken.

The rest of them walked in silence back to the house.

After a cup of coffee and a time of quiet conversation, Leo said, 'Come on, let's get dressed, I believe we have an appointment this morning. No more sorrow.' He kissed his sister's cheek.

When they left the house an hour later to drive to the hospital, the sun broke through the cloud, pale but nevertheless shining. It was the best the season had to offer, but it was more than enough.

Leo gave his sister away. Norris had no best man. Nevertheless, the bride and groom looked blissfully happy as Imogen turned Norris's wheelchair from the registrar to face the tiny group for the first time as man and wife.

There was to be no wedding breakfast. Norris was bundled back into his hospital bed by an anxious ward sister. The honeymoon would have to wait until the groom was well enough to be discharged. Imogen, glowing and lovely, perched on the edge of the seat pulled up to the bedside. It was enough to be together. At last, Dottie thought as she and Mrs Manderson threw rose petals over the couple.

Imogen bloomed. Her cheeks were pink without the help of anything from a jar, although her hair had been becomingly arranged by Dottie that morning. Imogen's eyes had been made up carefully to enhance their deep tones and long lashes. The dress was neither new nor fashionable, but it had a pretty elegance that suited the bride. All in all, Dottie thought, nothing else mattered. All that mattered was that happiness was there and had to be grabbed with both hands while it was possible.

Everyone came forward one at a time to shake Norris's hand. The bandage around his forehead lent him a noble air. His left hand gripped Imogen's as if he was afraid to let go.

'I'll telephone you tonight at Norris's flat. And you must remember to write to me as soon as you get back,' Dottie whispered as she kissed the blushing bride.

'I will,' Imogen promised. 'Thank you so much for lending us your car. I'll send a postcard from Devon.'

'They're having two weeks in Paignton, thought it will probably be at least a week before Norris gets the doctor's approval to go,' Leo said. 'When they return, I shall help with the removals. I'm letting them have a cottage on the estate. Oh, not a worker's cottage,' he amended, seeing Dottie's doubtful expression. 'No, it's one we used to let out to guests here for the hunting season. It's very nice, actually. Very cosy. It's one of a few that have been modernised, so it should be just the ticket. We had a long chat about it. Norris is going to let out the flat above the shop; it will give them a little extra income. What with one thing and another, they will have a comfortable life together.' After a pause, he sighed.

'It sounds perfect.' She put a hand on his arm. He patted her hand.

Dottie sensed his sorrow. 'I'm so sorry, Leo, for the way things have turned out.'

'Not your fault, old girl,' he said gruffly. 'And while

we're at it, I was an absolute swine to you. I'm very sorry. What we put you through, what we—what *I*—let you suffer. So very sorry, my dear. But this whole mess, you know. It started years ago. People marrying out of duty and not love. Against their inclination. So much bitterness.'

'True. Let's hope it's all over now. What will you do next?'

'I'm closing St Martins. Might even try and sell the place. Not sure. Give it a few months to make up my mind. I'd like to leave our place too, the memories, you know, but I've got to live somewhere, and at least Imogen will be nearby. Sir Stanley and I have always got on well, in spite of... He's going to need me over the next few weeks and months. No doubt you can understand what a shock this has all been for him. Well, and for myself, for that matter. And well, hopefully, given a bit of time...'

'Of course. Well do take care of yourself, Leo,' Dottie said. To her surprise he hugged her briefly.

'You too, dear. Sorry once again...'

'Oh it's all right, Leo. You did what you thought was best. It can't be helped now.'

Mrs Manderson came forward and kissed him on the cheek. 'Leo dear, if your uncle can be of any assistance at all, please don't hesitate to ask. Come and see us, a few days in London now and then would do you the world of good.'

'I will. Thank you.' He waved one last time and got into his car. As he rolled it away across the cobbles, he smiled and beeped the horn.

'Time for us to go too, Dorothy.'

Dottie smiled. Only her mother called her Dorothy. She put her hand through her mother's arm. 'Come on then, let's go and find William. I think he'll be in the pub.'

Mrs Manderson looked concerned. 'I do hope he's sober.'

Dottie laughed. 'He and Sergeant Palmer are taking tea.'

They drove away, leaving St Martins behind. Through the back window of the police car, Dottie watched the house recede, and vowed to never set foot in it again.

She hoped Leo would be all right. She made a mental note to telephone him as well as Imogen to let them know they had arrived safely. Imogen was moving into Norris's flat. She didn't want to be alone at St Martins, or to go to Leo's house. Besides, being in the flat would be more convenient for the hospital.

And when the new Mrs Clarke was back from her honeymoon, Dottie planned to ring Imogen regularly, and visit whenever possible. Dottie was thrilled that in spite of the situation, and having so very nearly lost him, Imogen had suddenly thrown aside her fears and taken the opportunity to marry the man she loved. Who knew, perhaps in a year or two, Leo might meet a nice lady who would make him happy. She did so hoped he would.

Another person she wanted to get to know better was Sir Stanley—she still couldn't bring herself to call him Father, not even in the privacy of her thoughts. But he seemed like a good person, and his sorrow over the recent events had taken their toll. She hoped to see him again in happier circumstances.

Dottie was so thankful to finally be going home. Yet there was one thing—one overwhelming truth—she struggled to accept. As she sat in the back of the police car, squashed between the suitcases and hat boxes, catching snatches of the stilted conversation taking place in the front, this one thing pushed its way into her thoughts.

It was William Hardy who had come to save her. William who had set aside everything and arrived when she needed him, needed his help.

In view of the fact that she had been arrested for murder, she didn't think she was being melodramatic in believing that he had saved her life. The unimaginable consequence of being found guilty of the murder of her mother's sister had loomed all too large, and she had been almost helpless. Certainly for three days, she had been near friendless.

Gervase had turned away from her. William had not. William had come to save her. Gervase Parfitt had remained in hiding behind his desk and had not lifted a finger to help the woman he supposedly loved.

Dottie had not expected that Gervase would ring people—important people—up in the middle of the night and demand her immediate release. It would have been nice if he had, she thought, and there was no denying one small, frightened part of her had wanted him just this once to use his precious name and his position to bend rules and to beg favours, for her, the woman he claimed he wanted to marry.

'Well, he's had that,' she said, 'I'm not marrying him now.'

'Did you say something, dear?' her mother called over her shoulder, raising her voice to counter the engine noise.

'No, mother,' Dottie replied. Glancing up she met William's eyes in the driver's mirror. Then he looked back at the road.

How could I have been so wrong, Dottie thought. She shivered. She felt cold inside. She had done something terrible, she saw that now.

Gervase had said she was naïve and too idealistic.

'No one can be perfect,' he'd declared, rather pompously she admitted now, 'and if you expect your husband to be perfect, well my dear, you're setting yourself up for a fall.'

This brief lecture had fallen on her because she'd told him that 'a friend' had let her down by failing to reveal private knowledge that affected her family. She hadn't wanted to say too much, and although Gervase had assumed she was referring to a male, he hadn't insisted on knowing the man's name. Another fact he claimed credit for, adding,

'If this person had gained the information by being in a place of confidence, then how could they reveal what they knew without the confidante's permission? One never betrays a confidence, it's a matter of honour.' When they'd first met, she'd told him about Diana, grief-stricken as she was by the final outcome of that situation, and he'd been sympathetic, full of concern. But she had never told him how she came to be in Scarborough in the first place. Never mentioned William's revelation on the train from Scotland.

With an inward sigh, she watched it all play itself through her head again, like a newsreel at the cinema. William, proposing, her thrilled acceptance, their blissful moments, the kisses, the foolish promises, the sheer heady wonder of feeling overwhelmed by love. And then—those fateful words, the lurching disappointment, the fear, the sense of betrayal and loss. The numbing doubt: was he really the man she thought he was? William, angry, upset. Herself, rejecting him, getting off the train, cold.

Naïve. And too idealistic.

Dottie felt swamped with shame. So much had happened since the summer.

The car bumped on the road, and Dottie steadied

herself by clutching at the back of the driver's seat. Her hand was inches from his shoulders and neck.

She liked his shoulders; she always had. When he'd put his arms around her, she'd felt as if she were being hugged by an enormous bear of a man. It was the shoulders that gave that impression.

She liked his hair too. She was glad he didn't Brylcreem it down smooth all the time as most young men did. She knew that was probably a habit dictated by lack of money, but she approved it. Until recently he'd been rather hard up, and old habits had a way of hanging on. Fair hair. Thick and wavy. Like Gervase's, though different too. Gervase's hair was straighter, thinner, and had a tendency to flop once it grew a bit. How had she ever mistaken Gervase for William that first time she'd seen him? They were nothing like one another.

Then there were the cheekbones. Quite high, with a natural emphasis, that she thought vaguely Scandinavian. Coupled with that hair, it was a devastating combination.

And his eyes. Blue. Not cold, but expressive as the sea. They could be disconcerting, she knew, seeming to look right through you, making you feel you couldn't back away. And what man had any right to have long thick eyelashes like that?

His eyes flicked up to the mirror again and met hers. He slowly winked at her. Such a small thing, but it made her heart sing. They were still friends! She beamed at him.

If her mother had not been in the car, Dottie would have liked to touch the back of his neck. Unless she looked in the mirror, that was all she could see of him. There was a gap of perhaps two inches between the top of his collar and the start of his hair, very short and very fair at the nape. She wanted to put her fingers there, stroke the skin, feel the bristles of the short hairs against her fingertips. Perhaps push her hand up a bit so that her fingers could really tangle in his hair, draw him in closer to her, close enough to...

There was a muffled curse as the car suddenly veered wide and he had to bring it back to the right side of the road. He mumbled an apology, just as her mother said sharply, 'Really, William, dear!'

As he reached up a hand to adjust the mirror, Dottie wondered, when had her mother started calling him *William*, let alone *dear*? It was exactly the way her mother addressed George, Dottie thought, almost as if her mother thought of William as a member of the family, like a son. The penny dropped. Oh. Not a son. But a *son-in-law*.

Dottie glanced up, but the new angle of the mirror defeated her attempt to catch his eye. Feeling disappointed she went back to looking out of the window. Her heart was soaring. William had come down to Sussex intending to save her and save her she certainly had.

They stopped for petrol after an hour, and whilst the young garage assistant was filling up the tank, Mrs Manderson turned in her seat to speak to her daughter.

'I told Janet and Cook to leave us out some sandwiches and a flask of coffee. I imagine we'll be very glad of a hot drink when we get home.'

Dottie nodded absently to these domestic arrangements and glanced in the direction of the driver.

Hardy got out of the car and stretched. Not that they'd been travelling for long, but he felt he'd done nothing but sit for the last few days; his back and shoulders were cramped with knotted muscles.

He exchanged a few words with the young fellow filling up the car, then leaned inside the car to ask Dottie to pass him his wallet from his jacket pocket.

She did so, her fingers finding the familiar worn-smooth leather of his old wallet, the one she'd discovered when nosing about his room back in those summer months that felt so long ago. As she passed it to him, their fingers briefly touched, she felt a tremble go through her and her eyes looked into his. Her heart did a little flip of joy.

His grip tightened on the wallet and he snatched his hand away as if she'd burnt him. Too quickly he straightened and bumped his head on the car roof, swearing instinctively and at the same time, dropping the wallet in a puddle.

Mrs Manderson immediately said, 'Language, William dear!'

He apologised. He shook the water off his wallet, paid the attendant, then there was nothing for it but to get back into the car. He let off the brake and they rolled back out onto the main road. Dottie saw that the back of his neck was flushed as red as his face.

As the countryside and villages rolled by, Dottie's thoughts returned to their previous theme and expanded on them. I've wasted six months, she told herself. Six months when I could have been William's fiancée, perhaps even his wife by now. Or perhaps a spring bride. I could—she gulped. She was only saying the words in her head, but even so she almost choked on the emotion. I could have been his wife by now, living with him in Mrs Carmichael's old house, choosing curtains and china with him, making it a home.

They came to a junction and he glanced in his mirror. It had somehow reverted to its previous position, although she hadn't noticed him move it.

His eyes found hers again in the glass.

'How is your sister getting on up in Matlock?' her mother was asking him, whilst Dottie was staring at him, and thinking, I could have lain in his arms every night.

Her mother added sharply, 'Oh, do be careful of that car, William. I'm sure you're not fully attending to the road.'

He apologised and moved the mirror again. Which was probably just as well, Dottie thought as she leaned back in the seat, her chin propped on her hand. As the scenery flashed past, her thoughts ran in circles, unable to move beyond her knowledge of having done something incredibly foolish on the train all those months ago. She dashed away a tear, glad he had not been watching her at that moment.

They stopped again for a late lunch six miles from London. Conversation was general, with William and Dottie avoiding looking at one another or speaking of anything other than the weather and the good time they had made and the lack of traffic. Mrs Manderson politely failed to notice that there was any tension.

For the last section of the journey, they had all lapsed into complete silence. It was growing dark by the time they reached Scotland Yard. William went inside for a moment to drop off his papers and to call a cab for the ladies.

Mrs Manderson kissed his cheek, an act that astonished her daughter. Dottie would have liked to kiss him too, but he held out his hand to her in an unmistakably distancing manner. She shook his hand and thanked him politely for all he'd done. As if they were strangers again, she thought. The cab arrived. William helped the driver to put their luggage inside.

They hesitated, looking at one another awkwardly. Mrs Manderson simply said, 'Goodbye dear, thank you for everything you did. We're all so grateful. Do come and see us next time you're free for dinner or tea.'

'I shall, Mrs Manderson, thank you. Give my regards to everyone.'

He turned to look at Dottie again.

'Can we drop you anywhere?' she asked. 'How are you getting home?'

'Oh, I'm waiting for...'

Just then there was the sound of a car horn, and they stepped back as a vehicle swept to a halt beside them, perilously close to mounting the pavement.

'Ah this is my lift,' he said. He looked a little sheepish. 'Well, goodbye, Dottie.'

She wanted to hug him or kiss his cheek. But he gave her a quick wave, opened the door of the newly arrived car and got into the passenger seat. To Dottie's dismay, she saw a woman behind the steering wheel. A young, blonde woman. As William got in, she leaned over and directing a glance straight at Dottie, she tilted her head and kissed William full on the lips. They drove away and Dottie stood there wondering what had just happened to her heart.

'Dottie?'

With a sigh and a shrug Dottie got into the cab. 'Oh Mother. I've been such a fool. And now it's all too late.' She leaned against her mother's shoulder, fighting back the tears.

'Nonsense, dear. It's never too late unless you give up entirely.' Mrs Manderson rapped on the glass. 'Drive on, please.' She leaned back to put an arm around her daughter's shoulders.

The driver let off the brake, and the car gently

rolled out to the main road to join the evening traffic. At least, Dottie thought, I'm going home.

THE END

ABOUT THE AUTHOR

Caron Allan writes cosy murder mysteries, both contemporary and also set in the 1920s and 1930s. Caron lives in Derby, England with her husband and two grown-up children and an endlessly varying quantity of cats and sparrows.

Caron Allan can be found on these social media channels and would love to hear from you:

Facebook:
https://www.facebook.com/pages/Caron-Allan/476029805792096?fref=ts

Twitter:
https://twitter.com/caron_allan

Also, if you're interested in news, snippets, Caron's weird quirky take on life or just want some sneak previews, please sign up to Caron's blog! The web address is shown below:

Blog: http://caronallanfiction.com/

Also by Caron Allan:

Criss Cross – book 1 of the Friendship Can Be Murder trilogy

Cross Check – book 2 of the Friendship Can Be Murder trilogy

Check Mate – book 3 of the Friendship Can Be Murder trilogy

Night and Day: Dottie Manderson mysteries book 1
The Mantle of God: Dottie Manderson mysteries book 2
Scotch Mist: Dottie Manderson mysteries book 3 a novella
The Last Perfect Summer of Richard Dawlish: Dottie Manderson mysteries book 4
The Thief of St Martins: Dottie Manderson mysteries book 5

Easy Living: a story about life after death, after death, after death

Coming Soon – 2020/21

The Spy Within: Dottie Manderson mysteries book 6

Rose Petals and White Lace: Dottie Manderson mysteries book 7

Coming soon: 2020

Thanks for reading!

Made in the USA
Monee, IL
04 August 2021

74972194R00210